# Also by Sandhya Menon

*When Dimple Met Rishi*
*From Twinkle, with Love*
*There's Something about Sweetie*

# Of CURSES and KISSES

## SANDHYA MENON

Simon Pulse

NEW YORK  LONDON  TORONTO  SYDNEY  NEW DELHI

SIMON PULSE

An imprint of Simon & Schuster Children's Publishing Division
1230 Avenue of the Americas, New York, New York 10020
First Simon Pulse hardcover edition February 2020
Text copyright © 2020 by Sandhya Menon
Jacket illustrations copyright © 2020 by Petra Braun
Jacket hand-lettering copyright © 2020 by Saskia Bueno
All rights reserved, including the right of reproduction
in whole or in part in any form.
SIMON PULSE and colophon are registered trademarks
of Simon & Schuster, Inc.
For information about special discounts for bulk purchases, please contact
Simon & Schuster Special Sales at 1-866-506-1949
or business@simonandschuster.com.
The Simon & Schuster Speakers Bureau can bring authors to your live event.
For more information or to book an event, contact the Simon & Schuster Speakers
Bureau at 1-866-248-3049 or visit our website at www.simonspeakers.com.
Jacket designed by Sarah Creech
Interior designed by Mike Rosamilia
The text of this book was set in Tiempos Text.
Manufactured in the United States of America
2 4 6 8 10 9 7 5 3 1
Library of Congress Cataloging-in-Publication Data
Names: Menon, Sandhya, author.
Title: Of curses and kisses / by Sandhya Menon.
Description: First Simon Pulse hardcover edition. | New York : Simon Pulse, 2020. |
Summary: Told in two voices, Jaya Rao, an East Indian princess, and Grey Emerson, an English
lord, suffer the effects of a centuries-old feud when they meet at an elite Colorado boarding school.
Identifiers: LCCN 2019012497 | ISBN 9781534417540 (hardcover)
Subjects: | CYAC: Vendetta—Fiction. | Blessing and cursing—Fiction. | Dating (Social
customs)—Fiction. | Boarding schools—Fiction. | Schools—Fiction. | Princesses—Fiction. |
Students, Foreign—Fiction. | Colorado—Fiction.
Classification: LCC PZ7.1.M473 Of 2020 | DDC [Fic]—dc23
LC record available at https://lccn.loc.gov/2019012497
ISBN 9781534417564 (eBook)

*For the cursed and the brave*
*who refuse to bow to the stars*

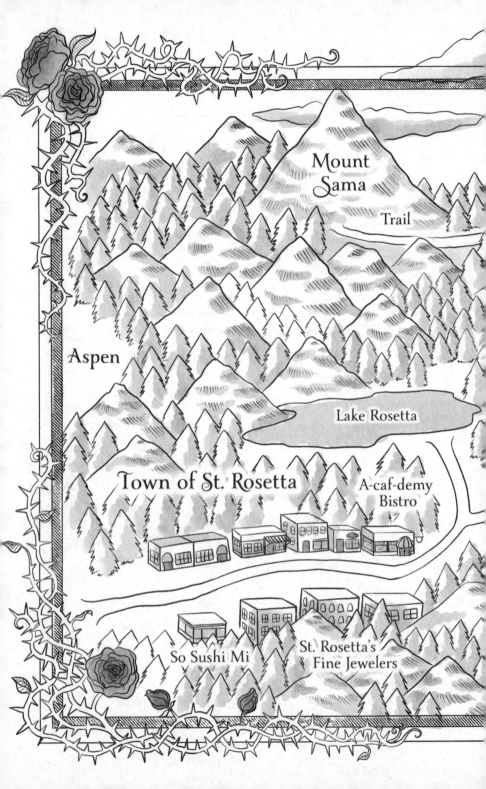

He fell into despair,
and lost all hope.
For who could ever learn
to love a beast?

—Beauty and the Beast

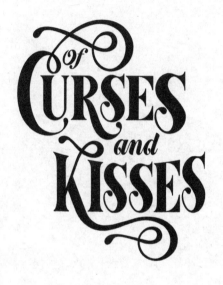

# CHAPTER 1

Just outside Aspen, Colorado, nestled between the sentinel mountains and an inkblot lake, lies St. Rosetta's International Academy. Its sweeping spires, creeping ivy, and timeworn brick turrets often lead visitors to remark that it looks like a venerable castle from an old European city. The Academy would be Princess Jaya Rao's home for the next year.

While she was there, Jaya had one mission: break an English nobleman's heart.

But first she had to fall in love with him.

# CHAPTER 2

# Jaya

Being a princess wasn't as glamorous as the media might have you believe. If the courtiers introduced her, say, in this fashion: "Her Royal Highness, Princess Jaya Rao of the Imperial House of Mysuru," most people would immediately picture Jaya cooing to birds and shaking hands with friendly mice, tiara glimmering in the summer sun. The entire Disney enterprise had a lot to answer for, in her opinion.

Jaya's reality was actually quite different. It was always, "Jaya, the townspeople want you to feed their lucky elephant so it'll win in the races tomorrow. Oh, and by the way, the elephant is in musth, so watch your dress" or "Jaya, the Prime Minister of Oppenheim is morally opposed to butter, so you cannot have any at breakfast either."

But it was all right. She was the heiress to the "throne" of Mysuru. (Technically, India was a democracy now, not a monarchy, but Jaya's family used to be the monarchy in this region and still carried the title.) Jaya understood that she would, at some point, have to grasp the reins. She'd have to take care of the city she lived in, just as her father had for years and her grandfather did before him. India wasn't supposed to have royal families—except the open secret was that they were still there, and people still looked to them to be benevolent, firm, and fair. Non-royals depended on them for jobs, for charity, and for a million other reasons Jaya was still learning. Maybe because of this, the Raos were placed upon a pedestal. They were, fairly or unfairly, expected to be perfect in every way; the common citizens needed them to be. The Raos family name and the royal traditions that bound them were everything.

And that was precisely why she had to do what she was about to do. She might be a princess, her parents' firstborn child and the heiress ascendant to the throne, but that wasn't all of her story.


They stood in the grand marble entrance with their small bags. Jaya tipped her head back to look at the enormous crystal chandelier suspended like a dewdrop above her head. The rose pendant hung heavy from her neck, eighteen rubies glinting like watchful eyes, reminding her why she was there.

Isha whistled, low and long, and Jaya glared at her. She cut off mid-whistle, looking only slightly abashed. "Nice setup," she whispered, but her words echoed anyway. "Nicer than our last boarding school in Benenden, even. And the English *really* know boarding schools."

The wall before them was adorned with flags of more than three dozen countries. A gold-plated sign above them boasted "Our students come from around the world!" Jaya's gaze was drawn automatically toward the flags she knew very well—India, of course, along with the US, UK, UAE, China, Japan, Mauritius, and Switzerland. She'd spent summer holidays in all these places and lived in most of them, reading in cafés and parks while Isha foraged through thrift stores, searching for gears or batteries for whatever contraption she was working on.

The floor was drenched in sea-green tiles inlaid with gold, a splash of oceanic beauty here in the mountains. Jaya had heard it rumored that these were a gift from the Moroccan king half a century ago, when his son had been exiled here after an embarrassment of some kind. She hadn't ever unearthed what that scandal was—St. Rosetta's was *very* good at burying what they didn't want found—though she felt a kinship with the king. He wasn't the only one who'd shouldered the responsibility of protecting a wayward family member. Jaya's eyes fluttered to Isha unwittingly, and she forced them away.

Isha gripped her arm, pointing to the wall on their right. "Look!" she whispered. "Is that . . . ?"

They ogled a cluster of colorful paintings, large and small, that contrasted with the Moroccan tiles, depicting smooth desert landscapes that lifted off the page and caressed the eye. "I think so," Jaya whispered back, thrilled. She wasn't sure exactly *why* they were whispering. Maybe because they were in the presence of greatness? It was probably why people felt compelled to whisper in libraries, too. "Georgia O'Keeffe spent a semester here as a teen, and later donated paintings to the school as a thank-you."

Before Isha could respond, thunderous footfalls came rushing down the opulent marble stairs that faced away from them. Without even turning to look, Jaya could guess from the boisterous, deep laughter that it was a couple of boys, though the sheer amount of noise could also indicate a herd of buffalo.

"Come on," her sister said, tugging her forward.

Jaya grasped her wrist and shook her head. "Isha."

"What?" Isha said, her brown eyes wide. "I just want to get to know our schoolmates. We have to spend the next year or two here with them anyway."

As if Jaya trusted those innocent doe eyes. Isha thought she was much more naive than she really was. Lowering her voice, Jaya said, "And boys have gotten you in trouble in the past."

"That is so typical," Isha hissed. "You treat me like such a baby sometimes. It wasn't *boys* that got me in trouble. It was the stupid rules."

Jaya opened her mouth to respond—something scathing about the virtues of rules; she hadn't worked out the details yet—but a jovial voice interrupted.

"*Bonjour!* Are you beautiful ladies new?"

Jaya turned toward the rich French-accented voice. Two boys had rounded the corner and now stood before them. The tall, broad one who had just spoken smiled warmly, like he was greeting old friends. His skin was a golden brown and his straight dark hair hung to his shoulders. Jaya was fairly good at guessing ethnicities, and she thought he was likely a blend of Southeast Asian and Western European.

Isha set her bag down and stepped forward before Jaya could stop her, proffering a hand. "Isha Rao. This is my sister, Jaya. I'm a sophomore, and she's a senior." They shook, and Jaya managed not to wince at Isha's firm handshake, a reminder of her sister's . . . indomitable spirit.

Jaya pushed her annoyance away. It wasn't *entirely* Isha's fault. No one would've known what Isha was up to if the loathsome Emersons hadn't set her up. Why blame Isha for the Emersons being a bunch of grunting troglodytes wrapped in aristocratic finery? Just thinking of it made Jaya want to strike something.

(Not that she ever would. That behavior wouldn't be befitting the heiress to the Rao dynasty.)

The Emersons and Raos had been at it for a long time. In fact, Jaya and Isha's father, or Appa as they called him, said he couldn't remember a time when the clans *weren't* fighting. In the mid-1800s, during the British colonization of India, the Emerson family had infamously stolen a beloved and sacred ruby from one of Mysuru's temples. Even after India had achieved independence, the Emersons refused to return the ruby, claiming it had belonged to them all along.

But Jaya's great-great-grandmother got the last laugh. She cursed the ruby, something about it bringing misfortune to the Emersons and eventually resulting in a termination of the bloodline. She also made sure to circulate the news about the curse far and wide—far enough and wide enough to reach the Emersons. To make them sweat and rue the day they'd cheated the Raos, ostensibly.

Obviously, Jaya didn't believe in the legitimacy of the curse. She was a child of the twenty-first century. Still, her great-great-grandmother's generation *had* believed in it, and for many years Jaya hadn't understood why her relative would curse an entire lineage to end. Yes, they'd stolen a ruby, but that had been in the 1800s. Why, in the mid-twentieth century, would her great-great-grandmother have done something so cruel?

Then Appa had explained to Jaya how much pain and suffering there had been during the British Raj. By stealing the ruby and then refusing to return it, the Emersons hadn't just taken a jewel. They'd seized a piece of vital Indian history they had no claim to. Then, even when the British finally gave India back to her people, the Emersons had kept the ruby as a token of their superiority, of their arrogance, of their ultimate victory. It was this final insult that Jaya's great-great-grandmother had been unable to abide. Remorselessness was absolutely cause for execration.

Now Jaya finally understood her great-great-grandmother's rage. It was nearly impossible to look the other way when someone hurt something you cared for so deeply and refused to atone.

She set her bag down like Isha had and forced herself to smile. "How do you do? We're new this year."

"*Oui*, I thought so!" The boy slung an easy arm around Isha, and Jaya struggled not to tear it off. Isha hated her overprotectiveness, and Jaya was trying to be better about it. "It is no problem at all. I shall get you very comfortable. I'm Leo Nguyen, a senior as well. And this"—he gestured at a scrawny, short Indian boy who was intensely focused on his phone and refused to look any of them in the eye—"is my good *ami* Rahul Chopra."

Jaya studied Rahul's snub nose, the fringe of his eyelashes, the hint of stubble at his chin. Leo seemed friendly and outgoing, properly socially groomed by his parents. Rahul, on the other hand . . . His shirt was baggy, his pants were too short, and the colors clashed, as if he'd just picked clothes at random.

Something about him seemed familiar to Jaya; she was sure she'd met him before. Thanks to Amma's gentle but insistent coaching on royal etiquette, she'd made up a visual cue to remember him. "Rahul Chopra," she said slowly as it finally came to her: a shy boy in front of the winglike building of the Delhi Secretariat. "Is your mother Mukhyamantri Arti Chopra? The chief minister of Delhi?"

Rahul nodded and sneaked a glance at her before looking down at his phone again, his fingers tapping rapidly at the screen. With a slight prickle of sympathy, Jaya remembered his awkward fidgeting from their previous meeting. It wasn't easy to forget someone who drew as much attention for being different as Rahul did.

"You're Rajkumari Jaya Rao," he said. "My mother knows your father. We met six years ago, at the wedding reception for Nehika and Pritam Gupta. You were wearing a beaded red *lehenga*, and your sister, Isha, was in a matching yellow one. I would say more, but I'm very invested in the outcome of this chess game."

Jaya gawked at him, though every well-mannered bone in her body told her not to. "You're playing chess? That fast?" His hands were practically blurry with the speed of his moves. "Surely no one could make moves that quickly?" Jaya looked at Leo, sure Rahul was pulling her leg.

Leo laughed. "Please. Do not get him started on how chess is just a formalized logic system."

Rahul said immediately, "Chess *is* just a formalized logic system. If you look at the discreet graph, for instance—"

"Wait. How did you remember what we were *wearing* when we met? That was so long ago!" Isha said. Oh yes. Jaya had been so distracted by his swift chess fingers, she'd failed to see the more alarming part of what he'd said.

They all stood there in awkward silence until Rahul coughed.

"I . . . I have a knack for remembering details," Rahul said, still not meeting their eyes. "I'm not being creepy. That's what some people say, but my brain just works differently from most others'. I suspect those people don't understand the neuroscience of memory—"

Leo interjected with a sudden laugh and clapped Rahul on the back. "*D'accord*," he said jovially, though his smile looked like

Appa's when a teacher told him Isha excelled at physics but had the lowest grade in home economics. "Let us not distress the new girls on their first day. There will be plenty of time for them to hear the rumors on their own."

Isha and Jaya glanced at each other, and then Jaya forced a laugh of her own. "You haven't distressed us at all. I'm glad we made such an impression on Rahul." It was coming back to her now, the reason Rahul's parents had sent him away from the public eye in India. He was too different, too strange, to be a politician's son. She'd known that some of the villagers in rural Delhi thought his mother had been cursed before he was born, due to her "mannish" (read: ambitious) nature.

"Wait just a moment. Did you say 'Rajkumari'?" Leo said to Rahul, turning to look at them with renewed interest. "As in, *princess*?"

Here it was, the inevitable question Jaya was prepared for. Even at St. Rosetta's. She shook her head. "Rahul's too generous. India doesn't have an authoritative monarchy anymore, but yes, we do come from the Rao family that used to rule Mysuru in South India."

Leo grinned. "*Chouette!* We have a member of the British aristocracy here—Grey Emerson. Or Lord Northcliffe, to use his official title. Do you know him? Perhaps there is some kind of royal family network?" He laughed jovially.

A dozen responses flew into Jaya's head. *Know him? Not personally, but I'm no stranger to the tears and heartache his family caused mine.* Or *No, but my fist would love to make acquaintance with his jaw. Could you point me in the right direction?* But, of course, she kept her thoughts to herself.

The thing was, refusing to return the ruby wasn't the last of the Emersons' transgressions. Far from it, actually. Perhaps as payback for the "curse" (British aristocrats tended to be as superstitious as Indian royal families, Jaya knew)—or perhaps because they were just cruel—the Emersons regularly released vitriol into the Indian tabloids about the Rao family. Not that the Raos just sat there and took it. Jaya remembered more than an occasion or two when they'd struck back at the Emersons in various business dealings and political connections—all warranted, of course. It was a seesawing, back-and-forth enmity that was second nature to both clans.

This time, though, the Emersons hadn't gone after the adult Raos like they usually did. This time they'd gone after Isha. And, unfortunately, this time everything the tabloids had printed, everything the Emersons had leaked to them, *was* true.

Jaya remembered asking Kiran Hegde, fellow trusted royal from a different clan in the Indian state of Karnataka, why the Emersons had changed their modus operandi. "It doesn't make sense," she'd said to him on the phone. "Something feels off. Why now? Why Isha?"

"I don't know," Kiran had said. "Why don't you call and speak with the journalist on staff? The man who wrote the article? He probably won't reveal his source, but he might give you a hint about what the Emersons are up to."

So Jaya had done just that. She'd called the tabloid, spoken to the reporter, and asked him who was behind the leaked picture of Isha. She remembered distinctly how that smug, greasy little man had paused before saying: "Would it come as a great surprise if I said it was the male heir of a family that finds you Raos particularly deplorable?"

"You mean a male *Emerson* heir," Jaya had said, fuming, her hand clenched around her cell. "I suppose I knew that all along.

Which one of them was it? And why did they come after my sister?"

"That I cannot say," the reporter had said, practically cackling with glee. Jaya imagined him in his stuffy, crammed office, his feet jauntily up on the desk. "But can I get a quote about how you're dealing with the story? Do you feel a lot of rage, Jaya? And what about Isha? Is she still 'drowning in a bottomless well of mortification'?"

She'd pressed "end" without saying another word.

Kiran had been right to instruct her to go to the source. Recently, Amma and Appa had been hinting that Jaya marrying Kiran might be a good political move for the Raos. It made sense. He was the firstborn son of the well-placed Hegde royal family. An alliance would only strengthen both estates. When the time came, Jaya would be happy to do it.

Now, at St. Rosetta's, Jaya felt Isha's sharp gaze on her, and took her time answering. She inhaled slowly and deliberately, trying to calm her rubbed-raw nerves. Then, pushing her hands into the back pockets of her jeans, she said slowly, "I've . . . heard of Grey Emerson. Is he here?"

"Yes, and he has disappeared again as he does," Leo said, exchanging a glance with Rahul that Jaya didn't understand. "But we can introduce you on Thursday, the first day of classes. Please come sit with us in the senior dining hall during breakfast."

"We have the table all the way to the back and right," Rahul added helpfully.

"That's nice of you to include Jaya!" Isha chirped.

In spite of her cheerful tone, Jaya could see the worry in Isha's eyes. All summer long, Isha had seen the embers of anger burning in Jaya's heart. She was no stranger to the way any mention of the Emersons had flushed Jaya's cheeks, fevered her eyes. Now she was worried how Jaya would react to the knowledge that an Emerson went to this school.

But that wasn't all Jaya saw in her sister's eyes. Jaya recognized Isha's anxiety, too. As was her nature, Isha had been quick to forgive and forget the Emersons' deception; she'd just wanted to move on with her life. But Jaya had seen how the scandal had left her usually effervescent sister flat, dull, empty. She'd worried during Isha's blackest period that she wouldn't come back to her whole. Now, in Isha's eyes that were just a bit too wide, in her smile that was just a bit too stiff, Jaya saw Isha's memories of that time resurface.

But Jaya would be her shield now. No Emerson would ever hurt her sister like that again.

Jaya smiled her most convincing smile at the boys. "Yes, thank you," she said. "I'd really like that." And she'd worried finding a way to get close to Grey might be difficult.

"Heyyyooo, what up?"

A pale-skinned girl with cropped, flame-red hair bounded up to the boys, her smile ebullient. Even dressed in distressed denim shorts and a cropped white T-shirt, she carried herself with the effortless grace and easy nonchalance of someone who was used to being popular and well liked. At nearly the same height as Leo, who Jaya guessed was about six feet tall, she towered over both sisters. Her green eyes wandered over them slowly. "New meat?" she asked, glancing at her friends.

Rahul pushed his glasses back, his mouth twitching with what looked like eager energy. "This is Rajkumari aka Princess Jaya and her sister, Princess Isha," he replied. Jaya got the feeling he liked things "just so;" one of those people who believed rules and norms existed for a reason. They'd get along just fine. "Princesses, this is Daphne Elizabeth McKinley."

"More blue bloods?" Daphne Elizabeth said, cocking her head. Her accent was American, Jaya noticed. Isha and Jaya shared a mostly British accent that came with having attended schools all over the world that emphasized the virtues of the Queen's English accent. The irony was that they'd been back in India for less than a year before disaster struck. Perhaps they should've stayed away.

"Don't we have enough of those?" Daphne Elizabeth continued. But her voice was gently teasing, inviting them to join in.

Taking her cue, Jaya laughed. "Apparently not."

Daphne Elizabeth grinned. Her gaze falling to Jaya's pendant, she whistled and leaned in. "I like your pendant."

Jaya smiled. "Thank you. My father got it for me."

"And look who is talking about blue blood," Leo said, rolling his hazel eyes. To Jaya and Isha, he added, "Daphne Elizabeth is the heiress of the McKinley dynasty."

Jaya saw the revelation on Isha's face mirror hers. "McKinley Hotels!" Jaya said, smiling fondly. "*Love* your heated towels. Wrapping up in one after a long day is the best feeling."

A group of boys, other seniors from the look of them, walked past them and toward the French doors to their left. Daphne Elizabeth's eyes followed them. "Glad to hear it," she said, forcing her gaze back to Jaya. A tinkling sound permeated the air. "Oh, that's my cell. I'll catch you guys later. Ta!" And off she went, pulling her cell phone from her pocket.

Leo looked after her, shaking his head. "*Elle est toujours presée.* Rushing, rushing, rushing." Turning to Jaya and Isha, he said, "All right, we were going to help one of our friends unpack. You ladies are welcome to go with us . . . ?" He tossed a questioning look at Rahul, who nodded.

"Oh, well, thank you," Jaya said. "But I think we need some time to unpack too, and rest after our flight."

"Okay," Rahul said, already turning away.

"Dr. Waverly! New people!" Leo called out. Jaya turned to see a middle-aged woman with pale, fragile-looking skin turn to survey them from across the entrance hall. When she caught sight of the sisters, recognition flashed across her face and she began to hurry over. Leo waved and followed Rahul to the doors. "See you tomorrow in the dining hall!"

Isha turned to Jaya. "What was that about Grey Emerson going here?" she said, speaking quickly, before the headmistress was close enough to overhear. "Jaya . . . did you know about that? Because I'm pretty sure Appa and Amma don't." Isha was supposed to call her "Akka," the honorific title bestowed upon elder sisters. But Jaya didn't have time to argue that point.

She arranged her face into the most nonchalant expression she could. "Of course I didn't know. And we probably shouldn't tell Appa and Amma. I mean, what's the point of worrying them? We'll just keep out of his way and he'll keep out of ours, okay? Remember, we're supposed to lie low." She was a rather good liar when she wanted to be, but still, her heart pounded. If Isha told their parents, she'd be utterly—

Never mind. The word that came to mind was too improper to mention.

Isha bit her lip, studying Jaya carefully. Finally, she nodded. Jaya breathed out a silent sigh of relief, thankful for Isha's younger-sister-level trust in her.

"Okay," Jaya said, putting an arm around Isha and squeezing her. "Besides, I won't let it be a problem. I promise."

Dr. Waverly's heels echoed across the lavish Moroccan tiles as she made her way to them. "Princess Jaya and Princess Isha," she said deferentially in a mid-Atlantic accent, bowing slightly. "I'm Dr. Christina Waverly, the headmistress here at St. Rosetta's International Academy. We are honored to have you join us. I am so sorry we had no one waiting for you. I was informed that you wouldn't be arriving until much later tonight." She paused, her gaze lingering on the rose pendant, as most people's did. "Oh my. What a *beautiful* piece of jewelry."

Jaya smiled in her most gracious manner, channeling Amma. "Thank you so much. My father acquired it at a gold *souk* in Dubai."

"He has exquisite taste." Jaya could tell Dr. Waverly was trying her hardest not to stare at the rubies. The necklace's strangely mesmerizing effect was what had enchanted Appa in the first place.

"Thank you," Jaya said again. "Oh, and please call me Jaya and my sister Isha. We decided to take an earlier flight from Munich. You couldn't have known."

Dr. Waverly nodded, the double strand of pearls around her neck clattering together. She was clearly a jewelry aficionado herself. Folding her hands neatly against her navy skirt, she asked, "I trust your travels were uneventful?"

"They really were," Jaya answered quickly, nearly forgetting her manners and asking if Dr. Waverly could show them to their rooms already. She had so much to plan. If this were a fairy tale, she might be cackling while bent over a bubbling cauldron. Except, obviously, she was the heroine in this one.

"Excellent," Dr. Waverly said, gesturing toward an open, wood-paneled archway. "Then I can take you both up to your dorms. Of course, with Isha being a sophomore and you being a senior, you will be in different wings." She smiled apologetically. "I did speak to the Maharaja about it."

"Yes, he told us," Jaya said as they wound around the large hall. Across from them, a fireplace soared to the ceiling. She could've easily walked in with her arms spread wide and had room to spare on either side.

"That is so cool," Isha said, following her gaze. "How much snow do you get here?"

"It's not uncommon for us to get close to thirty inches in December and then again in the spring," Dr. Waverly said, smiling a little. "We encourage students to take advantage of the shopping trip in late October to go into Aspen and buy winter gear. It gives you a chance to get to know your cohorts better off campus as well."

Jaya had no interest in shopping or getting to know her cohorts, though of course Dr. Waverly couldn't have known that. No one did. Jaya's only interest was Grey Emerson.

One thing she'd come to realize—sabotage wasn't always cloak-and-dagger. It wasn't always dead-of-night escapades, or masked people swathed in midnight and stars. Sometimes it looked like this: ageless mountains that kept watch and saw all. An elite boarding school 8,800 miles away from home. And somewhere deep inside, an unsuspecting aristocrat.

# Grey

Grey sat back against the rough granite on Mount Sama and looked down at the tiny town of St. Rosetta, shops and small buildings dotting it like thorny burrs. In the distance, he could make out the bigger neighboring town of Aspen. In a couple of months, everything would be covered in a heavy coat of snow. Grey liked the snow; he felt perfectly hidden in its thick, cold folds.

The wind whipped around him, nine thousand feet in the air, and Grey closed his eyes, reveling in the chill. Thursday was the beginning of a new school year—his last. Summer was already melting into fall, and soon he'd turn eighteen. He swallowed, trying to distract himself from the thought. Eighteen meant . . . complications. Complications he didn't want to think about right then.

This summer had passed him by somehow. The other students and teachers had all flown home. Leo, whose parents were surgeons who traveled the world fixing up people who couldn't otherwise be fixed, flew out and met them wherever they happened to be. Daphne Elizabeth, whose parents ignored her the entire summer and then lavished her with gifts right before she left, which she'd grudgingly admitted made being ignored almost worth it, still went home whenever she could. And if her parents didn't want her, she'd go visit some other family member. Even Rahul, whose parents rented a tiny chalet in France every summer because he was too "odd" to live with them at their home in Delhi, took the summer to be with family.

When Leo had left, he'd frowned at Grey. "When are you going home?"

"Tomorrow," Grey had said, looking away.

"*Ouais, mais* . . . If you don't have any place to be, you can come to Thailand with me. We could go snorkeling."

Grey had shaken his head. "No. But thanks."

Leo, like Daphne Elizabeth—or DE as almost everyone called

her—and Rahul, was clueless about the curse, the reason Grey was never invited home. They knew Grey didn't like talking about his family or his home, so they never brought them up.

But never bringing them up didn't change the truth: that something dark stalked him, had stalked him since birth. That the Rao curse might have already claimed someone he cared about, and he was terrified it would claim him next. Maybe other people would find it odd that Grey, a well-educated, not-quite-eighteen-year-old, would believe in such a thing. But what choice did he have? When other kids were learning their ABCs and "Twinkle, Twinkle, Little Star," Grey was learning the words to a familial curse. Ever since he could remember, he'd been told nothing, *nothing*, was as important as the curse was. So the least he could do to atone for his mother's death—for which he took full responsibility—was to keep away from the manor, to keep his father cushioned from the reminder. He didn't blame his father at all.

The only real place Grey felt safe, like he couldn't hurt anyone, was in the mountains. The great towering stone, jutting out from the earth like vengeful gods, felt indestructible. They'd been there millennia before Grey, and they'd be here long after he was gone.

His cell phone beeped in his pocket. Grey frowned; he'd forgotten to silence it.

**Where are you?**

It was Leo. The other students, even those who, for some unknown reason, considered themselves his "friends," were all back for the semester, but he'd purposefully made himself scarce. Being alone over the summer always did something to him—the longer he spent alone, the more alone he wanted to be. Sometimes he imagined the world without him. Would anyone really miss him when he was gone? By all accounts, his existence was a cosmic mistake anyway.

**Out,** he typed back.

**Oh, oui, out,** the response came back immediately. **That makes everything clearer.**

Grey waited.

**We met someone interesting,** Leo, used to Grey's cryptic silences, added. **Princess Jaya Rao and her sister, Isha. You know them? They seemed to know of you.**

Grey felt a jolt of shock travel up his spine. The Rao sisters were *here*? But why?

He took a breath. He'd lived under the shadow of the Rao curse his entire life. He distinctly remembered being dropped off at St. Rosetta's when he was almost six years old, about to begin kindergarten. In Dr. Waverly's leather-and-brass office, his father had looked him in the eye. Dr. Waverly was waiting outside, giving them some privacy to say their goodbyes.

"Listen to me, Grey," Father had said solemnly, and Grey had known whatever he was about to say was important. He'd listened very closely. "You'll never be like the other children here, even though many of them are outcasts themselves. You're . . . different. You'll always be different." Father's face had contorted ever so slightly. "The Raos have seen to that. This is your burden to bear."

Grey still remembered his confusion. "But I want to make friends," he'd said.

Father had grasped him by the upper arm, hard. His water-colored eyes bored into Grey's. "You must keep to yourself," he'd said, each word slow and deliberate. "You hurt Mother because of what you are."

Grey had stared, aghast. Of course Mother was dead, but had *he* killed Mother somehow? Why had no one told him before now?

"The curse," Father had said, still looking at him in that unsettling way. "Do you remember what I've told you about your curse?"

Grey nodded, his mind still reeling with what he'd just learned, about his hand in Mother's death. But the poem was ingrained in him. Father had taught it to him when he was very young. He remembered the curse.

"The curse has tainted your blood. It's like a virus." Seeing Grey's incomprehension, he'd grunted impatiently. "And because of that, you won't ever have any friends. People will sense there's something wrong with you; they'll hurt you. Best to keep your distance and save yourself the pain. Do you understand?"

Grey had nodded again, trying to grasp what was being said. The curse . . . the curse had caused Mother to die. Already, he could feel a tiny hardening in his heart, like it was growing a protective shell. He wouldn't cry. He didn't need to cry.

Letting go of Grey, Father had gotten up abruptly and walked to the door. His hand on the knob, he'd said without turning around, "You can come home at the holidays." And then he'd left. Grey was never invited home for the holidays.

And now the Rao sisters were here. But . . . so what? St. R's was a popular school with international students of checkered backgrounds. If anything, their sudden appearance should be a reason for curiosity and interest, not alarm. The universe didn't revolve around Grey.

Vaguely, he responded.

Well, you can meet them at breakfast Thursday, Leo typed. But do you want to meet for dinner tonight? Just us guys and DE?

# CHAPTER 3

# Jaya

Dr. Waverly, Isha, and Jaya approached another set of stairs at the north end of the building. These were wide, with carved mahogany balustrades, and covered in a rich red-and-tan carpeting. A large skylight overhead let in sunlight that fell in dappled squares on each step. Jaya trod on the patches of light, feeling the warmth beaming through her shirt and seeping through her shoes.

Two very young-looking students passed them, going down. They smiled politely at Dr. Waverly, darting curious glances Isha and Jaya's way.

"Hello, girls," Dr. Waverly said. To the sisters, she continued, "This environment can take some getting used to, but I want you to know the faculty and staff at St. Rosetta's are committed to your success. We're always here to meet any of your needs. The front office is staffed twenty-four hours a day, seven days a week, during the school year to cater to our international students and families. We have students from a hundred countries around the world, you'll be interested to know." Jaya bit her lip to keep from smiling; Dr. Waverly sounded exactly like the official school brochure. "We're very flattered to have people of your caliber choose us, Prin—Jaya."

**No,** Grey typed, and put away his phone. Leo would no doubt be hurt, but no doubt he'd forgive Grey. *Why,* Grey wasn't sure. It wasn't like he gave him or Rahul or DE anything to hang on to. Maybe they thought of him as charity. Grey ground his teeth, his jaw set. Let them think of him whatever they wanted to. They were immaterial. They had to be.

He sat back against the boulder behind him and closed his eyes. The time had almost come for him to step out from his hideaway, as it did every year.

"Of course," Jaya said, reciting the response she'd practiced with Amma a dozen times before they left. "It's essential that we attend an Ivy League university in the US, and our parents feel St. Rosetta's will best prepare us to do so."

"And after we graduate, we can sit on the same charity boards as our mother and drink chai with the same boring ladies every afternoon," Isha muttered under her breath. When Jaya darted a warning glance at her, her face was smooth and impassive. She even batted her eyes for good measure. It was exactly this kind of attitude that had gotten them into the situation they were in in the first place.

"I'd say your parents chose wisely, but I am, of course, quite biased." Dr. Waverly laughed quietly and led them to what a gold-lettered sign proclaimed to be the SOPHOMORE WING.

"Thank you," Jaya said as Isha poked around. "I think Isha and I will be okay from here."

"I could show you your room in the senior wing, if you wish . . ."

"No, that's all right." Jaya smiled. "I can find it myself. It'll help me get a feel for things, if you don't mind."

Dr. Waverly studied her for a moment before smiling back. "Independence. I do respect that." She handed Jaya two keys. "Those are printed with your suite numbers. Classes begin at eight a.m. Thursday, which gives you a day and a half to settle in. The office has notified me that your uniforms are ready for pickup and they're finalizing your schedules now. That should be everything you need for your first days. Please let me know if I can be of service."

Once Dr. Waverly disappeared down the stairs, Jaya turned to survey the sophomore wing. Isha was already perusing a bookcase to their left. The wall nearest Jaya was lined with photographs in gilt frames. A sign informed her that these were just a few of the notable people who'd graduated from St. Rosetta's International Academy. There were kings and queens, prime ministers, presidents, famous novelists, musicians, artists, and a few A-list Hollywood actors and actresses.

Jaya wandered into the common area where a couple of students lounged, talking or texting on their phones. More than a century of students' feet had worn silk-smooth grooves into the wood. The floor-to-ceiling windows along one wall overlooked the rolling greens of the campus with the purple-black mountains beyond. Green velvet sofas and gold armchairs were arranged strategically in front of a fireplace.

Isha was pawing through the books when a girl with curly dark hair looked up at her from a plush maroon settee and said, "Hey."

Isha turned, her smile instantaneous and warm. "Hi."

"I'm Raina. Are you new here?"

As Isha began to forge a new friendship—a skill that had always come easily to her but seemed like magic to Jaya; *her* best friends were made from words—Jaya walked up and pressed the room key into her hand. Isha barely glanced at her as she said, "Thank you."

"I'll be up in my room," Jaya murmured as the round-cheeked, pale-skinned girl prattled on about which teachers were the best and which meals Isha should be wary of in the dining hall. Jaya got the feeling her jaw muscles were well exercised. "Text me when you're ready to eat."

Isha nodded absently and then launched into a battery of questions.

Jaya walked up two more flights of stairs, feeling slight misgivings at leaving Isha, even though she knew she'd be perfectly safe.

She couldn't help it; the need to protect Isha had been ingrained in her since she was young and they'd wander the palace grounds together as children.

Homes didn't get much safer than palaces—with bodyguards and grounds guards and shifty-looking men who tailed Appa and never took off their sunglasses . . . They were told to call them "uncles," but someone had once told Jaya they were highly trained bodyguards. And when she was younger, they'd even had chained tigers along the borders of their land. (The tigers ate ninety pounds of raw meat at each meal. It hadn't escaped Jaya that she'd weighed exactly that much at that age. She didn't go anywhere in the vicinity of the tigers again after that realization.)

So, yes, palaces were safe. But even so, Jaya was constantly alert so Isha wouldn't fall in one of their many ponds or wander off into the forest beyond their property. When Isha leaned too far out a high palace window, eager to study a parrot perched in the mango tree outside, it was Jaya who grabbed the back of her tunic and pulled her back in, refusing to let go until her sister's feet touched safe ground once again. While Isha flew down the marble stair banisters when Amma wasn't looking, Jaya would run behind her, one hand out just in case Isha needed her.

Isha was as unburdened by fear as Jaya was cautious. Even though they were only two years and two months apart, Isha seemed so much younger, so much more naive. As the eldest, it was Jaya's responsibility to make sure Isha was always safe. And earlier this year, she'd failed completely in that duty. Bodyguards and tigers didn't guarantee safety against every danger facing a royal family. Not even close.

When Jaya emerged onto the senior wing, she saw Dr. Waverly was right about the floors being identical. Even the common area was the same as the one on Isha's floor, except for a popcorn machine in one corner. A few students sat talking on the sofa, but none of them glanced up as she walked past. Jaya followed the hallway to room 301, and used the key Dr. Waverly had given her to let herself in.

Her room looked comfortable enough. A bed made neatly with soft green linens was tucked into the corner. An ornate-but-functional desk, ready with the newest Mac laptop and a lamp, stood across from it. Jaya walked to the picture window and gazed down into the gardens, her hands shaking just the slightest bit as it finally hit her.

She was *here*. She'd crossed a big hurdle already, without even trying: she'd met people who knew Grey Emerson and had been invited to sit with them. As far as Appa and Amma knew, they'd gone to St. Rosetta's to get away from the constant media attention, to give Isha a break from the relentless circus her life had become, thanks to Grey's family. Jaya felt only slightly guilty at having withheld some very important information from her parents. And just a touch proud. She could have been a spy if she wanted to. (But naturally she didn't. That wasn't a fitting profession for a royal.)

The scandal had broken right before summer vacation, and the public outcry showed no signs of remitting. Appa's face had been drawn and sallow. "I really do think the wisest course of action is for you to go with Isha to St. Rosetta's International Academy. They're used to this kind of thing there. It's the best place for her now, Jaya. At least until everyone forgets. The astrologer says you'll be safe there."

"I agree with you, Appa," Jaya had replied, though hearing the once-proud Maharaja Adip Rao concede defeat made her stomach curdle like sour milk. The blood of so many great Rao rulers ran through Appa's veins, and hers. They were cut from the same cloth; surrender didn't even usually occur to them.

That was when Jaya had realized that the Emersons hadn't just sullied her sister's reputation; they'd stolen something sacred. They'd tainted the essence of her family, the very pride and honor and strength that made them who they were.

When the school year start date was a week away, their St. Rosetta's welcome packet had come in the mail. In it were log-in details to a private online group for students at the Academy. Jaya had logged in, wanting to see who else she might recognize—the world of elites was smaller than you'd expect, really—when she'd seen it, in the *E* section. Her eyes went right to his name, like a soldier spying the glint of an enemy rifle.

**Name:** Grey Emerson

**Formal Title:** Lord Northcliffe of Westborough

**Added:** 5 years ago

**Status:** Inactive, never logged in

Unlike everyone else's profile, his didn't have a picture. It was annoying; Jaya had been unable to find a single recent picture of Grey Emerson online, even with extensive googling. She couldn't remember hearing much about him at any of the many events she'd attended over the years, except perhaps that his father, the duke, was an awful man. And that his mother had died in childbirth when Grey was born.

But that was information about his parents, not really about him. It was like he *wanted* to stay hidden. Still, this much was true:

an Emerson went to the very school Appa had picked, that their astrologer had picked. And not just any Emerson . . . the male heir of a family that found the Raos particularly deplorable. Just like the journalist had told her. The very person who'd brought so much pain to her family. The coincidence was remarkable. So much so that she began to wonder . . . was it a coincidence at all? Perhaps this was fate, finally smiling on the Raos. Perhaps it was an opportunity, perfectly laid out in Jaya's path.

Right then, staring at the screen, Jaya had known his presence at St. Rosetta's meant something. Something big. There was no question; she would take the opportunity, as anyone would. A dark little sapling of a plan began to form in her mind.

But if this *was* an opportunity, what was it an opportunity *for*, exactly? In the week following her discovery, Jaya had racked her brain. What could she do to Grey Emerson to exact her revenge? She'd thought of and discarded: poisoned tea, a carefully placed arrow to the heart, and laxative cake. All too obvious.

And then, one day while she was in her room getting dressed, it had come to her.

Jaya'd spun in a slow circle, until she was facing the mirror on her dresser. Looking at her reflection, she'd said, "What weapons do I have at my disposal?" Her bare hands, and nothing else. She blinked and watched her reflection blink back. *You have gorgeous hair*, she heard one of her governesses saying. And an aunt had once said to her mother, when she thought Jaya wasn't listening, "You'll have to keep an eye on this one, Parvati. Boys are going to be chasing her from the time she turns fourteen."

Hmm. Jaya had walked closer to her reflection. She *did* have a rather symmetrical face, and wherever she went, plenty of suitors.

Who was it that said, "Beauty is a weapon; a smile is its sword"? Could she use that against Grey Emerson somehow?

And then it came to her almost immediately.

"You could break his heart," she whispered to her reflection. "You could make him fall in love with you and wreak havoc on his life, just like he wreaked havoc on yours. You could teach him to never come after the Raos again." Yes, she could certainly do that. The Emersons had shown her that emotional pain was infinitely worse than physical agony.

Now, as Jaya explored her new quarters, she thought about the decision she'd made. She felt a faint stirring of guilt, like leaves in a light breeze, at the thought of the extreme deception she'd be carrying out. But in the next instant, she pushed it away. An eye for an eye, that had always been her motto. She could let Grey Emerson believe she was the only one for him. She could pose as his perfect "other half." She could be toxic and cancerous on the inside, but beautiful and serene on the outside. She could slowly infiltrate his life until he had no choice but to love her. And then she'd break his heart completely. Let Grey Emerson feel the torment of a shattered soul. Let him take it back to his father, to the entire Emerson clan— the Raos weren't as meek or helpless as they seemed to think.

But . . . could she really pull this off?

Jaya walked to the dresser and ran a finger along its polished stone top, considering the enormous task before her, feeling the thrill of purpose, a twinge of anxiety at the unknown. Grey Emerson had to have a lot of poison in his heart for what he'd done to the Raos. But Jaya was certain that if she pretended she had no doubts about him, if she pretended to be suitably submissive and sweet and smitten, his giant male ego would have no hope but to fall for her.

But in order to get him to that place, Jaya would have to work extremely hard. And what did she know about love, really? Or how to make a boy fall? She was completely out of her depth, a gladiator hoping to disguise herself at a debutante's ball.

Well, at the very least, this whole thing with Grey— *pretending* to be in love—could be practice for the real thing. Jaya had known from a very young age that she was meant to marry another Indian royal. Someone like Kiran Hegde. He knew what Jaya's life was like, what was expected of her. The Raos and Hegdes had a good relationship, likely because the Rao dynasty was slightly bigger than the Hegde dynasty and they shared little competitive interest, being historical allies. There was no need to be unfriendly when you already had the better piece of pie.

And, of course, Kiran had proved himself to be a valued ally when he'd connected Jaya with the journalist to get to the bottom of who was behind the scandal. They had a lot in common. Tradition and decorum were important to the both of them, for instance. Kiran wanted to go to an engineering college, which was somewhat interesting. And they both . . . well . . .

Jaya bit her lip and regarded herself in the mirror. The truth was, she wasn't exactly attracted to Kiran, not in the *strictest* sense of the word. Physically, he was gorgeous—tall enough, dark, and princely. But there was no emotional spark between them at all. According to Amma, that'd come later. What was important was that they had a solid foundation to build on.

Kiran had the same expectations for himself as she did for herself. To him, there was nothing more important than the Hegde line. He could wax on for hours about the strength and virility (that he'd want to talk about the latter Jaya found. . . baffling, but she let it slide) of the Hegdes and how they were meant for even bigger things. Kiran might even be more passionate than Jaya about his position, which she found rather pleasing. *There* was something that could bind the two of them together. After Isha's scandal, things had gotten a little . . . quiet with Kiran. A little cooler, probably because he was worried how being scandal-adjacent might affect the Hegdes. But Jaya was confident she could bring things back on track.

Perhaps when she was done with Grey Emerson, Jaya would even be a master flirter (but still a subtle one, so as to not be gauche). She was okay at it, but she knew she had room to improve. If only that had been one of the courses she'd studied at any of the private schools she'd attended over the years.

Jaya sighed and turned away from the mirror, pacing restlessly back toward the window. She would've never guessed the first time she fell in love, it would be a lie. There would be no fairy-tale Prince Charming for Jaya. But that was exactly what had to happen. In order to weaken Grey Emerson, Jaya had to get him to be vulnerable with her. And what made boys more vulnerable than love?

But there was something missing. How could Jaya get close enough to Grey to make this work? She grasped her ruby pendant, remembering a perfect spring fragmenting into a vicious summer.

Appa had bought the necklace in Dubai in March. Before he'd left, he'd asked her what she wanted, and Jaya had said a red rose. Of course, Appa, being the generous, lavish man he was, had bought her a 24-karat gold-and-ruby rose pendant on a slender gold chain instead. It was stunning; eighteen rubies as big as her pinkie nail coiled in a tight spiral to the center, each ruby a cleverly stylized petal. Jaya had never seen anything like it. When Appa had handed it to her, nestled in its pale cream velvet box, she'd gasped. He'd smiled fondly. "Yes," he'd said. "That was my precise reaction when I first saw it. A beautiful jewel for my beautiful gem of a daughter." It had been an idyllic time, mild and slow and happy.

But then . . . then the earth shook. Grey Emerson had come after Isha for no reason at all. The maliciousness of the photos and rumors he'd fed to the press had taken them all by surprise. Never in recent memory had things been this ugly. What had he been doing in Mysuru that summer anyway? Had he gone there specifically to see how he could hurt the Raos? But why now, and why Isha?

Jaya took a deep breath, steadying herself. These were questions she'd get answers to one day soon. But for now, how was she going to make sure she had enough time to work on Grey Emerson? Yes, she was eating breakfast at his table on Thursday, but what after that? How could she ensure she was in his orbit enough to make him fall?

Something Dr. Waverly said flashed through her brain, a sudden firework of inspiration. *The office has notified me that your uniforms are ready for pickup and they're finalizing your schedules now.*

Smiling, Jaya slipped her cell phone from her pocket and began to dial.

Outside her window, the grasses swayed gently in the summer mountain breeze. In the distance, a stone fountain gurgled happily, its water sparkling in the late-afternoon sunlight. It was peaceful and calm here. A haven.

# Grey

For fuck's sake. Couldn't a guy just sit and read in peace?

Grey glanced over his shoulder. At the other end of the long room, the repellant Alaric Konig and his minions, Lachlan McCoy and that redheaded douchebag Martin Stromberg, rounded on a sophomore. Grey couldn't remember the sophomore's name, but then again, Grey didn't *want* to remember his name.

"Nice uniform," Alaric said, his blond hair carefully styled in a strange wave on his head. "I'm pretty sure that's the one I donated to Goodwill last year."

Martin snickered. "Yeah. And those shoes are the ones *I* donated."

Nice one, Martin. Real original.

"Leave me alone," the sophomore boy said. "I'm just trying to study."

"Right, because otherwise they'll take your scholarship away." Alaric walked closer to the sophomore's table and flipped his book shut. "Uh-oh. How're you going to study now?"

Grey groaned softly. He didn't *have* to get involved; he knew that. But letting those assholes get away with this would really annoy him. He sighed and rose from the table, walking over just as the sophomore got up from his chair, puffing up his chest, strutting with a wannabe alpha-male swagger.

Grey rolled his eyes. *Yeah, kid. Like your skinny ass could take on those two.* Still, you had to admire that kind of spirit.

He felt the tone of the room shift as he walked closer and the four students noticed his presence. Grey had that kind of effect—because he was 6'4" and 220 pounds of muscle, most dudes didn't want to mess with him. They could tell he could handle himself. And if you found him on your side, well, you tended to feel a whole lot better about your situation.

"What do *you* want?" Alaric asked, but Grey saw his eyes touch on Lachlan and Martin, reassuring himself that there were three of them.

"See that book over there?" Grey said, pointing back to his table. "I really want to get back to it. So if you could leave this kid alone and just mosey on out of here, I'd really appreciate it. Don't you have some hair product or other to buy?"

"Think you're funny?" Alaric asked, tossing his head so his gelled hair bounced a tad. "This doesn't concern you, okay? I'm talking to Scholarship Boy here."

Wide-eyed, the sophomore was watching them like they were on TV.

"See, now that's the kind of thing I need you to stop," Grey said, stepping closer. He smiled a little, but his eyes were cold, remote.

Alaric pulled himself to his full height, which was still three inches shorter than Grey. Even counting his hair. Grey Emerson wasn't the least bit worried. He *was*, however, getting pretty irritated.

A weight lifted off Jaya as she ended the call and slipped her phone back into her pocket. She could scarcely believe it had worked, but she wasn't one to poke and prod at a good thing. That it had been so simple to get herself into each and every one of Grey Emerson's classes was just further proof, she knew, that she was meant to be here. That she was meant to exact this revenge.

Well, it was all taken care of now, which meant she could do something just for her. Jaya smiled. She knew where she wanted to go.

Libraries had a unique magic. No matter what country Jaya was in, no matter how far away from home, the glossy wood tables, the smell of book glue, and the whispers of riffling pages always welcomed her back like old friends.

Pushing through a set of heavy double doors on the first floor of the West Wing, Jaya came to an abrupt stop, a soft gasp escaping her lips.

St. Rosetta's library, encased in plush, velvet silence, was three stories tall, with a large, circular first floor. Proud pillars flanked the curving staircases on either side. Jaya stood just inside the doors, her head tilted back, reveling in the breathtaking beauty of the old polished wood, the soft lighting, the enormous stacks of books towering over her. It was an ocean of words, and she stood on the seafloor, letting it wash over her before she made her way to the staircase.

As she idly scanned the shelves on the second floor, the sound of heated voices brought her pause. She tilted her head to listen.

Rounding a corner, Jaya found herself at the entrance to a darkened area. Her eyes were immediately drawn to five boys standing by a large window on the far side of the room. If the raised voices weren't enough of a sign, their crossed arms and tense shoulders definitely said this was not a friendly conversation.

"I'm just curious," a tall guy with a narrow face and gelled blond hair was saying. He grinned, but there wasn't a shred of affection or humor in it. His friends, a red-haired boy and a brown-haired boy, grinned sycophantically back. Jaya casually positioned herself behind a large potted plant so they wouldn't see her. That way, she could run and get help if things got too out of hand. "What's a scholarship worth these days, anyway? Or was it supposed to be a secret?"

"I'm not ashamed of being a scholarship student," a younger white boy with dark hair responded, fists clenched at his sides. His accent was American. "If anything, it shows that I'm here on my own merit. My daddy didn't have to buy my way in."

The blond boy and his two friends took a step closer to the younger boy. "What did you say?"

"*Chill.*" The word was a growl, rumbling and low. Jaya's attention flitted to the fifth boy, the one who'd spoken. He was huge, also white, with an American accent.

The tallest boy had wild, shaggy dark hair, the tips colored a light brown. He wore ripped jeans, and his big feet were clad in old sandals. There was something feral about him, reminiscent of a wild animal. Or a beast.

The feral boy put his hand on the blond boy's chest and held it there, not pushing, but not giving, either. "Why don't you go calm down before this turns into something you really don't want? If I remember, you've got only one fight left before they expel you. I don't think your father would look too kindly on you getting kicked out from your third school in four years."

"You want to be careful who you're talking to like that," the blond boy said, he and his friends turning to the feral boy.

Smirking, the tall boy leaned back and crossed his arms in

one lithe movement. Powerful biceps pressed his shirtsleeves taut. His eyes, a startling, brilliant blue, flashed, and Jaya knew instinctively that if the other boy were to take him on, he'd win easily. "You know, Alaric, I'll take my chances. In my experience, most snakes aren't venomous."

The boys all stared at each other for another minute, the air crackling with the energy of a fight. Jaya held her breath.

The tension collapsed when the blond boy, Alaric, shook his head and turned away, his silent friends following in his tracks. They passed right next to Jaya as they walked out a door on the other side of the darkened area, but none of them noticed her behind the plant.

"You didn't have to do that. I can take care of myself."

The other boy cocked his head. He was enormous, built like a bear, and he dwarfed the slighter, younger one. "Sure, kid." He began to turn away.

The younger boy straightened up. "My name's Elliot."

"Congratulations." After a pause, the feral boy glanced over his shoulder. "Stay away from those three. And if I were you, I'd clear out of here in case they decide to come back."

Elliot crossed his arms. "Why should I have to go? They were the ones who bothered me. I was just in here studying."

The older boy sighed. "Doesn't matter. Alaric's an asshole and he's gonna be looking for revenge. I'm not sticking around to watch out for you. So if you know what's good for you, get out." Without waiting for a response, he walked off.

Elliot stood looking after him for a long moment. Then, sighing, he gathered his books and slid them into a backpack. Slinging the bag onto his shoulder, he followed the older boy out.

They both passed by Jaya on their way out the door on the far side, but just like Alaric and his friends, neither of them seemed to notice her presence. She stood there a moment longer, smiling a little to herself. She always did like when the underdog won. Even though that blue-eyed feral boy seemed rather grumpy, like a bear with a thorn in its paw.

Sliding out from behind the plant, Jaya walked to the nearest stacks. Nonfiction: Renaissance. She was reaching for one of the books when a deep male voice broke the silence. "Every man is surrounded by a neighborhood of spies."

Jaya jumped and spun around, heart slamming against her rib cage. A hulking figure stood in the doorway, but backlit as he was, Jaya couldn't see his face. Her tongue stuck to the roof of her mouth like glue.

"Who are you?" the figure demanded, walking forward slowly, features finally materializing.

It was the feral boy from just moments before. His head was cocked, electric blue eyes focused on her the way a wolf might study an interloper in the forest. Though Jaya's pulse pounded furiously, she attempted a joke to defuse the situation, taking a page from Amma's etiquette book. "Do you always go around quoting Jane Austen to strangers you meet in libraries? It's very charming."

He didn't return her smile. His eyes were hooded, guarded, and his jaw was dotted with a few days' worth of dark stubble. As he walked closer, graceful and silent, Jaya noticed how his broad shoulders took up the space with authority. His eyes seemed to alight on her rose pendant, like almost everyone's did. Unlike everyone else, a shadow passed over his face as he took it in. His expression cleared so quickly Jaya could almost believe she imagined it, and he said, "You still haven't told me why you were spying."

Jaya crossed her arms and gazed straight into those lupine eyes, feeling her nerves fade and her temper bristle. How dare this scruffy, angry boy question *her*? And looming over her like some schoolyard bully? "I wasn't spying. I hid there in case you needed help."

He huffed, and what looked like a smile hovered at his lips. "Not likely."

Jaya shrugged. "Well, I didn't know."

The boy's expression softened a bit at that, and his shoulders relaxed. "No, I suppose you didn't." After a pause, he added, "You're new?"

The tension between them dissipated. "I am. My name's Jaya Rao. I've only just arrived here, and so I thought I'd explore. I knew I'd love the library."

She waited for him to introduce himself, but he just nodded at the sign behind her. "You like Renaissance-era nonfiction?"

Jaya smiled a little, always happy to talk about books. "Of course. Although I read just about anything."

"Then I highly recommend *The House of Medici: Its Rise and Fall*," he said, walking toward the table where he'd apparently left his cell phone.

"Jane Austen and *The House of Medici*?" Jaya was impressed he was familiar with the latter; it wasn't exactly light reading. The book charted the eventual decline of a wealthy, powerful family in Florence. "Well, thanks," she said. "But I've already read it."

He didn't look back as he lumbered toward the exit. "You could always read it again."

She frowned at his back. "Pardon me, but you haven't introduced yourself." He kept walking, as if he didn't hear her. "Hello?" Jaya heard the double doors shut with a muffled thump.

How rude. Some people just didn't have the same breeding she did, she supposed. And she was hard-pressed to remember an odder encounter. Why would this absolute stranger care whether or not Jaya read some old book? Maybe it was an omen, him recommending it. Royal families were rather prone to superstition, and she wasn't an exception. Maybe the mention of the Medici family meant the Emersons would fall into decline as surely as the Medicis did. Or perhaps the boy was just rambling because he wasn't used to human company. He certainly looked the part of the misanthropic recluse.

Jaya shook off the bizarre incident and turned back to the bookshelf, still happy. She was surrounded by books. Heaven couldn't be marred that easily. She'd read until she was sated and then see where the day took her.

# Grey

So that was Jaya Rao.

Grey sat back in the recliner in his room an hour after their encounter, a small stack of animal science books on the end table at his elbow. She was smaller, more harmless-looking than he'd expect for someone from such an evil genetic line. He stared out the window at the gardens below, wondering again why she was here. St. Rosetta's International Academy was a fine institution, but he knew from experience—he'd been here more than a decade now—that most students who transferred in this late in their academic careers had something to hide. St. Rosetta's was a holding cell for the wayward teens of high-profile parents, a place they could be kept safe and away from the public eye until they were old enough to be sent even farther away to college—or until fate intervened. Grey should know.

Grey's own father didn't want to see Grey, didn't want to see his wife's eyes in his son's traitorous face. Grey could understand. He'd been a newborn when his mother died, but he alone had been responsible for her death.

Grey stood and walked to the floor-to-ceiling windows. There, down below in the garden, he saw Jaya Rao sitting on a bench, her face serious, thoughtful . . . and guarded. Her slender fingers played with the pendant at her throat. Something about it had tugged at him when he'd first noticed it in the library, sparkling against Jaya's throat. . . . A blanket of unease settled over Grey.

"Why are you here? And what are you hiding?" he murmured, his breath fogging the glass.

# CHAPTER 4

# Jaya

Isha still hadn't texted by the time Jaya was finished at the library, so she decided to explore the gardens she'd seen from the window in her dorm room. She could use the time to plan her first meeting with Grey Emerson on Thursday, and nature always calmed her. When Jaya was in elementary school, Appa had the palace groundskeepers set up a little bench by the roses where she could spend her summers reading in peace and quiet. It had been her own private sanctuary, away from Isha's troublesome antics, though neither of them said that out loud. Jaya smiled at the memory.

Outside, she walked along a small, winding path. The hedge along the pathway shielded her from anyone who might walk by, and she sat on a bench shaded by two large pine trees, pleased by the privacy, her thoughts returning to Grey Emerson.

Things had fallen into place well so far, Jaya had to admit. She'd been worried about how to insinuate herself into his social group, but it had worked out seamlessly when his friends took care of that. It *had* to be a sign from the universe; she was meant to break Grey's heart.

It wasn't uncalled for, not in the least. There was a running joke in the Rao family: What zodiac sign did the Emersons share? Gemini, because they were all so incredibly two-faced.

But she could play that game too. Thursday morning, the first day of school, she'd begin phase one of her plan. She would flirt and banter to the best of her ability; she'd stroke his ego and smile sweetly at him despite the poisoned arrow in her heart.

Jaya thought of how proud Appa would be of her for defending their family's honor. Once the Emersons had a taste of their own medicine, he'd forgive her instantly for not being candid about her plan.

Glancing down at her rose pendant, Jaya discovered one of the eighteen rubies was missing. She stared at the empty socket, her stomach dropping. She'd worn this necklace for months without incident. She was normally so careful with her things, and to lose a gift from her father? Oh God, Appa. He was going to be beside himself; he couldn't abide irresponsibility. Jaya got down on her knees and began to look.

It was like the stone had disappeared. Five full minutes later, she was still searching under the bench for the missing stone when hurried footsteps crunching down the path startled her out of her thoughts. Jaya saw a flash of red through gaps in the hedge, then heard the sound of someone breathing heavily. She sat quickly back down on the bench. "No, *stop.*" The voice was full, round, every syllable like ripe fruit. She'd heard it only a couple of hours before—Daphne Elizabeth McKinley. "I told you, Alaric, it was a summer-only, messed-up thing. We shouldn't even be out here talking."

Alaric? Could it be the same Alaric from the library?

"Then let's not talk," a smiling, husky, familiar male voice said. Yes, definitely the same boy from the library, although he was being much nicer now (for obvious reasons). His accent was a mixture of American and something else, hard to place, but Jaya thought it might be German. All she could see were his polished black shoes. Jaya considered clearing her throat or sneezing. She didn't want to take part in any inadvertent snooping.

There was silence for a moment. Jaya braced to step out and announce herself when she noticed their shoes moving closer and closer together.

Oh, fantastic. She squirmed—quietly—on her seat.

It wasn't hard to work out what was happening. Isha had sneaked innumerable Harlequin romances from their governess's room—and Jaya had once peeked at one, her young curiosity changing quickly into shock. Plus, palaces came with their share of drama—cooks with maids, bodyguards with village women, governesses with older, visiting cousins (now *that* one had been interesting). If past experiences had taught her anything, it was that her best move was probably to stay here, quietly. Hopefully their . . . *moment* . . . would be over quickly so she could get back to her daydreaming. She wished she had a book to while away the time.

"Look, I can't do this, okay?" Daphne Elizabeth again. "You made your choice when you decided not to break up with her. I can't be your booty call when Caterina's not around."

Jaya sat up straighter in spite of herself: intrigue. She may be a royal, but she *was* only human.

"Daphne—"

"I'm serious. Just leave me alone." But her voice wobbled, and Jaya didn't think she really meant it. Not all the way down, where it mattered. Her expression must've been fierce, however, because shiny-shoed Alaric didn't argue.

Jaya heard retreating footsteps, counted silently to ten, closed her eyes and sighed in relief, and stood.

She found herself face-to-chin with the willowy Daphne Elizabeth. Clearing her suddenly dry throat, Jaya looked up to see shock mingling with anger on Daphne Elizabeth's freckled face, like ink spreading in a cup of water. "You! Were you . . . *spying* on me?"

What was it with people in this school and their obsession with spying? Daphne Elizabeth seemed liable to break Jaya in half and throw the pieces into the bushes, however, so Jaya spoke hurriedly. "No, I wasn't, I promise. I was sitting here when you both began your . . . conversation, and then it was too late to say anything. I didn't want to embarrass you."

Daphne Elizabeth smiled a ghost of a smile, her eyes green fire. "Well, lucky you—you've stumbled onto primo gossip your very first day. Nothing endears you to people more, at least at our school." She raised her arms, waving her fingers dramatically. "Tell people what you heard and watch yourself rise in the social ranks like magic!" Dropping her arms, she sighed, resigned. "And watch *me* be destroyed by Caterina LaValle," she mumbled to herself.

Jaya straightened her shirt, tilted her head back, and looked Daphne Elizabeth right in the eye. "I don't know about the other people at this school, but *I* am a Rao. I would never stoop to that level." Her regal pose was only slightly marred by Daphne Elizabeth's height advantage.

Daphne Elizabeth tensed and studied her for a long minute, as if she didn't know whether or not Jaya was laughing at her. Finally, her shoulders relaxed and she blinked a few times, looking away. "It's just so messed up. I never thought I'd be the kind of person to . . ." She paused. "He already has a girlfriend and I . . . People would never forgive me if they found out. I mean, Alaric and Caterina are an institution at this place. They're the kind of couple everyone wants to be." She bit the inside of her cheek, her eyes searching Jaya's. "You probably think I'm a total mess."

"I don't," Jaya said honestly. "I don't know Alaric and Caterina, and I don't know you, but I *do* know what it's like to have a secret you hope no one finds out. And I know what happens when people do."

They started back up the path in unspoken unison, their feet crunching loudly on the gravel.

Daphne Elizabeth ran a hand through her short crimson hair. Her nails were painted bright green with small diamonds dotting the tops. Smiling at Jaya as they entered the cool interior of the school again, she said, "I like you. I hope you'll come sit with us at breakfast tomorrow."

It was the second invitation she'd received from Grey Emerson's social group. They seemed nice, the kind of people she might actually be friends with if circumstances were different. Jaya wondered how Grey had managed to fool them all. "Thank you. That'd be wonderful."

"Well, I better go get unpacked. I hate leaving it for later." Daphne Elizabeth made a face, half-rueful, half-resigned. "See ya."

Jaya spent another fifteen minutes fruitlessly searching for the missing ruby under the bench. Where had it gone? Rubies didn't just *disappear*. Appa was going to be angry. She'd have to have it replaced before she saw him again.

Sighing, Jaya made her way back around the building, to the stairs.

• • •

Jaya walked up to the senior wing again after texting Isha that she was ready to eat. Inspired by Daphne Elizabeth, she went to her room to unpack while she waited. She stood undecided for a moment, looking at herself in the mirror. The necklace hung at her throat, its one empty socket mocking her. Should she put it away in her drawer to keep it safe until she could get the ruby replaced? Jaya stroked it. It was a reminder of home, a reminder of happier times. She didn't want to part with it yet. She'd just have to be more careful. Nodding firmly to herself, Jaya walked to her suitcase. But before she'd even begun unpacking it, there was a knock on the half-open door. Jaya turned to see a girl with peach-pink cheeks and long blond hair in a braid leaning through the doorway and staring at her unabashedly.

"G'day," the girl said in an Australian accent. "I'm Penelope Grant, your neighbor in 303." She pointed her thumb to her right.

"Oh, hello! It's so nice to meet you. I'm Jaya Rao."

"I know," Penelope breathed, baby-blue eyes wide. "I heard that you're a . . . princess?"

Daphne Elizabeth wasn't joking; gossip and rumors really did seem to fuel St. Rosetta's. Jaya had been here all of three hours. "It's nice to meet you," Jaya said with a modest smile.

Penelope walked in and sat at the edge of Jaya's bed, still looking up at her in awe. "I'm Australian, so say the words 'royal family' and I'm rapt."

Jaya laughed.

"Oh," Penelope said, her smiled fading a bit as her eyes widened. "That is an *exquisite* pendant. I've never seen anything like those rubies."

"Thank you," Jaya said, caressing it very gently, in case any of the other rubies were loose. "My father—"

She was interrupted by a piercing squeal ringing out from somewhere down the hallway. She and Penelope looked at each other for a moment before rushing out to follow the screeching.

The door to room 315 stood wide open. A beautiful dark-haired girl dressed in a stunning emerald-green ball gown was twirling in the center of the room. Two others, both more pale-skinned than her, sat on her bed, watching her with slack-jawed admiration.

"I can't believe Daddy did this!" the girl gushed in a smoky, Italian-accented voice. Tossing a phone to one of her friends, she said, "Take my picture so I can send it to Alaric. I want to make him drool a little." She laughed throatily as she twirled.

Just as Jaya began to realize who she was looking at, Penelope whispered, "That's Caterina LaValle, the only daughter of Italian American multimillionaire Matteo LaValle. There are rumors he'll be running for the Senate soon. Anyway, people call her Queen Cat behind her back. . . . She kind of rules this school."

Caterina LaValle, as in the Caterina-and-Alaric "institution" Daphne Elizabeth had just told her about.

Caterina looked up once her friend had taken her picture. "Oh, hi there," she said, flashing a brilliant smile. She ran her fingers through her mahogany hair, and it cascaded back down in undulating waves around her shoulders.

"Hi, Caterina," Penelope said, her voice breathy with defer-ence. "This is Princess Jaya. From Mysuru, in India. She's new."

"Just Jaya," Jaya corrected easily, smiling. "Jaya Rao. Pleased to meet you."

"So, what do you think of my dress?" Caterina asked,

pirouetting for them. "A custom Valentino. Daddy had it packed in with my things as a surprise. It's for our Homegoing dance later this year."

"It's beautiful," Jaya said, and meant it.

It was the kind of dress that dripped money, even if you couldn't put your finger on why. As Jaya took Caterina LaValle in—her model cheekbones, hair like a silken waterfall down her back, flawless makeup that looked airbrushed on—she realized the repugnant Alaric had chosen someone exactly the opposite of her to have his summer dalliance with. Jaya suddenly felt horrible for Caterina, with her shiny teeth and expensive ball gown.

"Well, excuse me," she said, turning to go, a combination of pity and guilt squirming in her stomach. Jaya might be poised for some major Emerson sabotage, but this girl was an innocent as far as she was concerned. She didn't enjoy knowing about Alaric and Daphne Elizabeth when Caterina didn't. "I should finish unpacking."

"Wait." Jaya felt a hand on her shoulder and turned to see Caterina.

"Penny, come here," one of the girls on the bed called, waving a magazine. "Tell me if this hairstyle is too much."

Penelope, obviously thrilled to be included, pushed past them and into the dorm room.

Caterina stood close to Jaya, still smiling, though her eyes glinted with something dark and sly. "Beautiful pendant," she said, nodding appreciatively at Jaya's throat. "You have good taste."

"Thank you." Jaya smiled. "The credit belongs to my father, though."

"Mm." Caterina cocked her head. "You know, I once visited

Kerala with my father on a business trip. I spent a good amount of time at a resort with Sri Devi Nair, one of the daughters of the royal family in that region."

"I know Sri Devi," Jaya said carefully, unsure of why, exactly, they were having this conversation. A few girls walked past, waving and calling out to Caterina. She responded with a dignified bow of her head but kept her eyes on Jaya. "My family and her family are old friends."

Caterina twirled a lock of hair around a slender finger, the tip of which was doused in pale purple nail polish. "She said that royal families still wield a lot of power in India and even beyond its borders. They're well respected."

"I suppose that's true."

Caterina leaned against the doorframe, the fabric of her gown rustling with the motion. She could've been posing for *Teen Vogue*'s "Dorm Chic" issue. "I know you're new here, Jaya, but I want you to know something. I always take care of my friends." She waved an insouciant hand, and her perfume wafted to Jaya. It was something soft and clear, petals drenched in dew. "Ask Sri Devi if you like. I've helped her out of a jam or two, and she's done the same for me. It can be really helpful, having friends who care."

Jaya met her calculating eyes. She'd known people like Caterina LaValle before. They dealt in the currency of tit for tat; their world ran on you-scratch-my-back-and-I'll-scratch-yours. When one was wealthy enough to buy nearly anything, favors and good graces became a much more valuable currency. But best of all for Jaya's purposes, they usually had their fingers on the pulse of wherever they were, and the uncanny ability to feel secrets fluttering under the thin skin of normalcy. Caterina LaValle, Jaya was sure, could be a very, very helpful ally indeed. Or a formidable enemy. She smiled her most PR-friendly, royal smile. "Any friend of Sri Devi's is a friend of mine."

Caterina grinned and leaned forward to air-kiss her. Jaya returned the favor. "Excellent," she said, pulling back to hold Jaya at arm's length. "I know we'll get on famously."


"Caterina must've really liked you," Penelope said, that same note of awe in her voice once they were back in Jaya's room. "She isn't usually so welcoming."

"We share a mutual friend," Jaya said vaguely, putting her shirts away in her dresser. Her heart sang. She was taking all of what had happened so far—Grey Emerson attending St. Rosetta's and Leo, Rahul, and Daphne Elizabeth asking her to sit with them at breakfast on Thursday—as extremely good omens. It was as though the universe were conspiring to help her bring Grey Emerson to justice. Jaya thought of herself as a logical, practical person, but she couldn't help seeing omens everywhere she looked. It was part of growing up in an Indian family. She thought again of the ruby falling and dismissed it. She couldn't afford to get negative now.

"Knock, knock!" Isha stood at the door, grinning. "Oh. Hello," she said to Penelope. "I'm Isha, Jaya's sister."

"Hello!" Penelope said, holding out her hand.

Isha clasped Penelope's hand with both of hers. "Ah, that Australian accent! It's one of the things I loved most about Sydney when we studied there." She paused, the dimple in her chin giving her a mischievous-yet-cherubic look that had gotten her out of many a scrape. "Well, that and the boys. Australian boys are so adorable."

Jaya tossed her a meaningful glance, eyebrow raised. "Are you ready?"

"Where are you going?" Penelope asked.

"To grab an early dinner at A-caf-demy," Isha explained, naming the café all St. Rosetta's students frequented, according to the brochure (the punny name Jaya didn't care for—it was rather puerile). Then, seeing the way Penelope's face fell a little, Isha began, "Do you—"

"So we'll be seeing you soon," Jaya cut in, turning to Penelope. She didn't want Isha inviting Penelope along. There were matters she needed to discuss with her in private.

Penelope paused, looking a little like a droopy bloodhound. "Right. Cheerio. I'll just catch up with you later, then."

"Wonderful." Jaya smiled and waved. She'd apologize later.

A-caf-demy Bistro was nestled at the base of the rolling hill on which St. Rosetta's main campus sprawled.

Jaya glanced at Isha, stifling a yawn and shivering lightly as they walked along the path in the fading light of dusk. It got cold quickly in the mountains when the sun went down, something she remembered from a visit to the Alps. Her travel-foggy brain had still neglected to remember to bring a sweater on the walk, and Isha didn't have one either. Jaya wouldn't have minded a nap to help with the jet lag, but she'd need to stay awake until later tonight if she wanted to adjust as soon as possible. She had to be as alert as she could be when she met Grey Emerson for the first time.

Isha was dressed in a T-shirt Jaya was very familiar with, one she'd *promised* Jaya she'd throw away. Jaya opened her mouth to say something, but then she realized Isha was playing rather morosely with the hem. She watched, worry clouding her brow.

It wasn't a big sacrifice for Jaya to leave behind her friends in Mysuru—she didn't have that many to begin with. But Isha, being Amma's daughter, was the quintessential social butterfly. Everyone was heartbroken that she was leaving—the teachers, the custodians, the principal, and the students—though obviously they understood why.

Jaya spent countless moments wishing the Emersons had found something horrible to say about her instead. She hadn't had as far to fall as Isha did. Everyone—the media, friends, royal families in other parts of India—was always paying attention to the vivacious, beautiful, talented Isha. When she fell, she fell in full view of her audience, making the humiliation so much worse. Evidently, it was exactly what Grey Emerson had been counting on. God, the vitriol he must've imbibed from his family over the years to execute something this ruthless!

Jaya put her arm around Isha as they turned onto a small road. No cars were visible at all, a far cry from their bustling hometown. Aspen trees towered on either side, their leaves whispering in the slight breeze. Jaya took a breath, preparing herself to say what needed to be said. "Ish, I know things haven't been easy for you these past few months. But we came here for a clean start. So this is just a gentle reminder, before our first day at this school . . ."

Isha sighed. "I know, Jaya. Keep my head down. Do what's expected of me. Appa already gave me the lecture."

Jaya tried not to let her temper rise. "It's not a lecture, Isha. Our father was only doing what he thought best. The whole reason we're here is because—"

"Because of who I am." Isha tried to say it defiantly, like she didn't care, but the catch in her voice gave her away. "I know you want to go home. You had to leave everything behind because of me. The Hegde family probably heard what happened, and propriety is so important to Kiran and his parents . . ." She stopped talking for a second before continuing. "I'm sorry, Jaya."

Jaya stopped in her tracks and turned Isha toward her. "*No.*" She ducked a little to look right into Isha's eyes as she spoke. Isha had gained a lot of height quickly over the past two years, but was still three inches shorter than Jaya's 5'4". She tried to look away, but Jaya cupped her chin. "All this isn't because of who you are. It's because of who *we* are. We're royals, and the rules are different for us. That's why Gr—those *Emersons*"—Jaya spat out their name like it was a curse—"came after you. And why it's so important that we keep a low profile now, that we do what's expected of us. One of them goes to our school. We can't afford to let our guard down again." She took a breath. "As for the Hegde family, don't worry, Isha. It'll all work out, somehow or another."

They began walking again, in silence this time. Isha was the first to speak, her voice suspiciously over-bright. "Quick question: What if I want to take robotics engineering? I was looking in the course catalog and it looks so fun."

Jaya stared at her sister, who was simultaneously the most intelligent and most stupid person she knew. St. Rosetta's International Academy had a whole catalog from which students could pick electives. Options ranged from *French Cooking* to *A Study of the History of Russian Ballet* to *Principles of Global Finance*. But, of course, Isha wanted to take robotics engineering. "That is not advisable, Ish."

"Why not?" Her voice had a hard edge to it. "Plenty of Indian women are engineers."

"Yes, but they're not royals," Jaya reiterated, trying to be patient in spite of her temper beginning to stir and crackle again. She tried to remember that she'd always found it easy to grasp that the rules were different for her than they were for others, simply by virtue of her blood. Isha, though, had fought against her birthright since she was a toddler, screaming "No!" and flinging off her gold bangles before any major event at the palace. Should Isha know better by now? Yes, she should. Did she? No, she absolutely didn't. But perhaps Jaya could point that out gently, with the extreme diplomacy that had been ingrained in her since birth. She needed a light touch here.

"Isha, are you completely *mad*?" she blurted, her voice getting louder with each word she spoke. Sometimes a light touch was overrated. "The Emersons had pictures of you cavorting with those *men*—mechanics in a motorcycle shop!—covered in oil and dirt like some vagrant. Not to mention you were kissing one and hanging all over him and drinking alcohol! Not to mention, you're wearing the very same T-shirt you were wearing that day! I thought you agreed to get rid of it. You're lucky the angle of the shot didn't allow for that quote to be readily seen. That would've been just one more thing for our people to latch on to. One among many." Her cheeks burned at the memory. She'd stared at the pictures for so long, trying to deny that it was *her* little sister in them. "You looked like some—" Jaya stopped to take a breath. "It's in our best interests to show you as a respectable member of the royal family."

"They weren't men, and I wasn't *cavorting*!" she said indignantly, apparently having forgotten her apology of only seconds ago. "You make a mistake *one* time and—" She stopped, taking a breath. "You know I really liked Talin—*and* his crew. What's wrong with kissing someone you like? How does showing my feelings make me a bad person? And this T-shirt? What's so bad about it?" She looked down at it. It was a tight-fitting white baby-doll T-shirt with bold black font on the front. NO GODS, NO MASTERS. Jaya had googled it. The slogan was about *anarchy*. And extreme feminism. Both things a royal Indian woman should definitely *not* appear to support. Seeing Jaya's thunderous expression, Isha hurried to continue. "They were boys my own age, and I was helping them with their business. Not everyone in India can afford school, Jaya. You know that. Some people have to earn a wage from childhood. I'm an excellent mechanic. I was helping them earn enough money so they didn't have to close the shop! Talin knew I was a good mechanic; it's why they agreed to let me help out in the first place. Can't you see I was doing a good thing?"

Jaya put a hand to the bridge of her nose and pressed, trying to take control of her anger. The only problem was, "pressing" had turned into "shoving," until she was afraid she might accidentally deviate her septum. "I know all that. You told us. But it doesn't matter. You saw how it was, with the news turning it into a scandal and people questioning your character and our family's honor! Amma was completely alienated from the boards she chairs. And have you forgotten how horrible you felt, how much people whispered and pointed and laughed until you couldn't even leave the palace grounds? You're a Rao. You just can't behave like that, and you can't have those kinds of interests when you're born into a royal family. It's a privilege—"

"You sound just like Appa," Isha said angrily. "I just want to be me."

Jaya wanted to shake her. Did she think Jaya enjoyed being whisked off to a strange place for her last year of high school? Did she think Jaya liked having to always be the responsible one, the one who thought of what was best for the family, while Isha impulsively did whatever made her happy without a care for others?

Jaya took a deep breath and collected herself. "Let's let this go for now," she said, forcing herself to speak calmly.

Isha didn't respond for a full minute and Jaya let her have her space. Isha had a short fuse; it burned fiery hot when she was angry, but cooled down fast too. Jaya, on the other hand, was a slow burn, content to let the embers of anger simmer for months before she took action.

Sure enough, Isha turned to her a minute later, smiling slightly. "You're right; let's let it go. I think I'm going to like it here. I've already made a ton of friends on my floor. And Raina, that girl who was talking to me in the common room? I think she has best friend potential." She threaded her hand through Jaya's and Jaya squeezed her fingers.

They walked in relative silence the rest of the way, inhaling the fresh, cool breeze rolling off the mountains in the distance as they huddled closer to ward off the encroaching chill. Lake Rosetta was off to their right somewhere, buried deep in the woods like a glassy jewel waiting to be discovered. This place was different in almost every way from their home. Still, with her sister by her side, Jaya didn't feel so alone.

# CHAPTER 5

# Grey

Any young gentry walking by the West Wing at St. Rosetta's International Academy would have witnessed a curious sight: a large silhouette in the window of the West Wing tower, padlocked against intrusion since nearly the inception of the school.

Grey paced the diameter of the tower's interior, a single lantern on the floor illuminating just enough so he wasn't completely blind in the dark. He'd been coming here since middle school, when he'd learned how to pick the ancient lock. The administration at St. Rosetta's was oddly sentimental about old stuff and held on dearly to the way things had always been done. The lack of electronic locks on this door was one example. It had worked out well for him, obviously—not once had he ever been questioned about the tower. It always amazed Grey, how easy it was to break arbitrary rules and how human beings paid so little attention to one another.

It was nearly two a.m., but he couldn't sleep. He just couldn't stop thinking of Jaya Rao. Why was she here? He was gripped by a certainty that it had something to do with him, but he couldn't put his finger on why. Was it just the fact that her family had cursed his—actually, likely him, specifically?

And that pendant?

He'd finally figured out what it was and why it had struck a chord with him—the cursed ruby. It was something constantly whispered about in the ancient manors on the Westborough estate. Although they didn't like to speak of this shameful event, the Emerson family had once, back in the 1800s, stolen a ruby from one of the ancient temples in Mysuru, in the Indian state of Karnataka. The thievery had been orchestrated by Grey's own great-great-grandmother, who'd had her footmen undertake the task. This was back when the British still ruled India, and although some members of the extended Emerson family tried to pooh-pooh it as some kind of centuries-old Indian vendetta, Grey believed it completely—the British were infamous for stealing all manner of precious artifacts from their colonies.

Because of the provenance of the ruby and how sacred it was, a member of the ruling Mysuru family—one of the matriarchs of the Rao family, in fact—had cursed it. There was even an actual poem, a prophecy the Rao matriarch had uttered. His father was so obsessed with it, Grey knew it by heart:

> *A hallowed dream stolen,*
> *A world darkly despairs*
> *A storm, a life, a sudden death*
> *Heralds the end, the last heir.*

> *As the glass rose dims,*
> *So the hope of redemption*
> *Eighteen years, one by one,*
> *Until what's left is none.*

*Mend that which is broken*
*Repair that which is severed*
*Or the Northcliffe name is forsaken*
*And shall vanish, at last, forever.*

His mother had died in childbirth because a storm—apparently the worst the town had seen in a hundred years—had prevented the doctor from getting to her in time. Grey's father was out of town on a business trip. He'd never forgiven himself, or Grey.

Grey remembered when he'd first learned what the curse really meant for him. Father had flown to St. R's for a mandatory parent weekend the school did for kids under the age of thirteen. Grey was twelve; it would be their last mandated time together. By this time, six years after being dropped off as a kindergartner, Grey and his father had drifted apart—already, he felt more like a distant relative one equated with the holidays than the person who'd helped give Grey life.

He and Father had gone to a hot-air balloon event the school was hosting. Grey remembered wanting to float above the treetops, to feel the wind whipping his face and hair, the exquisite thrill of the experience being that high in a colorful balloon that felt like it should exist only in a dream. He couldn't wait for his turn.

Then Father had turned to him and said, unsmiling, "Let's talk." He'd walked away from the lines of kids and their parents waiting, past a grove of aspens and pines, and toward Lake Rosetta. It was quieter there, with the excited chaos and laughter like a distant memory behind them.

Grey watched his shoes sink in the soft dirt on the bank of

the lake; he felt the afternoon sun warm the back of his neck. He knew whatever this talk was about, it wouldn't be good. By then he'd already distanced himself from Father, had come to think of him as a relative who sent money for clothes and books and occasionally called, when he remembered to.

Without preamble, his father, never a man of many words, said, "The curse. You know of it, of course. But I think the time has come to tell you the whole truth, Grey. I have every reason to believe that when you turn eighteen, you will die." He gave Grey the news like a jaded oncologist might tell a cancer patient there was nothing more he could do, that medicine had done its best and still it wasn't enough. The news was delivered briskly, without warmth, without ambiguity.

Grey stared at him in the bright sunlight, threads of silver in the duke's hair glinting. The air, smelling of deep water and dark mud and creatures that slithered, unseen, was cloying in his nostrils. "What?"

"Don't say 'what.' It's very middle-class," Father said, frowning. "The curse is very clear that our lineage will end. I believe it will end on your eighteenth birthday with your death."

Grey pushed his shaking hands into his pockets. He nodded, not giving way to the panic that was clashing its incessant cymbals in his ears. He knew he'd get more out of Father if he kept his composure. "So . . . you think the curse says I'll die in six years."

"Yes," Father said.

"And you believe it."

"Yes." His father's eyes, two ice chips, held his. "I have no reason not to. The curse predicted the storm. It predicted your hand in your mother's death. *You* are the last heir it speaks of, Grey."

"I—"

"Now, let's get back to the balloons," Father said, striding away from him, one hand in the pocket of his trousers. "Just a few more hours and we can put this weekend behind us."

Over the years, Grey had traversed all the many stages of grappling with something like that, over and over again: disbelief, shock, anger, despair, belief, numbness. He'd finally arrived at a nihilism that felt much more manageable. *Was* the curse real? No one else would understand it except his father, but Grey felt, deep inside his bones, that it was. It was as much a part of him as his title or his blue eyes.

The big question was, why had it been so easy for Father to forsake him? Was it because it made no sense to invest in something that wasn't going to last very long anyway? Because he saw Grey's mother in Grey's blue eyes, too painful a reminder of what he'd lost? Grey wished he could turn his back on his father, wished he could tell him he was cruel and ruthless and Grey deserved better. But his father was the only one who truly understood who—what—Grey was. And that meant something.

One thing Grey couldn't overlook: his eighteenth birthday was coming up. Time was ticking down, faster and faster.

In an attempt to avoid the curse, the Emerson clan had sold the ruby to a master jeweler in the Middle East. (Of course, they could've just apologized and returned the ruby to Mysuru in an attempt to overturn the curse, but by then there was too much bad blood between the Raos and the Emersons.) For generations, that's where the trail had ended.

Maybe the rose pendant was a total coincidence, but Grey had to admit it *was* pretty damn strange that Jaya Rao, of all people, happened to have one. But why wear it here? To taunt him?

Ever since he'd seen the pendant on Jaya when she sat in

the garden, he couldn't stop thinking about it. Letting a groan of frustration echo against the stone walls of the tower, Grey clamped his fists to his head. He needed answers. Was that ruby pendant the cursed one? He couldn't just keep churning like this, an ocean tossed around by storms.

As the night wore on and the stars above twinkled like glass shards in black velvet, Grey Emerson knew he had to take action. He had to unearth the truth about Jaya Rao and why, exactly, she was here.

# Jaya

Sunlight splashed from the sky into Jaya's room and onto her face. She groaned and rolled over, forgetting if it was the beginning of a new day or the end of an old one. And then she did remember: oh yes. The last two days were gone in a haze of exploring the school and its grounds (and keeping a close eye on Isha). It was now Thursday: the first day of school. The day she'd begin working her charms on Grey Emerson. A horde of spiteful butterflies began to assault her nervous stomach.

Jaya checked her phone: 6:15 a.m. Her alarm was set to go off in fifteen minutes, so she turned it off and sat up in bed, looking out the window at the gardens dotted with dew below. The day she'd been awaiting was finally here.

After she brushed her teeth, took a shower, and arranged her hair in a crown braid (the better to feel queenly with—everyone knew a future queen trumped a duke's son), she dressed quickly in the Academy uniform she'd picked up at the administrative office the day before: a deep maroon blazer, white shirt, maroon tie, and gray skirt. Not the most imaginative uniform she'd ever worn, but at least it went nicely with her pendant. And she wasn't really there as a student, not anymore. Jaya was a human Trojan horse, and this helped her blend in nicely. If her life had a soundtrack, it'd be thrilling and ominous, full of a dark but powerful energy.

Picking up her bag full of new books, Jaya closed the door quietly behind her. She only passed two other students on her way downstairs; few students seemed to be awake yet. She'd be early to breakfast; Leo, Daphne Elizabeth, Rahul, and Grey Emerson probably wouldn't be there, which was excellent. She needed the time to mentally bolster herself. You never went into battle unprepared, and you never let the enemy take you by surprise. The Raos may not wage wars for land anymore, but like Appa always said, the wisdom of her ancestors ran in her blood.

When Jaya got down to the sophomore wing, Isha was already waiting in the luxuriously appointed common room, reading a book about Eleanor Roosevelt. Her hair was in two ponytails that cascaded past her shoulders, and suddenly, Jaya saw her as she'd looked at seven years old. In spite of being a fireball of mischievous (and annoying and frustrating) energy, she did have her moments. Deep down inside, Isha was still just a little kid, innocent and sweet and much too trusting. Jaya's heart swelled.

It wasn't right what the Emersons had done, coming after a young girl. Jaya balled her fists, breathing hard, and at that moment Isha looked up and frowned. "Why do you look like a constipated bull?" she asked.

"I have no idea what you're talking about," Jaya said, blowing out a breath and picturing her anger dissipating in a cloud above her. She stepped forward as Isha put the book away and gathered her bag. "You've got dark circles under your eyes. Did you sleep at all last night?"

"No," Isha said, linking her arm through Jaya's. "I was too excited."

"You know, most people might be anxious about the unknown . . . moving to a school nine thousand miles away from everything they know, et cetera?"

Isha laughed. "We've done it so many times before, it's not exactly like I don't know what to expect."

"True."

"You're up early too. Besides," Isha added, "I'm weird."

Jaya snorted. "You don't have to tell me." When Isha elbowed her, she continued. "But seriously, Isha. Just remember, it's okay to miss your friends. When the excitement dies down, you'll probably be homesick. You've been through a lot lately."

"I know," Isha said softly, her eyes downcast. She laid her head on Jaya's shoulder for a second. "But I have you. So."

"And I have you," Jaya said, squeezing her hand, drawing strength from Isha without her even knowing it.

The heavy wooden doors to the dining hall opened soundlessly beneath Jaya's hands, and the girls slipped inside. Isha gestured to an arched entryway to their left. "The sophomores eat in there, I think." She waved, and before Jaya knew it, she was gone.

Suddenly Jaya felt very alone and very small. It was not a feeling she was used to or particularly cared for. "I am Rajkumari Jaya Rao," she said aloud. "Daughter of Maharaja Adip Rao." The effect was altogether unremarkable. She still felt small, and now she also felt stupid for talking to herself.

Jaya stood in front of the enormous main entrance hall and looked around, gathering herself for a bit. After a few moments, Jaya navigated her way alone to the cavernous senior dining hall, which was currently empty of students. Bright sunlight angled in through the tall windows, drawing sharp lines of shadow throughout the space, which was dotted with round wooden tables arranged in concentric circles. Above her, the sleek steel fixtures that would normally bathe the room in warm light were turned off. Toward the north end of the hall, waitstaff bustled at glossy steel-and-tile food stations.

*Okay,* Jaya thought. *I'm here. I can do this.* She set her bag down at a nearby table.

"Hello," she said quietly. "Hello, Grey. Pleased to meet you." She threw her head back and practiced a flirty, throaty laugh. She'd watched several videos online about it and was fairly sure she had it down. "Hahaha," Jaya said more loudly. Then, clearing her throat, she tried again. "Hahahaha, oh, stop." She added a coquettish hand wave for good measure.

Yes, that was good. Very good, in fact. Charming, graceful, and natural. Grey Emerson would be drawn immediately in. He'd lean forward and say—

"What are you laughing at? And why are you waving your hands around like that? Bugs are pretty rare at this altitude."

Jaya jumped and let out a rather unroyal scream. A pair of glittering blue eyes was watching her from another table in a shadowed corner.

"What in the—oh! H-hello." She took a deep breath. "You scared me half to death."

The big, bearlike boy from the library nodded once but gave no apology. Rude. So rude. "Do you often make yourself laugh?"

"Only when my company's lacking," Jaya said stiffly, trying to recover a modicum of dignity. God, how embarrassing. What else had he heard?

This feral boy, whoever he was, was making a habit of catching her off guard. Although . . . Jaya narrowed her eyes. He looked different this morning. Almost presentable. His hair was mostly neatly combed today. Dressed in his uniform, he appeared a lot more civilized and a lot less lupine, though his eyes were just as piercing. And he still exuded a self-possessed authority. A leather satchel sat on the table beside him, embossed with the monogram *GE*.

When realization finally hit, she gasped, the sound echoing in the near-empty room. This boy, the one who'd been so kind and brave in the library, was . . . "*Grey Emerson?*" Collecting herself quickly, she added in a more dignified tone, "Erm, I mean, Lord Northcliffe?"

Grey raised his eyebrows at whatever he heard in her tone. "Grey is fine."

He spoke with a completely inappropriate brusque informality, as if he were an overworked government employee rather than the son of the Duke of Westborough. Jaya wrinkled her nose in distaste until she remembered her purpose at this school. No matter how furious she was at Grey Emerson and his family, she had to pretend he was the best thing she'd seen all day. Jaya forced a laugh, still going for throaty and flirty. So what if he'd seen the rehearsal? He'd probably enjoyed it.

"I'm surprised you didn't tell me who you were yesterday. My family is well acquainted with yours, naturally." She couldn't help it. Her voice sizzled with reproach.

Grey Emerson frowned. "Likewise." He drummed his large fingers on the tabletop. "The legendary Raos. Creators of chaos and misfortune."

"What?" Jaya said, all intentions to be flirty completely evaporated. "So you've told yourself a little fairy tale, have you, where the *Raos* are the villains?" She walked closer to him, even though her brain was throwing up bright red flags: STOP! DO NOT APPROACH! CAUTION! "And where does all the pillaging and plundering your people have done fit into your fairy tale? Please enlighten me."

He just sat there all slouched, one of his long legs spread out in front of him like he were sitting in a hookah bar. Ugh. "That was a long time ago," he said, his voice clipped and hard. "And yet somehow those of us who weren't even alive then are still being held responsible. You'd think *your* people would let go of the acrimony."

Jaya laughed disbelievingly. The arrogance! The hypocrisy! He clearly didn't think she knew he was behind everything. "Yes, you'd think, wouldn't you? Except you—" Ooh. Careful, Jaya. She'd been about to say, *Except you went and splashed my little sister's indiscretions in the tabloids, you big ogre.* Keep your eyes on the larger goal. Don't let this prickly boy get under your skin so easily. She tapped her pendant lightly with a fingertip, a reminder to herself of her duty. Slowly, the soft conversations of the few other students in the dining hall began to filter into her consciousness. Forcing a smile and a deep breath, Jaya said, "You're right. How about we let all of that go? Perhaps forgiveness can start with us." She tried not to vomit.

Grey Emerson didn't respond. Which might've been because his gaze was riveted to the pendant at her throat. She was standing near his table now, close enough for him to see it clearly. "That's . . . an unusual pendant." He was studying her face now, a little too intently, though Jaya couldn't decipher his expression.

"Thank you," she said, even though what he'd said wasn't quite a compliment. Laying a finger on it gently, she added, "My father bought it for me in Dubai."

Grey fiddled with a napkin on the table, but when he saw her watching his fingers, they went still. "Did the seller tell your father anything about its origin? Where it came from or where the rubies were sourced from . . . anything like that?"

Jaya frowned slightly at the strained urgency curling around the edges of his words. He was clearly past the conversation of their family feud and onto something new. "Ah . . . no, not that I know of. I didn't really ask him."

Grey's face was pinched in frustration, like he wanted to ask her more questions but didn't know how. How incredibly odd. "I . . . I . . ." He stopped and took a breath, shaking his head as if to clear it.

Jaya studied him for a second. There was definitely something off about him and the necklace; she wasn't imagining it. She filed the information away for later. Suddenly she remembered his comment about *The House of Medici* the day before. It was hard now *not* to see the message there. He wanted the Raos to collapse into decline and decay just like the Medicis had.

Jaya kept her expression congenial, though every facial muscle hurt with the effort. "May I join you there at your table?"

Grey shrugged. Jaya waited for a more polite invitation, but there was none forthcoming.

"Thank you," Jaya managed to say warmly as she picked

up her backpack and went to sit by him. There was something secretive about Grey Emerson. But it wasn't *just* about what he'd done to the Raos recently. The way he held his body, just slightly angled away. His strangely intense reaction to her pendant. The way his eyes studied her from behind a wall of wariness and, dare she say, fear . . . There was something very odd happening here. Jaya had to force her shoulders to relax once she was seated. Her arms had goose bumps, as if her body knew she was sitting next to a scorpion. Smiling, she turned to face him. "It was really nice of you to stand up for that other boy yesterday. In the library, I mean."

Grey waved a big hand—*paw* might be a more suitable term—and looked away. "I don't condone bullying," he said shortly, as though he didn't want to talk about it.

*That's ironic, considering what you did to my sister,* Jaya wanted to bite back. Instead of speaking her mind, though, she leaned toward him and spoke quietly, like she was telling him a secret. "I still think it was really brave."

Grey glanced at her, a little surprised, as if he wasn't used to people noticing his nicer qualities. Probably because he didn't have too many. After a pause, he asked, "Don't you have a little sister?"

Jaya stared at him for a moment. He was toying with her, of this she was sure. Her nails suddenly wanted to be embedded in his skin. "Yes, I do," she said carefully. "Isha. She's in the sophomore dining hall with her friends."

He grunted in response. It would be hard drawing him out, Jaya could already see. "Why do you ask?" she managed to say in a light, offhanded way.

"Leo mentioned it."

OF CURSES AND KISSES    71

Right. Leo had "mentioned it." As if Grey Emerson wasn't keenly aware of everything the Raos were doing. He was good, she had to admit. But she was better.

Jaya said in a lilting voice, "Oh, Leo, of course! Your friends were so kind when Isha and I met them earlier. I've been warned that there'd be all kinds of cliques and people waiting to stab you in the back with their heirloom swords at St. Rosetta's." She trilled a laugh. "That's why I'm so glad I have someone like you—and your friends—to show me the ropes. I hope we have some electives together."

Grey narrowed his eyes, as if he were trying to see through her facade. Jaya held steady. He couldn't know she knew. She needed to play things just right. For good measure, she put her chin in her hands and batted her eyes at him a little.

Finally, he ran a jerky hand through his hair, as if her incessant flirting was flustering him, and said, in a low voice, "I have archery first period."

"Me too!" Jaya widened her eyes in mock surprise. "But I don't know the first thing about archery. I'm a little worried about that class." She crinkled her nose, partly to play the role of innocent ingenue and partly because it rankled her to lie about this. She was actually an incredible archer. Grey Emerson, on the other hand, was probably terrible. Just look at those gigantic hands. As if they could handle a bow and arrow with the gentle finesse the instruments demanded. But there was no point complaining now. She'd known the price when she'd enrolled in his archery class. "Can I sit with you?"

It hadn't been hard to find out what classes Grey had. One phone call from Jaya in her dorm room, pretending to be the Duke of Westborough's secretary to the administrative staff at

St. Rosetta's was all it had taken. She'd requested that the family's dear friend, Jaya Rao, be placed in all the same classes as Grey Emerson, and since she'd been able to give them all of her identifying information, it had been rather simple.

"Sure," Grey said gruffly, after a pause, looking up at Jaya from under his eyelashes. His blue eyes lit briefly on her rose necklace and then flitted away.

Jaya touched him lightly on his bare forearm. Wow. She hadn't realized it was possible to have such a muscular forearm. "Thank you! That's so nice. I'll feel so much better having someone to guide me."

Grey lifted his arm from under her hand to scratch at his chest, so her fingers were left suspended in midair. He couldn't even conceal his dislike of the Rao family to endure some light flirting. No matter. She'd wear him down eventually. She had lots of practice being nice to people she hated and who hated her, thanks to her royal training. "Here's my schedule," she said, pulling it out of her backpack and setting it on the table between them. "I wonder if we have any other classes together."

Jaya watched his eyes run down the piece of paper. "Huh. We'll be together the entire semester. Every class." He said it abruptly and kind of shiftily, as if he couldn't quite make her out. "What's your deal?" he asked after a pause.

Jaya raised her eyebrows. "I beg your pardon? My deal?"

He waved a hand impatiently. "Raos don't like Emersons. Emersons hate Raos. So why are you being so nice? What's your angle?"

Wasn't he about fifty years too young to be so cynical about life? Jaya smiled her best and brightest smile. "I told you, Lord Northcliffe. I think forgiveness could begin with us." Good work,

Jaya. She should write self-help books and travel the world healing nations.

He crossed his arms, his biceps bulging. His overall expression told her he didn't quite believe her. But his eyes held hers just a little too long, and Jaya knew she'd played her first move well. He *could* be hooked, even if there was a caginess about him she'd have to work on.

Jaya kept smiling as they talked, hoping he wouldn't see the angry outbursts she was swallowing quicker than the scalding coffee she'd poured herself. She willed him to be hypnotized by her smile, her brown eyes, her easy banter.

The rose pendant glittered at her throat in the rising sunlight, throwing red embers of light across Grey Emerson's skin.

# Grey

There was something about the way she was leaning in to him, her smile just a touch too wide, her eyes just a bit too . . . blinky.

Grey was used to girls flirting with him. He didn't know what it was—his brooding, dark demeanor, perhaps, or maybe the way he was always just a little too tall and a little too broad for any space he occupied. Or maybe it was just the title of nobility he carried. Whatever the case, he cycled through the same steps with nearly every new girl who walked through the gilded double doors of St. Rosetta's:

Girl: Flirt

Grey: Pretend to not notice

Girl: Touch Grey

Grey: Cough and step aside, just a bit too far for her fingers to easily brush him

Girl: Smile

Grey: Glare

The only exception to that cycle so far had been Daphne Elizabeth, who was now one of his self-proclaimed "friends," along with Leo and Rahul. Instead of telling him all the ways in which he could screw himself, DE had latched on to him freshman year, convinced that he needed someone to take care of him. He found her annoying and tolerable in equal parts, though he'd never tell her about the tolerable part. When she'd made it clear she would rather read *War and Peace* a thousand times over than date him, he'd relaxed and let her talk to him. Sometimes.

Yeah, new girls flirting with him was normal. But something about Jaya Rao struck him as very slightly off. It was like she was playing a part, not truly flirting because she found him attractive. And then there was the fact that she had transferred in this late into her high school career, little sister in tow. Lastly, there was the matter of the necklace. Why did she have a ruby pendant shaped like a rose that her father had gotten in Dubai, of all places? Given the story of the stolen ruby and the curse her family had placed on his, that was too big a coincidence. A Rao so willing to befriend an Emerson would be rare enough. But a Rao wearing a ruby rose pendant, being overfriendly *and* registered for the same classes as him? Something was definitely not right.

Grey studied her, but didn't see guilt or sadistic smugness. Just some B-grade flirting. His eyes dropped to the pendant again—and he froze. "A ruby's missing," he said, his voice sounding faint and wooden even to his own ears.

The words of the curse sizzled in his brain.

> *As the glass rose dims,*
> *So the hope of redemption*
> *Eighteen years, one by one,*
> *Until what's left is none.*

Each ruby on Jaya's pendant represented a petal of the red rose. Was this what the curse had meant all along? Eighteen petals, falling?

Jaya, unaware of the frantic pounding of his pulse, glanced down. "Yes, I know; it went missing yesterday. I'll have to get it replaced soon."

"How many rubies are there?" Grey asked, his voice weird and wooden again.

"Eighteen," Jaya said. "Well, seventeen now, I suppose."

Eighteen. Just like the curse. And once they'd all fallen . . . Grey would die. Just as his father had always said. Here it was, the countdown, right in front of his eyes. After all these years, it was real. The curse was real. Grey felt his face pale.

"Are you all right?" Jaya asked.

Grey couldn't even bring himself to nod.

There was something about Grey's expression that reminded her of a person in shock. She'd once seen a picture of a survivor of a horrible car crash, and they'd had the same wide eyes, the slightly sallow face, the expression like they couldn't quite believe this was reality.

Why did he care so much about whether or not she lost a ruby, anyway? She'd expected him to be a lot more focused on Isha or the Raos' disgrace, even in a circumspect manner. But Grey Emerson seemed strangely obsessed with her pendant.

"Good morning, royals and noble-type people!"

Grey and Jaya looked up at the same time to see Daphne Elizabeth flitting toward them. Leo and Rahul followed behind at a statelier pace.

"Hello, Daphne Elizabeth," Jaya said, smiling her best royal smile. Other students were beginning to filter in, and she had to raise her voice to be heard.

"How are you this morning?"

"Fan-freaking-tastic," Daphne Elizabeth replied, grinning. She turned to Grey and studied him for a moment. "What's your problem?"

"Nothing." Abruptly, he pushed his chair back and staggered off.

Daphne Elizabeth looked after him. Jaya watched him get swallowed by the growing numbers of hungry seniors, then turned back to his friends. "I'm not sure what happened . . . I hope I haven't offended him in any way."

Leo and Rahul turned to follow him.

"Well," Daphne Elizabeth said, blinking and smiling at Jaya even though Jaya could see she was worried about Grey. "I'm starving. Wanna grab some breakfast? The from-scratch buttermilk waffles are to die for."

"Certainly." Jaya tossed a glance over her shoulder as they

walked. Leo and Rahul had joined Grey over by the coffee and tea counter. None of them were actually ordering anything, though. Their heads were bent together, and they were deep in conversation.

Interesting.

Very interesting, indeed.

# CHAPTER 6

# Grey

Jaya's pendant losing a ruby was bringing everything that was wrong with his life, with *him*, into sharp focus. But he couldn't speak to anyone about it. Leo, Rahul, and DE didn't know anything about the curse—or how Grey had murdered his own mother. No one would understand that. It was just one more way he was different from the rest of the student population at St. Rosetta's. Actually, make that the rest of the human population, period.

Now Grey shrugged off their concerned questions and kept his back turned to them. "I'm fine. I just want some coffee. Okay? Go back to the table." He reached for the silver cafetière and poured himself a mug of black coffee.

Leo folded his arms across his chest. "*C'est des conneries.*"

"Leo thinks what you just said, in an attempt to placate us, is bullshit," Rahul provided.

Grey kept his back turned. "Yeah. I got it. Thanks."

"So are you going to be honest with us now?" Leo inquired, his eyebrow arched.

Grey gulped down his coffee and set the mug down. "No,"

he said, looking back toward Jaya, graceful hands crossed on the table as she listened to whatever DE was saying. "I'm not."

What he was thinking but didn't say was that being alone all these years might as well be a death sentence. His family was thousands of miles away. He had people, who, for some reason, kept trying to be a part of his life, but he kept them at a distance too. He didn't know how to be close with people. Being kept apart from his family because of what he'd done to his mother had taught him that he was toxic. Inherently damaged.

So maybe the curse was meant to kill him on his eighteenth birthday, but in many ways, Grey felt like his life had already ended. In so many ways, he'd already experienced a kind of death: the death of himself. The death of whatever he might once have had inside him, the freedom to be kind, the freedom to be a friend, the freedom to love with abandon and without fear. In so many ways—with every single passing day that he lived like this, keeping everyone at bay, going days without saying a single word to another soul—Grey didn't really count himself as one of the living. In so many ways, he was fully and without question, the beast his father said he was.

He heard Leo sigh and mutter something in French, and after a moment both he and Rahul walked off back to their table. They'd given up on him.

Grey's eyes stole across the large hall to Jaya again, to the pendant he saw faintly twinkling at him in the light, as if it were able to read the tenor of his thoughts. If he stole it, perhaps returned it to its rightful place in the temple in Mysuru, would it keep the curse at bay? Or had the ending to his story already been written, long before he was born?

# Jaya

They'd just gotten their waffles—blueberry for Daphne Elizabeth, strawberries and cream for Jaya—when she saw them. Caterina and Alaric.

Daphne Elizabeth had been in the middle of telling her about the annual fall trip to Aspen, when everyone in their class went shopping together. Apparently, last year Alaric had face-planted in the snow on the way back to the bus, and his dad had sued the city unsuccessfully. This year Alaric's dad had reserved a company to come out the day of the trip and shovel all the snow within fifty feet of anywhere Alaric might go. Basically the whole town.

"Alaric's dad is just so over-the-top protective," Daphne Elizabeth said, sighing. "Must be nice to have parents who actually give a shit," she added quietly.

Jaya made the appropriate sympathetic noises, though her eyes surreptitiously followed the couple. Daphne Elizabeth hadn't noticed them yet, and she wanted to keep it that way for as long as possible.

Caterina and Alaric wore the same school uniform as everyone else, but somehow they looked like they could be strolling down a red carpet instead of walking inside a dining hall full of loud teenagers. Caterina's hair was done perfectly in those same cascading waves as the first time Jaya had seen her. A diamond-studded clip held back the front of her hair, and her makeup was still just as flawless, though she'd toned it down for school. Short of hiring a makeup artist to camp out with her in her dorm room, Jaya could never manage such perfection with her makeup.

Not a hair was out of place on Alaric's head either. He wore a big Gucci watch, and his skin was tanned like he'd spent his summer at some posh seaside resort, probably in France, because that's where people like Alaric and Caterina usually went. Appa thought France was full of rude, stuck-up people, but Jaya secretly loved it. When she and Isha had gone to boarding school in Amsterdam for a year, she'd sneaked away with friends on a mini-vacation to Paris and her parents had never been the wiser. Of course, that was before she realized how irresponsible that was for the first child of a royal family. She'd never do something like that now.

Daphne Elizabeth's words petered out as she noticed the happy couple too. Well, Caterina was happy, anyway. Alaric appeared too smug to be "happy," in the strictest sense of the word.

"Oh," Daphne Elizabeth breathed as Caterina and Alaric walked past and stopped by a table to speak with a few people. It sounded like a little moan of pain. Though he couldn't possibly have heard her over the din of chattering first-day seniors in the dining hall, Alaric glanced at her, his gaze stuttering just a moment before it moved slickly away.

Jaya put a hand on Daphne Elizabeth's arm and led her back to their table. The boys were already back, with bagels and fruit. Grey was brooding over a cup of coffee. Black, of course, to match his bitter personality. "I'm sorry," Jaya said to Daphne Elizabeth, because she didn't know what else to say.

"It's not your fault," Daphne Elizabeth said, setting her plate down with a bang.

Leo raised his eyebrows. "What's going on?"

Jaya shot a glance at Daphne Elizabeth, who waved a hand. "He knows. They all do."

"Oh." Leo sat back and popped half of an entire bagel into his mouth, chewed, and swallowed. It was like watching a magic trick. "A-la-dick?"

"That is *not* his name," Daphne Elizabeth hissed. Then, looking over her shoulder, she added, "And oh my God, could you please come up with a less obvious code word?"

Leo held up his hands in surrender. "You told her?" he asked Daphne Elizabeth.

She blew her red bangs out of her eyes. "Jaya kind of saw. I didn't have a choice."

"You shouldn't worry. I'm an excellent secret-keeper," Jaya said, and at that, Grey gave her a look. She was about to say something when he spoke, interrupting her train of thought.

"The best way to get over him is to force yourself to stop having feelings for him," Grey said, glancing at Daphne Elizabeth.

Daphne Elizabeth rolled her eyes and tucked into her waffle. "Right. Because it's just that easy."

"Maybe it's not easy, but it is that simple," Grey said calmly, sipping his coffee.

"Seriously?" Daphne Elizabeth laughed. "You can't just *force* yourself to stop having feelings for someone."

"Au contraire," Jaya put in. "I agree with Grey." She tossed him a brilliant smile, which he decidedly did not return. To Daphne Elizabeth, Jaya continued. "The heart must be ruled by the head. It makes for more successful unions and outcomes." This was why she'd taken her parents' hints about Kiran Hegde, naturally.

Grey turned those bright blue, stormy eyes on her, appraising. Jaya found herself noticing the slight shadow of stubble on his square jaw. "Right. It's not easy. But yes. It *is* a matter of willpower."

Daphne Elizabeth shook her head. "The heart doesn't work like that," she countered. "It's no one's servant. And sometimes . . . sometimes the person you love, as bad an idea as he might be, is the only one in the world who really, truly sees you."

"Sometimes the heart doesn't have the luxury of doing whatever it wants," Grey said, almost angrily. Jaya wondered what that was about. "Sometimes there are outside mandates on what the heart can or cannot do."

Much as she despised Grey Emerson and all he stood for, Jaya understood that. She had known from when she was very young that there were acceptable suitors and unacceptable ones. Kiran fell into the former category, and Grey, for instance, fell into the latter.

Daphne Elizabeth sighed loudly and stuffed her mouth with a waffle. Once she was done chewing, she said, "Fine. Let's just agree to disagree, then."

Grey blinked and his shoulders relaxed. "Right," he said. "Let's."

Leo, Rahul, and Daphne Elizabeth spent the rest of breakfast talking about which teachers Jaya would love and which ones she should watch out for. Grey just sat quietly and drank his coffee. Jaya found herself laughing along to his friends' jokes and asking questions, warming to them. She realized with a prickle of guilt that at the end of all this, when they realized what she'd done to Grey, they'd probably hate her forever. But there was no way to avoid that.

Just as Rahul finished telling them about a numerical scale he'd devised over the summer to measure the likelihood of any teacher revoking privileges (St. Rosetta's didn't do detention, which was much too plebeian; rather, the teachers simply revoked off-campus and on-campus privileges), a woman in a gray chignon appeared at the head of the dining hall and rang a small, insistent silver bell.

"Time for class," Daphne Elizabeth said, sighing. "I have English . . . with Alaric and Caterina. I'll get to see them sitting together and writhing all over each other the rest of the semester. Yay, me."

"I'm sorry," Jaya said, infusing as much warmth into the sentence as she could. "Will I see you back here for lunch?"

"Yep," Daphne Elizabeth responded as they all stood with their plates and mugs. She was putting on a brave face, but Jaya could see the bleakness in her eyes.

"And we are off to the magical land of computer science," Leo said, motioning to himself and Rahul. "*Au revoir.*"

Rahul paused, staring down at his feet. One of his shoelaces was untied, but he didn't seem to notice. "Wait a minute. Daphne Elizabeth?"

She looked back at him.

"You have Mr. Thomas for English, don't you?"

"Yeah?"

Rahul pointed a finger upward and spoke quickly, like he was in the middle of a great breakthrough. "Mr. Thomas assigns seating for people who're disruptive the first week of class. If you can make Alaric and Caterina talk to each other, especially loudly, you won't have to worry about them sitting together the rest of the semester."

Daphne Elizabeth frowned. "How do you know this?"

"I had him last year," Rahul explained. "And with careful attention to dining hall gossip, I've noticed the pattern every year. Last year it was Daryl and Misha who were separated, the year before that it was Lilah and Anna, and the year before that it was George and Paithoon. I remember them talking about it."

Daphne Elizabeth shook her head. "Wow, I always underestimate how useful a perfect memory can be. Thanks, buddy. But I'm not sure how to get them to talk noisily enough so Mr. Thomas hears them."

"Get them to argue," Rahul said almost immediately. "Caterina is powerfully strident when she's angry about something. And one thing Caterina and Alaric tend to argue about is social events. Just this morning, I passed them on the stairwell arguing about the color of Alaric's cummerbund for the winter formal. Caterina wanted him to wear a deep green, to match her dress, but he didn't seem to want to talk about it at all. So if you—"

"Bring up the winter formal at all, they're probably going to throw down!" Daphne Elizabeth said. "You know, I think I can handle that." She grinned suddenly, her perfectly straight white teeth on display. "Thanks, Rahul. You're like an expert on Caterina, and um, I appreciate it."

He nodded, turned rapidly on his heel, and left. Laughing quietly, Leo followed.

Jaya looked at Grey, her eyebrows raised, as they both began to amble toward the exit too. "Wow. That was really impressive."

The corner of Grey's mouth lifted a little. He may have been attempting to smile. "Rahul doesn't speak much, but when he does, it's like he's channeling Sherlock Holmes. Or Einstein."

Jaya studied his expression. "You have really great friends," she said. "And you know what they say—you can tell a lot about a person by the friends they keep."

Abruptly, his expression shuttered again. "Those aren't my friends," he said, turning away. "Come on, we're going to be late." And he loped off, leaving her two steps behind.

# Jaya

"Correct archery technique is something you can only learn with practice," Ms. Bayer said from the front of the class. "And from listening in lecture. Therefore, I expect you to give me your undivided attention whenever you're in class. I don't care if you're sick, if you're missing home, or if you went against your better instincts and ate the deviled eggs from the dining hall. If you thought this was going to be an easy elective, I am sorry you were misinformed."

An ex–Olympic gold medalist, Ms. Bayer was an intimidating woman. Though she was slender and on the shorter side, you could tell she had shoulder and arm muscles that could snap your neck in half if you just looked at her wrong. According to her, her genetic makeup was "fifty percent Nigerian, fifty percent Iranian, and one hundred percent all-American badass. Yes, I'm aware that adds up to two hundred percent and no, that's not a mistake. I don't make mistakes. Do not test me." Jaya didn't think anyone had any intention to.

Grey was sitting beside her at the double desk, scribbling in his notebook. Jaya cleared her throat as Ms. Bayer turned to the whiteboard to write something. "That was quite intense," she said, laughing quietly.

Grey looked up from his notebook. "Yes. But she really knows what she's talking about." He went back to scribbling again.

Hmm. With his cryptic nature, he might be a tougher nut to crack than she'd originally given him credit for. Jaya playfully leaned in. "So, what are you doing? Writing in your diary?"

Grey pulled the book closer to his body. "Nothing."

Jaya sat back up in her seat, watching him from the corner of her eye thoughtfully. What secrets was Lord Northcliffe guarding so closely?

# Grey

There was no way it was a coincidence that Jaya Rao was in every one of his classes. And yet, when she asked to sit beside him in every class, instead of immediately saying no and distancing himself, he'd said yes every single time. Why? Because he was an idiot. There was something about her wavy black hair, her full mouth that tipped so easily into a smile. The way she possessed a self-assured grace as she moved through the world, relaxed in the knowledge that she owned all she saw and that which she didn't own yet, she would eventually.

The girl was trouble; he could sense it. Being alone and having to watch out for himself all these years had attuned Grey's senses. He knew when someone was blowing smoke up his ass. And Jaya Rao definitely was. But about what? Either she was an incredible actress or she had no idea what the rose pendant represented. So what, exactly, was she doing here? And why was she so interested in him?

Grey had made a list in his notebook about all the things he knew about Jaya Rao and the things he suspected about Jaya Rao in an attempt to arrive at a logical conclusion.

Things he knew:

1. She and her sister had come here senior and sophomore year respectively, which probably meant they were running from something.
2. She was being overly flirty, strangely dismissive of the generations-long Emerson/Rao feud.
3. She was wearing the ruby pendant that he was pretty sure was *the* ruby pendant.
4. She was somehow in all his classes.
5. She really sucked at archery.

Things he suspected:

1. Jaya Rao was a sadistic mastermind, and she'd come here to torture him with the ruby pendant, eager to make him watch as each ruby fell.

Sure, it seemed far-fetched. But it fit why she was being so friendly. As for what she was running from? That he didn't know. Unless . . . unless she was running *to* something. Specifically, him, to show him the pendant. But was that too bizarre, even for him?

They were walking across the impeccably manicured green to their last class of the day, Russian Literature. The sun hung lower in the sky, a bright, blazing ball that hurt his eyes.

They passed Alaric Konig walking with his henchmen, Lachlan and Martin, as usual, and all three glared at Grey. He glared back, unflinching, unblinking, until they broke eye contact.

"You haven't told me yet why you're here," Grey said, once he was past their group.

Jaya adjusted her tie and frowned at him as if she were confused about something, but the laugh she produced was completely at ease. She was used to being a media darling back home, he supposed. "You know why," she answered, batting at him with a small hand. "My parents wanted us to get the best education—"

"Yeah, I know that's the party line. But there are a million other schools they could've sent you to. And if a boarding school was what they were after, the UK does those way better than the US." He paused, listening to their shoes rustle in the grass. He was saying a lot, maybe more than he should, certainly more than he usually did. But he wanted answers. "St. Rosetta's has . . . a reputation. The administration has done a good job covering it up, but it's still out there. If you transfer in in the middle of the year or in the middle of your high school career, say . . . you're usually running from something."

She turned to look at him, her face defiant. "Is that why you're here? Are you hiding something?"

Grey looked away. "I didn't say that was true of *all* the students here."

"You didn't answer my question."

"You didn't answer mine."

They'd stopped walking and were now glaring at each other. Every trace of humor and flirtation was gone from her demeanor, and Grey knew he'd hit a nerve.

"Jaya!"

They both jumped at the female voice. A short, younger student was running toward them, waving, her smile huge and carefree. Even though the way they carried themselves was completely different, Grey saw the resemblance in the younger girl's features as she got closer.

"Isha," Jaya said. Grey saw the look she was darting him; she was clearly uncomfortable. "Shouldn't you be going to class?"

"Sophomores have study hall this period," Isha explained. "Mrs. Price told us we could go to the library today since it's the first day and all. That's where I'm headed." She looked at Grey and beamed. "Hi," she said, sticking out her hand. "I'm Jaya's sister, Isha."

He took her hand. "Grey Emerson."

The girl's—Isha's—smile slipped for a second. Grey watched with increasing perplexity as she rallied an unconvincing facsimile of it back onto her face. "In-indeed. Nice to meet you."

Grey dropped her hand. Something told him there was more behind her reaction to him than just the Emerson/Rao feud. But years of self-imposed isolation made it easy for him to keep his true feelings off his face, which remained a blandly neutral mask.

"You should go to class," Jaya said quietly.

"Okay," Isha said, glancing at Grey. That strange fake smile was completely gone now. Another benefit of watching people but hardly ever interacting with them: Grey could read their energies pretty easily. Isha was a ball of barely suppressed confusion and anxiety, whereas Jaya seemed . . . protective. And maybe a little defensive. "Bye." Isha walked off quickly, missing the previous bounce in her step.

Grey turned to Jaya. The late-afternoon sun glimmered in her black hair like gold dust. "What's going on?" he asked her as she gave him that confused look again before breaking eye contact, like her attention was gripped by a group of students in the distance. But if he had to guess, he'd say she couldn't meet his eye. If she were anyone else, he wouldn't care. He'd chalk it up to humans being humans. But Jaya was a Rao, which meant she was potentially . . . dangerous.

After a moment, meeting his eye again, Jaya said, "How do you feel about ditching class on the first day?"

Grey hesitated. "Why can't you just tell me here?"

A small smile played at the corner of Jaya's lips. "Are you afraid I might attempt to assassinate you, Lord Northcliffe?"

Something about the way she said it didn't sound entirely like a joke. Grey crossed his arms and waited. Jaya shook her head. "It's . . . a bit of a story," she said, looking off into the distance. Turning back to him, she said, "Please. I'd feel better in private."

On the one hand, he trusted Jaya Rao about as far as he could throw her (which actually might be pretty far, considering their size differential). On the other, he really wanted to know what this Rao heiress had to say. "Fine. Follow me."

# *Jaya*

What was he playing at? Why was he asking her why she was here? The first and most obvious reason: he was a sadistic, evil jerk, and he wanted to see her writhe in pain. But . . . that didn't really fit with what she was seeing on his face. His expression was curious but guarded—not eager, not gloating. Which was throwing her a bit.

Obviously she wasn't going to tell him she knew about his involvement. Whatever his angle was, she'd unearth it eventually.

A couple of silent miles away from the school now, they walked up a forested path together. Through spaces between the aspens and birches and blue spruces they went, Jaya inhaling the scent of pine and thin mountain air. She glanced at Grey more often than she would've liked, but it was impossible—frustratingly so—to gauge what he was thinking. His face, as always, remained as impassive as stone.

"This is beautiful," she panted, looking around them at the secluded, hidden trail winding ever upward. "I'm surprised there isn't anyone else here."

"Not many people know about this path," Grey said shortly. He was surprisingly nimble as he clambered over small stones and fallen logs in their path, his big feet steady, as if he'd had years of experience. Occasionally he'd stop and wait as Jaya labored to catch up with him, but he never offered her a chivalrous hand. She didn't know whether to feel relieved or irritated.

"How did you find it?" she persisted. He was a man of so few words, he might as well be an empty book. She needed *some*thing to grab on to if she was to make headway with her plan.

"I like to wander," he said simply, offering no further explanation.

Which was just as well, because the path then took on a much steeper incline, and Jaya realized they were climbing up a small mountain. Her lungs, not yet acclimated to the altitude, could only expend enough air to keep her alive and upright.

Once they were finished climbing, Jaya took in the view around her, genuinely appreciative. Grey had brought them to a vantage point halfway up the mountaintop. Although she was wheezing from the climb, even the black spots dancing in front of her eyes couldn't mar the majesty of the panorama. The town of St. Rosetta lay under them like a peacefully sleeping child.

"Incredible," Jaya whispered, holding on to her tie as the wind tugged insistently at it.

"Mount Sama. It's been my favorite place since I was about twelve," Grey said, staring straight ahead at the horizon. "There's a quietness here you can't get anywhere else."

Jaya studied his profile—the dark hair that, though it had been combed neatly at the beginning of the day, was now hanging in his eyes; the strong jaw dotted with black stubble; the straight royal nose. Grey Emerson was, she reluctantly conceded, quite handsome and rather intelligent. But he was strangely antisocial, too. Why did someone who'd so heartlessly thrown Isha to the wolves also need quiet meditativeness on a mountain? Why did he isolate himself from people so much? She'd expected Grey Emerson to be overtly cocky, arrogant, vicious. She had to play archaeologist, to delicately chip away at the dust and debris and stony exterior until she got to the truth underneath.

He turned to her. "So," Grey said, his remote blue eyes giving nothing away. His square, straight jaw was hard.

"So." Jaya took a deep breath of the cool air. "Something happened, back home." She let a shadow of the vulnerability she really felt show, the morsel of truth. But no more than that; if he realized she knew about his involvement, he'd never let her get close to him. "With Isha. Isha's our maverick, I suppose." She smiled a little, but her eyes remained watchful. Would he smirk? Give away that he knew exactly what she was talking about? But he just continued to watch her, expressionless. "She's always been one to dance to her own songs. Isha thinks our traditions are silly."

"Unlike you." He narrowed his eyes and crossed his arms, as

if he was taking everything she said with a grain of salt. How very obnoxious.

"Unlike me," Jaya agreed, though even divulging that little bit of honest information about herself felt like too much, like giving the lion a waft of blood when you're trapped alone in a cage with him. "Anyway, she befriended this group of boys near where we lived. They were her age, and they ran a motorcycle repair shop. Isha's pretty mechanically inclined, a skill Appa really wishes she'd keep more under her hat. She was constantly messing around with Appa's cars in the palace garage, bribing the mechanics with cigarettes and snacks so they wouldn't say anything to him. Tinkering with cars isn't very becoming of a female royal, you know—greasy hands and ball gowns don't mix." She paused, waiting for a flicker of recognition. She'd read somewhere that your eyebrows don't lie; when faced with someone or something you recognize, they rise very slightly. Grey's eyebrows looked like he'd had a shot of Botox recently: immobile. Was he just *that* good a liar? She supposed that wasn't completely surprising; deception ran in the Emerson bloodline, after all.

"Anyway," she continued, "the boys told Isha one day that they were having trouble keeping their doors open. Their father had taken ill, and with one man down, they just weren't able to fulfill customers' needs like they used to. People were beginning to take their bikes to the rival shop. The boys were worried they wouldn't be able to support their family anymore, or get their father the medical attention he needed."

"Ah," Grey said, and Jaya thought she saw a ghost of a smile at his lips. "Isha to the rescue?"

Jaya began to bristle but then noticed that, strangely, there was no sarcasm or smugness in his voice. If anything, he looked

OF CURSES AND KISSES

vaguely impressed. Frowning slightly, she said, "I suppose you might say that. She began cutting classes so she could assist at their shop during the day. She's very good; she just made sure to stay in the back where customers wouldn't see her. Even if no one recognized her as a Rao, people would definitely remark on a female mechanic. The boys were sworn to secrecy, and they had a reason to keep the secret. She managed to keep it going for several weeks by forging a letter from our mother to her teachers, saying she was ill but would be back soon."

"So what happened?"

Hmm. Jaya studied his face. Still no trace of that sadism she kept waiting for. If Grey Emerson was putting on a show, he was an actor on par with Meryl Streep. What was he doing? Why did he need to hear all of this in her words? Feeling a bit like she was playing a game of chess in the dark, Jaya went on, her eyes tracking his every facial twitch. "Isha got careless. A newspaper reporter, ah, just happened to be passing by the shop one day and saw her, covered in motor oil, drinking, and kissing one of the mechanic boys. He snapped some pictures and the story ran the next day. That was it. Just a teenager acting like a teenager and now our entire family has to pay." She let her gaze bore into his as she said it, hoping, even if he didn't show it, that he'd feel the wicked blade of guilt stabbing into his heart.

"That was it?" Grey asked. "She drank and kissed a boy and that was enough for people to condemn all the Raos?"

"Perhaps you forget how conservative the Indian working class can be."

Grey inclined his head, allowing that. "And the British upper class," he muttered. "Continue, please."

Jaya let out a shaky breath, remembering the horror of it all.

"The public outcry was . . . I couldn't believe it. People were accusing our parents of raising wayward daughters, questioning whether we were meant to lead because we obviously lacked the moral fiber required of a royal family. Anytime we went into town, shopkeepers would make cruel remarks under their breaths. People pointed and whispered and yelled rude things. It didn't matter that we had bodyguards with us and they protected us from anything more serious. They just kept doing it anyway. It was like they wanted us to know how much we'd let them down, how unworthy we were."

Grey moved a half step closer, and in doing so, blocked the wind. As if he were her protector. Ironic, considering what he'd done. "I'm sorry," he said quietly.

Jaya studied him, eyes narrowed. What was he apologizing for, exactly? "It was awful," she continued, holding his gaze. "I've never seen our father so . . . beaten. He couldn't even look at Isha. My mother was crying all the time. And Isha . . ." She shook her head and paused for a moment. "The light went out of her eyes. I was afraid, *really* afraid, for her. She completely retreated into herself. It was like she couldn't believe the world could be so cruel, that people could be so savage. It called into question everything her eternally optimistic, idealistic heart believed in. I was afraid she'd never come back to me. I was afraid our family would fracture right down the center." Jaya stopped short, remembering who she was talking to. She straightened her shoulders. "Anyway, when our father suggested that we leave to go abroad before any of the serious papers picked up the story, I agreed straightaway."

Grey's face cleared a bit. "That's why she looked so uncomfortable."

"Right. Exactly."

OF CURSES AND KISSES    97

"But why here? Why did you choose St. R's?" Grey asked.

Was he afraid that Jaya had another agenda? A brisk breeze tugged at her hair, and she tucked it behind her ears before continuing as earnestly as she could. He had to believe the story she was telling if she was to get any closer to him. "You've probably heard how superstitious Indian royal families can be. Well, my father consulted with our palace astrologer, and he suggested we go to a boarding school surrounded by mountains and hidden by aspen trees." Jaya waved a hand at herself. "Thus, here we are."

Grey studied her for a second. "A royal astrologer, in effect, chose where you went to school?"

Jaya nodded, feeling a thrum of anger at the disbelieving judgment in his voice. What did he know of the Raos and their traditions? "Perhaps it sounds superstitious to you, but paying attention to the stars is rather important to my family."

Something passed over Grey's face, a shadow of a fleeting emotion Jaya couldn't catch. "'Fear is the main source of superstition, and one of the main sources of cruelty.'"

Jaya felt her hackles go up. Was he calling her family fearful and cruel? After all the Emersons had done? Did he know nothing of his own checkered history? How dare he! The pompous, arrogant . . . She forced herself to take a surreptitious deep breath.

He glanced at her. "That's a quote by Bertrand Russell. I've always remembered it."

Bertrand Russell. A British philosopher. Maybe he should read outside his own narrow lane. "Oh," Jaya said, smiling, even though inside, every nerve ending sparked with anger. She needed to be careful, she reminded herself. Very, very careful. She reached out and took his hand, squeezing it briefly before letting go. Grey, she noticed, stood numbly and didn't reciprocate, like he wasn't used to human contact. Jaya chose to ignore his odd reaction. "Grey . . . may I ask one favor?"

He nodded once without speaking.

She stepped a little closer to him; he didn't step back. "Please don't share this with anyone. Let us leave it behind." Glancing down at her feet, she continued. "It's just . . . there's so much vitriol out there about us, about her. We really need a break from it all." She batted her eyes at him, made her lips just a touch poutier, as if she were in danger of crying at any moment.

Just as she knew he would, Grey's gaze slipped to her lips, then back up to her eyes. He nodded. Jaya held back a triumphant smile. She would be *great* at PR, but just like espionage, that wasn't an occupation that was royal-approved.

Grey cleared his throat. "Sure. I promise."

When Jaya spoke, she spoke honestly. "Thank you. This is so important to me. There's nothing I wouldn't do for Isha. Absolutely nothing."

CHAPTER 7

# Jaya

Four days into the school year, everyone seemed like they were getting into the routine of being on strict schedules again. Even Alaric's unfailing arrogance had calmed down a bit, though he still liked to remind all the teachers, the other students, and himself that he was "heir to a multibillion-dollar company that deals in ideas so that the common man doesn't have to think." Jaya had asked Daphne Elizabeth what that meant. Apparently, Alaric's parents had made their fortune commercializing thirty-six previously under-utilized parts of deceased cows.

Jaya was on her way to the dorms—she and Daphne Elizabeth had made plans to study together—when Isha ran up to her on the steps outside the building. "Hi!" Jaya began, but Isha's face was reminiscent of an oncoming thunderstorm.

"You can't avoid the topic anymore," Isha said, hugging a book to her chest.

"What topic?" Jaya asked, feigning innocence.

Isha cocked her head, and for once her cherubic face was completely serious. "I've been trying to talk to you for days about Grey Emerson, and you just keep telling me you've got a headache or you're in a hurry to go somewhere or that we'll talk about it later. Well, it's later."

Jaya sighed. "You already knew he went here. Leo told us that first day—"

"Yeah, but why were you hanging out with him? Why are you talking to an Emerson after all the crap you had to say about their family?"

Isha's clear brown eyes pierced hers, and Jaya knew she was on quicksand here. She had to think fast or she'd sink in a pit of her own lies. "Because I . . . I don't think it's right to judge people based on what their family's done. You know that." Ugh, that was really weak. Perhaps she wouldn't make a great spy after all.

Isha stared at her, her mouth slightly open. "Are you joking?" she said finally. "That's literally your personal slogan. 'You are your family and your family is you.' Isn't that what you always say?"

Although impressed that Isha had actually been paying attention all those times Jaya lectured her, Jaya knew she was in a crisis moment. There was *no way* she could tell Isha the truth—that she wanted to make Grey Emerson fall in love with her so she could break his heart. Isha would never understand. So, instead, Jaya made something up on the spot. "All right, all right. The truth is . . . the truth is I'm keeping him close. Trying to find out what he knows, et cetera."

Isha's face relaxed, and with it, Jaya's shoulders. "Oh. That makes sense." She paused, nibbling on her lower lip. "And? What does he know?"

*I don't know!* Jaya wanted to say. *It's maddening. The guy's either the best actor I've ever seen or literally the most clueless human on the planet.*

But which was it? If past Emerson behavior was any indication, it would be the former, no question.

Jaya did her best to smile in a reassuring big-sister way. "Don't worry, Isha. I've got it all under control."

Later that week, Jaya sat in Daphne Elizabeth's giant papasan chair, working on her Latin vocabulary, while Daphne Elizabeth sprawled out on her bed, a mad mess of notebooks and pencils and textbooks and papers all around her. They'd been studying for about thirty minutes when Daphne Elizabeth sat up and looked at Jaya, a pencil tucked behind her ear. "I'm bored," she said, reaching into her bag to get out a stick of gum. After offering it to Jaya, who shook her head, she popped it into her mouth.

"Hmm," Jaya said. "I suppose we could take a quick break." She got up and stretched, then sauntered over to Daphne Elizabeth's desk. There was a picture of her and Alaric in a group of people taped to the wall, and under it, a stack of books and picture frames filled with photographs of Leo, Rahul, her parents, and even a horse. "That's a beautiful horse," Jaya said.

"That's Polly," Daphne Elizabeth said, smiling fondly. "She's a Clydesdale. The high point of my year is when I get to go home and ride her."

"I can see why," Jaya said as her eyes lit on a medal. It was small and silver, with an embossed bow and arrow on the front. "Archery?" she said in surprise.

"Oh, that. Bayer told me to take part in some competition last year. I got second place."

"I love archery. I won a trophy for it once, at a boarding school in Britain," Jaya said, feeling a pang for a hobby now gone. "I've considered doing it in college, too."

"Cool," Daphne Elizabeth said, lying back and staring at the ceiling, her red hair bright against her white sheets.

Jaya studied her; she clearly had something on her mind. "Everything okay?"

"Sure," Daphne Elizabeth said. "Rahul's advice is still working. Alaric and Caterina aren't sitting together anymore in English, so they can't really talk in the one class I share with both of them."

"Ah," Jaya said, sitting back down in the papasan and picking up her book. "But?"

Daphne Elizabeth nibbled on her lower lip and turned over to face Jaya. "I just never thought I'd be that girl. The other woman." She said it mockingly, but Jaya could see pain in the lines that bracketed her mouth. "It's so freaking cliché."

"Why don't you change it?" Jaya asked. "If you really feel like your life's a cliché and Alaric isn't worth it, I mean."

Daphne Elizabeth laughed a little, her chin propped in her hand. "You make it sound so easy."

"That wasn't my intention." Jaya paused, thinking about Grey Emerson and how she was letting her instincts—spitting sparks, roaring with anger—lead her where she needed to go. "I suppose I just mean people's instincts rarely lead them astray."

"I can't tell if it's my instinct or my hormones that led me down this path," Daphne Elizabeth said morosely.

Jaya paused and then turned a page in her book. "I see."

"What do you mean?"

"Hmm?" Jaya continued to read.

"Jaya." Daphne Elizabeth waited until Jaya met her eye reluctantly. "What did you mean by 'I see'?"

Sighing, Jaya crossed her arms on her book. "Well, I . . . I don't understand why you feel the need to be with Alaric, that's all."

She thought again about Alaric in the library, that first day she'd met Grey without knowing it. How Alaric's face had been a twisted sneer of entitlement and elitism when he'd bullied Elliot before Grey stepped in. She considered telling Daphne Elizabeth what she'd seen, but she didn't know her very well, and Jaya was afraid she'd shut down completely. She already looked on her way there, with her arms crossed, leaning away from Jaya.

"You have so much to offer, Daphne Elizabeth," she continued. "You're funny, you're beautiful, you're kind . . ." She didn't add, *When it comes to Alaric, though, you seem to forget all that*, but the unspoken thought hung in the air between them. Jaya waited, worried she'd overstepped her bounds.

Daphne Elizabeth didn't speak for a long moment, her face a mask of defensiveness. But when she looked up at Jaya, perhaps seeing the lack of judgment in Jaya's expression, the fight went out of her eyes. Running a fingernail along a crease in her bedsheet, she sighed. "I don't know. I guess . . . I feel like Alaric was the first person to really see me. I mean, sure, I've dated other guys before, guys who got off on the fact that they were dating the McKinley heiress. But it never felt like this. For some reason, when I'm with Alaric, he doesn't seem like he's looking through me. He tells me all the time that when he saw me, it was like a gong went off in his head and he just knew." She uncrossed her arms and played with a pencil on the table.

"Knew what?" Jaya asked, expecting Daphne Elizabeth to say, *He loved me.*

Instead, she said, "That he had to have me."

Jaya paused. "He . . . he had to 'have' you?"

Daphne Elizabeth waved a hand. "That sounds bad, but the

way he said it, it really felt like he meant it. You know? Like, that he just had to have me in his life. He pays so much attention to me, Jaya. I'm not invisible when I'm with him."

Jaya leaned forward and put a hand on Daphne Elizabeth's ankle. "You're not invisible at all, Daphne Elizabeth."

The girl smiled a little. She tried to make it look brave and nonchalant, but it just looked sad. "Maybe not to you, but try telling that to my parents. Sometimes I swear I'm half human, half a pane of glass." She rallied. "But it's okay. I know they're super busy, super important people and all that. They've been telling me that my whole life." She shrugged. "But on occasion, it's just nice to be *seen*, you know?"

Jaya forced a smile. "Mm." She turned back to her book.

"And what about you?" Daphne Elizabeth, who clearly had no intention of either studying or letting Jaya study, asked. "Anyone you've got your eye on?"

"Well . . ." Jaya looked up from her book. "There is someone . . . but I'm taking my time with him." *Taking my time burrowing into his life*, she thought, but didn't say. *Like a little rabbit. A little, vengeful, heartbreaking rabbit.*

"Well, he's a goner, whoever he is," Daphne Elizabeth said, laughing. "You're what they call a hot-tee with a capital 'tee.'"

Jaya sometimes failed to understand about a third of what Daphne Elizabeth said, but she got the gist of this. Twirling her pen thoughtfully, she said, "That's what I'm hoping."

A few days later, Jaya stood on the outdoor archery range with Grey, her hair blowing slightly in the light breeze. Using the hair elastic around her wrist, she tied it back in a sporty ponytail and turned to him, shrugging. "This is so hard." She giggled, even though just saying the words was anathema to her very soul. "I just cannot remember what Ms. Bayer said, and I don't want her shooting me with an arrow."

"Hmm," Grey said. His target was about seventy-five yards south of them. "Let me see you do it."

Jaya irritably pulled the arrow up to her mouth, smiling a slightly rictus smile. "Like this?"

"No," he said brusquely. "Pull it under your chin. Remember?"

He wasn't being condescending in the least. Still, she'd easily been the best archer at her last few schools. And now, to pretend like she had no clue what she was doing? It really, really stuck in her craw. If she were being completely honest, Grey's square stance wasn't even that good. *She* should be teaching *him*.

"No," Jaya said now, doing her best damsel-in-distress move. She tried to laugh helplessly, but there was an edge to it that she hurriedly tried to round out. "Could you show me? Please?"

Grey stepped behind her (he was positively *looming*. God, was there any reason for anyone to be that tall and broad?) and guided her arms. "Like . . . this," he said, positioning her the right way.

She relaxed against him and smiled. "Thanks, Grey."

He said nothing.

# Grey

Jaya was resting her body lightly against his, and it . . . it felt strange. Good strange, but still strange. It was like she was just finding reasons to touch him. The thought wasn't completely unpleasant. But it also didn't make sense. Sure, they'd built up an acquaintanceship over the last week and a half. It was kind of impossible not to—she was in all of his classes, she sat with his group of friends for all of their meals. Her story and emotions about her sister's scandal had seemed real enough. But she was a Rao. Her pendant was still a big question mark hanging around her neck. If he knew what was good for him, he'd stay away from her. Completely away. And yet . . .

"Time to wrap up!" Ms. Bayer called from down the line of students. "Put your gear away!"

Grey stepped back from her quickly, muscling past the slight but alarming reluctance he felt.

Jaya turned and smiled up at him. "Until next time, then." She sashayed off to her station, which was right next to his, and looked over at him as she put her gear away. "So, I was wondering, are you going to the back-to-school mixer next Saturday?"

Grey dropped his arrow into the quiver. He hated school-sanctioned "fun" activities like these. "Yes," he said tightly. "It's mandatory." Because Dr. Waverly thought if they didn't go, they'd all turn into hermits.

Jaya studied his expression. "Is it quite that awful? We get to dress up and mingle on the rooftop, don't we? I've heard it's really beautiful." Jaya put the rest of her gear away and then walked back over to Grey's station.

"Dressing up and mingling on rooftops? Not my thing."

She laughed, the breeze tugging on a strand of her hair that had come loose from her ponytail. "So if I come talk to you, you'll walk away?"

Grey watched her for a moment, hesitating. Then he turned away without answering.

# Jaya

Later that evening, Jaya and Isha were meeting downstairs by the fireplace in the lobby to go off campus for dinner. But when Jaya finally made it downstairs (she'd been reading the latest young adult rom-com in her room and had completely lost track of time), she almost didn't recognize her baby sister. Isha was wearing a sweatshirt so baggy it slipped off one shoulder, her lacy halter bra strap on display.

"*Isha*," Jaya whispered, hurrying to her side. She yanked on the neckline of Isha's sweatshirt, but it didn't help; the thing just slid back down again. "What on earth are you wearing? Where did you get this?"

Isha pulled on it and smiled. "I got it at the airport store in Denver. Cool, huh?"

"The day we flew in? Where was I?" Jaya asked, frowning at it.

"In the bathroom." Isha batted her palm frond–like eyelashes.

Sighing, Jaya said, "You better hope Appa never finds out."

"How would he?" Isha retorted. "You're not going to tell him, are you? You wouldn't do that to your baby sister."

Jaya rolled her eyes and put her arm around Isha's shoulders, mostly to cover up her bra strap. "I suppose not. Anyway, where do you want to go to eat?"

"Ooh, Elliot told me about this really delicious sushi restaurant downtown. He says it's pretty good for being a thousand miles away from the ocean and eight thousand feet above sea level." She laughed uproariously, as if Elliot were the most hilarious person she'd ever encountered.

"Elliot." Jaya's eyebrows knitted together without her permission. Isha had been spending a lot of time with that boy. Just yesterday she said Elliot and she had lain on the hilly green by the astronomy building and just watched the clouds float by. The clouds. Float by. Like Isha had ever cared about floating clouds before.

"Yeah," Isha said, fiddling with the gold ring on her finger. Amma had given them matching ones when each of them turned thirteen. "He's my friend. I asked him if he wanted to come tonight, but he'd already made plans with Carlos."

Oh, he was her *friend.* Of course. Just like Romeo was Juliet's friend. "The sushi restaurant's downtown?" Jaya said, instead of the million and twenty things she really wanted to say about Elliot. "I don't know. It's getting dark out and that's ten miles away."

Isha laughed. She actually *laughed* at Jaya. Her older sister. "'It's getting dark.' You sound like you're fifty, Jaya. Come on. We're young."

"Our age has nothing to do with it," Jaya said serenely, even though her blood pressure was rising. Why was Isha always so quick to flout the rules? To do whatever she wanted? "It's not safe to go traipsing around a town that you don't know. We're still getting acclimated. We don't have an escort."

"St. Rosetta's has a car service!" Isha said, sighing. "The driver will literally drop us off right at the door; we can set it up right now. You know the office is open 24/7. It's not that hard."

"I could be your escort."

Isha looked over Jaya's shoulder at the bearer of that deep, rather growly voice and smiled hesitantly. Even though Jaya had managed, in the interceding days, to convince Isha that Grey knew nothing of the scandal (there was no reason for *both* of them to constantly be on high alert. Also, if Isha believed Grey knew nothing of the scandal, Jaya could socialize with him without Isha getting suspicious), it was understandable that she was a little unsure of him.

Jaya took a breath and turned around with the sweetest smile on her face. "Grey!" she said, in a hearty so-nice-to-see-you voice. "We couldn't trouble you that way." Like she was going to let him anywhere near her little sister.

He was dressed in his after-school outfit—ratty long-sleeved T-shirt with some obscure-but-certain-to-be-cool band logo on the front, his big feet clad in boots that looked like they'd been run over by several buses, his jeans hanging just so from his hips. His hair was unbrushed and mussed. Annoyingly enough, it gave him a certain savage charm.

Sticking his gigantic hands in his pockets, Grey shrugged, broad shoulders moving easily under his shirt. "No trouble," he said. "Sushi sounds good. I'm hungry." It struck Jaya that he spoke like a Neanderthal in a cartoon, in stunted sentences and abrupt monosyllables, a good bit of the time. Rather strange for a nobleman.

Isha glanced at Jaya. "Okay. Let's do it, then." That she was willing to give him a chance wasn't entirely surprising to Jaya. That was Isha, never prejudging people for where they came from. And maybe she'd decided Grey Emerson would be unable to mastermind a vicious scandal. He could barely manage to string two sentences together. She had a point, but Jaya wasn't yet ready to arrive at the same conclusion. Grey Emerson might just be an extremely good saboteur.

Grey raised his eyebrows, asking Jaya for permission to come, and Jaya bowed her head, giving it. Besides, if he, the most committed recluse Jaya had ever come across, wanted to come to sushi with them, that was a sign her plan was working, wasn't it? Even though she was tired of all the flirting, perhaps she was nearer the finish line than she'd thought. The idea filled her with a burst of renewed energy. "Excellent. Thank you, Grey."

# Grey

He tried not to stare at her—or at the pendant, minus one ruby— as they rode in the Escalade. Sure, Jaya Rao had seemed truthful when she told him about the scandal with Isha and why they'd come here to St. Rosetta's. But that didn't mean his guard was down. She still wore the pendant. And the fact that both Rao sisters were here, at St. R's, in the middle of their high school careers? More than a little unsettling.

He clenched his fists on his thighs. Was that the *only* reason he'd volunteered himself as their escort? Grey wasn't one to lie to himself. Somewhere in some dusty corner of his mind that was beginning to light and spark as it hadn't ever done before, he knew the whole truth was a lot more complicated. He stole a glance at Jaya Rao, her smooth brown skin, her laugh that was both confident and sexy, her obvious protective love for her little sister. Yeah, the truth was a lot more complicated.

It felt strange, going out to dinner with them when he barely knew them. He rarely went out to get food with DE, Leo, and Rahul, and then only when they begged and pleaded and wouldn't take no for an answer. He felt his social muscles, stiff from lack of use, creaking and snapping every time he tried to make conversation. Jaya and Isha carried most of the conversation seamlessly; they were probably used to it from all their training.

Grey sat back against the seat and let their inane chatter wash over him as the car hurtled toward the restaurant. Whatever Jaya Rao was here for, he'd get to the bottom of it.

# Jaya

So Sushi Me was dimly lit and somewhat grimy, tucked away on a shop-lined avenue in downtown St. Rosetta. Grey insisted on tipping the driver himself and wouldn't let Jaya reimburse him, which she found both irritating and strangely charming. The waitress led them to a table by the window (that overlooked the parking lot) and left them with their menus.

"It's not much to look at," Grey said. He was seated across from Jaya, alone in his ripped vinyl bench. Which was probably wise; he took up the entire thing on his own. "But the food is good."

"That's what my friend Elliot said," Isha put in, because evidently, she couldn't go more than fifteen minutes without mentioning Elliot.

A flicker of recognition crossed Grey's face at Elliot's name, but then he nodded seriously. "Then Elliot has good taste."

*Don't encourage her*, Jaya wanted to sigh. Instead, she leaned in and smiled. "So. What do you recommend here, Grey?"

"The *masago* is my favorite," he said. "But I think the seaweed salad is their most popular one."

"Mm. I think I'll go with your favorite."

"I'll get the *unagi*," Isha added.

Grey signaled to the waitress that they were ready, and then they all placed their orders.

It was kind of . . . interesting how he just took charge. Some women might find that attractive, but Jaya herself merely noted it as a student of social patterns. He was still the enemy, no matter how chivalrous or confident or how much of a sushi expert he was.

"So, Isha," Jaya said, because she was the elder sister and it was her duty. "How are your studies coming along?"

"Great! I checked this book out of the library, and it's all about how to weld parts together to build a robot. It's fascinating!"

"Oh dear." Jaya tried not to let her face show how horrifying she really found the thought of Isha building robots.

"Have you read about the origami method?" Grey asked, looking interested in spite of himself.

"Oh, you mean where you practice with paper before you do it on metal? To get the basics of building the body down?" Isha replied. "Yeah, I have. I have this great book by David Cook."

"*Robot Building for Beginners*," they both said at the same time. Isha smiled at him across the table. Jaya could see that Isha was beginning to warm to Grey, simply because he showed an interest in her completely inappropriate hobby. And speaking of completely inappropriate hobbies, did she have to talk about it to the *very* person who'd brought her down in flames for another one of her inappropriate hobbies? (Well, two others, if you counted "boys" as a hobby.) Not that Isha knew about Grey's involvement in her scandal, but still.

Still, this wasn't unsalvageable. So far, Isha hadn't divulged anything tremendously harmful that Grey could use. Jaya just needed to step in and manage the conversation. Maybe pivot it to draw *Grey* out more.

She scrunched up the paper her straw had been encased in with rather more force than was strictly necessary. "Oh, I didn't know you were into robotics too, Grey."

He grunted without saying anything further, but Isha pressed on. "Have you taken the robotics elective?"

"Robotics I, last year."

Isha waited for more details. *Ha*, Jaya wanted to say. Don't hold your breath. The boy hoards his words like they're air and he's in outer space without a helmet.

Grey shifted in his seat, as if he were gearing himself up for what he was about to say next. Jaya watched, fascinated. "I didn't take Robotics II, but an engineer from MIT comes in to teach the second half of that class. You get to set up a think tank and lab and brainstorm some of the most pressing problems plaguing robotics." He sat back, as if exhausted from the effort of saying all those words.

"Wow," Isha said, her eyes shining. She obviously hadn't noticed how bizarre their dinner companion was. "That's so cool."

Jaya laughed politely. The last thing Isha needed to do was join robotic think tanks. Forget building robots, she should be focused on rebuilding her reputation.

"Thanks for telling me about it, Grey," Isha continued.

"Sure," he said. After a pause, he added, "Have you heard of Next?"

Isha shook her head. Jaya wanted to reach across the table and stuff her paper napkin into Grey's mouth. Was he just baiting Isha into divulging information that showed her interests were completely unsuitable for a young royal woman? *You've already shown everyone in Mysuru that*, Jaya thought, gritting her teeth.

"They're a nonprofit based out of Denver, and their mission is to get more women into STEM fields—"

Thankfully, the waitress interrupted them by bringing out their plates of food. When she was gone, Jaya said, "Ooh, all of this looks so yummy." She beamed a little savagely at Isha. "Eat!"

Isha rolled her eyes and tucked into her *unagi*. "Mm, this *is* good," she said. "How's yours, Grey?"

He grunted and shoved a *masago* roll into his mouth.

"I'm going to look into Next," Isha said after swallowing a mouthful of *unagi*.

"No, you're not," Jaya found herself snapping.

Grey looked from her to Isha and back again. "They have a good website."

Jaya tried not to snarl at him. "That's not the point, is it? Our family has certain expectations of us. It's important we adhere to them." Jaya drank a sip of water and waited for Isha's repartee, but amazingly enough, she was quiet. Good. Maybe Grey would think she agreed with Jaya.

They ate in silence for a minute, and then Grey said, "Familial expectations aren't always the only way or even the right way." He said it like he was biting off each word, like it caused him physical pain.

Jaya couldn't help the venom that tinged her words. "That's strange for a British nobleman to say. Aren't you governed by rules and etiquette?"

Grey held her eyes. "Doesn't mean I believe in them."

Jaya sat up straighter. He was making her angry, even though she knew she should hide it for the sake of the bigger goal. "Well,

OF CURSES AND KISSES    115

we believe in ours. Our family is *everything* to us." She could feel Isha's eyes on the two of them.

"Family shouldn't be everything to anyone," Grey said shortly, stabbing another roll into his mouth and chewing violently. His eyes never left hers. "Family can be unreliable. Family can hurt you."

Jaya narrowed her eyes. What did he mean by that? But before she could ask him, he threw his napkin down and stood. "Excuse me," he said, then walked abruptly toward the bathroom.

"What was that about?" Isha asked after they'd watched him disappear into the far side of the restaurant.

"I don't know," Jaya said thoughtfully, drumming her fingers on the table. *But I intend to find out.*

# Jaya

Not half bad. Saturday, the night of the mixer, Jaya leaned in close to the mirror and studied her reflection. She'd artfully arranged her curly hair in a half bun, and she wore a Wendell Rodricks dress in wispy pink-and-gold layers that exposed half her back. Pairing the dress with high-heeled gold glitter Manolo Blahnik pumps had been a great idea too. She'd worked hard on this look and it said, in a very casually flirty tone, "Hey, Grey. I'm gorgeous and funny and interesting and into you. You'd be crazy to not go out with me." She was getting better at this.

And maybe she was imagining things, but she could swear he was beginning to respond to her a little. Granted, it was a bit hard to tell with him. He spent so much of his time in silence.

She got the feeling he was completely comfortable being quiet, just watching the world.

It was all right, though. If she could handle elephants in musth, she could handle one antisocial son of a duke.

Smiling, Jaya straightened her ruby necklace.

Her phone rang with the video-chat tone, and before answering, Jaya shrugged into the shimmery bolero that went with her dress. Her parents' faces smiled at her from the screen.

"Hi, Appa, Amma!" she said, pressing "answer." A twinge of homesickness prodded at her when she saw their loving, comfortably familiar faces.

There was a knock on her door and Isha entered, wearing a black dress with lime-green bows along the back, her hair straightened so it hung to her waist. She bounded up to the phone and waved at their parents.

"You both look so pretty!" Amma said. "Is the mixer tonight?"

"Yes," Jaya answered. "It should be fun!"

"Don't talk with boys," Appa said immediately. "Just say it's against your culture."

Isha snorted, and Jaya elbowed her off-screen. "Yes, Appa," she said demurely.

"Isha, that means you, too," Amma said. "Don't forget what happened not too long ago."

Isha was immediately more serious. "I remember," she mumbled.

"Jaya, you'll take care of her, won't you?" Amma said.

"Of course I will," Jaya replied, putting an arm around her sister. "That's my job."

Isha rolled her eyes and groaned. "Why can't you all stop treating me like I'm six years old?"

OF CURSES AND KISSES    117

"You'll always be my baby," Amma said, smiling fondly at the two of them.

Appa took a more serious tack. "How are things there? Has anyone said anything . . . ?"

"No," Jaya responded, equally seriously. "We're fitting in well."

"Even though Grey—" Isha began, but Jaya quieted her with a look. There was no need to mention Grey at all. It would just upset their parents.

"Hmm?" Amma asked, leaning toward the camera. "Even though what?"

"Even though gray . . . gray skies prevail, we shall see it through!" Isha said, smiling brightly.

"Erm, yes, victory will be ours," Jaya said, adopting an equally bogus, cheery-to-the-point-of-being-scary grin. "Anyway," she continued. "We should probably go. But we'll call you soon!"

"Okay, take care, both of you," Appa said. "We'll talk to you soon."

"Bye, *chinnu*," Amma said in a wobbly voice, her eyes shiny. *Chinnu* was her term of endearment for her two daughters, and hearing it made Jaya feel a little sick at the thought of the lie she'd just told.

She pushed the "end" button and turned to Isha. "Wow." She blew out a breath. "Good save there."

"Mediocre save," Isha corrected. After a pause, she said, "Why we can't tell them about Grey Emerson, again?"

"Because we don't want to worry them," Jaya said. Guilt squirmed in her stomach like a nest of snakes. She abhorred lying, generally. It was crass and craven and behavior not befitting a royal. But wasn't all fair in love and war? This was definitely war. Grey Emerson may not know it yet, but Jaya certainly did. "What's the point, when they can't do anything about it?"

"Right," Isha said thoughtfully.

"Anyway. Are you ready? We're supposed to be in the ballroom in seven minutes. Dr. Waverly will probably send out a search party if we're late." Dr. Waverly had been on edge ever since they'd announced the mixer, warning people repeatedly that if they "cavorted" in an "inappropriate manner" at any time, she'd put their entire school on lockdown. Jaya felt a prickle of sympathy for the headmistress. It couldn't be an easy task—managing students who were used to getting everything they wanted the instant they decided they wanted it, while also keeping their extremely powerful, wealthy parents happy.

Isha looked at her silently for a long moment, as if she could sense that Jaya was holding something back. But then, sighing, she stood.

The two of them walked arm in arm out of the room, and Jaya thought, *It'll be all right soon, Ish. You'll see.*

CHAPTER 8

# Grey

Grey stood by a large potted plant in a corner of the sprawl-ing rooftop of the main building, watching everyone laugh and socialize—something he'd never quite gotten the hang of. Elliot, the kid from the library and Isha's friend, talked animatedly with a group of other sophomores. Grey was glad, in spite of himself. He'd noticed the boy last year, too, always walking by himself around campus. He'd probably had a hard time fitting in, being one of the only scholarship people at St. R's. Grey got what it meant to be different, apart. Which might sound weird coming from a rich, white, British-born male aristocrat, but Grey had never felt part of anything. He'd always thought of himself as an island, existing outside of the continent of human relationships. Elliot looked over, caught his eye, and waved. After a moment's hesitation, Grey raised his own hand in a kind-of wave.

A cloud of laughter rose up from another group in the cor-ner and Grey's gaze passed over them. Everyone was a glitzier, more animated version of themselves tonight. Grey couldn't help feeling the slightest edge of boredom, of ennui. Every year was the same. The freshmen were fresh-faced, the sophomores were finally getting into the groove of things, the juniors were all about hooking up, and the seniors would spike the punch at some point. Same show, slightly different actors. Did none of them notice? Did no one except him see how . . . how pointless it all was?

"Yo." Daphne Elizabeth grabbed his elbow, jerking him out of the spiral of his thoughts. "You okay? You look like you're watching the most depressing movie in the universe."

Grey straightened. "I'm fine."

Batting her feathery glued-on eyelashes, DE looked down at her distressed retro prom dress. "How do I look?"

Grey studied her. She'd ripped holes in the silk fabric so her cleavage and stomach were exposed. "Good," he said blandly.

She grinned. "Loquacious as usual, huh? Well, thanks. This used to be my nana's, so I thought I'd repurpose it."

Leo appeared at his elbow and tutted at DE. He'd worn his long hair down and was dressed in a very flashy blue suit. "And does Nana know that you have so mercilessly 'repurposed' her dress?"

DE smiled slyly. "What she doesn't know won't hurt her, right?"

"Yes, yes, I suppose so. But enough of that because I have exciting news: I am ready to find a girlfriend," Leo said, throwing up his hands just as Rahul walked up. *He* was dressed more conservatively, like Grey, in a black suit, although he was wearing a tie and Grey had decided to go open collar. Honestly, Grey thought, he just couldn't be bothered with a tie for the sake of two or three mind-numbing hours of standing around.

"Congratulations?" DE said to Leo, raising an eyebrow. "Got anyone in mind? I might want to warn her."

"I have compiled Leo's requirements for a partner from several conversations and have come to the conclusion that the only true requirement is that she have a pulse," Rahul said, completely deadpan.

"Why do you say this to me?" Leo asked over DE's guffaw, ostensibly hurt, though his mouth twitched. "Okay, okay, I do confess this: my requirements have been very lax in the past. But this year I will find my one true love!"

"True love is an abstract, illogical social construct that likely does not exist," Rahul countered. "There's no biological imperative to support the concept of true love."

Leo sighed, then, turning to DE, he said, "Well, at least things are going better for you, *mon amie*. I have seen Alaric and Caterina fighting a lot recently. You must be very happy, *non*?"

DE flushed and looked away. "Not especially."

"But you and Alaric—" Leo began.

"Well, that doesn't mean I think it's all candy hearts and unicorn farts, okay?" DE snapped. "Do you think I like being the reason for someone's heartache? Do you think I'm a total bitch?"

Leo looked taken aback. "*Non*," he said carefully. "I do not think that at all."

DE put two fingers to the bridge of her nose. "I'm sorry. I shouldn't have . . . I need a drink."

As she walked away, Leo said, "Hmm. That ship, it has a crack in its foundation."

"Ships don't have foundations. Buildings have foundations," Rahul said, and began to walk off. "I'm hungry."

Leo, apparently back to his usual optimistic state, grinned and rubbed his hands. "Okay. Would you like to go with me to execute Mission Find-a-Partner, Grey? I really feel this is the year for us."

"No, thank you," Grey said, putting one hand in his pocket. "I'm going to hang out here."

After only the slightest hesitation, Leo shrugged and walked off after Rahul. Grey wondered how much longer it'd be before they decided Grey wasn't worth the trouble. He could see DE, Rahul, and Leo remaining friends through college. He, on the other hand, wouldn't even make it *to* college.

Grey was wondering if he should go back to his room when Jaya Rao glided in. And, without quite realizing it, he forgot to breathe.

# Jaya

Jaya walked through the open set of double French doors with Isha. It had been chilly on the walk over, but several large outdoor heaters had been placed all over the expansive rooftop, making it almost balmy. Although, maybe it wasn't only the heaters. There were almost two hundred people here. Jaya took off her bolero and stuffed it into her bag as she and Isha looked around.

It *was* beautiful, Jaya had to admit. She'd been to her share of gorgeous functions at the palace, of course, but this was different. Perhaps because she was surrounded by her peers rather than stuffy old officials and her parents' friends, Jaya felt a thrum of excitement. She felt like a proper teen tonight, not just Rajkumari Jaya Rao. Smiling, she took in the ornate white stone railing and dozens of large potted topiary plants, draped with thick strands of twinkling lights that cast a golden glow on everything. There was a large table to her right, on which snacks and drinks of every kind were on display. Waiters in tuxes walked around with canapés and glasses of punch on silver trays. Hidden speakers thumped out party music that vibrated the stone floor under Jaya's feet. Above her, the star-sprinkled night sky stretched on, infinite.

Couples and groups of people were clustered around the rooftop, everyone's faces shining. The girls sparkled with makeup, expensive jewelry, and anticipation. The boys—hair slicked back or hanging in their eyes carefully—smirked with a practiced nonchalance, but their glowing cheeks gave them away too. There were teacher chaperones present, but they kept themselves tucked away, talking quietly to each other.

"Hi, Elliot!" Isha called from beside her, and the shorter white boy from the library, now surrounded by a group of students—sophomores, from the baby-faced looks of them—waved enthusiastically. "I'll see you later, okay, Jaya?" Isha said, and before she could respond, her little sister had danced off to join the boy.

Jaya opened her mouth to call after her little sister and then closed it again. She had other, more pressing business to get to at the moment. Where was Grey Emerson?

It was like thinking his name had summoned him. Jaya took a glass of punch from a waiter, turned slowly to survey everyone, and found him gazing directly at her. Her breath caught in her throat. He had one hand in his pocket, the other circled loosely around a glass of his own. He'd left his hair shaggy, hanging on his forehead. The open collar of his shirt hinted at his broad, nicely defined chest, and the well-cut suit jacket hugged his muscular frame. Those were all lovely details, aesthetically pleasing things meant for others—like that group of students in the corner, who were not-very-surreptitiously watching him and making not-so-subtle innuendos. (Jaya noticed everything. It was a gift and a curse.) But his eyes . . . his eyes were locked on Jaya.

She stood still, watching as he made his way toward her through the crowd, a head taller than everyone else, his bright sapphire gaze locked with hers. Her heart pounded. Why was he looking at her like that, like she was both the journey and the goal? Maybe her plan was working better than she thought. But this time, calling her plan to mind didn't give her purpose and confidence, as it usually did. Jaya blinked and looked away, tucking a lock of hair behind one ear as she felt him draw closer.

"Hello," Jaya said. She could smell his cologne: leather and pepper and woodsmoke.

Grey nodded, his intense gaze never leaving her face.

Jaya took a drink, not because she was thirsty, but because his eyes, those wild eyes, all storms and thunder and crashing waves, unnerved her. Normal people didn't look at you like that.

She waited, but Grey didn't rush to fill in the silence. He just continued watching her.

"So this is a St. Rosetta's mixer," Jaya said, in a voice that sounded about two octaves higher than her normal one. God, was she starting to *sweat*?

"It is," Grey agreed. He was just standing so close because it was loud here, Jaya told herself. After a pause, he added, "You look . . ."

She waited, heart hammering.

". . . nice," he finished, and she felt a little thud of disappointment. Which, of course, was because she needed him to fall in love with her in order for her plan to work, and "nice" wasn't exactly a sizzling proclamation of love.

"Thank you." Jaya smiled her most charming smile, forced her eyes to shine like he'd called her this generation's Mona Lisa. "You look really great in a suit." He did, too; *that* was no lie.

Grey pulled on his cuffs and said disparagingly, "I've learned it's a good idea to have at least three suits or tuxes on hand if you're a male student at St. R's. The administration likes to make us dress up so they can photograph us and convince our parents back home we're following in their 'civilized' footsteps."

Jaya regarded him in surprise. "I don't think I've ever heard you say so much at once," she said before she could stop herself. "You must feel rather strongly about it." That had been a veritable speech for Grey Emerson. Had he ever said so many words, apart from when he was talking to Isha about robotics?

He grunted and looked away.

"But anyway, there's nothing wrong with following our parents, is there?" Jaya said, trying to get him to open up once more. She shouldn't have called attention to his verbosity at all. "I think my parents' footsteps are respectable ones to want to follow."

"Yes, but . . ."

Jaya waited.

"Don't you ever feel the need to do something different with your life than what they expect?" His voice was so low it rumbled inside her chest.

"Different?" Jaya laughed at the very idea. "'Different' is for artists and celebrities' kids. I've always known, since I was a small child, that it'd be up to me to carry on the family legacy. I've known I needed to go to an Ivy League university, major in business or finance, and return back home to run Appa's estate. Simple."

Grey raised an eyebrow. "Simple? More like incredibly boring."

Jaya straightened her spine, her eyes drilling into his. "*Boring?* Did you really just call my life boring?"

Grey looked at her for a moment, as if he were weighing whether he wanted to say what he was really thinking. "I'm calling your life *plan* boring," he said finally. "That's an important distinction. Don't you find it . . . stifling to have your entire life mapped out according to someone else's plan? Don't you want to define for yourself who you are rather than just taking someone else's word for granted?" He pushed a hand through his hair. "Don't you have a mind of your own, or do you believe everything your father tells you?" He spat the last question out rapidly at her, his words like bullets from a machine gun. But somehow she got the idea he wasn't just talking to her. Well, regardless of whomever he intended that message for, he was being remarkably, flagrantly rude. Then again, what else could be expected from an Emerson?

Jaya's temper rose like water that was dangerously close to spilling over a dam. She tried channeling Amma and counting backward from one hundred by sevens, but she was barely at ninety-three when she found herself snapping as the dam burst, "*My* father is a well-respected, honorable member of society, unlike some other people's!"

There was a dangerous silence as they both glared at each other. Then, very carefully, like his own temper was only hanging on by a thread, Grey asked in a low voice, "What do you mean by that?"

Bollocks. He'd earned every word of that comeback, naturally, but Jaya'd lost sight of the plan. And that was very, very bad. *Keep your eyes on the prize, Jaya, my girl,* her inner critic said, shaking her head and tutting. *Recover yourself immediately.* "Nothing," she said, trying to calm her breathing and putting on a smile that felt very flat and very small. Why did this boy get to her so easily? "Nothing. Just that other people here, their fathers . . . I don't know. I've heard stories. That's all." *You arrogant, bloody son of a duke.*

Grey studied her for a long moment, like he didn't quite believe her. Nevertheless, the fire went out of his eyes. She felt her cheeks warm and her temper cool at his obvious suspicion and coughed politely to distract from it. "So, ah, Grey," she said. "What's your plan, then? After you graduate?"

A strange look passed fleetingly over his face. "I have no plans."

Jaya frowned, interested in spite of herself. "But . . . what about your estate? Westborough? Don't you want to manage that, help the duke run it?"

Something dark and shadowed settled over Grey. "That's not in the cards for me."

"But surely your family would want—"

"I don't speak with my family," Grey said tersely.

"None of them?" Jaya frowned, remembering his words at the sushi restaurant. *Family can be unreliable. Family can hurt you.*

"No," Grey said, his jaw hard. "None of them."

Jaya felt a flickering doubt, like a guttering flame, inside her. Was it possible that Grey really didn't speak to his family? That his seeming lack of knowledge about the Rao scandal wasn't an act or a devious ploy she couldn't work out, but simply the truth? But . . . then who had the journalist in India been talking about? Was there another young Emerson who might've fed the papers this story? Perhaps. Jaya didn't know every single member of the Emerson family tree.

She studied Grey's profile, feeling a hint of misgiving. If he truly had no idea what his family had done . . . did he deserve to be punished for it? But had the Emersons given Isha any such consideration? Had they thought of her as an innocent?

"Why don't you speak to your family?" Jaya asked, bringing her mind back to the conversation at hand.

Grey was opening his mouth to respond when Samantha Wickers accidentally whacked him with her shoulder. Samantha, a senior like them, had curly strawberry-blond hair piled into a high updo and was nice enough, Jaya supposed, but right then she wanted to slap her.

"Oh, crap!" Samantha said, her blue eyes going wide. She was holding a plate filled with hors d'oeuvres in her hands. "I'm so sorry, Grey. I didn't see you there."

Jaya kept her eyes on Grey, desperately wanting to go back to their conversation. Damn it. He'd been about to say more—she'd felt it. But he was looking at Samantha bloody Wickers now, and the moment was shattered.

Leo materialized right behind Samantha, as if he were a ghost and Sam the Ouija board. He grinned appreciatively (and, Jaya was sure, what he thought of as "winningly") at her, but Samantha seemed rather oblivious to Leo's presence.

"Would anyone like a taste?" Samantha said, smiling around at all the people nearby, holding up the tray of crackers with jam or cheese on them. Samantha's mother was the owner of the Wickers Jam empire, and according to Daphne Elizabeth, they had more money than a small European country. She thrust the tray at Grey, and more out of a wish to protect his face rather than an actual desire to taste the food, Jaya thought, Grey took one.

Jaya took one too, just to be polite, even though what she

really wanted was to take that plate from Samantha and fling it over the railing into the blackness beyond. "Mm," she said, nodding.

Samantha beamed at Grey and Jaya. Behind her, Leo's brow furrowed. Samantha still hadn't noticed him or offered him a cracker. "Peach champagne jam on brie. I helped my mom's company come up with the flavor this summer." She turned to Grey. "What do you think?"

"I think I don't like peach. Or brie," Grey said curtly.

Jaya struggled not to stare. Did he have no social training whatsoever?

Samantha's face darkened. "Well, I think that's just ru—"

Leo lunged forward, pushing Jaya slightly aside. He grabbed the remaining crackers off Samantha's plate and shoved them in his mouth as Grey and Jaya watched, agog. "Do not listen to Grey, Sam. He does not know what he is speaking of. *Mon dieu*," he said with his mouth full, "these are *incroyable*, Samantha! Well done! What is your secret! You must share it with me!"

"I . . ." Samantha looked down at her plate and then at Leo, who was staring at Samantha with what could only be described as a feverish light in his eyes as he crunched away. Jaya hid a smile behind her hand.

"Sam!" a girl called from across the rooftop. "Come here a sec!"

Samantha tossed a final, bewildered "what's wrong with you" glance at Leo and Grey, then walked off. Leo watched her go, his face sagging.

Jaya drank a huge gulp of punch and said, "That was . . . interesting."

"I was flirting!" Leo said, waving his hands around. "I was

being interested in what she is interested in! Is this not how you win over people?"

Jaya stared at him. "That was . . . *flirting*?"

Leo frowned a little. "*Oui*," he said, a little uncertainly. "Did it not . . . come through that way?"

"Well, not exactly . . . ," Jaya said.

Leo sighed. "I do not understand."

"It's okay," Jaya said sympathetically. "Dating is really complicated." Unwittingly, she tossed Grey a look—only to find he was looking at her, too.

"Perhaps," Leo said, oblivious to the two of them. "I suppose I will go get a drink." He walked off, his shoulders hunched and sad.

Jaya turned to Grey, a small smile at her lips. "So . . ."

Before she could formulate a diplomatic question to steer the conversation back to Grey and his family, Isha came walking up and wrapped her arms around Jaya's waist. "Hello!" she said to Grey, who nodded back at her. After the sushi-dinner bonding exercise, they seemed to be on fairly good terms.

Jaya smiled. "Hi, Ish."

"I want you to meet my friend," Isha said, gesturing behind her.

Jaya noticed Elliot standing behind her. "Oh, hello." She held out a hand. "I'm Jaya Rao."

"Elliot Brown," he said, shaking her hand. His grip was firm and dry. Impressive. She'd met heads of state whose handshakes felt like playing that Halloween game where you stuck your hands into bowls with your eyes closed and tried to guess what disgustingly slimy object you were touching. "Nice to meet you."

"Guess what?" Isha burst in breathlessly, before Elliot was fully finished speaking. "I'm switching from study hall to robotics engineering."

Jaya stared at her younger sister, who had clearly lost her grip on reality. "We talked about that, Isha," she said, careful to keep her expression smooth and her voice cordial. It was something she'd had to practice over the years. People, she'd come to realize, did not want to see princesses fighting or bickering or being petty. They wanted to see a royal family calm and in control, always civil and smiling. "Remember? You don't want to"—her eyes darted to Elliot—"overburden yourself with robotics. Besides, isn't it too late to swap now, nearly two weeks into the semester?"

"No, it's not," Isha said, grinning at Elliot. "Elliot convinced me to talk to Dr. Waverly"—she pointed vaguely toward the French doors—"and she said she wanted me to be 'adequately challenged.' She could see from my entrance tests that I had 'quite the aptitude for science and technology.' So she's making an exception." Isha squealed and clutched Elliot, who looked equally thrilled. "Isn't it great, Jaya?"

"Oh, so it was Elliot who moved this along," Jaya bit out, still smiling, though she thought she could feel the points of her canines gleaming. Clueless Elliot who had absolutely no idea how much her sister needed to lie low and not generate more gossip with her robotics classes and friendships with boys. This would be fabulous news for virtually anyone else, but Isha could never return to the Rao estate and practice *robotics engineering*. "How lucky for us. Would you excuse us a moment? I need to speak with my sister." She grabbed Isha by the elbow.

"Why?" Isha said, glaring at Jaya now, probably having sensed where she was going with this. "Don't you have people from your own grade to talk to?"

Jaya was opening her mouth to issue a stern warning about

disrespecting your elders when Grey's voice cut across hers.

"It's a great idea," he said behind her.

Jaya turned slowly, still smiling through her rising temper. Never in her life had she met anyone who could get under her skin like Grey Emerson. He was a very tall, extremely well-dressed splinter. It was beginning to give her a headache. "I beg your pardon?"

"It makes more sense to take a heavier class load your soph-omore and junior years, so you have a lighter senior year," Grey said. "Plus, Isha clearly has a natural talent for robotics. She knows a lot more than most Robotics I students do at this time of year, so she won't be behind."

"That's exactly what I said!" Elliot beamed, apparently proud of himself for having thought the same way as Grey Emerson.

"Smart," Grey answered in an offhand way, and Elliot looked like he was ready to pop with pride, like one of those poisonous puffer fish.

"Okay," Jaya said, still trying to be congenial even though the vein in her temple felt like it was going to explode. "But we just transferred in, and I don't want Isha overdoing it." She made a meaningful face at her thickheaded little sister. "Remember when we talked about that . . . sweetheart?"

"You worry too much," Grey said from behind her.

Jaya snapped her head around to glare at him. What? *What?* Who did he think he was, the worry police? What concern was it of his if she fretted over her only sister? Like he should even talk after what his family—

"Yeah, you worry too much," Isha said. "Ooh, is that the new Rihanna song?" she added suddenly, because obviously she had the attention span of a gnat. Grabbing Elliot's arm, she dragged him off to the dance floor, saying, "Let's get the whole group to dance together!"

Jaya watched her go for a moment and then put her fingers to her temples.

"May I suggest a pair of clamps to cut the cord?" Grey said, and she heard the derision in his voice.

She turned to him. "Forgive me for caring about my sister's reputation," she said more harshly than she'd intended. If the intention was to seduce him, fighting with him certainly wasn't the way.

There was a pause during which Jaya tried to get her breathing back under control. *Don't let him get under your skin, Jaya. Burrowing is for leeches, not tall, handsome British aristocrats.*

Grey smirked. "So I'm a handsome leech?"

Jaya's cheeks flamed. She'd spoken out loud by accident and now Grey Emerson looked extremely pleased with himself. "You wish," she snapped, before she could think better of it.

Grey's lips twitched. He was trying not to laugh. *Insufferable.*

Jaya closed her eyes for a moment, letting her irritation float away. When she opened them, she realized couples all over the rooftop were coming together. Rihanna had morphed into some romantic ballad she hadn't heard yet. Damage control, that's what she needed. She was letting him ruffle her too easily, and she needed to get back to playing the part of insipid love interest.

Putting on her most bashful, charming smile, she said, "Grey?"

He looked at her.

"I'd love to dance." She cleared her throat delicately. "As friends, of course."

"Dance?" he said abruptly, as if the concept was alien to him.

"Yes," Jaya said, reaching for his hand slowly. He didn't pull away when she entwined her fingers with his.

They stared at each other for a long moment, assessing, she the trainer, he the wild horse. Just when Jaya was sure he was about to pull his hand from hers, he set his glass down on a nearby table and led her to the dance floor, his face impassive.

# Grey

Grey didn't know *exactly* what had come over him, why he'd listened to Jaya Rao. Maybe it was something about the fiery passion in her dark eyes when she spoke about her sister, the way she'd turned on him, breathing hard, hair blowing in the breeze, brown skin glowing golden by the lights on the rooftop. Her scent kept wafting over to him, florals and spice, and he had a hard time concentrating. Or maybe it was because he was getting to her. And for some reason, that pleased him.

He should keep his distance from Jaya. She was a Rao, for one, and that pendant around her neck was another reminder of why this was a bad idea. And also, just like she'd said, he tended to talk more when he was around her. It was like all the thoughts he usually kept inside himself, like mismatched socks in a forgotten drawer, came tumbling out, eager for companionship and pairing. Yeah, he *definitely* should keep his distance from her.

But when he felt her small, soft hand in his . . . How long had it been since he'd had any genuine human contact? Since any person had shown more than a passing interest in him, in being near him, in wanting him in their immediate proximity? He was like a starving man who'd just been offered a delicious morsel of food. Pathetic.

He walked out onto the dance floor, aware that Jaya was close behind. When he turned to her, her eyes met his with a hint of apprehension, as if she were just as aware as him that this was possibly a very bad idea. But she stepped closer to him anyway.

Grey's arm snaked around Jaya's waist, his fingers resting loosely on her bare back. Her skin was like sun-drenched silk, whisper-soft and almost burning with heat. She stepped in closer, her hand reaching high to perch on his shoulder, her small body brushing his. The sky was a cupped hand above them, sprinkling stars that glimmered in Jaya's thick black hair.

The music tinkled, and she floated in his arms silently. Grey knew he was a good dancer—it came naturally to him—and she let herself be guided along, her feet keeping up with his.

# Jaya

Well, it was now or never. If she wanted to move the plan forward, opportunities didn't get much more perfect than dancing cheek to cheek. "You're a good dancer," Jaya said, looking up at him from under her eyelashes. That was sexy and flirtatious, wasn't it? "Your past girlfriends must've really loved that."

Grey's fingers increased their pressure just very slightly on her bare back, and goose bumps sprouted on Jaya's arms and legs. *Yes, he has manly hands. Yes, his shoulders are really nice and he's towering over you in a rather sexy way, but, dear brain, can you please focus on the task at hand?*

"I don't have any past girlfriends," Grey replied.

Jaya didn't know what to make of that. "You . . . you don't have any past girlfriends?" Then understanding dawned. "You mean to say you've never dated?"

"Correct." Looking at some spot over her head and in the distance, he added, "And I'd like to keep it that way. I don't want to date."

She stutter-stepped. He just looked at her, impassive as always. "You don't want to date . . . this semester?"

He twirled her once, and when she was face-to-face with him again, said, "Ever."

"Oh." Jaya frowned. "But . . . why?"

"I just don't date." But the way he said it, his eyes over her head once more, his mouth set in a thin line, made her think he meant he *couldn't* date. Her gut told her it had something to do with what he was beginning to say earlier, about not speaking with his family. Intriguing.

"Did you hear that?" he said suddenly, his head cocked.

Taken slightly aback by the change in topic, Jaya shook her head. "Hear what? If you mean the music, I think everyone hears it."

His eyes dropped to her pendant. Her smile faded as she saw the look on his face. It reminded her of that time in the dining hall—the same look of shock, of disbelief. "Two more rubies," he said, his voice strangled. "Two more rubies have fallen."

Jaya's gaze automatically dropped to her pendant. "Oh no," she said, gently touching the empty sockets. "I've been thinking about just leaving this in my room until I can take it to a jeweler to get repaired—"

But when she looked up at him, he was shaking his head. "I was dancing with you," he said, "and then two more rubies fell."

"I'm not sure when they fell, exactly . . . ," Jaya said, not seeing the connection. She was about to ask him to explain what he meant when Daphne Elizabeth rushed by, looking nervous. The last strains of the song rang out at the same time, and a freckle-faced boy in her literature class—Adam? Alan?—came up and tapped Grey on the shoulder. "May I cut in?" he asked, smiling at Jaya.

*No, you may not!* Jaya wanted to yell. But she was fairly sure Aiden was the son of some famous diplomat.

Grey stepped wordlessly back to let the boy take his place.

Jaya forced her frustration down and let the new boy take her hand. Grey disappeared toward the far corner of the balcony.

As Jaya let herself be swept around in a waltz, her gaze snagged on Daphne Elizabeth again, who was now covertly looking over one shoulder and stepping through the French doors and into the interior of the building. Jaya scanned the rooftop. Caterina was engrossed in conversation with a group of other seniors, and Alaric was nowhere to be found.

When the song ended and the boy (Albert??) bowed deeply at his waist and took his leave, Jaya walked to the corner of the balcony where she'd seen Grey disappearing to.

He was gone, like some kind of superhero afraid of being unmasked. But why? They'd been talking and connecting—as much as Grey Emerson was capable of connecting with people, anyway. Jaya had felt like she was finally getting somewhere with him. And not just that, but she was finding herself . . . rather intrigued by Grey and whatever secrets he held so closely. Also, what had he been saying about the missing rubies in her pendant?

"Have you seen Grey?" Jaya asked Samantha Wickers, who was talking to a very tall girl in a killer Alexander McQueen, but she shook her head.

She looked around the rooftop, feeling uncertain, as she usually did after a conversation with Grey Emerson. Like she was two steps behind in a very complicated dance. Jaya let out a breath. What now? Well, she kind of had to visit the ladies' room. Perhaps she could take a moment to do that and regroup.

She sought out Isha, who was now gulping down water, spilling some of it down the front of her dress. Her hair was disheveled and sweaty from all the "dancing" she'd been doing. Clearly Isha had no interest in reforming her ways. Robotics engineering, flirting with that boy, dancing completely inappropriately. Why did Isha care so much about such trivial things? Why couldn't she just conform?

There were so many things Jaya wanted to say, but she wouldn't say them now. She didn't want to make a scene. Besides, she was a little . . . weary. Taking care of Isha, making sure she didn't do yet another unsuitable thing, shielding her from another impending scandal, was a full-time job. And sometimes, very occasionally, Jaya felt a little resentful of all that responsibility. Sometimes she caught herself thinking, *I'm only eighteen. I really don't care about whether or not Isha's skirt is too short. Let her do whatever she damn well pleases.*

Only very rarely, and only when she wasn't thinking clearly, obviously.

"I'm going to the ladies' room," she said to Isha now. "Will you be okay for a few minutes?"

Isha waved at her. "Yeah, that's fine—oh my God, did Stewart just stuff an entire tray of salmon mousse canapés into his mouth?" She squealed and ran over to her friends.

Sighing, Jaya walked to the French doors.

# Grey

Two more rubies. Two more rubies were gone. And it had happened when he was dancing with Jaya Rao. As if the old Rao matriarch were laughing at him. It wasn't a coincidence; it couldn't be. The pendant had to be the one. Grey pushed his hair back, angry. What kind of world was this, where he was held responsible for the repugnant actions of his ancestors?

He groaned in agonized frustration as he strode off, pissed at himself. Why had he danced with her? Why had he even come to this fucking mixer in the first place?

Grey followed the twists and turns of the West Wing blindly, letting his furiousness with himself guide him. His hands shook; he had a problem when it came to Jaya Rao. He always said too much. He felt like he was constantly on the verge of blurting everything out, like his lips were a faltering dam against his words. He remembered his father saying, all those years ago, *You're . . . different. You'll always be different. The Raos have seen to that. This is your burden to bear.*

Climbing a set of stairs, he stopped at a tufted bench in an alcove on the third floor. The administration had made little seating areas here and there for students to rest. This one abutted a giant floor-to-ceiling window that showcased the rolling hills, but right then, all Grey could see was inky blackness. He looked at his reflection in the glass, his nostrils flared, his jaw hard, eyes wild like a horse that had been spooked. Pushing a hand through his hair, he jumped up and took off again. He needed to calm himself, and he knew where to go to do it.

# Jaya

Jaya was lost. The bathroom by the rooftop had a line, so she'd wandered deeper into the building, trying to find a more deserted one. Now she found herself by a large spiral staircase, and not yet ready to go back to the rooftop, she began descending it. Her brain kept turning over the way Grey had disappeared; something was going on with him. This secret he was keeping . . . What was it? And why did it seem to cause him so much pain?

On the heels of those questions came another thought: How could she break the heart of someone who was already in so much pain? Jaya felt an immediate rush of guilt at the thought. How could she even think of abandoning the plan? What mattered wasn't Grey or his pain, but her sister and her family. She was a *Rao*. The Emersons were not her problem. But then . . . why did she feel so unsettled? Why were her instincts telling her to pause, to take stock?

Conflicted, Jaya followed the main corridor of the third floor. It turned left and then right and left again. Lovely. She'd have to find a directory map and work out where she was if she wanted to get back to the mixer.

Jaya was just considering turning around when something caught her eye. Up ahead in a small alcove, a tall figure sat on a bench. It was difficult to see who it was from there, but Jaya walked forward quickly along the carpet—and stopped short.

CHAPTER 9

# Jaya

"Daphne Elizabeth?"

Daphne Elizabeth spun around, her green eyes wide. She was wearing a beautiful vintage-style dress that was aggressively ripped up (on purpose?), and her fists were bunched around the tulle of the skirt. "Oh." She put a hand on her chest. "H-hey. Hey, Jaya. I thought you were . . ." She shook her head. "Never mind. What are you doing up here?"

"I was looking for a bathroom." Jaya smiled. "What about you?"

"Hey, I saw you dancing with Grey," Daphne Elizabeth said, but her cheeks were now a bright pink and she wouldn't meet Jaya's eye. "That's a first for him."

Jaya didn't remark on the obvious avoidance of her question because she was quite pleased with the direction the topic change had taken them. "I asked him, and he agreed. Although, I couldn't help but wonder if he—if there's something bothering him. He seemed . . . disconcerted. And then he left."

Daphne Elizabeth shook her head. "Yeah, I love Grey, but man, he's the tortured soul of our group."

Jaya sat on the bench next to Daphne Elizabeth. "And why is that? He said he doesn't date, but he made it sound like—like he *can't* date, perhaps."

"You're telling me," Daphne Elizabeth said. "We've all tried to get him to open up about that, but he won't. It's like he's punishing himself for no reason." She paused. "Or no reason that he trusts us enough to share with us, anyway." Her gaze suddenly shifted to something behind Jaya's back. She swung her feet around and sat up straight. "Um . . . I've got to go now."

Jaya turned around just as someone stepped around the corner, out of sight. Someone with shiny black shoes, a very nicely cut black suit, and blond hair. She turned back to Daphne Elizabeth. "Alaric?"

Daphne Elizabeth put one finger to her lips. Her candy apple–red lip gloss shimmered under the recessed lighting overhead. "Don't judge me." She said the words lightly, but Jaya sensed a weightiness just under the surface.

"No judgment," she said honestly.

"I *have* thought about what you said to me the other day in my room, you know, why I feel the need to be with Alaric?" Daphne Elizabeth said, playing with the tattered hem of her dress. "I can't stop thinking about it, in fact."

"And?" Jaya prompted her gently, sensing there was an "and" floating between them.

"And . . . I still don't know why. Every time I think about how we're doing this to Caterina, how I'm complicit in something so mean and heartless, I feel sick to my stomach. But then there's this other part of me, and that DE? *That* DE really wants the attention Alaric throws her way, everyone else be damned." She bit her lip. "I'm afraid the other DE is getting louder. Sometimes I think I should just break it off with him. But then I think about being alone again, having Alaric look through me, being totally invisible to him just like when I go home . . ." She shivered a little. "I can't keep away from him, Jaya." She hung her head. "Maybe there's something wrong with me."

"There's nothing wrong with you. Absolutely nothing. But, Daphne Elizabeth?"

Daphne Elizabeth looked at her. "Yeah?"

"Being thoroughly invisible to Alaric doesn't mean you'd be invisible to me. I'll be here to hang out with you or talk or go shopping. If you want to, I mean." Jaya shrugged, feeling a little awkward.

Smiling faintly, Daphne Elizabeth stood and squeezed Jaya's shoulder. "Thanks. That really means a lot."

Jaya watched Daphne Elizabeth disappear around the corner after Alaric, her mind drifting to Grey.

She sat back, lost in thought. Grey wouldn't—couldn't?—date anyone. He wasn't planning on managing the Westborough estate and he didn't speak with his family. But why? What linked all of those things together?

# Grey

His feet carried him to the far west corner of the West Wing as if they had a will of their own. He needed the tower, *his* tower. Grey unlocked the heavy door in the dark corner, and shutting it behind him, he stood in the near complete darkness and closed his eyes. The blood rushed in his ears, roaring like an indignant ocean. *Unfair.* He tried not to let himself go down the self-pity path too often, but sometimes the sheer unjustness of the entire situation hit him between the eyes.

He was seventeen (almost eighteen, but that was a problem for another day—maybe a day too soon). He'd danced with a girl who wanted to dance with him. Why was that such a crime? Why did it have to be so . . . so fraught? Why couldn't he, like all the other guys there, just decide to dance without being weighed down by all the other shit?

The room was lightless and silent, as familiar to Grey as his own name. Chest heaving, he put one foot on the step he knew was right in front of him and wound his way up, into the tower in the sky.

Grey stood suspended above the world, looking out through the big, curving windows. The tower was dank and always cold, no matter the time of year. He was sure more than a few bats and other undesirables made their home up there in the soaring ceiling rafters and musty corners, which should instinctively make him want to stay away. But Grey knew he belonged.

He slid his phone out of his pocket and dialed. The reception through the heavy stone walls of the tower was unreliable, but it would have to do.

"Grey?" His father's voice crackled down the line, sounding like he was in another dimension, rather than on another continent.

"Hello, Father." They were both silent, their awkwardness with each other a dance they did every time they spoke, which, thankfully, wasn't often at all.

"Well, what is it?" The words were terse, as if Grey were an underling who'd called to break bad news of a financial investment. "What's happened?"

"Nothing's happened. But I—I need to know something."

"All right." Cautious now. Could he hear the urgency in Grey's voice?

"The ruby you told me about, the one that was cursed by the Rao matriarch."

"Yes?" The first half of the word cut out, so it sounded like his father had hissed down the line.

"How would one know if they found it? The cursed ruby?"

More crackling. "Why do you want to know?"

"Could you just answer the question?" He pushed an impatient hand through his hair as he paced.

"Well, we know it was broken up and put into a rose-shaped pendant. The curse talks about the rose 'dimming,' so I suppose it would involve the undoing of the rose in some manner. I imagine that would mean the metal tarnishing beyond repair or a clasp or chain that keeps breaking or—"

"Or the rubies falling out," Grey said quietly.

"Yes, or that. Why do you ask?"

"I was just curious. That's all." Grey didn't share anything of himself with his father, and this was no different.

The sudden hiss of static made Grey wince. He held the phone away from his ear for a moment. When it fell silent again, he brought it back. "Father? Are you there?"

But there was no response. No signal. Grey pressed the "end" button and stood staring out the windows at the blackest night beyond.

# Jaya

The mixer had progressed to a much louder state of debauchery by the time Jaya found a bathroom and a directory and made her way back. She'd been hoping to find Grey had returned, but looking around, she knew he'd never subject himself to *this*. People were dancing in more alarming gyrations than ever, and a few couples had drifted off to corners to, erm, be intimate. Jaya could tell from the swells and bursts of laughter and screeching that someone, somewhere, had sneaked in alcohol. The teachers were noticeably absent, as if they'd given up trying to rein all this in. Thankfully, Isha was still dancing with her friends and seemed to be fully in control of her senses (except for her sense of propriety, but Jaya didn't think she could blame that on alcohol).

Jaya had barely stepped back onto the rooftop when she felt a thin, cold hand on her upper arm.

"Have you seen Alaric?"

She turned to see Caterina LaValle, her dark brown eyes glittering under false eyelashes. Caterina wore a red, one-shouldered cocktail dress with a sprinkling of diamonds along the hem and six-inch-tall gold-and-red ombre Jimmy Choos. As usual, she looked like she'd stepped off the pages of *Vogue*. Her breath had the telltale metallic scent of strong alcohol, though, and she held a cup full of pink liquid, her bright red nails resting against the glass.

A male voice cut in before Jaya could answer. "H-hey, Caterina." They turned to see Rahul, his eyes fixed on Caterina, his flat, greasy hair falling onto his forehead. "And Jaya."

Caterina's eyes rested only briefly on Rahul. "Hello." Turning back to Jaya, she said, "As I was saying—"

"I—I like your, the red. It's very witchy." Rahul pushed his glasses up. Jaya noticed the tips of his ears had gone red.

Caterina turned back to him, raising an imperious eyebrow. "*Witchy?*"

"In a good way," Rahul rushed to add. His ears were practically flaming now. Neither Jaya nor Caterina said anything for a long moment. Jaya couldn't think of *what* to say. No amount of royal training had prepared her for this.

"E-everyone loves Halloween," Rahul blurted into the quiet.

Leo materialized from nowhere. "Do you want to go get a drink, my friend?" he said quickly, putting an arm around Rahul's shoulders.

"No, not really," Rahul said, but Leo practically dragged him away.

Jaya itched her eyebrow. What on earth was all that? Finally, turning back to Caterina, she shook her head and said, "You were saying?"

"Alaric." Caterina blinked and looked around. "I don't see him."

Jaya tugged at an earlobe, making her chandelier earrings dance. "Ah . . . he's . . . perhaps he's in the bathroom? Or getting some fresh air outside the building?" The memory of Daphne Elizabeth rushing off to follow someone with very shiny black shoes flashed through her brain. She hoped her expression wouldn't give her away. Daphne Elizabeth had become a friend of sorts. She couldn't tell Caterina the truth, not without it feeling like a betrayal.

Caterina pursed her hot pink lips. "We're on a *rooftop*. And he's been gone a half hour."

"Right." Jaya swept her gaze around the rooftop. Where were Caterina's friends, anyhow? Shouldn't she be talking to them? A clot of people moved out of the way, and Jaya caught sight of three girls, Heather, Imogen, and Rebecca, all seniors, all Caterina's friends, laughing in a group of people on the other side of the rooftop. Jaya got the feeling Caterina had purposely left them behind to come talk to her. She turned back to Caterina. "I really can't help, I'm afraid. So, how is your semester going so far?"

"Okay," Caterina said after a pause. Then, straightening, "Marvelously, as a matter of fact. I'm throwing a charity gala on a yacht the end of November. You'll get an invitation." She took a sip of her drink.

"Oh, are you?" Jaya said, relieved they'd moved on from Alaric. "How lovely!"

Caterina waved a well-manicured hand, careful not to spill her drink. "Well, it's what we do, isn't it? Galas and balls and event upon event for charity. Noblesse oblige and all that."

Jaya smiled. "What charity are you raising money for?" Amma loved fundraising for charity. She'd probably be interested when Jaya told her about the mixer later (a very sanitized version that wouldn't involve Grey Emerson at all, naturally).

"One World," Caterina said. "The gala's going to be spectacular. I'll have a party planner and two different caterers—oh, and a bartender, of course. Alcohol loosens the purse strings." She smiled a little.

Jaya nodded as one thumping song merged into the next. After a pause, she asked, "What does One World do?"

Caterina's eyes focused on her with an intensity. "Sorry?"

"The charity," Jaya said, wondering just how much Caterina had had to drink. "One World? Who do they serve?"

"Children around the world who live in poverty," Caterina said, her chin thrust out. The lights on the pillar behind Jaya reflected in her eyes like amber jewels. "And before you say anything else, let me tell you that 385 million children live in extreme poverty. It's a really pressing problem, one from which we're lucky to be isolated."

Jaya wondered if she'd missed something. "Right," she said finally. "I think that's wonderful, actually. My mother loves charitable giving," she added, unsure of why Caterina seemed so oddly protective of her charity. "I'll ask her if she's heard of them."

"Mm. Good. Yes, do that." Seemingly satisfied, Caterina took a deep drink. She blinked hard, as if she were now seeing through a haze of alcohol. She swayed the tiniest bit on her feet. "Jaya," she said. "Why do we love?"

Jaya struggled to adjust to the change of topic. "Perhaps to feel less alone?" she ventured.

Caterina appeared to consider that. "Yes. Yes, maybe you're right." She paused, thinking. "I love Alaric."

Jaya nodded, uncertain. Next to them, a group of freshmen burst into peals of laughter and moved away onto the dance floor. "I'm sure you do."

"But sometimes I wonder if there's someone else for Alaric," Caterina said, like Jaya hadn't spoken. She blinked, her eyes bleary and red-rimmed from drink. "When I talk about the things I'm interested in, I see the way his eyes glaze over. Sometimes he doesn't answer when I ask him a question. And do you know what he said when I asked him if he thought he could get a cummerbund to match my green Valentino dress for the winter formal?"

"No. What?" Out of the corner of her eye, Jaya noticed that Caterina's friends were looking at them. But none of them made a motion to walk over.

"He said, 'Who fucking cares about the winter formal, Caterina? Who knows what we'll be doing by then.'" When Jaya didn't respond immediately, Caterina pressed on. "Why do you think he said that?"

Jaya wondered briefly how she managed to get herself into these situations. It was a talent, really. Suddenly she wished she could have a sip of whatever Caterina was drinking. "Ah . . . perhaps because he's not a planner?"

"No," Caterina said, shaking her head. She gestured with her drink, and a drop landed on Jaya's arm. She discreetly brushed it away. "No. He wants to break up with me, Jaya. I'm sure of it."

"I'm sorry," Jaya said, unsure of what else to say.

But Caterina appeared not to hear her. "Do you know anything?"

Jaya frowned. Why did Caterina always appear to speak in riddles? "Know anything?"

Caterina grabbed her upper arm again, with her free hand. "About Alaric," she said, dipping her head so her face was close to Jaya's now. "And . . . Daphne Elizabeth."

Jaya's heart pounded. She waited, not willing to say anything just yet. Someone on the rooftop whooped.

"I don't like asking for favors," Caterina said, the edges of her words blending into one another. "I don't like to rely on anyone else. But there's no one else I can ask." Her eyes drifted over to her friends at the other side of the rooftop and then back to Jaya. "But you're new here, Jaya. You're in Daphne Elizabeth's group, but you're not best friends with her, are you? You haven't been here long enough for that. So you could help me. Tell me what you know."

"Caterina . . . ," Jaya began, unsure of what, exactly, she was going to say. She had a feeling she was seeing Caterina in a very rare state of disarray. She had to play her cards just right so she didn't embarrass her. "I . . ."

"I can't sleep," Caterina said quietly, her face open and lost in a way Jaya had never seen it. "I can barely eat. Please. You have to be honest with me."

Jaya disengaged Caterina's hand from her arm, feeling a pang of guilt and warring loyalties. On the one hand, it was clear Caterina was suffering. On the other, Daphne Elizabeth was her friend. And she, too, in her own way, was suffering. "I'm sorry," she said, looking right into Caterina's eyes. "Truly. I can't imagine what you must be feeling."

Caterina waited, expectant.

"But . . . I can't get in the middle of this," Jaya said gently.

Caterina's expression cleared. In a matter of moments, she seemed taller somehow, her face closed off again, her eyes cold. It was like Jaya's words had burned off the alcohol in her blood. "So you won't help me."

"Cater—"

Caterina held up a hand. "You know, Jaya," she said. "You could've sided with me on this. I always take care of my friends, I told you that. Instead, you've decided to oppose me."

"Just because I don't want to get involved doesn't mean I oppose you," Jaya said, holding Caterina's gaze.

"Is that what you think?" Caterina replied, a hint of a smile at her lips. Then she turned and swept away, her regal exit only slightly ruined by the way she swayed unsteadily on her feet.

A chilly breeze whipped over the rooftop, raising goose bumps on Jaya's arms as she watched Caterina merge back in seamlessly with her group of friends. She stood rooted to the spot, unable to shake the feeling that things were about to get a lot more complicated with Caterina LaValle.

# Grey

Mr. Martinez knew how to get their attention, all right. He had one of the only classrooms in the science building that opened out onto a balcony, and he used it to his full advantage. Every day since school began, he'd had them put their chairs outside—once even when it was thirty-five degrees. He claimed the brisk breeze and fresh air kept students paying attention longer, especially today, the day before the trip to Aspen.

It was working for everyone else. They were all more engaged, leaning in to Mr. Martinez's demonstration, whatever it was. The man was the world's biggest introvert—he wouldn't even make eye contact going up or down the stairs when you said hi—but get him talking about physics and he got extremely animated, almost lively.

Grey looked toward the horizon, at the heavy snow clouds doing their best to smother the mountains. Without his explicit permission, Grey's eyes stole across to Jaya—and the pendant at her throat. It had been a little more than a month since the mixer, and although he'd been holding his breath, no other rubies had fallen. It was like they were waiting, biding their time.

Jaya Rao continued to try to advance their friendship, but he still hadn't been able to figure out why. He kept her at a distance, though. It was for the best.

Now the rubies glinted in the muted light of the colorless day, their red shine searing his retinas. They were mocking him. His fingertips dug into his thighs. The pendant knew who he was; it knew he was near. It *knew*.

". . . allowed me to pull the tablecloth off without disturbing the bowls? Mr. Emerson? Grey?" A pause. "Or do you only answer to Lord Northcliffe?"

Grey blinked, vaguely aware that he was supposed to do something, that everyone was staring at him and tittering. Jaya turned to look at him and he found himself meeting her gaze, tinged with concern at whatever she saw in his expression. After a pause, she made an urgent motion at him—eyebrows raised, nodding her head, gesturing with her hand—but he had no idea why. He felt weirdly detached from everything, as if he were an onlooker watching a train hurtling toward a cliff and its inevitable conclusion.

"Inertia," Jaya said in that crisp, clear voice of hers, turning to face Mr. Martinez. "An object at rest will remain at rest until an outside force acts on it." She glanced at Grey and tucked a lock of hair behind her ear.

"Nothing changes if nothing changes," Grey mumbled, forgetting where, exactly, he'd heard that.

"Yes! Good. Very good." Mr. Martinez went back to his demonstration.

Grey and Jaya locked eyes again. There was something in

her gaze, something that said her answer had to do with more than just physics.

After class, as they were all hauling their chairs back into the classroom, Jaya said, "You're going to Aspen tomorrow to shop for winter gear, aren't you, Grey?"

He blinked. "Why?"

"Dr. Waverly said she has tickets to that ski resort up there, if people want to go after they're done shopping." She set her chair down, her eyes downcast. She was smiling. "I . . . would like to ski, but I don't really want to do it alone."

Grey didn't let his face show any emotion. Jaya Rao was compelling in some ways. When she let her real self shine through. When it wasn't all mindless chatter and eye batting. When she got mad and said what she really thought. But Jaya Rao was, above all, a Rao. The entire reason he was . . . the way he was. And that pendant she wore? It really didn't want him anywhere near her. Who was he to fight that? "DE skis."

Jaya studied him, her smile fading. As if she might be genuinely disappointed at his rejection. "Okay. I'll ask her, then."

Nodding, Grey set his chair down and turned away, ignoring the slight regretful tug in his own heart.

# Jaya

Grey Emerson had turned her down.

Jaya stood looking after him, feeling equal parts confused, unsettled, and mildly irritated. This past month since the mixer had been mostly progress. Although she'd felt fissures of doubt crack through her plan at the mixer, Jaya had somewhat reluctantly decided to continue with it because, really, there was no other choice. Between a stranger who'd orchestrated her sister's scandal and her entire family, who was she supposed to choose?

So while Grey was still his gruff, standoffish self, occasionally she'd gotten glimmers of *some*thing from him this past month. A response to a question or a comment that felt genuine, less guarded. She'd been moving in the right direction. Or at least, she thought she had. He wasn't supposed to turn her down. He was supposed to fall for her, head over heels, heart and soul, all of that. *And you're feeling just the slightest bit disappointed at his rejection*, a small voice deep inside her whispered. *Denial doesn't become you, Jaya.*

She scoffed at the inner voice. Disappointed? Princess Jaya Rao was *never* disappointed, let alone by an Emerson. If Grey Emerson thought she was going to be put off that easily, he was wrong. Jaya knew she just needed to chip away a little bit longer. Success was right around the next bend, calling her name over its golden shoulder.

Later that day, Jaya set her laptop down on the polished wood desk in the library. The wind howled outside, announcing winter's steady encroachment. Jaya felt safe, ensconced in the warm cocoon of books. They had a big test coming up in calculus, one Leo had called "epic." Hearing it in his French accent had caused Rahul to ask him to repeat himself about seventeen times, which had then sent Daphne Elizabeth into peals of laughter.

Jaya smiled at the memory. Things had changed immensely since she'd first arrived at St. Rosetta's. She now had friends here, something she'd never thought possible. They wouldn't be her friends after she'd successfully executed her plan, but at least she had them for now. That was something.

She turned on her computer and logged into her email account. There was one unread message (from Kiran; he never texted and refused to use his phone to email people out of some unfathomable sense of propriety and etiquette).

From: Rajkumar.Kiran.Hegde@urmail.com
To: jayaohjaya@urmail.com
Subject: Hi from Kiran

Jaya,

It has now been nearly four months since Isha's incident this summer. Things have died down in the Media, but not entirely. When you both left, it picked back up again.

My Family has had some doubts about our possible Alliance, but don't panic. I believe I have calmed them down. I still believe an Alliance could be beneficial to both royal estates. Of course, how this all plays out remains to be seen.

Anyway, I wanted to tell you I am thinking of you. How is Aspen? I am sure the Boarding School situation is not ideal. Girls in trouble need their Parents, we all know that. But stay

strong for your Family. You are the Heiress,
and as an Heir myself, I believe we must do
what's best for our Kingdoms.

I will write again soon.

Sincerely,

Rajkumar Kiran Hegde

Jaya tried not to glare at her computer screen, but it was a trial. Although she and Kiran did indeed share many things in common, she'd forgotten about Kiran's propensity for acting like he was a concerned uncle, rather than her peer. Kiran was one of those guys who thought Jaya's X chromosome stood for "xplain things to me." Things that were currently irritating Jaya about his email:

1. The gratuitous and, to be honest, puzzling use of random capitalization, probably meant to evoke a commanding air.

2. That sanctimonious tone Kiran had when talking about their "alliance." (Or, rather, "Alliance.") *How this all plays out remains to be seen?* As if he and his family were conferring a great favor upon the Raos by even considering them still. Despite the recent . . . problems . . . the Raos were still more powerful than the Hegdes would ever be.

3. Girls in trouble need their parents. Supposedly "we all" know that. Really, Kiran? I must've missed the announcement when you earned your PhD in Expertise on Women, Even Though No One Asked for Your Opinion.

4. Who signed their personal emails with their complete royal title??

Before she could stop herself, her fingers were flying across the keyboard, tapping out a response.

> Dear Kiran,
> I AM SorRy mY faMILy siTUAtion haS Been sO HarD on You. WHAT Can I DO to MaKe It BetTer? YoU Are The GUY, so CleArLY You KnOw BeST.

Jaya sat back, breathing harder, and stared at the screen. She really, *really* wanted to send the message. But she knew that wasn't how royals were supposed to act. Sending the email was something an uncouth brute like Grey Emerson would do. She, on the other hand, was Jaya Rao—always poised, always self-possessed.

Jaya sat thinking for a few minutes, absentmindedly playing with her tie. Then she typed a more appropriate response to Kiran's email.

> From: jayaohjaya@urmail.com
> To: Rajkumar.Kiran.Hegde@urmail.com
> Subject: Re: Hi from Kiran
> Hi Kiran,
> It was nice to hear from you. Thank you for the update re: Mysuru. I'm disappointed that the media continues to libel my family, but as you said, this is for the best. I'm staying strong for my parents and Isha.

How was the meeting with the tax attorney?
Your previous email about the land taxes on
your estate was fascinating. You're right, if the
Hegde/Rao estates were merged, we might well
make the accounting easier.

All right, I must go. I hope you're well. Give
my best to your parents, won't you?

Regards,

Jaya

Jaya closed her laptop and sighed at the notion of an "alliance" between the Raos and the Hegdes. Not that it was completely bizarre. In fact, for so long, it had seemed the right thing to do, the way forward that would benefit both their families. But now, with some time and distance (and honestly, looking over their tepid email history), Jaya found herself waffling.

A lifetime with Kiran? Someone she had no spark with, no friendship with? Someone who, as far as she could tell, was only with her also out of a sense of duty? Whatever would they talk about over dinner—tax laws? Whether or not the crops were getting enough rain? The very thought bored her nearly to tears. And didn't Kiran deserve better too?

Jaya took a breath as she pulled out her textbooks. Well, it wasn't like she needed to make these decisions now. She had years and years.

# CHAPTER 10

## Jaya

Saturday, the day their class was taking a trip to Aspen, was finally here. On her way out to the bus with Penelope, Jaya stopped at Isha's dorm to say goodbye. This weekend was seniors only, so she was leaving Isha here by herself, much as she hated to. "Be good," Jaya said, infusing a special significance into the words as she put her hands on Isha's shoulders.

Isha, still in her Bob's Burgers pajamas, sighed and leaned against her doorjamb. "I *will*."

Jaya smiled stiffly over her shoulder at Penelope, who stood off to the side, waiting, pretending very hard not to be listening. Turning back to Isha, Jaya said, "So, what are your plans today?"

Isha gave Jaya a look. "I'm going back to bed. And then I'll probably go get my nails done with Raina. And after that I'll eat lunch; I'm thinking a burrito. Maybe with avocado spread, maybe not. But if my itinerary changes, I'll be sure to text you."

Jaya looked at Isha's guarded, defensive face, at her unkempt hair, and felt a tug of sadness. How had their relationship devolved to this? Couldn't Isha see that her older sister just wanted to take care of her? Jaya felt a familiar weight pressing down on her shoulders. She wished, fleetingly, that she could kiss Isha on the cheek and be off without any reminders or warnings. Sometimes she felt like Isha's parole officer, not her sister.

"Okay," she said softly. She didn't have the energy for an argument. "Then I'll let you get back to bed."

Isha didn't even say goodbye before she closed her dorm room door. Sighing, Jaya turned around and smiled at Penelope. "Ready?"

They walked outside together, both of them bundled in their coats and mittens. It was an especially opportune trip, because Jaya needed to get her necklace repaired. Perhaps she could find the time to do that on this trip. She hadn't dared to wear it in a couple of days, just in case the rubies began falling again.

A giant, shiny black bus stood at the curb, waiting. "Whoa," Jaya whispered when she climbed aboard behind Penelope. She'd been on luxury buses before, but never one quite like this.

This bus had sumptuously padded leather seats that looked like they belonged on armchairs in ancient libraries, neon lights that lit everyone up in bright colors, mirrors along the walls, and polished black floors. It was like the designers had tried their hardest to make it look like a nightclub rather than a bus.

Penelope laughed as they took their seats, Jaya next to Daphne Elizabeth and Penelope next to a Haitian girl named Trinity and some of Trinity's friends. "It's a limousine bus," Penelope said. "It's even got—"

"A bar! *Ouah!*" Leo cried.

"A bar stocked with hot chocolate and soda," a blond, middle-aged female teacher Jaya didn't know said wryly. "Have a seat, Mr. Nguyen."

Leo sighed theatrically and slid in next to Daphne Elizabeth and

Jaya. Rahul followed. "Can you believe this fascism?" Leo said, and Daphne Elizabeth shrugged. "Will you two go to the slopes after?"

Jaya looked around for Grey but didn't see him. Surely he wouldn't just stay in his dorm and abandon Aspen completely? "Erm, yes," she said. "Daphne Elizabeth's going skiing with me. Have you seen Grey?"

"I texted him seven minutes ago, but he hasn't answered yet," Rahul said. "Maybe he won't come this year."

Jaya felt a thud of disappointment. Which was clearly because Grey was impeding her plan by keeping himself isolated this way.

"Skiing?" Leo said scornfully. "You need to snowboard! That is what Rahul and I are going to do."

Jaya raised an eyebrow. "Didn't you tell Sam Wickers you were going skiing? Something to do with the fact that she's a black diamond skier herself?"

"Allow me to share what I have learned about wooing hot girls," Leo said, leaning forward. "You must get your foot in the door when you can or—"

A loud, authoritative female voice spoke from outside, interrupting him. "No! My father's assistant cleared this well in advance. I'll be riding in my own car with Alaric. See, that's my driver, Pietro."

An affected male voice, with a slight German accent that made Daphne Elizabeth stiffen in her seat: "Caterina, please do not make such a scene. Let's go in the bus."

"Alaric, why can't you just for once be on my side?"

"Ms. LaValle, we simply cannot allow you to make your own accommodations. I don't know who your father's assistant spoke to in the office, but Dr. Waverly has made it quite clear that no deviations are permitted. Not for anyone."

"Okay, fine. Then I'm just going to go sit in my car. What are you going to do? Drag me out?"

The blond, middle-aged teacher on the bus stepped down to see what was happening.

"You're being ridiculous." Alaric's voice floated in to them. It was low and furious. Jaya could barely hear it.

"Don't call *me* ridiculous! This *situation* is what's ridiculous! We're not preschoolers! Pietro is a professional driver!"

Alaric ascended the stairs of the bus, pushing up the sleeves of his chunky taupe sweater. "Ridiculous," he muttered again as he went to sit by all his—and Caterina's—friends. "She's a spoiled brat," he said loudly to Lachlan. "Maybe her dad should've made her walk to Aspen." All of them snickered.

Daphne Elizabeth looked decidedly uncomfortable, her cheeks pink. Jaya's gaze traveled from Alaric's smug face to Lachlan's, and then at Heather, Imogen, and Rebecca. Not a single person in Caterina's group was standing up for her. Jaya remembered what she'd said on the rooftop, at the mixer. *I don't like to rely on anyone else. I don't trust anyone, you see.* The question was, were they untrustworthy because of their natures or because Caterina kept them at a remove? To Jaya's trained eye, Caterina's "friendships" seemed more like business transactions. Everyone served a purpose; there was no inherent loyalty like in Grey's group. Perhaps Caterina was this way to prevent herself from getting hurt . . . though, ironically, it looked like she was getting hurt now precisely *because* of the way she treated the people closest to her.

Jaya glanced out the window at a smoky gray Tesla SUV, its windows tinted so dark, no one could see inside. A red-haired male teacher gave a thumbs-up to the impassive driver behind the wheel, and he took off. Jaya imagined Caterina inside, alone and small, desperate to not feel anything, and felt a pang of pity for the girl.

As she turned back around, her hand automatically went to her throat—and came up empty. She realized with a lurch that she'd forgotten to fetch the necklace from her dresser when Penelope had knocked on her door.

"I'll just be a minute," Jaya said to the red-haired teacher as she flew down the steps and past him on her way back to the building. "I'm so terribly sorry!"

She thought she heard him mutter something like, "Is it winter break yet?" but she couldn't be sure.

# Grey

He wasn't going. He waited as the bustle in the hallway got quieter and quieter and finally completely stopped. Then he threw on one of his many pairs of bland sweaters and pants and walked out of his room.

It was summer-level quiet in the senior wing. No one else had stayed behind. Rahul had texted him a few minutes ago, but Grey was hoping he'd forget about him in the chaos of the morning. Going on this trip wasn't mandatory, and he'd already spoken to Dr. Waverly about staying behind last night. He hadn't told anyone else because he hadn't wanted to defend his decision—or worse, for anyone to feel obliged to convince him to go.

All the other students were probably sitting in the limo-bus St. R's got every year, already eager for a break from the monotony of classes that had only just started. Even Jaya. Thinking about her made him feel less alone. It didn't make any sense, considering how they bickered about very basic values. They had seemingly nothing in common and yet . . . Jaya was as tied to her family's expectations of her as he was to his. For completely different reasons, but still. She was in a straitjacket of their rules and decrees too, even if she didn't know it. And knowing Jaya, even if she realized it, she'd probably *enjoy* wearing the straitjacket as part of her royal couture. It was ironic, too, that he should feel any sense of camaraderie with her, considering her bloodline and the harbinger of his curse she'd brought with her.

Grey steeled himself for what he was about to do. Taking a deep breath, he walked down the empty hall and made a right into an interconnected hallway. The girls' dorms were all here, twenty-five doors spooling out in front of him. Grey walked forward, his eye on Jaya's door. It was an unspoken St. R's custom that no one ever locked their doors. Friends came and went as they pleased, and if anyone needed privacy, they'd just hang a tie from their doorknob. The administration wasn't crazy about this, but there wasn't much they could do to force people to lock their doors.

Grey had never particularly cared about the open-door culture one way or another. Right now, though, he was infinitely grateful that he could steal into Jaya's room unnoticed. A sudden pulse of guilt and shame heated his face as the doorknob turned easily under his hand and he slipped inside. He'd never considered himself a thief. He'd never ordinarily do something as underhanded, as dishonest, as taking another person's belongings without asking them. But these were not ordinary circumstances. This was literally life and death.

Jaya had said at the mixer that she might begin keeping the pendant in her room because the rubies kept falling out. And then he'd noticed that she hadn't been wearing it these past couple of days. Once he'd realized that, Grey knew what he had to do—what any normal person in this situation would do. He wasn't sure at all that she'd left it in her room today, but he also knew he'd never have another opportunity like this one. She was going to Aspen to ski—if she was really worried about the necklace, she'd leave it here. That was all he had to go on, and it was thin as a newly formed skin of ice, but he was hanging on to it nonetheless.

He *had* to get that necklace and fix it somehow. He'd lain awake too many nights, sweating and plotting and worrying about the fucking curse. Maybe the answer was finding a good jeweler to repair it and sending it anonymously back to the temple in Mysuru from which it had been taken. Or maybe he should just destroy it completely.

Or maybe, a very pessimistic voice inside his head thundered, maybe it was too late now that the rubies were falling, especially since three of the original rubies were lost completely. Grey didn't know. What he *did* know was that he couldn't just watch the thing count down his fate and sit there idly, letting the curse happen to him. He was utterly done with being sent away, with having his life course already decided, with feeling like he'd been born simply to cause heartache to his parents and live a life devoid of love or companionship only to die young. Because if that was true . . . what was the point? Of anything? What was the fucking point?

Breathing harder, he stalked to the far corner of Jaya's room and rummaged through her desk. A few neatly opened letters from home, sachets of lavender-scented potpourri, stationery with her initials embossed in gold at the top. Grey squeezed his eyes shut for a moment.

Pulling himself together, he turned to her vanity, careful not to look at himself in the mirror. The top was organized neatly with her perfume, makeup, and an ornate silver jewelry tray all arranged parallel to each other. A few necklaces were looped carefully around the corner of the mirror. None of them were the ruby pendant. He opened the first drawer—and stopped short. A black velvet bag sat there, looking innocuous enough. But he imagined he could feel something . . . a kind of dark energy, pulsing through the fabric.

Grey took the bag out and gently shook out its contents into his palm. The heavy rose pendant lay waiting, its tightly coiled center now completely bare, the remaining rubies grinning at him like a handful of bloody teeth. He wanted to throw it across the room. He wanted to rip each remaining ruby from its socket and crush them under his boot. Instead, he picked the pendant up carefully, intending to slide it back into the velvet bag to take with him, to decide what to do with it in the safety of his own room.

*Ping!*

Grey wasn't sure at first where the sound had come from. Then he looked at the pendant and understood. Another ruby had fallen, bringing the total to four missing. As he traced its path and saw it roll under Jaya's vanity, he heard the noise again, twice in quick succession. And when he looked, he saw two more rubies had fallen. Twelve rubies remained in their sockets.

As he stared at the rose pendant, his stomach twisting, he was suddenly sure it was fully aware who was holding it. It was as if the thing wanted to punish him, to show him that it wasn't at all surprised that he, a thieving Emerson, had crept in here to try to steal it yet again. Only now the ruby was fighting back.

Terror turned Grey's bones to mush. He felt certain that by the time he got the pendant back into its bag, all the rest of the rubies would've fallen and his fate would be completely sealed, a month and a half in advance of his eighteenth birthday.

"No, no, no, no," he whispered as he pushed it as gently as he could back into its bag, into its Pandora's box. With shaking hands, he set the velvet bag back into the drawer and slid it shut. He caught sight of himself in the mirror then, his forehead shiny and damp, his eyes wide, his cheeks pale and hollow. He looked like someone who'd gotten terrible news at the doctor's. He looked like someone whose life was ending.

There was a sound down the hallway, as if someone had just come up the elevators. Grey jerked his head up, his heart thundering now for different reasons.

# Jaya

Jaya stepped off the elevator, walking quickly down the hallway to the senior girls' suite. She'd get the pendant, and maybe she'd walk over to Grey's room and see where he was. He couldn't just hide away in here. He had to go to Aspen.

A familiar knot of guilt formed in her stomach as she walked. Grey Emerson was obviously very troubled. Continuing to execute the plan felt a little . . . cruel. But what was she to do, just let this opportunity go? It had landed in her lap, as if the fates themselves had conspired to bring the Emersons to justice. Emotion had no place in this. And yet revenge was supposed to be sweet. Why, then, was the inside of her mouth so ashy and bitter?

Jaya reached her door, turned the doorknob, walked in, and stopped short.

Grey Emerson stood in the middle of her room, his blue eyes wide, wild. He was dressed in a charcoal sweater that hugged the hard planes of his chest and stomach, and loose jeans. Strands of his dark hair hung in his eyes, and there were bags under his eyes that said he hadn't slept well. Stubble dotted his upper lip and jaw.

*Stop staring at his stubble, Jaya,* her inner critic said, exasperated. *There are more important matters at hand.*

"What the hell are you doing in my room?" Her paralysis breaking, Jaya took another step inside and noticed her dresser drawer was open. Had she left it open? "Are you *snooping* through my things?"

"What?" Grey said. "No!"

Jaya turned back to him and stepped forward, her pulse high. "Then what? Why are you in here? It is *not* okay to go into someone's room when she isn't there. Do you understand that? I could have you expelled."

"I was . . ." Grey looked away and pushed a hand through his hair, not finishing his thought.

Jaya walked over to her open dresser drawer. Nothing seemed to be rifled through. The velvet bag was still there, right on top, unmoved.

"I'm sorry," Grey said quietly, his face leaching of color.

"For what?" Jaya walked closer to him and narrowed her eyes. When he was silent, she pressed on. "Grey. You can't just walk into my room without permission and not answer my questions. This is unacceptable!"

His mouth opened and then closed again, his fists clenched at his sides. "I know."

But he didn't say anything else. "Were you looking for things to send to the tabloids?" Jaya asked, her voice hard.

"No!" He looked genuinely shocked. "I would never do that. Never."

In spite of her extreme skepticism toward all Emersons (indeed, she even doubted most of them were fully human), she believed Grey. He looked . . . physically sick. Like someone who was too swept up in their own thoughts to go snooping around for salacious gossip. "What, then?" she asked, unrelenting. He'd been in her room without her knowledge. She deserved to know why. "My dresser drawer is open. What were you looking for?"

After a long pause, both of them staring at each other, Grey spoke, so softly she could barely hear him. "Your ruby pendant."

"Why?" Why had he been so obsessed with her pendant from the beginning? What was going on?

Outside, the bus horn honked three times.

"That's the warning," Grey said faintly. "They're leaving in five minutes."

They studied each other, and for once Jaya let her expression mirror his once-more impassive one. "Fine," she said. "But you're coming too. We can finish this conversation in Aspen, when you tell me why you were skulking around my room."

"I wasn't *skulking*."

"That's the least important part of everything I said."

Finally, Grey nodded once. "All right." He walked forward and brushed past her, striding out into the hallway.

Jaya watched his retreating figure for a moment, then reached into the drawer and pulled out the black velvet bag. She peeked in briefly—the necklace was still ensconced safely inside. Slipping the bag into her coat pocket, she followed Grey Emerson down the hallway, her mind churning.

# Grey

As they took the elevator down and crossed the large entrance foyer, Grey wondered why he was doing this. Technically, Jaya Rao couldn't force him onto that bus. Sure, she could get him expelled like she'd threatened—and then where would he go? Definitely not back to his father—but he had a feeling she wouldn't. She was as interested in finding out why he'd been in her room as he was in keeping the reason from her. And now, thanks to his stupid guilty conscience, she knew it had something to do with her pendant. Damn it.

The truth was, he *had* been snooping in her room. There was no going around that, and he had no right to be. He was clearly in the wrong. And so, caught in a weak and guilty moment, he'd found himself agreeing to go to Aspen and confess to Jaya exactly what it was that he'd been doing in her room.

As they walked, he glanced at her sidelong to find that she was looking at him, too. He forced his eyes away and lengthened his stride, so he was ahead of her as they pushed the doors to walk outside toward the bus. Yes, she wanted the whole story. Yes, she had a right to ask. But still, Grey couldn't imagine himself telling her. He hadn't told a single soul in all of his nearly eighteen years. How was he supposed to change that for a Rao, of all people?

His mind turned back to the pendant, as it always did. The Raos had cursed the ruby. Jaya shows up to St. R's wearing it. How could there not be a connection?

Grey recalled all the times he'd asked Jaya about her pendant. She'd never once looked guilty, never once said anything to hint at the fact that she might know where it had come from or what it meant to him. Besides, she'd thought he was snooping in her room so he could sell information to the tabloids. She hadn't mentioned the pendant at all. So her having it was probably just another weird thing to add to the list of weird things that had plagued Grey since he was born.

"There you are," Mrs. Wakefield, the Russian Lit teacher said. She was waiting just outside the bus, her brassy blond hair blowing in the breeze. "Come on, you two, we're ready to go."

He climbed up the steps, feeling Jaya right behind him. As he'd expected, everyone was on the bus already. (Except Caterina, who apparently was in her Tesla, according to what Alaric was saying. Who knew what her problem was besides an insatiable thirst for drama.) Grey took a seat across from DE and Penelope—one of the only few seats remaining—and Jaya promptly plopped down beside him. He kept his body rigid, and his eyes out the window in front of him.

"Where were you?" DE asked, reaching over to kick his foot with hers.

Grey flushed as he slid his foot out of the way. "Upstairs."

DE snorted. "Upstairs!" she said to Leo, who was on her other side. "That explains everything."

Leo shook his head and went back to talking to Rahul. There

was an awkward pause while DE and Penelope waited for Grey to tell them more, which he didn't. And then Jaya cleared her throat and began to speak in that very classy, very Jaya way about dresses or dancing or something.

He glanced at her out of the corner of his eye as the bus began to move. Why the assist? But if she saw him looking, she gave no indication. Feeling equal measures of gratitude and guilt, Grey settled against the plush seat, leaned his head back, and closed his eyes.

About twenty minutes into the drive, DE leaned forward and said to him, "Who are you taking to Homegoing?" and Grey realized the dance had been the conversational topic the whole time he'd been alternating pretending to be asleep and staring out the window at grazing cows and sheep.

Feeling waves of *something* coming off Jaya and pointed in his general direction, he kept his voice neutral when he answered, still looking out the window. "I'm not going."

"Homegoing" instead of "Homecoming" was another one of St. R's "fun" events. Since St. R's had to be different in everything they did as a proclamation of their elitism and inherent superiority, they'd decided to instead have "Homegoing," the biggest event of the season. Homegoing was a winter formal, and everyone dressed up in their designer best and took a date they'd been gathering the courage to ask out since the beginning of the school year.

"You are not going to Homegoing?" Leo this time. "Why not? *Mon ami*, it is our chance to blow off steam after finals, *non*? It is the biggest event of the year. *Everyone* goes."

"Well, I guess it's going to be everyone minus one this year," Grey said, turning to look at him.

Jaya was studying him, her eyes slightly narrowed, as if she couldn't make him out.

"You have to go," DE said.

Grey turned his gaze on her. "Have to? I don't remember seeing that in the school handbook."

DE rolled her eyes and looked at her phone. On her other side, Alaric was talking about his limited-edition gold-plated Lambo to Lachlan McCoy. He could almost have passed as a little boy bragging about his new Hot Wheels car.

They were silent for a long moment, Grey looking out the window while his attention was laser-focused on Jaya. She was ostensibly looking straight ahead too, but Grey could tell her attention was elsewhere. Finally, in a voice so low he almost didn't hear it, she said, "You're going to tell me."

He jerked his head to look at her. "What?"

She turned her cool brown gaze on him. "I can feel it; you're going to try to wriggle out of telling me what you were doing in my room. About my pendant."

Feeling the beginnings of panic, Grey glanced around at the other students, but they were all intent on their own conversations. Jaya was speaking low enough that it was hard enough for him to hear her over the bus engine and the chatter of the other students, but still. "I'm not wriggling out of anything," he said, pushing a hand through his hair. He *had* been tempted to avoid her, but that was too cowardly. It wasn't how he rolled. "I'll tell you everything, okay? I promise."

She raised an eyebrow. "When?"

"I just need to think." Grey leaned forward, resting his forearms on his thigh. He needed to get up the courage, figure out the words to say. How did you *begin* to explain something like this?

"Meet me at the Forest Lakes Lodge tonight, seven o'clock."

Jaya looked at him, assessing. Satisfied with whatever she saw in his eyes, she nodded. "Okay. Seven o'clock, sharp."

With a hissing sigh, the bus stopped. Everyone began to chatter loudly, all at once. Grey looked out the window at the parking lot of the large Aspen shopping plaza St. Rosetta's always took them to. "Go time," he said softly.

# CHAPTER 11

# Jaya

Jaya watched Grey lope off by himself, as she'd known he'd do. Even though she shouldn't, she felt sure he'd meet her when he said he would. Soon she'd know exactly what was going on with him.

One thing had become clearer: what Grey had said at the mixer before he disappeared—about how he couldn't date and how he wouldn't run the Westborough estate because he didn't speak to his family—*was* connected to Jaya's pendant, just as she'd guessed. It had to be. *How*, Jaya was eager to find out.

"So, I think we need to talk," Jaya said to Daphne Elizabeth now.

The chaperones had set them loose with instructions to meet back at the bus that night at ten, but for now they were free to go wherever they pleased. She and Daphne Elizabeth had immediately joined up, and Rahul and Leo had gone shopping together at one of the big department stores. She and Daph were taking a shopping break at La Maison du Chocolat, a Parisian chocolate shop. Daphne Elizabeth's father owned a large portion of stock in the international company because she loved their stuff so much.

Daphne Elizabeth bit into her fudge brownie. "Oh my God. Wow." She closed her eyes as she chewed. "Mmm, no I'm totally listening. It's just that I'm also having a foodgasm."

"Erm . . . ha. Yes. Of course." Jaya never knew how to respond to Daphne Elizabeth's often crass, rarely appropriate jokes. Then she ate a truffle and her taste buds almost exploded on the spot. "Oh *my*. You're right. This is absolutely divine."

"You're literally the only person our age I know who says 'oh my' unironically."

Jaya frowned. "What do you mean?"

Daphne Elizabeth bit back a laugh. "Nothing. Anyway, back to what you were saying. We need to talk about what?"

Jaya crumpled up the thick paper cup her chocolate had come in. "You have to tell—"

But Daphne Elizabeth's phone beeped, cutting Jaya off. She pulled it out of her pocket. Studying the screen, Daph muttered, "Great." She turned her phone around to show Jaya.

**Your father and I have to jet to Milan over Christmas. We think you should just go to Nana's—or maybe just stay at St. Rosetta's? We'll pay the extra boarding fees. xxMitzi**

Jaya frowned. "Who's Mitzi?"

"My mother," Daphne Elizabeth said, snorting. "She thinks 'Mom' makes her sound old."

"But . . . do you celebrate Christmas?" Jaya asked, and Daphne Elizabeth nodded. "Oh, Daph, I'm sorry."

Daphne Elizabeth shrugged. "I'm used to it. This has happened before. It's fine."

Jaya could not think of a single sadder thing. On impulse, she found herself saying, "Why don't you come visit my family? If you want to, I mean? We don't celebrate Christmas, but we do go to a different country every winter break."

Daphne Elizabeth stared at Jaya. "Seriously? You'd do that for me?"

Jaya smiled. "I bet I could even convince my father to put up a Christmas tree wherever we go and do a gift exchange."

Daphne Elizabeth shook her head. "That's so sweet. I mean, I'll probably just go to my aunt's in France for most of the break, but maybe I'll come visit you, too."

Jaya smiled. "I'd love that."

When Daph went around the table to give Jaya a hug, Jaya wrapped her arms around her, too, even though she wasn't at all what they called "a hugger." She thought again about what she'd been meaning to talk to Daph about—Caterina and Alaric. But maybe now wasn't the time. It wasn't as though Caterina had done anything else, after their tête-à-tête at the mixer. Perhaps the whole thing would blow over.

The bell above the door tinkled, and Jaya glanced up to see Sam Wickers walking in, looking cheery as usual in a bright yellow sweater and light pink pants. She was on her way to the counter when she noticed Jaya and Daph and turned on her heel.

"Hey, guys," she said, waving at them with her free hand. The other one held at least six shopping bags from stores all around Main Street.

Daph walked back around the table and took a seat. "Hey, Sam. What's up?"

"Hello, Samantha," Jaya said. "Would you like to pull up a chair?"

"Oh no, I'm just here to grab some brownies," she answered. "Um." She switched her bags from her left hand to her right and bit her lip, considering Jaya. "Okay, I have to know: Does Leo really get a dozen pots of jam at breakfast?"

Jaya stared at Sam for a moment, then glanced at Daph—who appeared just as confused as her—wondering if she'd missed something. ". . . I beg your pardon?"

Sam waved a hand and looked between her and Daph. "Leo. He told me he loves Wickers jam and that he gets, like, several pots of it at breakfast every day. I know you're new, Jaya, but I don't know him very well and you hang out with him every day. Is that just a really weird pickup line or what?"

Jaya nodded slowly. She could see Daph grinning in her peripheral vision. "Ah. Jam. Leo. Uh, no, he's not lying. He really does love his jam."

Samantha narrowed her eyes. "What's his favorite flavor?"

"Rhubarb," Jaya answered without hesitation. "He eats it straight from the pot with a spoon."

"Can confirm," Daph said, popping another chocolate truffle in her mouth.

Samantha beamed at them. "Rhubarb is one of my favorites too!" She laughed. "Sorry. Jam's just kind of my jam."

Jaya laughed also. "Hey, I understand. Family business and all that."

"Exactly." Samantha quirked her lips and ran a hand through her strawberry curls. "Is he a good guy, Leo? Do you like him?"

Jaya felt a swell of happiness for Leo. "Yes, Leo is a very good guy. I've come to think of him as a brother in a way. He's really warm, and he'd do anything for his friends."

"I've known him a long time, and seriously, dude, you can't do better than him," Daph said, tipping her chair back.

Samantha nodded, thoughtful. "That's good to know. Maybe I'll strike up a conversation with him soon."

"You should," Jaya said, smiling, glancing at Daphne Elizabeth. "He'd love that."

"He'll be over the fuckin' moon," Daph said seriously.

Sam flashed them a grin that she'd probably be wearing all day.

"So, you and Grey, huh? First Sam and Leo, now you guys . . . Must be something in the air," Daphne Elizabeth said, sipping her second hot cocoa (that was really more marshmallow than cocoa).

"That's ridiculous!" Jaya said immediately, feeling her cheeks getting warm at Daphne Elizabeth's insinuation. So ridiculous.

It was ten minutes till seven o'clock. She had asked Daph to come to Forest Lakes Lodge with her, just to help the time pass more quickly. They were all done with their shopping and didn't have to be back at the bus until ten o'clock. Daphne Elizabeth and Jaya were seated in gold velvet armchairs near the giant roaring fire. There was an enormous chandelier hanging right above them, made from what looked like real antlers. Hundreds and hundreds of them. How odd. What designer had thought, *I know what'll give this luxury resort a really classy feel. A grotesque amount of deer's head outcroppings!*

"We're just meeting up to talk about something important," Jaya added more calmly, leaning back. She didn't know why she hadn't told Daph about finding Grey in her room. He'd looked so . . . flustered, both in her room and on the bus, that Jaya had felt like protecting his privacy. Her feelings didn't make sense, however, and she was acutely aware of that. After all, Grey hadn't really cared about Isha's privacy when he'd leaked those pictures.

OF CURSES AND KISSES    *181*

"Mm-hmm." Daph chuckled, licking the marshmallow off her top lip. "'Important' like how does he look under his clothes important?"

"Daph!" Jaya said, scandalized.

Daphne Elizabeth laughed and hopped up from her chair. "Okay, dude, I gotta pee. Hot cocoa goes right through my system. And then I guess I'll take off. He'll be here soon, right?"

Jaya tried not to wince. "All right, then. I'll see you later, on the bus?"

Daph shot her a mock salute and rushed off toward the restrooms on the far end of the room.

The sky outside was a dark indigo, the pine trees mere shadows against it. Jaya got her cell phone out of her pocket and checked it. Nothing from Grey, and it was 7:01 now. Would he actually show up, then?

Glancing up from her phone, Jaya looked toward the entrance and felt every nerve fiber icing over. Caterina LaValle was gliding through the lodge with her friends, looking celebrity-fabulous in a full-length ivory coat and suede Prada boots. Her deep brown eyes were fixed steadily on Jaya. The warning there was clear: *I haven't forgotten your refusal to help and your continued alliance with the enemy. Not even a bit.* As Jaya watched, Caterina leaned in and said something to her friends, who nodded and continued forward, while Caterina pivoted and began striding toward Jaya.

Jaya sat up straighter, pasting a polite smile on her face as Caterina got closer. "Hello," she said, gesturing to Daph's newly vacated seat. "Would you like to sit, Caterina?"

She sat, although it appeared as if she were floating above her seat rather than perched on it like a mere mortal. "Jaya." She held her eyes for a long moment. "Interesting friends you keep."

Had she seen Jaya and Daph talking? "I suppose," Jaya said cautiously.

Leaning back, Caterina pulled off her calfskin gloves, one finger at a time. "Well, it's only that I saw you and Grey dancing rather close at the mixer. And today you two were the last ones to emerge from the building and climb onto the bus."

Jaya didn't break eye contact as she reached for her tea. She let the silence linger, waiting to see what Caterina was playing at.

"I have interesting friends too, you know," Caterina said, languidly crossing her long, slender legs. "You remember Sri Devi, of course? Being a part of the royal family network in India, she's well connected with all the royal families there." Caterina smiled placidly, and Jaya felt her pulse jump in her throat. "She seems to know so much—whose family's been feuding, which families might be poised for an alliance. It's all fascinating, I have to say."

Jaya took a sip of tea to wet her dry mouth. What did Caterina know? The details of the scandal? About Grey's involvement in it? That news of Jaya cozying up to an Emerson would be a devastating blow to not just her family, but their future alliance with the Hegdes—and therefore to the entire Rao dynasty. "Really?" Jaya said finally. "I didn't realize you were so well educated in Indian royal family affairs."

"Oh, I'm not, not usually," Caterina said, waving a hand. Her brown eyes were sharp, belying her seeming insouciance. "But when I thought about it, I realized I needed to know more. After all, as they say, knowledge is power." She smiled, showing all her brilliantly white, straight teeth.

"Indeed," Jaya replied, her heart thudding in her chest.

"Well, I must go," Caterina said, standing and looking down her nose at Jaya. "I'll see you soon, Jaya."

"It was a pleasure, Caterina," Jaya replied, forcing an easy smile.

With one last, long look, Caterina turned, her coat flying around her, and swept away.

Jaya set her tea down and sank back against her seat as she stared into the fire. That was a threat; anyone could see that. But what, exactly, would Caterina's next move be? She sat there for five whole minutes, gazing into the flames, looking for answers.

As the adrenaline left her body bit by bit, Jaya took a breath and turned—and then promptly forgot to breathe again, all thoughts of Caterina flying from her mind. It always surprised her, the surety with which Grey Emerson moved through a space, like he was claiming it for himself. People were watching him with a kind of quiet reverence and moving out of his way, but he didn't seem to notice. His eyes, those tempestuous, wild blue eyes, were locked on her.

"Hi," Grey said when he was close enough for her to hear him, to smell him. He'd brought in a scent like fresh snow and pine.

Jaya gestured to the empty chair. "Would you like to sit?"

He looked past her, out the enormous panes of glass that made up the far wall and faced the lit-up ski slopes. "Actually," he said, looking back down at her. "I'd like to ski. It might be easier to—I think it'll help me to clear my head." He stuffed his hands into his jacket pockets.

She studied his expression. It was haunted and ashamed, but it was also truthful. He really did want to tell her; he was trying to build up the courage to do it.

Any anger she'd been feeling toward Grey dissipated and was replaced by curiosity. Jaya nodded and stood. "All right. I'm game."

• • •

The ski lift ride up was magical. The air was crisp and clear and cold like a piece of dark crystal. As they rose higher and higher, Jaya's breath caught at the sight below them—the stone lodge was lit up in a thousand twinkling lights, the giant fountain in the courtyard staggering under a heavy blanket of snow. Ice crystals glittered in all the tree branches, like strands of diamonds.

"Wow," she breathed, forgetting for a moment who she was with. "Winter here really is enchanting, isn't it?"

Grey grunted in response.

The ski lift arrived at the top, and they both took their turns stepping off. Grey held his hand out to Jaya so she wouldn't fall. She looked at it in surprise for a moment, then took it and laughed. "God, this is a lot harder than it looks."

He glanced away, his face a cloud of turmoil at the conversation that lay ahead.

They moved out of the way of the other skiers on the lift, and Jaya realized they were still holding hands. They both wore thick gloves, but she swore she could feel his body heat seeping through. Grey seemed to realize what they were doing at the same time she did, and he pulled his hand from hers as if it were on fire.

"So," Jaya said, attempting to lighten the mood a bit. Maybe if she seemed approachable, it'd be easier for him to tell her what, exactly, was going on with him. "Are you a fellow bunny-slope skier, or do you like the black diamond stuff?"

"Bunny slope's fine." He turned to her, his ski goggles pushed up on his head, his expression a smidgeon more open. "Thanks for doing this. Skiing, giving me time." He paused. "Not getting me expelled."

"It's obvious there's something really bothering you, Grey," Jaya said. "And no, it's not okay that you were going through my things, looking for my pendant. But right now I'm more interested in what you're hiding. Because whatever it is, it looks like it's making you ill." She stopped, a little amazed at this burst of honesty from herself. There was something about the way he was looking at her, though, that called for it. As if he was so tired of hiding whatever it was he was hiding. As if he was on the precipice of telling the truth, if simply to unburden himself. It was a sentiment Jaya found herself identifying with. Subterfuge hadn't been nearly as easy on her conscience as she'd hoped.

Grey paled slightly at her words, then slid his ski goggles on. "Let's ski," he said quietly.

Jaya nodded and slid her own goggles on. She was so close to answers, she could taste them on the air like snow.

They made their way past the other skiers, all of their faces red beneath their ski goggles. The pathway was lit up brightly with overhead lights, and the slope was gentle and easy.

"There are quite a few young children here," Jaya commented, adjusting her ski pole. "That's a bit embarrassing."

Grey kept his voice light as he said, "You don't care what people think of you, do you?"

Jaya studied him under the night lighting. Shadows fell under his blue eyes but didn't dim their shine. His full mouth was set in a hard line despite the levity of his tone. "Actually, I do. I care very much."

"Why?"

"I'm a royal," Jaya said. "Reputation is half—if not more—of what we do. If people don't feel they can trust us, that we're . . . better than them, in some way, they're not happy. And if they're not happy, we can't lead the way we're meant to. Surely you know what I mean, being a duke's son."

Grey itched the side of his jaw, hard, with the back of his gloved hand, but didn't look at her. "I'm not better than anyone."

Jaya decided not to comment on the harsh, self-flagellating way he spoke the words. "Well, it's not that we're *better*, exactly," she said. "It's that they must *think* we are. They have to feel that we were born more able to cope with dilemmas and problems on a large scale. It makes them feel safe, taken care of."

"So it's all an illusion?" Grey asked, his grip on his ski poles tightening. Jaya was aware of people laughing and talking loudly on the slope all around them, but all the bustle felt distant, like it was happening on a TV screen instead of in real life. "And you're okay playing into that?"

"It's for the greater good. So yes, I am okay with it." For the most part. The parts where she was allowed to do only a very narrow scope of things and play the role of nursemaid to Isha, she wasn't so sure about, though she'd never admit that out loud. Jaya paused and adjusted her ski pole. "But you're not, I'm assuming?"

"Sometimes I get very tired of being who other people think I am," Grey said, a muscle in his jaw jumping. More quietly, he added, "But other times, I think maybe I'm exactly what they think I am."

Jaya noticed the switch from "who" to "what," but didn't call attention to it. "Who do other people think you are, Grey?"

He looked at her, blinking, as if he'd forgotten she was there. Shoving his ski poles into the snow with much more force than the action strictly required, he said, "It doesn't matter. Let's go."

He flew down the slope, and after a pause, Jaya followed.

They skied for the better part of an hour, Grey pushing himself to go, go, go, not stopping for a moment to speak with her, riding the ski lift up before she was done skiing down. On about the eighth round, Jaya held up her hand a quarter of the way down the slope. "I think I'm done for now," she said, wincing. "My legs feel like jelly."

Grey skied up easily beside her, no hint of discomfort on *his* face at all. "Okay." He began making his way to the lift, but Jaya put a hand on his elbow.

Pointing to a cluster of incredibly tall pine trees off to the side, nestled around a boulder in the darkness, she said, "Could we sit there for a little bit?"

Grey looked at the boulder and then back at Jaya, his eyes hooded and unreadable. "All right," he said finally.

# Grey

They sat in silence on the large boulder off of which Grey had swept a thick, fluffy layer of snow. Aspen sprawled below them, glittering and twinkling like a starlet bedecked in jewels. All the little kids had headed inside, presumably for dinner and baths and bed, and only a few quieter, older couples remained on the bunny slope.

"This is so beautiful," Jaya said, her brown eyes shimmering with the lights reflected up the mountain at them. "I know I keep saying that, but wow. It's like being on a movie set."

Somewhere below them, some dude whooped in pleasure.

Grey didn't say anything. The truth was on the tip of his tongue, an arrow waiting to leave the bow. He knew what he needed to say, but he also knew that once he said it, Jaya would change her mind about not being angry with him anymore. She'd drop the congenial act, strike a blow, tell him he was a miserable, wretched piece of shit for breaking into her room. He knew once the words left his mouth, she'd tell everyone that Grey Emerson was a sociopath or a thief or a miscreant of some kind, and that they should all stay away from him even more so than they did before. But he knew he needed to come clean, to confess, to tell her. She'd been gracious; she'd given him all day and gone skiing with him. It was time. He opened his mouth to begin.

"Hey." Jaya looked at him, her ski goggles pushed up on her ridiculous—and weirdly charming—pompom-adorned hat.

He gazed warily back. "Yeah?"

"You know what you said earlier? About playing into the illusion of being better than regular people? You asked if I was okay with it."

Grey nodded.

"I said I was, but the truth is . . ." She looked away and absent-mindedly patted down the snow beside her. "Sometimes I do get tired of it. Sometimes I think, why *can't* Isha just be who she is? And why can't I just do what I want? Is it *really* such a crime if she wants to take robotics classes?" She paused, biting on her glossy lower lip, apparently psyching herself up to say something. Curiosity pricked through the fog of Grey's dark mood. "Or . . . or if I want to, say, travel the world for a year after high school rather than going straight to college?" She glanced at him, her eyes wide, as if she couldn't believe she'd said that out loud. Before

Grey could respond, she was speaking again. "Anyway, adhering to all of these rules—and there are enough to fill a library's worth of books, believe me—is incredibly . . ." She took another breath, this one deep and tired. "Enervating."

Grey forgot his fear of reprisal for a moment. Jaya Rao, proper princess of all things prissy, wanted to travel the world instead of going to college right away? She had doubts about telling her sister she couldn't take robotics classes? "Hmm," he said finally. "I never would've guessed you felt that way."

"On occasion," Jaya said, turning to look at him. Her nose was red from the cold. "Not that I'd ever confess that to my parents. Appa—my father—would probably have a heart attack."

"Fathers have a way of dictating who you are," Grey said, more harshly than he'd intended.

They sat together for a while, pondering this.

Without quite making the decision to, Grey found himself speaking. "Do you know anything at all about your pendant?" he asked, staring straight ahead.

Also looking straight ahead, Jaya said carefully, "Well, as I told you before, my father got it at a gold *souk* in Dubai. But that's really all I know."

Grey studied her clear brown eyes. He believed her, he decided. And suddenly he *wanted* to tell her, almost more than he'd ever wanted anything in his entire life. He'd never considered telling anyone before, but the idea of telling Jaya felt . . . different somehow.

And how amazing would it feel, to set this burden down, just for a few moments? To share it with someone else for a bit? How sweet would the relief taste, if he were able to share this shameful, dark secret that had plagued him since he was born? How hilariously ironic, and maybe perfectly fitting, that the first person he'd tell would be the progeny of the one who'd cursed him in the first place?

Grey took a few lungfuls of the cold, icy air, tasting snow in the back of his throat. He moved his gaze from the city below them to Jaya's face as he said the next sentence, the first time he'd ever uttered it out loud. Grey was aware he was passing through a doorway, that he'd never be able to take this back once it was out there. But maybe it was time. "I killed my mother and my father believes I'm cursed."

# *Jaya*

Jaya stared at him, her blood going cold. She was suddenly aware she'd chosen a rather out-of-the-way spot to have this conversation with a very large man. "You . . . you killed your mother?" How had she not known this? Why hadn't anyone at St. Rosetta's told her? She'd always thought that Grey's mother had died in childbirth, not as a consequence of *matricide*.

Grey nodded. "She died in childbirth, bringing me into this world."

A sigh of relief whooshed out of Jaya. "Oh. *Oh*." She shook her head. "That doesn't mean you killed—"

His blue eyes flashed. "Yes, I did. It was all foretold. Because, like I said, I'm cursed."

Jaya frowned a little. "Cursed? What do you mean?" What was he talking about? Was that some kind of slang she was unfamiliar with? Then, as understanding dawned, her eyebrows shot straight up. "Does this have anything to do with my family? The ruby stolen from the temple in the 1800s?"

Grey dug his boots into the powdery snow. "I'm not surprised you've heard of it. It was your great-great-grandmother who cursed the ruby." Jaya could tell he was trying not to say it like an accusation, but he didn't fully succeed.

"Yes, but . . ." Surely he wasn't serious. Surely Grey, a well-educated boy in the twenty-first century, didn't believe in something as far-fetched as a curse. Jaya watched him for a second. He gazed steadily back at her. "Grey, that's just a story. No one in my family believes it to be true. My great-great-grandmother was angry; back then, a lot of Indians were angry with the British. They stole, they plundered—it was all so awful. The curse was just meant to strike fear into the hearts of those who stole the ruby."

"Do you know what it says?" Grey asked. "Have you ever heard the actual words she's supposed to have spoken?"

Jaya thought about it. "I know it had something to do with a future heir, but . . ." She shook her head.

He spoke the words quickly but clearly, the words coming as easily as if he were reciting "Jack and Jill." It was as if they'd been ingrained in him since he was a little boy, right alongside all the nursery rhymes.

> *"A hallowed dream stolen,*
> *A world darkly despairs*
> *A storm, a life, a sudden death*
> *Herald the end, the last heir.*
>
> *"As the glass rose dims,*
> *So the hope of redemption*

*Eighteen years, one by one,*
*Until what's left is none.*

"*Mend that which is broken*
*Repair that which is severed*
*Or the Emerson name is forsaken*
*And shall vanish, at last, forever.*"

The weight of the words hovered between them. Gooseflesh rose on Jaya's arms and legs. When she spoke, her voice was quiet. "What does it mean? Parts of it sound like riddles."

"I used to think that too," Grey said. "But things are starting to get clearer. The ruby my family stole from the temple was sold to a jeweler in the Middle East and then broken apart and placed into a rose-shaped pendant. You said your father bought your pendant in Dubai."

Jaya's hand flew to her throat, grasping for the pendant that wasn't there. "No—you don't think—my pendant holds the original ruby?" It seemed impossible. The ruby was stolen from the temple in the 1800s . . . and it coincidentally ends back up around her neck in the twenty-first century? What were the chances?

The wind whistled through the pine trees around them as Grey spoke. "I didn't really want to believe it either. All my life this curse has hovered over me. It's why my dad sent me to St. R's. My mother died because of me—*a storm, a life, a sudden death, herald the end, the last heir.*

"The night I was born, Westborough saw the worst storm it had seen in a century. My father was away on business, and he couldn't get to the estate in time. No one could, actually. My mother had to deliver me herself with the help of our housekeeper." Grey paused. Jaya could almost see the old story he must've been told all his life working its way under his skin, the guilt blossoming in his chest. "She died shortly after I was born." He swallowed and brushed more snow off the boulder with one hand. "The doctor wasn't able to come and she didn't get the medical care she needed. My father knew immediately . . . it was the curse."

As Jaya looked at him, at the wretched hopelessness on his face, the truth she'd begun to suspect blinked on in her mind, an old flickering light bulb finally coming to life: Grey Emerson could not have engineered the scandal against Isha. For one, he'd been nakedly, genuinely curious about why she and Isha were here. She'd searched his face for signs of recognition, deception, or gloating, and found none. At the mixer, he'd told her he wasn't speaking to any member of his family—and now she knew why. And hearing him talk about the curse . . . Jaya realized her previous half-joking thought in the sushi restaurant, that Grey wasn't capable of being a criminal mastermind because of his hermitlike tendencies, was probably quite true. He was a recluse because he thought he was damaged, because he'd been told all his life that he was worth nothing.

But if Grey wasn't behind the scandal, who was? Every certainty she'd had was unraveling.

The cold from the boulder began to seep in through Jaya's clothes. She brought her mind back to the present. "And you really believe in the curse?" she asked softly.

"I wasn't really given a choice; I was told what the truth was when I was very young, and I accepted it, like we all do. My father has always believed in the curse, very strongly. The Emersons have always believed in it, in fact, going back many generations.

Of course, when they first heard it had been cursed, they didn't want to return it to Mysuru. They were way too spiteful and small-minded for that, so they broke it up and sold it instead, hoping that would get rid of the curse." Grey took his ski hat off and pulled a hand through his hair, shaking his head. "Do you know how many times I've wished I wasn't an Emerson? How many times I've wished I was born an orphan, with no name and no title?" After a moment, gathering himself, he said, "Anyway, then I met you." He glanced at Jaya and back down at the city. "You had a pendant that fit the bill, but you didn't seem to know it. That first morning in the dining hall when you told me a ruby had fallen . . ."

"You left the table," Jaya mused, remembering the way he'd looked, like he'd had a bad scare. "I wondered why."

"I was completely and thoroughly shocked. I thought I had to be overreacting. I didn't know if you were playing a joke on me."

Jaya looked down at her hands and didn't say anything. Guilt squirmed in her chest. She *had* been playing a trick on him, just not the trick he thought.

Grey continued, oblivious to her thoughts. "And then at the mixer when two more rubies fell . . . I began to panic.

> *"As the glass rose dims,*
> *So the hope of redemption*
> *Eighteen years, one by one,*
> *Until what's left is none.*

"It's counting down to my eighteenth birthday in December. I can feel it. Every time I'm around your pendant, I can practically hear a clock's hands, ticking down the time until . . ." He turned to her, his eyes roving her face. "That's the reason I don't date,

Jaya. Once that last ruby falls, I'm . . . That's the end of me. The Emerson line is finished, and so am I." He looked at her. "At sunrise, I presume. That's when I was born."

# Grey

He hadn't meant to say all that, least of all to a Rao who was a direct descendant of the one who'd cursed him. And yet there it was. There was a certain openness to Jaya, something that invited confessions under the stars.

She shook her head slowly. "You . . . you believe you'll die? On your eighteenth birthday?"

"I have no reason not to believe it."

Jaya's face was full of pity. "Grey . . ."

"You might not want to feel too bad for me," he said, forcing a grim smile. He didn't want her feeling sorry for him, the cursed hereditary thief. "That's why I went to your room." He looked her right in the eye and said, "I wanted to steal the pendant. I didn't know if it would help, but I had this idea that I could have it fixed and maybe somehow return it to the temple in Mysuru. And maybe that would be enough, even with all the missing rubies. Maybe that was the way to *mend that which is broken* and *repair that which is severed*. I don't know. I don't know." He rubbed his cold face, then stopped and dropped his hands to his lap, looking straight ahead. "But maybe most of all, it means I am what my father says I am. Different. Cursed. Broken."

They sat in silence for a full minute. Saying those words out loud, Grey felt freer than he ever had before. But lurking under that open sky of freedom was a vast black ocean of shame and a surety that he was not just doomed but corrupt, too.

Grey glanced at Jaya, sitting, pensive, beside him. "You can yell. It's okay. Or you can leave. I'll understand."

She shook her head slowly. "I . . . I won't say it doesn't make me angry, that you were in my room without asking. That you wanted to steal a gift my father gave me, that might actually belong to my family in the first place." Her voice was hard as she said the last part, as if there were big things, like chunks of rock just under the surface, she wasn't saying. "But the point is," she said after a moment, her voice much gentler, "that you were desperate. We've all done things when we're desperate that we might not do otherwise."

"I somehow doubt that you, Perfect Princess Jaya, have done anything so crass as trying to steal someone else's necklace."

"Maybe not stealing," she said, shaking her head. She kept her gaze straight ahead too. "But I have planned to do things that I might never have considered under other circumstances."

"Really?" Grey was intrigued. "Like what?"

She looked at him, something burning in her brown eyes. She opened her mouth, paused, and then closed it again. "The details aren't important," she said quietly, averting her eyes.

They sat in silence another moment, and then Jaya said, "But wait a minute. You said you wanted to steal the pendant to end the curse, but you didn't steal it. I brought it with me." She patted her coat; presumably, the pendant sat nestled in an interior pocket.

"I didn't take it because more rubies began to fall out when I touched it," Grey said, his voice shaking slightly at the memory. "You'll see when you look at it. There are more rubies missing.

And the same thing happened when we were dancing, remember? Two rubies fell out. I feel like . . ." He didn't know if he should say what he really thought.

Jaya waited, watching him without speaking.

Well, he'd told her so much already. What was a little bit more? Needing to get it all out, Grey continued, in a rush. "I feel like it senses my presence, and it doesn't like when I get too close." He laughed mirthlessly. "I know. I *know* how that sounds, believe me."

Jaya stared out at the city lights, breathing steadily in and out. The slope was quiet now, almost deserted. Grey let her have her space. Finally, she turned to him, unsmiling. "I can't convince you otherwise, can I?"

"No," he said bleakly. "You can't." He paused. "Why did you bring it here, to Aspen?"

"I wanted to have some of the rubies replaced before my father saw I'd been careless with it." Glancing at her watch, she added, "Though I don't think I'll have the time now."

"You weren't careless," Grey said as the wind whipped against them. "It's me. I'm the reason." He took a deep breath. "I'll be eighteen in just seven weeks, you know."

"But . . ." He heard the edge of frustration in Jaya's voice; she was holding back what she really wanted to say.

"But you think I'm doing this to myself? That the curse is just a fabrication of my imagination and my father's? That this is all a self-fulfilling prophecy?"

"Yes!" she said, the word bursting out of her with the energy of her agitation. "How can you believe what he's told you, in this day and age? Don't you want something better for yourself?"

He turned on her, his temper flaring at the hypocrisy in her words. "Why do you care so much, anyway? What's it to you?" She looked at him, taken aback, no answers to give. "And anyway," Grey continued, anger like a flame inside his chest, "I could ask the same thing of you. Don't *you* want something better for yourself? Or do you want to be your father's puppet forever? What about *that* self-fulfilling prophecy, Jaya?"

She stared at him, her expression all ice and sharp edges, that earlier softness completely gone. "Here's the difference between my self-fulfilling prophecy and yours, Grey. Mine hasn't turned me into a thief. Mine hasn't made me some twisted, perverted version of myself! How about yours?" And she stood up and skied off, leaving him sitting alone, encased by drifting snow and darkness.

# CHAPTER 12

# *Jaya*

All of Jaya's righteous anger melted away, bit by burning bit, as she went back uphill to take the ski lift down by herself. She was too preoccupied by her own thoughts, by the echoing replay of their conversation, to notice the beauty of the wintry evening around her this time. As she traveled down she thought she glimpsed Grey in the near dark, head bent and still as a statue, but she wasn't sure.

Jaya felt the sickening churning in her stomach that came with having been needlessly cruel, with having lashed out at someone out of defensiveness and fear. Yes, he'd tried to steal her necklace. No, she didn't like it. But she understood. When he told her the story about the curse—the way he had the entire thing memorized—she'd understood how desperate, how unhappy, how scared he must be. She could see it in his eyes, the haunted, hunted look of someone coming to terms with news they had no framework to accept.

She didn't believe in the curse one bit. Jaya came from a world where ancient superstition and logic coexisted side by side quite nicely. It was a world where astrologers could pick your school for you based on the alignments of the stars, but you took anti-biotics when you were sick because you knew and accepted that medicine, that science, worked. The curse? It was obvious to Jaya that her great-great-grandmother had been consumed with pain and anger when she'd supposedly cursed the stolen ruby. Jaya had heard the story only once, a long time ago and then only in passing, because no Rao believed in it. She'd had no idea the Emersons did.

If Grey hadn't leaked the pictures like the journalist had said, who else might it be? Another Emerson? Perhaps the journalist was confused and meant it was an Emerson *aristocrat* and not nec-essarily an heir to their estate. And maybe the curse was behind it all. Perhaps that was why they'd lashed out at Isha. And why they always seemed to be coming for the Raos.

She shook her head as she got off the ski lift and made her way to the lodge, past the snow-caked fountain, passing under the stone arch lit up with a thousand twinkling lights. What the Emersons (whichever one was responsible) had done to Isha and her family was still unforgivable, of course. But Jaya had to won-der . . . how would Appa react if an Emerson had cursed *their* bloodline to end, had cursed Jaya to die? If he fully believed it were true?

How would *Jaya* react?

She took off her gloves and her coat, handing them off to the concierge as she made her way to the gold velvet armchair she'd been sitting in before, the one by the enormous fireplace. Star-ing into the flames, Jaya knew with absolute certainty that she'd lashed out at Grey like that because he'd struck a nerve. The truth was, she *was* scared. She was scared of the exact thing he'd said to her—that she was nothing more than a mouthpiece for her father. And she'd never confronted that fear before. And . . . Grey wasn't the only one who'd twisted and turned into himself. He wasn't the only one who'd done things he'd never have done under ordinary circumstances. Seeing him, the look in his eyes, the absolute heavy weight he carried on his shoulders day after day, the surety he had that he was doomed, damaged, destined for death, and knowing that he could never have orchestrated the scandal against Isha . . . Jaya had known then, on that boulder, that she could not carry her plan through. Not anymore.

What did this mean for her loyalty toward her family, toward her sister? How could she avenge the Rao name if she stepped aside this way? She didn't know. All she knew was that you sparred with an opponent in your own weight class. You didn't strike at someone in pain, someone who was already hunched over in agony, someone begging the fates for forgiveness.

She couldn't make this boy fall in love with her. She couldn't break his heart. Because if she did, it was her, not him, who was the beast.

# Grey

Grey walked into the lodge feeling bruised and paper-thin, like he was liable to rip in half at any moment. He shouldn't have turned on Jaya like that. He shouldn't have said the things he'd said; he'd been way over the line. But the things she'd said in return? The way he'd poured himself out to her. He'd lain himself bare, stepping over a threshold he'd never crossed before.

That had obviously been a huge mistake. This was why he held himself so carefully; this was why he refused to let people see who he really was. Because no one understood. Because no one could ever understand.

The attendant came up to him and took his coat, hat, and gloves and handed him a note.

Frowning, Grey opened it.

*Please forgive me. I'd like to talk, if you're open to it. I'm by the fireplace.*

*—Jaya*

Folding the note, he stuck it in his pocket and looked toward the armchairs by the fireplace, his heart thudding. Jaya sat there, looking right at him. She raised a hand in a hesitant wave. The embers of anger and shame in his heart began to die down at the look in her soft brown eyes.

Grey paused for a moment, and then, without conscious thought, his feet propelled him forward, toward her.

"Hi," she said when he got close. Gesturing to the chair beside her, she added, "Will you take a seat? I ordered us both hot cocoas, just in case." There were two cups topped with whipped cream on the table.

Grey took a seat, noting that Jaya looked relieved.

"Grey . . . I'm so sorry. What I said up there, that was cruel. I was defensive and angry and—" She broke off and shook her head, running a hand along her forehead. "You got under my skin. You have a tendency to do that; I'm not sure why." She didn't say it as an accusation, just as a statement of fact. It almost seemed like she was talking to herself. Grey felt a warmth in his chest. He *liked* that he got to Jaya Rao. Not much did. "Anyway," she continued, "it was vicious and mean-spirited, and I'm really sorry."

"There was no lie in it." Grey brought the cup of hot cocoa to his lips and took a sip, feeling the burn of the scalding liquid as it slid down his throat. "I'm exactly what you said I was."

"No, you're not," she said, sounding stricken. Leaning forward, she put a small hand on his. Grey stiffened, unsure what to do with the physical contact. It felt perfect; it felt dangerous. Noticing his reaction, Jaya withdrew her hand smoothly, a mistress of social graces. "You're not, Grey. You're scared, as anyone would be, in your situation. The truth is, that's not the first time I've wondered if that's what I am. A sock puppet for not just my father, but for my country, for a society that has a very narrow view of what a royal woman should be. Am I doing more harm than good by going along with it, by perpetuating the stereotype? And sometimes I get so tired of being the 'old guard' as it were, of playing 'keeper of the rules' with my free-spirited sister. I'm afraid it's hardening me into something I don't want to become." She shrugged her thin shoulders. "I don't know. I try not to consider all that too deeply—it's easier that way—and that's why your words struck a chord."

He studied her, surprised. "That's very honest of you," he said finally. "I appreciate honesty in people."

Her cheeks stained a deep red. "I don't know about that," she mumbled.

Grey settled against his chair, cradling his cocoa in his hands, and, after a pause, Jaya settled back against her chair too. They sat watching the fire together for a bit, until it was time to go.

# Jaya

In a somber mood, Jaya and Grey boarded the bus together at ten o'clock and took their old seats. Caterina's thinly veiled threats echoed distantly in her ears, but Jaya found she didn't much care in the moment. She looked at Grey sidelong as they settled in. It was strange, how different things were now. When she'd boarded the bus this morning, she'd been hell-bent on finding out what Grey Emerson was hiding. Now . . . well, now she knew. And it was like the wind had gone out of her sails. He wasn't the evil sadist she'd thought he was at all. Jaya wasn't quite sure what to do with that.

Daphne Elizabeth tromped onto the bus then and came to sit by them, looking gloomy. "Hey, guys."

"Hi." Jaya patted her arm. "Are you all right?"

Daph shrugged. "No. I'm feeling especially naive since Alaric chose to ride back with her." Daphne Elizabeth sighed and looked at the both of them, shaking her head. "I don't get it. Why can't I leave him alone?"

"Maybe it's the way his hair is gelled so much it looks like it's made out of concrete," Grey said, and Jaya elbowed him.

Daph raised an eyebrow. "Was that a *joke*, Grey?"

Smirking, he crossed his arms and lapsed back into silence.

"Maybe it's time you did leave Alaric alone," Jaya said, turning back to Daphne Elizabeth. "You're not happy, Daph. That's plain to see. And he isn't treating you right—either of you."

"That's easy for you to say, Jaya," Daph said, crossing her arms and looking out the window. She was clearly finished with the conversation. "But you're not in my shoes."

Jaya kept her silence, frustrated as she was. Grey settled in quietly as other students began piling on, everyone talking tiredly after a long day shopping and skiing. Jaya sat next to him in the neon-lit dark, her mind turning back to all that had happened that day.

When she'd caught him in her room, Jaya had not envisioned that it would end up like this: with her relinquishing the plan she'd been certain would avenge her family's honor. But what other choice did she have? Anyone reasonable would've arrived at that conclusion after seeing and hearing Grey's obvious agony. She glanced at his profile, lit pink from the neon lights on the bus, and felt a prickle of sympathy.

So now what? Where did all this leave her with her family? What would she tell them, or Kiran, who abhorred the Emersons as much as she did? What did it mean for her as the heiress to the Rao name and estate, if she was sympathetic to an Emerson?

Jaya leaned her head back against the window and closed her eyes. She felt like the ocean, once a storm had descended. Tossed about, churning, with no end in sight.

# Grey

Grey glanced at Jaya, who appeared to be napping, her head back against the window, her face bathed in pink light. She looked calm, peaceful, like a tranquil lake in Costa Rica. Grey, on the other hand, felt completely wrung out. He was an empty hull of a wrecked ship—shattered and adrift.

He'd never confided in another human like that before. All

the things he'd said to Jaya, all the weirdness he'd poured out on her, and she'd just . . . She hadn't judged him. They'd fought, sure, but then they'd talked and he felt good about it. He felt, strangely enough, like she'd listened. Like she'd truly *heard* him as no one else had before.

Glancing at her again, Grey felt his heart squeeze in his chest. *I like her,* he realized with a start. He really liked who she was, through and through. Alarmed and a bit disturbed by these feelings that were both unsanctioned and impermissible for someone in his position (not just cursed but also doomed), Grey frowned and looked out the window at the darkness.

A couple of days after the Aspen trip, Grey found himself in the aquatic center. He pushed himself to swim lap after lap, pulling himself through the water with his arms, his legs kicking effortlessly behind. Swimming helped him think. In the water, his mind went blank, all the thoughts that had been jostling and pushing for real estate falling quiet. The only sound he heard was the rhythmic splashing of the water. The only thing he felt was the balmy warmth of the heated pool.

He emerged at the shallow end, only to realize he wasn't alone. His goggles had fogged up, but he saw a figure in a bright fuchsia swimsuit standing above him. The figure didn't move; it seemed like they were waiting for him to do something. Grey pushed his goggles to the top of his head to find Jaya in a one-piece, ruffles along the plunging neckline. He forced his eyes to hers. "Hey."

She smiled, her eyes wandering over his naked shoulders as if she couldn't help it. A warmth spread through Grey's belly, and he squashed it with some effort. "Hi. Do you mind if I pop in for a swim?"

He waved his arm toward the empty lap lane next to his. "What it's there for."

She sat on the edge and let herself drop in, an effortlessly graceful royal mermaid. "Wow. I can't believe there's no one else here."

Grey looked out over the other six lap lanes. "Well, it's close to nine o'clock at night—one hour until the pool closes. It's usually deserted around this time."

Jaya began treading water. "Ah, I see. I got bored in the dorms, and felt like a bit of exercise, so . . . Hope you don't mind the intrusion." She held his gaze, asking his permission.

"You're not intruding." Grey slipped his goggles back on and, without another word, resumed his laps. This time his mind wasn't so empty.

He was too aware of her as he swam. There was a tentative ease between them now that wasn't there previously. Where before there had been a brick wall keeping them apart, there was now also a tiny window. Whatever he may have felt about the Raos, he couldn't ignore that Jaya Rao was the only one besides his family who knew all of him.

Jaya kept a much steadier pace than him, peacefully going back and forth. She seemed to enjoy just being in the water, as opposed to using it as a tool to outswim unwanted thoughts. She went for thirty minutes before she got out, shook herself off, and walked to the hot tub.

Grey considered her as he treaded water in the deep end. Her head was leaned back as she sat in the hot, bubbling water, her eyes closed, eyelashes resting on her cheeks. His heart thudded. He wanted to go sit by her. Should he go sit by her?

Without letting himself think too much, he swam over to the ladder, got out of the pool, and walked the few steps to the hot tub. Jaya opened her eyes when she felt him splash in next to her.

"Hope you don't mind the intrusion," Grey said, parroting her words from the pool.

She gestured to the bench beside her. "What it's there for."

A ghost of a smile at his lips, he took a seat. After a pause, he pointed in the general direction of her chest, not wanting to let his eyes linger there. "You're not wearing your necklace."

Jaya's fingers caressed the bare skin just under the hollow of her throat. "No. The rubies keep falling and I didn't want to make it worse." She glanced at him, her eyes soft. "How are you doing?"

He knew she wasn't asking about his general health. She meant "How are you doing since you think your life is ending?"

"I'm fine."

"I was thinking . . . ," Jaya said. "I might take it to get repaired. You know, just to see what, ah, what that does."

Grey frowned. "What it does?" Then understanding dawned. "Do you mean if it gets rid of the curse?"

She nodded.

Grey rubbed a wet hand along his jaw. "That's not going to help." It was a little endearing that she wanted to try, though.

"Maybe not," Jaya said. "But perhaps if the pendant really does know you're near like you told me in Aspen, it'll sense you trying to help." Seeing his skeptical face, she added, "Maybe it sounds silly, but I don't know how these things work. What can it hurt to try?"

He considered this. "Okay."

"Okay." She smiled, and for the first time, Grey realized just how perfectly bow-shaped her lips were. "I'll find a good jeweler. And ah . . . we could go together. If you wanted to, I mean."

Her expression was tentative, wondering if he'd reject her like he'd rejected her before. "Sure," Grey found himself saying, which was a surprise even to him. "That wouldn't be . . . awful." He was already kind of looking forward to it, in fact.

Her smile broadened and she moved infinitesimally closer to him on the underwater bench. "Not awful. I'll take that as a compliment. This is so beautiful," she added, tipping her head back to look at the stars through the paned glass roof. Her cheeks were stained a dark pink, strands of her hair coiled in wet curls on her neck.

Her hand rested lightly next to his on the bench; he could see it through inches of water. Her pinkie was so close to his, he could just twitch his finger and be touching her. His gaze drifted to her lips. They were close enough to be kissing. Did she want that? Did he? As if she could read his thoughts, Jaya looked over at him, her brown eyes soft and inviting. Grey's heart beat so loudly it was hard to hear his own thoughts.

What was he doing?

"I should go," Grey said, beginning to haul himself out of the hot tub.

There was no point. There was no point in getting close to Jaya Rao, in getting close to *any*one. He was . . . different from others. He was tainted. He couldn't allow himself to feel anything for Jaya Rao, and he couldn't let her feel things for him. It was as simple as that. So why the hell was he finding it so hard?

# Jaya

Jaya watched him as he made a motion to leave, her pulse pounding. Had they almost just . . . kissed? There had been *something* in the air. Why were her hands *trembling*, for God's sake? She'd found herself wondering what those lips would feel like molded to hers, what that sandpaper stubble might feel like against her cheek.

In the history of bad ideas, there had never been one worse than a Rao heiress kissing an Emerson aristocrat. And not just any Emerson aristocrat, but one who believed himself plagued by a curse that had originated with the Raos themselves. What would her family say? How would it reflect on her, on the Raos' reputation, the eldest daughter cavorting with an Emerson at boarding school on the heels of the scandal involving the youngest daughter?

Not to mention, now that she was sure Grey hadn't been behind Isha's scandal, she had a problem. She was back to square one, trying to figure out who'd been behind the leak. Perhaps she could reach out to the journalist in Mysuru again, offer to pay him for a name. It might be a different Emerson. Just another reason on a very long list of why it was a bad idea to edge emotionally closer to Grey.

He obviously had his own doubts too. Why else would he have jumped up like that to get away from her?

Still, Jaya found herself reaching out, placing a hand on his forearm, his muscles like steel cords under the skin. "Don't go," she said softly. The realization that she wasn't just being polite surprised her; she really didn't want him to leave.

He turned to her, strands of dark hair dripping water onto his face. "I . . . I can't . . ."

Jaya smiled. "It's okay. We'll just sit here and talk. Look, I'll even move over." She scooted a few feet so they were nowhere near each other anymore.

Grey paused for a second, studying her, and then the distance between them. Very slowly, as if he were waiting for her to change her mind, he sat.

Jaya nodded, feeling oddly happy. "Good. Now let's just enjoy the warm water, shall we?"

As the water frothed around them, she lay her head back, let her eyes slip closed, and took deep, calming breaths. Outwardly, she knew she appeared calm and in control, ever poised. Inside, she felt like a shipwreck survivor, on uncharted land she had no idea how to navigate.

The next afternoon, Jaya had just come in from the gardens, book in hand, when Penelope caught up with her on the stairs, going the other way. "Hello, Penny," she said, smiling.

"I've been looking for you! Has Caterina talked to you yet?" Penelope asked, her eyes bright.

"No . . . why?"

"Oh, I just saw her a few minutes ago and she says she has a surprise for you." Penelope's cheeks were pink with glee. "I'm not sure what, though. She said to tell you to go to her room."

Jaya's heart hammered. Unlike the innocent Penelope, she knew a surprise from Caterina was not a thing to celebrate. "Okay, thanks, Penny," she said, quickening her steps.

"Ta!" Penelope continued blithely running down the stairs.

Jaya walked quickly through the common room, noting in passing the smell of cooking popcorn, down the hallway with the dorm rooms, passing other students and smiling at them, though her mouth was rather dry. She clutched her book to her chest.

Perhaps Caterina wanted to apologize to Jaya. Well, maybe not to *apologize*—she doubted Caterina ever apologized for anything—but certainly to smooth things over. Maybe she'd thought about it and realized Jaya was only doing what any reasonable person would—that Caterina had put her in an uncomfortable position, asking her to rat on Daph. They'd talk about it, Jaya would say bygones were bygones, and that would be it.

She took a deep breath, smoothed down her sweater, and knocked on Caterina's door.

"Come in!"

Jaya turned the doorknob, walked in, and stopped, staring.

Caterina, dressed in a plum-colored sweaterdress and tan boots, sat at her desk. On the screen of the laptop in front of her were two familiar faces. "Jaya," Caterina said, smiling her most lovely, most carved-from-ice smile. "I believe you know my friends Sri Devi and Kiran? We were just catching up on Skype."

Sri Devi Nair, the daughter of one of the royal families in Kerala, the one Caterina had brought up again in Aspen. And Kiran Hegde, who naturally, Jaya knew well. Quite well. "What . . . ," Jaya began, not knowing what she was going to say. Her pulse hammered in her temples; her palms were suddenly very damp.

"Hi, Jaya," Sri Devi said while Kiran watched Jaya, unsmiling.

"H-hi," Jaya said, feeling more discombobulated than she had in her entire life. What would Amma do in a situation like this? She walked closer to the screen, to Caterina. "How are you, Sri Devi?"

"I'm well!" Sri Devi said. "Caterina was just telling us how well you're fitting in there. Sounds like you've met lots of interesting people."

Jaya swallowed. Had Caterina told Kiran she seemed to be getting friendly with Grey Emerson? And what had Kiran, in turn, told her? "Right. I have. Everyone's very . . . nice." She noticed Caterina's gaze on her.

"That's good," Kiran said, but he still didn't smile. "I'm glad everyone's so nice. And Isha's doing well?" His eyes held hers for a long, long moment.

"She is. Very well." Jaya cleared her throat into the silence.

"We were just saying goodbye," Caterina said, smiling flashily at them. "It's late where they are, you know? You missed all of our chat, unfortunately."

Jaya forced an easy smile. "Well. Maybe next time, then."

Caterina wiggled her fingers at them. "Till next time!"

She ended the call and turned to Jaya, her brown eyes sparkling. "You have such lovely friends, Jaya," she said. "They seem to like you so much."

"They're wonderful," Jaya agreed carefully, her eyes never leaving Caterina's face.

Caterina may not know anything of substance—how close Jaya and Grey had come to kissing, for instance. Maybe she, Kiran, and Sri Devi barely talked about Jaya at all. The important thing was for her to not mention Grey; Jaya knew this deep in the roots of her soul, like she knew never to eat the toxic fruit of the *othalanga* tree. This was a power move on Caterina's part, that was all. Surely this was just her way of saying, *Don't ever cross me. If I bothered to* really *dig into your private life, I could crush you like a bug under my boot heel.* Message received.

"I should go shower before dinner," Jaya said, making her way to the door.

"Good idea," Caterina said. "You never know what kind of dirt might be sticking to you."

They looked at each other. Jaya nodded, turned the doorknob, and left. She stopped in the hallway for a moment, her breaths coming faster, as if she were caught in a lightning storm no one had seen coming.

# CHAPTER 13

# Jaya

It was Saturday morning, a day and a half after the Skype ambush, and Jaya paced the length of Daph's room. They'd arrived at an uneasy truce after their confrontation on the bus in Aspen, both of them at an impasse. Well, it was time to break the impasse.

"What's going on?" Daph asked, tearing off a piece of fruit leather that was wrapped around her finger. She was dressed in yoga pants and a tunic sweater, ready for the weekend. "You seem really . . . stressed."

"I am stressed." Jaya stopped and looked at her. "Look, I have to tell you something that I should've told you a while ago, and you're probably not going to like it, but things have now come to a head and—"

"Whoa, slow down," Daph said, her palms outstretched. "Start at the top, darling. Tell me everything."

Pulling the sleeves of her sweater down, Jaya turned to her. "Okay. You have to tell Caterina about you and Alaric."

Daph paled. "What? Jaya, you know I can't. Why are you saying this?"

"Because *I'm* in her crosshairs now. She talked to me at the mixer, and again at the lodge in Aspen, and now . . ." Jaya took a deep breath. Caterina could ruin everything if she told Kiran that Jaya and Grey were an item. He'd tell her parents, who'd be furious, of course, with good reason. This could jeopardize everything, and it had to stop. Now. "I haven't told her anything about you and Alaric, but she knows I know something, and she's not taking my silence too well. I don't have to tell you, Caterina's not someone I want as my enemy."

Daph stood and walked to her window, looking down at the gardens below. Jaya gave her some space. After a long pause, she turned around and looked Jaya in the eye. "I'm so sorry she's coming after you. I never thought—I'll take care of it. I'll tell Alaric we need to come clean."

Jaya's shoulders sagged in relief. "Really?"

Daph smiled a small, sad smile. "Really. It's about time anyway." Her eyes got misty. "I'm so sorry you got dragged into it, even a little. I know Caterina was probably not very nice to you about it. I feel like absolute shit, you know? I wish I could just stop, just walk away from Alaric." She sniffled. "Do you know how many times I've told him I want to tell Caterina? Or begged him to?"

"So why haven't you, then?" Jaya asked, not unkindly.

"He's always got some excuse, you know? Either he's stressed about some test or Caterina got bad news from home or . . ." She shook her head and dabbed at her eyes with a napkin. Looking right at Jaya, she said, "Haven't you ever lied for someone you loved? Even if it meant hurting someone else?"

Jaya felt herself still. "Yes," she said finally, when she'd found her voice again. "Yes, I have."

Daphne Elizabeth gave her a watery smile. "It sucks, and I feel so totally weak, but . . . this is it, though. This isn't fair to you now, and I never wanted anyone else pulled into it. It's over; one way or another, we're going to tell her."

Jaya nodded. After a pause, she said, "Thank you."

# Grey

It was Saturday afternoon, and Grey and DE were headed back to the main building from the library. Grey had just returned a few books and was meeting Jaya in the lobby so they could take a car to the jeweler in town together. He had no idea what DE was up to tonight; he hadn't asked. She'd basically just latched on to him when she saw him, which, strangely, he didn't mind too much for a change.

Winter was definitely here; they were both huddled into their jackets as ice-edged wind cut at their faces and ears. DE typed furiously on her phone, probably talking to Alaric. Bits of her brilliant red hair showed from under her pale green beanie. "So, Grey," she continued, looking briefly at him as they walked. "I think it's pretty clear that Jaya's buried an arrow from her bow deep into your heart."

Grey snorted as he tucked his hands into his coat pockets. "If she hits anything, it's only by accident."

"What?" DE asked, confused.

"She's a terrible shot," Grey explained as they passed a group of laughing freshmen. "I had to give her archery lessons." He smiled at the memory of them at one of their very first archery classes.

"Oh. Weird," DE said, going back to her phone.

"What is?"

"It's no big deal," she said, shaking her head. "I was sure she told me she'd won a trophy for it or wanted to do archery at college or something. It sounded like she was pretty good." She tossed him a smile. "I'm probably just remembering it wrong, though."

"Yeah," Grey said, frowning slightly. "Probably."

"So what are you doing tonight? Anything fun?"

"Ah, just going into town to run an errand," Grey replied as they walked up a small hill toward the main building. Another stiff breeze shook the line of aspen trees on either side of them.

"Oh, you're going alone?" DE said. "Need some company?"

"I'm not going alone." He could feel her green gaze on the side of his face. Reluctantly, he added, "Jaya and I are going together."

DE snorted and he glared at her. Trying her best to get her smile under control, she said, "Right. Of course you are."

Grey rolled his eyes and lengthened his stride to leave her behind, but he could still hear her laughing.

# Jaya

A week and a half after the "almost kiss" in the hot tub, Jaya waited in the lobby of the main building for Grey. She'd already requested a car from the school's service, and now she stood by the fireplace, warming her hands. A few other students lounged on the chairs around her, talking or texting, but Jaya kept to herself, lost in thought.

It felt like a good way to spend a Saturday evening, going into town to try to get her necklace repaired. The fact that she was going with Grey, though, she wasn't too sure about. Not after what Caterina had done.

Jaya had to be especially careful now, how and where she was seen with Grey. For instance, he'd texted her that he wanted to return a few library books. Normally she would've asked to walk with him, but she'd forced herself to stay at the main building instead.

She looked over her shoulder for signs of Caterina but saw none. Relaxing a bit, she turned back to the fire. Getting into a car with Grey in public was probably not the smartest thing to do if her objective was to prove there was nothing at all between them (which there wasn't) and that she didn't like him (which she didn't), but she'd already invited him and didn't want to rescind the invitation. That was needlessly cruel. Besides, Jaya was hoping getting the necklace fixed might help him. Not that she believed the curse was real, of course, but there was such a thing as a placebo effect, wasn't there? Perhaps Grey would see it fixed and believe the curse was gone.

The front doors opened then, letting in a burst of cold air. Jaya turned to see Grey enter, with Daph close behind him, and she walked toward them. "Hi."

"Hey," Grey said, nodding but not smiling.

"Jaya, do you have a minute?" Daph said, grabbing her elbow.

"Erm, of course." She turned to Grey. "The car should be outside in another minute or two. Do you want to wait there and I'll meet you?"

He nodded and turned on his heel to head back outside.

Jaya turned to Daph. "What's going on?"

Daphne Elizabeth cleared her throat, two bright spots of color on her cheeks that Jaya didn't think had to do with the cold air outside. "Just wanted you to know I told Alaric that either he needed to tell Caterina about us or I would."

Jaya stood up straighter. "And?"

Daphne Elizabeth held out her cell phone. "He gave me her cell number." On the screen was a text message, sent the day before.

**Caterina, this is Daphne Elizabeth. We need to talk. Alaric and I have been dating. I'm sorry we haven't told you before now. I know this is so shitty, but it just happened and . . . I'm sorry. Truly sorry.**

There was no response text.

Jaya looked up at Daphne Elizabeth. "She hasn't replied?"

"No, but she was glaring at me in class today, so I'm sure she saw it." Daphne Elizabeth let out a breath. "It feels good to have gotten that off my chest. Really good."

"So what's the plan now? Will you talk to her, since she hasn't responded?"

"No, I'd better not. I'm going to let it rest. Ball's in her court now. She might need a while to digest the text . . . or plot my murder." Daphne Elizabeth laughed, but there was a hysterical, nervous edge to it.

Jaya put her hand on Daphne Elizabeth's shoulder. "I'm proud of you for doing that," she said.

Daph smiled. "Thanks."

"And has Alaric said if he'll text her too? Or talk to her? Is he with her right now?"

Daph shook her head. "No. After that stunt she pulled in her car the day of the Aspen trip, they haven't been hanging out too much. He says he'd rather not rattle her cage right now."

Jaya nodded, though she thought Alaric was quite possibly

the biggest coward she'd ever met. "For what it's worth, I don't think it was a stunt, what Caterina did. Perhaps she just wanted to spend some time with Alaric; she was probably hoping he'd ride with her."

Daphne Elizabeth looked abashed. "Oh." She twisted the fringe on her scarf. "Right."

"Daph," Jaya said, leaning forward. A group of students came in from outside, and Jaya and Daph moved out of the way, to the side. "You could get another boyfriend, you know. Someone else who'll love you and treasure you and respect you the way you deserve. Someone who won't ask you to do the heavy lifting while he does . . . well, whatever Alaric's up to right now." She paused, half hearing Amma's voice in her head: *Do not meddle in other people's relationships, Jaya.* "And maybe you don't need a boyfriend at all right now," Jaya pushed on, because she wanted to say this to Daphne Elizabeth, because she actually cared about this girl. "Maybe you could take some time for yourself, to work out what's important to you. It doesn't all have to be on Alaric's schedule."

Daph smiled at her, her green eyes tinged with sadness. "Thanks, Jaya." On impulse, she reached out and gave her a hug. "Now, you better go. I know Grey's probably getting pretty desperate." She laughed.

Jaya glared at her. "We're just running an errand."

"I know, I know, that's the party line," Daph said, still chuckling as she turned around and made her way to the stairs.


The car pulled up to the curb on a quiet shop-and-tree-lined street a few miles from campus in downtown St. Rosetta, near the sushi restaurant she, Isha, and Grey had eaten at so long ago. Now Grey tipped the driver quickly and slid out. Jaya followed, her boots crunching.

She looked over her shoulder as if she expected to see Caterina hiding behind a tree, fully aware she was getting a little paranoid. She hoped that seeing Daph's text would ease Caterina's anger a bit, but the fact that she hadn't replied bothered Jaya. She glanced at Grey as they walked down the sidewalk. It would make the most sense for her to not even be here with him. And yet she couldn't bring herself to actually take action that would make him leave. What was that about?

"Here it is," she said as they walked up to a familiar quaint stone shop decorated with ivy garlands and lights. Jaya had seen the picture on their website; it looked like something a hobbit might live in, but in a good way. A sign outside said ST. ROSETTA'S FINE JEWELERS.

Grey held the door open for her.

The shop was much larger inside than the exterior suggested. Their footsteps echoed on the marble tile floor, and Jaya breathed in the dry scent of the heater mixed in with some subtle herby fragrance.

"This is beautiful," she said, looking around at all the stately glass cases, in which jewels as big as her fist glittered in colors of the rainbow. She walked over to a display case on the right, in which an intricate gold hair clip that looked like it was made from lace rather than metal sat on a pale blue velvet pillow.

Grey read a little sign by the case. "It says most of these pieces are custom-made. You can't find work like this anywhere else." He studied the hair clip with her. "Wow, he's really talented."

"I thank you for that compliment."

Jaya turned to see a short, white-skinned man with a perfectly trimmed goatee and small, neat hands smiling at her and Grey. He wore one large signet ring on his pinkie and a gold rope necklace around his neck. "Princess Jaya, I assume? I am Silas, the resident master jeweler and proprietor of this establishment."

"Yes. We spoke on the phone earlier this week." Jaya smiled and held out her hand. "Just Jaya, please. And this is Grey Emerson."

Silas enveloped Jaya's hand in both of his. His suit rustled just a little as he moved, a thick, lush sound that told her it was bespoke. "I think honorifics add a bit of elegance to a conversation, don't you?" he asked her, his eyes twinkling.

"They do." It was hard to disagree with Silas. He was the perfect mixture of soft-spoken and confident. "In that case, this is Lord Northcliffe."

Grey shifted, as uncomfortable with his formal title as if it were a scratchy, ill-fitting shirt.

Silas beamed. "Excellent." Letting go of Jaya's hand, he asked, "So. What can I help you with today? You said on the phone you're having some issues with a necklace?"

"Yes." Jaya reached into her coat and gently extracted the rose pendant from the velvet bag. Beside her, Grey stiffened as if she were handling a viper. "My father got this for me in Dubai recently, but as you can see, the rubies have been falling out."

"Hmm." Silas took it from her and walked over to a little mahogany workbench in the corner. Clicking his jeweler's glasses into place, he maneuvered a bright work light into position. Tutting quietly to himself as he examined the pendant, he said, "Oh, dear. This is very unusual indeed."

"What's that?" Jaya asked.

"Well, you see, the prongs that held each of the missing rubies have pulled away from the main body of the rose," Silas explained, pointing out the prongs to Jaya. "It's rather strange for the prongs to do that without assistance, although I have seen that happen in rare circumstances. You say this is a new piece? Has it been handled roughly?"

"I only got it a few months ago, and I've been very careful with it."

"Hmm. Unusual. Very unusual."

Grey took a step away from the pendant. Jaya wondered if he knew what he'd done or if it had been a subconscious reaction.

"Do you think you can replace the rubies and fix the prongs?"

"Well, yes. But without knowing the cause, I'm afraid the same thing may happen to the new rubies."

Jaya nodded. "I suppose that can't be helped. Could you do anything to protect against the prongs getting wrenched away like that?"

"I could bend them into place and perhaps anchor them with a tiny bit of jeweler's epoxy. And I can do the same for the rest of the prongs as well, while I'm at it," Silas said thoughtfully. "Could you give me an hour?"

"Of course. We'll keep ourselves busy until then."

Silas smiled as he slipped her rose pendant into a velvet pouch. "I'll see you both again shortly, Princess Jaya, Lord Northcliffe."

They stepped outside into the cold early-November air, and Jaya glanced at Grey. His face was unreadable, preoccupied. "You okay?" she asked as they began aimlessly up the sidewalk, burying her hands in her coat pockets.

"Fine." He paused, ran a hand through his hair. "The prongs . . . they were pulled away. That's weird."

Jaya shrugged. "But not supernatural. I'm sure that happens to jewelry sometimes. Besides, Silas is going to fix it." She wanted to reassure Grey, she realized. But she also wanted to not be out here on the street, where anyone driving by might see them together.

Across the street, the warm, glowing lights of a small bookstore called Bookingham Palace beckoned. Enclosed, small, decidedly unglamorous, and somewhere Caterina wasn't likely to be. Perfect. Putting her hand on Grey's arm, Jaya smiled. "Let's go in there."

There were few dark moods books couldn't fix.

Entering into the cozy warmth of Bookingham Palace, hearing the soft jingle of the bells on the door, Jaya felt her worries melting away. Smiling, she took off her coat and let the buzz of various conversations settle over her like a balmy wave. The store wasn't very big, but it was packed to the gills with books of every kind, as well as gifts for the upcoming holiday season like Santa mugs and peppermint bark.

They walked to the right, and Jaya began browsing the latest young adult romances. After a moment, she looked up at Grey, who was following her with his coat draped over his arm. It was clear he was still lost in his own head. "What do you like to read?"

"Historical biographies, mostly."

She gave him a wry look. "Really?"

He raised an eyebrow. "Are you judging my reading choices?"

Jaya's cheeks got warm. "Of course not," she said quickly. "What's your favorite biography, then?"

"Hmm, that's hard to say. Probably . . . *Bertie: A Life of Edward VII*, by Jane Ridley. He was sort of a black sheep of his family, and not a very nice person, from all accounts." He said the words blandly, but Jaya detected an undercurrent of something.

They lapsed into silence then, alone in the narrow space between the shelves. But this silence wasn't like the usual silences as they walked to and from class. This silence felt . . . tangible. Jaya noticed her breathing quickening as she realized how close they were really standing to each other. The din from the other shoppers faded. She could see the faint dark stubble along Grey's jaw; his blue eyes blazed as he studied her brown ones.

*What are you doing, Jaya?* a little voice inside her head said. *This is a repeat of the hot tub incident! Is that what you want?*

*No, of course not!* another part of her brain replied. Considering how much harm Caterina could do if she were to tell Kiran anything, it would be downright irresponsible. And besides Caterina telling Kiran, Jaya herself didn't think it was right. She was an heiress, for God's sake. She had responsibilities to her estate and her people and her family name. Grey Emerson didn't factor in to any of those responsibilities. Right. She was going to step away. Step. Away. Right now.

Jaya found herself stepping in closer to Grey.

Suddenly, he turned on his heel and began to walk away from her.

"Where . . . where are you going?" Jaya said, dazed, to his retreating back.

He glanced at her over his shoulder. "To find a book."

"Right." Jaya paused, choosing her words carefully. "It *is* customary to let your shopping companion know where you're going before you just take off."

"Oh." Grey looked genuinely taken aback as he turned to fully face her. He was so broad, he took up all the room between the two shelves on either side of him. "I'm . . . going to find a book." He paused. "Like that?"

Jaya hid her smile behind a hand. "Just like that. I'll see you soon."

Grey nodded once, turned again, and walked off.

She watched him go, slicing his way through the crowd. More than a few people stopped to watch him, but he didn't seem to notice. What a waste, she thought. To be born a natural leader, only to feel that you were inherently poisonous, someone to be hidden away at all costs. In spite of herself, she felt a shot of anger toward his father.

*Careful, Jaya*, her internal critic piped up. *You're acting like you actually care about the boy.*

*I don't* care *about him*, she thought scornfully back at the internal critic. *I'm just . . . feeling the normal amount of concern that any human being would feel.*

*Oh, good*, the internal critic said snidely. *What a disaster any* real *feelings would be. Could you imagine?*

*No*, Jaya thought somberly. *I couldn't.*

It was fine. She was here running an errand with Grey, and after this, they didn't need to have any more interactions besides civil, acquaintance-level ones. She'd continue to keep her distance from him in class, she wouldn't walk with him anymore, and she'd make sure Caterina had absolutely nothing to feed Kiran or anyone else back home. She'd do the right thing because she was a Rao princess, and that's what she always did.

Jaya walked to the register a few minutes later, armed with three new books, all the first in series she hadn't read yet. Looking over her shoulder as she paid, Jaya saw Grey loitering by the front door with a bag. He was studying a small stuffed pug on a rotating rack by the door, and she bit back a smile at the sight of the tiny, soft animal in his giant bear paw.

She went up to him and tapped him on the back. He turned and a small smile caressed his lips. Jaya felt a tiny spark of surprised joy; it was one of the few times she'd seen Grey Emerson smile at anyone, let alone her.

"Hey."

"What'd you end up buying?"

They pushed through the glass door and back out into the cold, both of them putting on their coats. Grey pulled a paperback book out of his plastic bag and showed it to her.

"*Napoleon: An Exhaustive History*," she read. "Er, great! I'm glad that looks, ah, interesting to you."

Grey snorted. "Right." He put the book back. "I also got this." Grey pulled out another book, a hardcover this time.

"*Twenty Places to See During Your Gap Year*," Jaya read.

"It's for you," he said gruffly, thrusting it at her. "Just in case you decide, you know, to do it."

Jaya took the book, feeling ridiculously touched. "You . . . you bought this for me?"

"Because of what you told me on the school shopping trip," he said, frowning down at her. "How you think about—"

"I remember," Jaya said softly. "Thank you, Grey. This is very thoughtful."

He waved her off, his cheeks going pink.

In her coat pocket, her cell phone rang. She pulled it out and answered it.

"Princess Jaya? It's Silas from St. Rosetta's Fine Jewelers."

"Oh, hi, Silas." That was fast. She raised her eyebrows. "Is it ready so quickly?"

"I think you'd better come on back to the shop," he said in a strange voice. "I've something to show you."

"Okay." Jaya met Grey's eyes. "We'll be right there."

# Grey

Grey's hands shook while he stood by the spotless glass cases of opulent emerald earrings and blushing garnet rings, waiting for Silas to emerge from the back room. The recessed lighting caused all the gems to twinkle, as if they were winking at him, beckoning him closer. No, thank you. He'd had enough of jewelry to last a lifetime, probably more.

He loosened his uniform tie so he could breathe better, and looked over at Jaya, who smiled hesitantly at him. It had been nice of her to invite him along, especially considering (1) she thought the curse was bullshit and (2) it was *her* necklace.

Things had been different between them since the Aspen shopping trip—less tense, less fake, more real. Jaya wasn't finding reasons to touch him anymore, nor was she laughing that throaty laugh all the time. It was like some barrier of inauthenticity had crumbled between them on that ski slope when they'd yelled at each other. Grey was glad. Dishonesty was one thing he couldn't stand. His father might've been cruel, but he'd never lied to Grey, at least. He'd always been up-front about how he felt about him. Grey respected that.

And somehow, seeing the *real* Jaya Rao, Grey was realizing

a little more every day how much he was coming to enjoy their time together. He was still a misanthrope, but she didn't seem to mind his misanthropic ways. And when he caught sight of her waiting for him after class or in the common room before breakfast, it made him . . . happy. He thought back to the night of the hot tub, or even just to earlier that same day, in the bookstore. For the first time, he was letting himself get closer to a girl. For the first time, he felt like any other dude in high school.

Grey was becoming more aware with every passing day that Jaya was changing him. Maybe because she was the only person who knew every part of him and still wanted to be around him anyway. Bit by bit, she was chipping at the block of stone he'd always surrounded himself with. Bit by bit, she was unearthing who he really was underneath. And to his astonishment, Grey was okay with that. He was kind of excited to see who he was underneath too, even if just briefly.

"Welcome back, Lord Northcliffe, Princess Jaya." Silas walked out just as Grey finished that last thought, snuffing out his brief spark of optimism. He held a big piece of black velvet cloth, folded in half and sandwiched between his hands, and gestured for Grey and Jaya to follow. "Here we are," he said, walking to his mahogany workbench.

Grey's legs felt like Jell-O as he made his way to the bench.

"Hello, Silas. So what seems to be the problem?" Jaya said, watching as he lifted the velvet cloth to reveal the necklace and turned on his work light so they could all see it better. "Wait." She peered closer. "You haven't added in any new rubies."

Grey stayed back and kept his distance, just in case. He could see fine from here.

"No, I haven't," Silas said, a rueful half smile on his face. "But it wasn't from lack of trying." From a drawer, he extracted a small metal box, which he opened with a small key he produced from his pocket. The box held six rubies. "I shall demonstrate for you, Princess." He sat on his stool and adjusted himself in front of the necklace. Next, he applied a dot of jeweler's epoxy into one of the empty sockets. Then, very carefully, using special tweezers, he set one of the rubies into the empty, epoxied socket of the pendant. It was a perfect job; Grey could see no visible imperfections at all. Silas looked up at the both of them appraisingly. "There. Now we'll let it set. Does that look all right?"

Both Jaya and Grey nodded uncertainly.

"Now," Silas said, reaching into an interior pocket for a gold pocket watch. Of course he had a pocket watch. "The epoxy instructions say to let it set for four minutes. We'll give it five just to be sure." He stood and walked to Jaya and Grey, who were standing by a brass statue of a knight.

"But what—" Jaya began.

"You'll see, Princess," Silas said. "Let's give it a few minutes."

"I'm not sure what we're doing," Grey said, trying to keep the impatience out of his voice.

"In just a few moments, Lord Northcliffe, I shall show you."

"Well, this is all very intriguing," Jaya said. "But if the product is defective in some way, I'm sure my father would want to know and take action. It's very important to him that the things he pays for are reliable."

"It's not that the pendant is defective, exactly," Silas said. "But perhaps your father should return it anyhow." He paused. "Are either of you . . . superstitious at all?"

Grey glanced at Jaya and found her looking right at him. He

turned to Silas. "Why do you ask?" he said carefully, keeping his face blank.

"There are many accounts, going back thousands of years, of cursed jewelry. More skeptical minds than mine have referred to these as 'irregular properties,'" Silas said. "The Delhi Purple Sapphire, the Hope Diamond, the La Peregrina Pearl . . . it is not unheard of. I wondered if either of you—"

A phone in the back rang. "Forgive me," Silas said, bowing slightly. "I shall return momentarily." And he walked to the back room again.

Grey turned to Jaya. "I wish he'd just get to the point."

A few minutes later, Silas hurried back, slipping his pocket watch back into his coat pocket. "Thank you for your patience. It's now time for me to show you why I called you here."

"Great," Grey said tightly. Jaya glanced down at his hands, and it was only then that he realized they were shaking again.

They walked with Silas back to the workbench and the necklace. Grey wondered if this was what it felt like being led to the gallows. His footsteps felt leaden; he felt like he must weigh a thousand pounds.

Silas went around the workbench and picked up the pendant very carefully. Then he tipped it over. The ruby, the one he'd set with epoxy, fell out.

"I don't understand," Jaya said. "I thought you used the epoxy to secure the ruby."

"I did, indeed," Silas said, his eyes watchful as he took in their expressions. "And I should note, this is the very same epoxy I use for all my projects. I've used this brand for decades now. It's never *not* worked before."

Grey swallowed and heard the clicking in his dry throat.

"So, what are you trying to say?" Jaya said, shifting beside Grey. Her tone was somewhere between disbelief and defensiveness.

Silas shrugged. "I'm not attempting to convince you of anything, Princess Jaya. I am merely showing you what I have experienced." His light brown eyes slipped to meet Grey's. "What do you make of this, Lord Northcliffe?"

Grey shook his head. He could feel Jaya's gaze on him. "I . . . I think I need some air." He glanced at Jaya quickly. "Will you finish this up and meet me outside?"

She nodded, her brow furrowed. "Are you all right?"

"Fine." He nodded in Silas's direction without quite meeting his eye. "Thank you for meeting with us, Silas. It, ah, must've been something I ate."

"Of course, Lord Northcliffe," Silas murmured.

Grey tried not to run to the door.


He paced outside in the frigid cold as the sun set on the mountains, plunging the world into shades of gold-dusted plum and rose-tinged blue. Why, of all the families in the world, did he have to be born to the Emersons? Not only were his ancestors morally repugnant, but his own father had virtually disowned him, and now . . . For the umpteenth time, Grey wished he could walk away from his life, from his father, from everything that felt like manacles around his wrists and ankles.

If there had been even a sliver of doubt in his mind about the pendant's provenance, it had disappeared completely. It was all true. He lived in a world where nanotechnology and ancient curses lived side by side. Grey barked a laugh, then was immediately afraid that he was losing his mind.

"Grey."

He spun around to see Jaya behind him. She held a small bag, and by its shape and heft, he could tell it held the velvet pouch that in turn held the necklace.

"Don't . . . don't jump to conclusions," she said, edging forward carefully, as if he were a spooked horse.

"The conclusions have already been handed to me," Grey said, pushing an agitated hand through his hair. "No jumping required."

"Grey, what we saw doesn't mean the pendant is cursed—"

"Then how do you explain it?" he asked, rounding on her. "Hmm? We were standing right there, Jaya." He thrust his arm out toward the store. "You saw him apply the epoxy."

She looked up at him, unflinching, her hair streaming behind her like a black silken flag in the cold breeze. "The epoxy was defective."

"The tube was half-gone," Grey said. "Silas said he uses it on all his projects. Don't you think he would've noticed that before?"

Jaya didn't say anything.

Shaking his head, he began to walk away, but Jaya put a hand on his elbow, stilling him. "Grey, please." After a pause, studying his expression, she said, "I'll put it away so you don't have to look at it anymore. Will that help?"

"No," he said quietly. "I want to see it every day. I *need* to see it right now. It's in the darkest corners that things seem the scariest."

"Are you sure?" There was a wrinkle of concern between Jaya's eyebrows. "You want me to put it on right now?"

"Yes," he said. "I want you to put it on right now." Grey took a deep breath and turned on his heel, rubbing a hand along his jaw. "And I also want to get out of here."

Jaya slid the pouch out of the bag and pulled the necklace out carefully. Grey held his breath. It twinkled at him, laughing coyly, darkly, under its breath as Jaya fastened it around her neck and put the velvet pouch away. "Okay?" she asked him.

"Fine," he said curtly. There was the bitter taste of panic in the back of his throat, and he swallowed compulsively, trying to get rid of it. "Let's go find the driver. He should be parked around the building."

He took off down the sidewalk, hearing her footsteps as she hurried to keep up.

# Jaya

Jaya was worried about Grey. She couldn't help but look at him every so often as they walked along the sidewalk, toward the car. She could tell he needed air, and time to think. Yes, it was a little strange, what Silas had shown them. But . . . Jaya shook her head. There *had* to be an explanation of some kind. She glanced down at the pendant. It looked completely innocuous, like all her other jewelry. It was inanimate, powerless.

But she knew Grey was convinced, perhaps because of the messages he'd received since he was a little boy, that the curse was real. She remembered their conversation on the ski slope and her mind automatically went to the messages she and Isha had always received: Princesses are always polite. Princesses do what their families need them to do, not what *they* want to do. Women in royal families cannot be anything they want. Women in royal families must be quiet, virtuous, well behaved, and congenial.

She'd tried not to question them. If she ever felt doubt about any of it, she pushed those doubts away as quickly as possible, as if even *thinking* them was treason. So how was it fair for her to expect Grey to eschew what he'd always been told? And if she expected him to do it, then should she be doing the same?

Feeling discomfited, Jaya pulled her coat around her. *It's not your problem anymore*, she told herself sternly. *The errand is done. It's time to let this go. Grey Emerson is simply an acquaintance from this point on, remember?*

Jaya swallowed as they got to the car and the driver hopped out to open their doors for them. Yes, she remembered right then why getting close to Grey Emerson was a bad idea. The trouble was, she so often forgot when she was gazing into his blue eyes.

Jaya was dreaming. She was attempting to climb a very tall tree, some manner of pine, but she was a quarter of the way up and couldn't find any more limbs to grasp. Appa was on the ground below her, yelling instructions. "On your right! It's right there! Take it!"

"I don't see it!" she yelled back down, but he didn't seem to hear her. He looked livid, she realized, and suddenly she was so nervous, she was trembling. Her knees were knocking together, and the sound echoed through the forest.

*Knock, knock, knock! Knock, knock, knock!*

Slowly, she drifted into semiconsciousness.

Someone was knocking very insistently on her door. Jaya opened her eyes, which felt glued shut, and squinted in the bluish darkness at the clock on her nightstand. It was four in the morning.

"What the hell?" she muttered to herself as she rolled out of bed and padded to the door in her thin nightdress. Surely Amma would understand the need for foul language at a time like this.

Grey stood on the other side, backlit by the light in the hallway. He wore a tight white T-shirt and plaid pajama pants. His hair was mussed; he looked like a big bear who'd just finished hibernating. *Sexy* was the word that popped into Jaya's mind as she took in his well-defined pecs, those enormous biceps that strained against his shirt. Naturally, she banished the word from her mind instantly.

"*Grey?*" she said instead, rubbing her eyes with her fists. Her voice was a croak. "Is everything okay? It's four a.m."

"I know." He paused, his eyes taking in the silk of her nightdress before he cleared his throat and looked away. Jaya felt an answering warmth seep through her. "Can I come in?"

"Oh. Yes." She waved him in, and he lumbered over to her window. "Look!" he said when she shut the door and just stood there, still sleep-dazed. His voice shimmered with a barely suppressed energy. "You have to see this."

Jaya pulled herself forward, wrapping her arms around herself. It was freezing. "What do you want me to see so bad—oh. Oh my."

The world had turned a soft, glowing white. Heavy curtains of snow were falling from the sky, the flakes thick and white and fluffy. The school grounds were already covered; the tree boughs bent and dipped. Jaya's windowsill had racked up a thick layer of snow, like cake frosting.

It had been a week since they'd picked up the necklace at Silas's. While Jaya had fully intended to devolve their interactions to mere acquaintance level, somehow she'd found herself unable to. She'd made rationalizations and justifications for her weakness—now that Caterina had Daph's text confession, surely she'd focus her energies on that and not on Jaya; she was just being kind to Grey because he was taking the news from Silas so hard; what was she supposed to do, admonish him like a stray dog when he walked with her after class?

And yet, through the mist of excuses, Jaya knew the truth. The more she saw of Grey—the *real* Grey, the one who made jokes and sarcastic comments and spoke about his fears of the curse—the more she liked him. Truly, truly liked him. And she hadn't been brave enough yet to contemplate the implications of that for her, as a Rao heiress, or for her parents, back home.

Sometimes she thought of the plan she'd first formed when she'd found out he attended St. Rosetta's. Whenever she did, shame threatened to engulf her. A few times, she'd considered telling Grey the truth about it all. But then she realized he wasn't the kind of person who'd take the news well. He was already so guarded, so expectant that the world would hurt him, and she didn't want him to retreat back into his ten-foot-thick shell. She was enjoying being the person he told when he made an A on the biology test he thought he'd failed. Was there really any point to telling him about the plan? What good would it do, really? She just wanted to put it behind her. Let the past be the past. Grey already had so many things on his mind.

"The first snowfall," Grey said, as if to her point. His voice carried a thread of so much poignant pain that Jaya was struck speechless for a moment. Her hand flew to her pendant in the next. Two more rubies had fallen in the night, leaving only ten rubies. "I wanted you to see it with me." He glanced down at her. "I know that sounds silly, but . . . my birthday's only a month away now."

"It's not silly," Jaya said, taking his fingers in hers and squeezing them just once and very briefly, knowing physical touch unsettled him. But when she began to let go, he tightened his fingers around hers slightly, and so she held on, her heart thudding in her chest. They were holding hands. Grey *wanted* to hold her hand.

They looked at each other in silence.

"Time's passing so quickly," Grey said, turning back to the glass. "Too quickly." After a beat, he added, "This snow feels like a harbinger of something."

"Then it must be a harbinger of something good," Jaya said firmly. "This is . . . magical," she added in a whisper, her breath fogging the glass. Jaya turned to him in the dim glow of the moon reflecting off all that white sparkling snow. "Thank you for waking me." As she spoke, the strap of her nightgown slipped down over one shoulder. She pushed it back up, her cheeks warm.

Grey's eyes were hooded in the darkness. "Will you go for a walk with me?"

Jaya studied his expression, so intense, so focused. She knew she shouldn't go with him; there would be no easy way to return from where he was inviting her. If she wanted to draw a hard line, if she wanted to place her responsibilities ahead of her heart, now was the time to do it. Now was the time to remember herself. She could do this. She could tell Grey Emerson no.

"Of course I'll go," Jaya whispered, her pulse pounding a warning she was too far gone to abide.

CHAPTER 14

# Jaya

They washed quickly and bundled up—Grey went to his room to do it—and stepped outside together. The world was asleep. It felt decadent, the air redolent with mystery, to be out at this time of night with a boy who felt like he'd stepped out of the pages of a fairy tale, whole and breathing.

Jaya tipped her head back and caught a snowflake on her tongue. "Yummy." Her voice was muffled, like someone was holding a scarf over her mouth. "I love that," she said, turning to Grey, who was watching her with a half smile on his face. "How the snow makes you sound quieter."

"When was the last time you saw it? Before Aspen, I mean?" he asked, sinking his boots into a fresh pile of snow.

"Two years ago, when we were in a boarding school in Amsterdam. That winter, we went to Switzerland with my parents. We stayed in a really cozy Swiss chalet and read books the entire time. No phone calls, no meetings, no one we didn't want to be around."

It had been one of Jaya's favorite holidays. Isha said the chalet reminded her of a gingerbread house. Appa was done with business earlier than he'd predicted, so they'd spent time together as a family for almost the entire two weeks they were there. Jaya remembered how, one night, their housekeeper had made them all creamy hot cocoas. The four of them had curled up in front of the fire and read their books in complete silence for hours. Jaya had never felt closer to her family, which was odd because they weren't even talking. Still, she'd felt herself go soft and pliable, like her edges were melting into theirs, like they were all just one heart beating in symphony.

Jaya blinked away the memory, feeling a sudden pang for her family, for that time of innocence and happiness. What would they think of her now, outside in the middle of the night with an Emerson?

"That sounds really nice." Grey looked at her, his thick, dark eyelashes dusted with snowflakes. The yearning in his voice was masked, but undeniable.

"I'm sorry you never had that with your father," Jaya said, hesitating just a moment before putting a hand on his.

He didn't pull away. "Thanks."

Her heart thudded at the look in his eyes, at the silence between them. After a pause, Jaya took her hand from his and said, "You're . . . different now."

Grey began to press his boots into snowdrifts again. "Yeah."

"What changed?"

He glanced at her, just for a moment. "You know what changed."

"Telling me about the curse?" Jaya guessed.

"That. And . . ." Grey looked at her more fully now. "You've changed too," he said frankly. They began to walk together, deeper into the trees. "After our blow-up in Aspen. You're less . . . blinky."

"Blinky?" Jaya said, raising an eyebrow. But then she knew in the next instant what he meant. He was talking about all her faux flirting before, when she was still executing her plan. Blinky. It was a less than flattering description. And not just that, but it made her feel . . . a little revolted at herself. She'd been trying so hard to "trap" Grey that even he'd felt it.

"Right," she said, laughing a little to cover up her discomfort. Should she tell him the truth about everything? Now would be a good time. But he'd literally *just* told her he was changing because of her. How could she tell him she'd gotten close to him in the first place only because she wanted to completely shatter his heart? How would that make him feel?

A sudden wind tried to make off with her scarf. Jaya shrieked, but Grey grabbed it just in time. Turning to her, he slowly draped the scarf back around her neck, his blue eyes holding hers, her skin coming alive everywhere his fingers touched. They gazed at each other for a long moment, Jaya's eyes falling unwittingly to his lips.

"Grey," she said, her voice breathless as she looked up at him. "You know the one thing I've missed the most about snow?"

He shook his head, his hands still on her scarf. "No, what?" he murmured.

She could *feel* the wicked gleam in her eye. Bending down, Jaya rolled up a snowball with the speed of lightning and lobbed it at Grey's torso. It exploded on contact, sending snow flying into his face and hair. "Snowball fights!"

"Hey!" he said, his eyes going wide. While she was busy laughing at him, he dumped two entire handfuls of snow on her head. *Big* handfuls.

"What the—" she spluttered, caught completely off guard.

She heard Grey laughing, snow crunching under his boots as he ran. She blinked the snow out of her eyes. "You'd better run, Grey Emerson! Because when I find you—" A snowball hit her, squarely in the chin this time, ice-cold precipitation going down her jacket and the front of her shirt. More laughing from behind the pine trees up ahead. "Oh, that is *it*!" Jaya said, rolling a snowball of what could only be described as epic proportions.

She ran off into the trees to the right and took cover, scanning the darkness for movement. They were about ten feet apart now. There was a crunching sound and a flash of Grey's red jacket. Jaya took aim and launched her snowball—catching him in the shoulder.

"Ha!" she yelled, triumphant. "Take that!"

Another flash of red, creeping closer to her. She rolled up another snowball and threw it, but it hit a tree. Jaya moved to another tree and silently picked up another snowball. Her heart was racing, her cheeks flushed with gleeful competition. Stepping backward, Jaya scanned the trees in front of her for the slightest movement, the sly snap of a twig or—

Grey grabbed her suddenly around the waist and bent down to speak in her ear. "Gotcha."

Grinning, she spun around in his arms and ground the snowball into his beanie, her hands coming to rest on his shoulders, her fingers brushing the back of his neck. "I'm counting that as a hit," she said. "Which means we're now tied."

"I guess so," Grey conceded as Jaya leaned back against the tree behind her, her heart racing with exertion and . . . something else. He stepped forward, his arms still around her waist.

Jaya tipped her head back, both of them breathing hard. He tucked a lock of hair that had escaped her hat behind her ear, his fingers lingering on the spot just below her ear. A brisk wind whistled through the trees, making her shiver. Grey stepped closer still, blocking the wind, his body heat enveloping her.

Jaya's smile faded as she saw the embers glowing in his eyes.

When their lips met, embers turned to flame. Jaya wrapped her arms around Grey's neck and he pulled her taut against his broad chest. He hadn't shaved yet that morning, and she felt his stubble scraping her lips, her jaw, her cheeks. Where before he'd been reticent and withdrawn, now he nipped at her lips with his teeth, pushing hard against her mouth, claiming her as his own in that wild, feral way. It was like every feeling, every hidden craving he'd kept behind his immovable mask was now out in the open, flooding every synapse. He'd finally lost control, and that knowledge drove Jaya mad. Their tongues clashed together, vying for control, two sworn enemies from feuding clans in each other's arms, overcome with desire. Jaya's blood sang, her body a symphony of longing. She was liquid fire, a drop of molten heat in his arms. In the darkness, with the snow swirling around them, she was sure she was on a tropical island, the sun blazing on her skin.

# Grey

They both pulled back at the same time, their eyes wide. Jaya's hand flew to her mouth as she stepped out of his arms, beside the tree. "I'm sorry," she said. She took a step back closer to him, and he wasn't even sure if she knew she was doing it. "I'm really sorry."

He didn't back away, like he knew he should. Like he'd done

before, in the hot tub or the bookstore. This time, he wanted to feel her soft, warm weight against him. This time, he didn't want to stop it. "Apology accepted." They studied each other in the near dark.

Jaya inched closer, just a breath away from him now. Before he could process it, she had her arms wrapped around his neck and he was bending down to brush her lips with his again.

She began to hungrily deepen the kiss, her soft lips parting, inviting his tongue in, her quick, panting breaths mingling with his. Grey tightened his arms around her waist, wanting to get closer, tasting her, letting himself be lost in her.

Something buzzed between them, insistent. It stopped, then started again. Finally, Jaya pulled back. "Sorry," she said, her voice husky, her lips slightly swollen from their kiss. "Let me just . . ." She pulled her cell from her coat pocket and looked at the screen. *Appa* flashed on the screen. Her father, calling so early? Jaya frowned a little. He must be confused about the time change.

"Do you need to get that?" Grey asked.

She looked up at him for a long moment, her eyes searching his, weighing something. Then she slid to reject the call, slipped the phone back into her pocket, and stepped back into his arms.

Grey's heart leaped with a happiness he didn't know was possible.

# Jaya

Grey rested his forehead on hers. They stood there in the snow, letting the white flakes cover them like confetti. Jaya smiled. She felt strange, exhilarated and full of wonder and filled with helium somehow.

"You know, when I first found out you were in all my classes, I thought it was a pretty weird coincidence. I was kind of suspicious, in fact."

Jaya's pulse pounded. "Really?" she asked, gazing into his eyes.

"Yeah, but now . . . now I think it was fate. If it was a sign, it was a sign of something really, really good." He smiled so brilliantly, he lit up the dark.

Jaya forced herself to smile back. How could she tell him the truth about why she was in all his classes and snatch his joy away? Was it really the most terrible thing in the world if he believed that it was all a sign from the universe? She leaned in and kissed him again, soft and slow, letting her body tell him everything she couldn't—that although she'd come here with bad intentions, she genuinely, truly cared about him now. She let her mouth tell him how much she wanted him; she let her thudding heartbeat reiterate that she would never, ever hurt him.

"So what now?" Grey asked when they broke apart, his voice barely more than a whisper. "Are we . . . dating?"

Jaya looked up at him, to see his eyes shining blue in the dark. "I don't know," she said, and then she heard herself laugh softly. "I don't know. How could I ever explain this to my father?" It was ridiculous! An Emerson and a Rao? Her parents would never understand. No one would. It was a terrible, terrible idea for so many reasons. And yet . . . yet somehow all she wanted to do right now was call everyone she knew and tell them how she felt about Grey.

"I guess we don't have to make any decisions right now," Grey said, but he was smiling a smile made of hope and excitement, one that mirrored hers.

"I guess for now we could just walk together," Jaya said, taking his hand and leading him onto a fresh path through the trees.

"Just walk together," Grey said in wonderment. "That sounds good."

Jaya lay in bed, smiling. She'd have to be up in an hour, and she'd only just gotten in from her walk with Grey, but she didn't even care how tired she'd be for the rest of the day. That kiss, her first-ever kiss (and then her second and her third), kept replaying in her head. The way Grey had looked at her, his eyes so hungry, so languid. The way he'd pressed his hands against her lower back, pushing her against him, his mouth warm and perfect.

It was ridiculous and bizarre and made as much sense as that leopard that had adopted an orphaned fawn as its own. Grey Emerson and Jaya Rao didn't belong together. Not on paper, anyway. But somehow, over the last two months, she'd begun to see that in many ways, she and Grey had more in common than she had with most other people. In many ways, they were cut from the same odd cloth.

But how on earth would she begin to tell people they wanted to date, not least of all her parents? What would the people of Mysuru think of their heiress running around with an Emerson? What about the alliance the Raos and the Hegdes had been counting on all these years? How could she ever be a revered ruler, one who appeared respectful of tradition, if she did something so outlandish? She couldn't; it was madness.

Jaya turned on her side, eyes gazing into the near darkness. On the heels of that thought, another, quieter one: But it could work, couldn't it? This didn't *have* to mean she was choosing

Grey over loyalty to her family or over her responsibility to her kingdom. She could show her family what she saw, that he had nothing to do with the scandal. That he was innocent. Besides, Isha liked Grey. . . . Perhaps she could be Jaya's "in" with their parents. And Jaya could show the people of Mysuru that she could date an Emerson and still be the heiress they needed. It would be difficult and challenging, but she wasn't afraid of hard work. Jaya could pull it off; she was sure of it. Most of all, Grey needed her. And she needed him.

Jaya laughed quietly in the dark, one hand going to her mouth, as if she were afraid someone might hear her joy and try to steal it. It was ludicrous and made her giddy and slightly dizzy, as if she were on the world's fastest, highest, swoopiest roller coaster. She had no idea how this could work, only that she desperately, desperately wanted it to.

On her nightstand, her phone buzzed to remind her she had an unheard voice mail. Oh, right. Appa had called her, hadn't he? She felt a brief flare of guilt at the memory of having rejected his call to get back to kissing Grey. Calling her so early in the morning, too . . . that was unusual for him. He didn't usually get the time zone so wrong. Picking up the phone, she hit the "listen" button.

And grew still as her father's rapidly spoken words filled her ear.

When she was finished listening, she let the hand holding the phone drop slowly to her lap and sat staring in the lifting darkness of early morning. As the minutes drifted down on her, collecting by her feet, forming sandcastles of time, Jaya's mind kept fighting what she'd heard. What her father had said. And what she was slowly coming to realize she had to do.

*There* has *to be a different way*, her inner critic insisted, sallow and worried, pacing the length of Jaya's mind. *Something else you haven't thought of, some workaround—*

But there wasn't. Jaya turned her head to look out the window at the lightening sky wearing streaks of gold in its hair. There was only one right answer, and she had to be brave enough to choose it.

# Grey

Grey stood on Mount Sama, watching Jaya make her way up the incline. He had a smile on his face that wouldn't go away, just imagining taking her into his arms and kissing her again, like they had last night.

His tie whipped over his shoulder in the wind and he tugged it back into place. What happened early this morning had been . . . a gift. Something he'd never dared picture for himself. Kissing a girl he really, really liked? He'd barely slept once he got back to his room, his mind turning over what had happened in brilliant color.

Then Jaya had texted him an hour ago, just before their first class, to ask if he'd meet her somewhere to talk. He'd suggested going together, but she said she had some things to do. She probably wanted to discuss the logistics of their . . . of them. Grey knew his days were limited; his eighteenth birthday was a month away. But the idea of spending the remaining weeks with someone he really cared about felt . . . It felt indescribable. It felt like the universe was finally, finally letting him have a sliver of happiness. And a minuscule part of him, one that he was too afraid of fully tuning in to, wondered if the universe might give him a pass on the curse, too. What if his life *didn't* end on his eighteenth birthday? What if Jaya was a signal of good things to come? Maybe it was just wishful thinking. But it was the first time in a long time Grey felt anything close to optimistic.

Jaya walked out onto the plateau, breathing hard, and Grey walked forward, smiling. "Hey."

She didn't smile back. There were dark circles under her eyes, and her hair wasn't nearly as neatly done as it usually was. "Hello, Grey."

He frowned, concerned. "Are you okay?"

Jaya huddled into her coat; it was zipped up to her throat, as usual, whereas Grey's was unzipped. "Thank you for meeting me here."

Grey studied her expression, but it was hard to read. "Sure." He didn't say anything else; he could sense that she needed the time to gather her thoughts. Grey's palms felt coated with ice.

Jaya walked a few steps away and leaned against a giant granite boulder. There was more space between them now. He turned slowly to face her. "Grey . . ." She swallowed, looked away, looked back at him. "Grey, what happened early this morning can't happen again."

His stomach dropped, as if he were falling from a very great height. "You . . . you changed your mind? About me?"

She flinched as if his words had a physical force. "No—I—I can't . . ." Taking a deep breath, Jaya spoke in a more controlled voice. "We can't be together."

"Why not?" he heard himself ask, in a voice that was rough as the rock they stood on.

# *Jaya*

*Why not?* There had never been a harder question in the history of the universe. And there had never been a simpler one.

Ignoring her heart, which felt like it was turning to stone in her chest, Jaya said, "We come from different worlds, Grey. I was foolish to forget that. I lost my head a bit this morning, but . . ." She blinked a few times, hoping he'd think she'd stopped talking to gather her thoughts and not because she was as dangerously close to tears as she really was. When she had a hold on herself again, she continued. "I've had a bit of family news from home. And it made me realize that—that what we were doing was childish. It was selfish. You're an Emerson. I'm a Rao. It couldn't ever work."

"That's it?" Grey said quietly. His blue eyes were searing, flaying her open, but she held steady. "You're just going to give up on this because we're from different worlds? Don't you think we're worth it, Jaya?"

Though his words were said with his characteristic detachment, Jaya detected a tremor just underneath. She knew he was masking his pain just as she was masking hers, and it took every ounce of strength she had to not run over to him and bury her face in his chest. She looked out over the edge of the mountain at the town of St. Rosetta, metal and glass glinting in the sunlight. "I'm sorry," she said. "My first duty is to my family and my people."

There was a long pause.

"Right," Grey said finally. When she looked at him, he was looking down at the town too, his jaw hard, his posture tense and stiff. He was shielding himself, she realized. He was shielding himself from her because she was hurting him. The thought made her want to scream. "Okay, then." He turned back to her after another moment. "Well, thanks for the courtesy of letting me know."

Without waiting for a response, he began to make his way back down the path to the bottom of the mountain, away from her.

"I'm sorry," she said softly to his retreating back. But the wind snatched her words from her mouth and flung them over the edge of the mountain and into the empty sky.

Jaya called in sick to the rest of her classes that day. When she got back to her room on legs that felt like pillars of cement, she called her father.

"Jaya," Appa said, alert even though it was the middle of the night for him. He likely wasn't sleeping much either. "Did you get my message?"

"I did." Jaya noticed remotely that her voice sounded robotic, as if she weren't fully human at all. There was so much pain flooding every nerve fiber that it appeared her brain had responded by shutting down all feeling completely. Grey's blue eyes, full of a deep hurt, full of rejection, flashed in her mind, and she turned away, toward the window, to stare at the rolling snow-covered hills with a focused intensity. It was impossible to believe where the day had taken her, where it had started. Her mind went blank again. "I've been thinking about everything you said. Sorry I didn't call back sooner."

"I just don't know what to do. The situation is—I've never seen it this bad before. That bloody journalist published another piece about Isha, about how she's—she's—"

"Pregnant," Jaya finished for him, in that robotic voice.

"Yes." Her father exhaled. "Supposedly that's why I sent you girls away so suddenly. They just won't let the story die! Why can't they just let it be? Our people are so angry. The invitation Amma had to a major political event in Mumbai is being rescinded—Jaya, we're losing footing."

"Yes, you said that," Jaya said, a distant part of her concerned at just how stressed her father sounded. She'd never heard him this way, so on edge, so thrown. "And you'd mentioned the Hegdes. They're getting cold feet?"

"Yes, yes." Her father took a shaky breath. "They say they're still on board for an alliance, but I could see it in their eyes—it's only a matter of time before they change their mind. And without their confidence in us, without their partnership . . . We stand to lose everything, Jaya. Our political position, everything generations of Raos have stood for, gone. Because of a complete lie." He paused. "It *is* a lie . . . ?"

"Yes, of course it is," Jaya said, shocked that Appa was even asking. Evidence, perhaps, of just how serious the accusations were.

"The first story about her wasn't," Appa mused. He took a breath. "Anyway, I don't mean to burden you with this while you're away, but—"

"But I'm the eldest daughter. The heiress." Jaya nodded, putting one palm up against the cold pane of glass. "I know, Appa."

"You're eighteen now," he said. "I think it's about time you took a more active part in what's going on with the dynasty."

"I agree. And I think I have a solution." Jaya's heart pounded against her rib cage, as if in protest. She ignored it.

"A solution?" Appa sounded more alert now. "What is it?"

Jaya closed her eyes. "My engagement to Kiran Hegde."

# Grey

Grey paced the length of the West Wing tower, the cold seeping out of the stones and into his bones. On the school grounds in the distance, he saw students in colorful coats and jackets sprinkled across the snow-covered grass like confetti. Laughing, talking, going about their day. He stood above them, apart, alone, trying to understand what had just happened.

He hadn't been prepared for the pain. Grey had forgotten what it meant, to care about people, to let them have the power to hurt you. He'd let her in; he'd given her the keys to his heart and she'd tossed them carelessly over her shoulder and walked away.

Grey screwed his eyes shut. Maybe he'd misunderstood. Maybe he'd let himself feel so deeply, but to her, it had always been a shallow dalliance. It was just a kiss. He was just a boy. Nothing more.

Or perhaps she'd reconsidered, come to see just how damaged he really was. Perhaps she knew someone like him didn't belong with someone like her.

Roaring to release the valve on his agony, Grey slammed his fists into the indifferent stone walls. How could he have been so stupid? How could he have *ever* thought she could love someone like him? He was an animal, a beast, and he deserved to die as he had lived—alone.

# Jaya

"Your engagement?" Appa said, sounding taken aback.

"Yes. Announce that preparations for the engagement are underway. Let the papers talk about that, how lavish the engagement ceremony will be, what we'll be wearing, how big the feast will be. Have one of the papers interview the Hegdes. People'll get sidetracked. It'll show everyone the Hegdes are very much still on board with allying with the Raos. And . . . and it'll keep the Hegdes from changing their minds. The announcement for the upcoming engagement has to be immediate, or it won't work." She swallowed and began to pace her room again.

"But, Jaya—you're still in school!"

"We won't actually be engaged until June, after I graduate. We'll need that long to get the palace ready anyway. But the buzz, the conversation, needs to happen now."

"I don't want you rushing into anything," Appa countered. "It's too fast."

"It's not too fast," Jaya forced herself to say. "I've known Kiran and I were meant to get married for years now. We're just speeding the timeline up a bit. It's for our family, Appa. It's for our kingdom. This is the right thing to do, and I want to do it. There's no other solution. You know it as well as I do."

"Well . . . okay. If you're sure, Jaya." Already Appa sounded less stressed. He saw what she did—that a royal engagement, the Hegdes with the Raos, would immediately turn the tide. People would be talking about the upcoming engagement and wedding, and nothing else, for the next couple of years. Isha's scandal would get buried in the avalanche.

"I'm sure," she said. "I'll call you soon to talk about the details."

Jaya ended the call and placed the phone on her dresser. To think that only a week ago she'd been concerned with bribing the journalist in Mysuru for more information, so she could continue to execute her revenge plan against whoever it was that had started all this. Jaya smirked. That was the least of her worries now. This was triage; she had to stem the blood, to revive her dynasty. Even if it meant binding herself to Kiran forever.

She studied her reflection in the mirror, her bloodshot eyes, the dark half-moons under her eyes, the unruly hair falling out of its ponytail. It shocked her to see that she almost didn't recognize the haggard, sallow young woman in the mirror. What weapons did she have at her disposal to protect her family from a crushing fate? Nothing at all, except her engagement to Kiran. Jaya blinked. She looked, she realized, utterly resigned to an end she didn't want, like someone with a grave and incurable illness . . . like Grey had looked standing over her dresser, when she'd found him in her room.

Jaya's gaze drifted to the ruby pendant, nearly half emptied of its treasure now. Was this how the curse worked? Had she been pulled into its orbit because of how she felt about Grey? Was it real after all? She knew it was her broken heart, her bleak future that made her question this. But still, one truth she couldn't deny: the rubies continued to fall. Only eight remained.

# Grey

Somehow a week passed, even though each day felt like a cold, flat copy of the one before it. Grey had an image of colorless ice cubes in endless white trays and blinked it away.

They were in physics, and he was sitting diagonally behind Jaya. He kept his eyes focused steadily on the whiteboard on which Mr. Martinez was writing something illegible, but sometimes, without his permission, his gaze would drift over to her, lingering on her hair, her shoulders, the way she gripped her pen. Her posture gave nothing away. He had no idea how she was feeling, or even *if* she was feeling anything.

But he knew the answer to that. No, she wasn't. If she felt even an iota of the pain he did, she would never have been able to do what she had. He was dispensable to her, just like he'd been to his father. There must be something inherently wrong with Grey's makeup that made people react to him that way. Was it the curse? Or had he been born this way? Gripping the edges of his desk, Grey turned his eyes back to his book and stared unseeingly at its pages.

# Jaya

Once the bell tinkled, signaling the end of class, Jaya watched Grey get up abruptly from his desk and cut his way through the crowd of students to the door, not looking back at her once. The entire class period, she'd held herself so stiffly, feeling his gaze on her skin as if it were his touch. She wanted so badly to turn to him, to take his hand, to place her ear against his chest and listen to the thudding of his heart. To ask him if his world, too, was soaked in tears and going up in flames.

She picked up her phone and looked at the email her father had sent her that morning. It was the copy of the engagement ceremony announcement that would run in the Mysuru papers that weekend.

*Maharaja Adip Rao and Maharani Parvati Rao announce with pleasure the upcoming engagement of their eldest daughter, Rajkumari Jaya Rao, to the heir of the Hegde house, Kiran Hegde, son of Maharaja Dilip Hegde and Maharani Aruna Hegde. The engagement ceremony will take place at the Rao palace in June, on an auspicious date to be determined by the palace astrologer. There will be a grand feast for all the people in the districts governed by the Raos and the Hegdes. Arrangements for the propitious event will begin soon.*

This was it; this was what she needed to do. Even though her world was on fire, Jaya felt an innate sense of calmness, that she was doing what her obligations and responsibilities dictated she must. This would show her people once more that the Raos were fit to govern them. This would save the Rao estate, one that had been managed so painstakingly, so lovingly, for many generations before her. This would ensure generations after hers would still know the joy of taking care of their beloved city. She would save her family, her dynasty, and her name in one fell swoop. She would make it right again.

Jaya got up slowly from her desk, putting her phone and her books back into her bag. She was at the beginning of a long, endless tunnel, with nowhere to go but forward.

# *Jaya*

It was a Saturday in November, more than a week since she'd made the decision to get engaged to Kiran. They'd had a short conversation a few days ago, mostly about the semantics of it all and when her high school semester would be over exactly. This wasn't a romantic move for either of them, and Jaya knew that. The cold practicality suited her new reality just fine.

It was now time to tell Isha about the engagement before the announcement ran tomorrow and their relatives began to reach out. Jaya finally felt able to talk about it to her sister, though she knew it wouldn't be an easy conversation, in part because she was still so raw herself. She didn't hold Isha responsible in any way for the engagement—this was simply something Jaya needed to do for the greater good, even if it meant hurting others she cared deeply about. Without her permission, Grey's face flashed into her mind, as it did many dozens of times each day, and she pushed it away. She wondered if this pain would haunt her for the rest of her life, like a long-ago broken arm that still ached when you bumped it against something.

Jaya sat at a table in a sunlit corner of A-caf-demy Bistro with Isha. The café was too bright with light and color, and the baristas behind the industrial-style counters were smiling garish smiles that made Jaya want to squint.

"So, how are you, Ish?" she asked, forcing her mind to the task at hand. "I feel like we haven't spent a lot of time together these past couple of weeks."

Isha took a sip of her cappuccino and wiped her foam mustache away with the back of her hand. Jaya winced, but didn't say anything. She didn't quite have the energy. "I know! Life has been so crazy. But I'm loving St. Rosetta's. I've made so many friends!"

"I'm glad you're happy," Jaya said, picking up her chai latte and taking a sip. "This is just what you needed. A change of pace."

"Yeah." Isha nodded heartily. "So, how's Grey?"

Jaya felt such an exquisite ache rack her frame that, for a full moment, she couldn't speak.

Isha frowned. "Are you okay?"

"Fine," Jaya managed to say. "I'm fine. Why are you asking me about . . . Grey?"

"Well, you said you were keeping an eye on him, right? And I've seen you guys walking to and from class together. Plus, you sit at his table and are friends with all his friends." She paused, as if she were unsure. "I just meant . . . how's all that going?"

Jaya took another sip of her chai latte. "It's . . . I've decided to stop all of that. Because I have some very important news."

Isha raised her eyebrows, expectant.

"Ish, I've decided to get engaged to Kiran Hegde." Jaya realized her palms were damp, and wondered why she was so nervous.

Isha stared at her for a moment. "What?" She set her cappuccino down with a crash, some of the coffee slopping over the side and onto the table. "*Now?* But . . . but why?"

"It's as good a time as any," Jaya said, folding her paper napkin into smaller and smaller squares. She'd once read that you couldn't fold a napkin more than eight times before the stress made further folds impossible. "The Raos allying with the Hegdes was always the plan."

"Yes, but why now?" Isha said. "You're not even done with high school!"

"Well, we won't be getting engaged until the summer," Jaya said. A barista came by to wipe down the table next to them and she waited until he was gone. "You know engagements happen with great pomp and circumstance in our part of the world; they take almost as much planning as weddings do. It's not just a matter of Kiran getting down on one knee and asking the question. So we're just announcing it now—getting the process started, as it were." And getting people talking about something besides Isha.

"But, Jaya . . ."

Jaya waited.

"Why—why don't you just wait a few more years? Or even, like, never?" Isha pinged her fingernail on her mug as she spoke.

There was no way she was going to tell Isha the truth about why she was hurrying. Her little sister didn't need to know that the scandal had continued to grow, like a malevolent fire that gobbled up the oxygen in the air and refused to die. Besides, she didn't want Isha to feel like any of this was her fault. It wasn't. This was about duty.

Jaya shook her head. "I'm ready now," she said. "I've already given Appa the okay. Amma's made about twenty calls today, trying to coordinate things already."

Isha took a thoughtful sip of her cappuccino. "You and Kiran."

Jaya nodded. "Yes."

"Kiran and Jaya Hegde."

Jaya swallowed the lump in her throat. "Mm-hmm."

"Jaya . . . are you happy with this decision?"

"I was the one who made this decision." Jaya hoped Isha wouldn't see the sidestep.

"But you and *Kiran*? Isn't that like marrying your actuary or something? To be honest, I thought—" She stopped short and looked at Jaya, a little abashed.

"You thought what?" Jaya asked, curious.

"I thought that you and Grey were . . ." Isha shrugged.

Jaya looked away for a moment. "Well," she said finally. "We're not. Kiran and I have some commonalities that Grey and I don't. This is what I must do as the heiress, Isha. It's what's best for the dynasty."

Isha sighed. "The rules are different for royals," she said quietly, parroting a line Jaya had said to her many a time.

"That's right." Jaya put her hand on her sister's. "They are. It's the way our world is." And they sat sipping their drinks, each of them feeling the weight of responsibility and expectation.

# CHAPTER 15
## Jaya

Later that evening, Jaya sat in an oversize papasan chair in Daphne Elizabeth's room, reading one of the books Jaya had picked up at Bookingham Palace in a happier time. The winter wind gusted in the pines and aspens outside the window as she huddled deeper into the chair, willing herself to be lost in the war scene she was reading. Once again, books were proving to be a solace.

Daphne Elizabeth was, at the moment, trying on and discarding outfit after outfit at her closet. "Hey, you know, Grey's going to Caterina's yacht gala next weekend too," she said. "I convinced him to."

Jaya looked up reluctantly from the dueling dragons on the page. "Yes, Leo told me." Daphne Elizabeth and Leo had tried every possible trick they knew to get Jaya to tell them what was happening. Jaya hadn't asked, but she guessed Grey was being just as tight-lipped as she was.

She didn't want to tell them about the engagement because she didn't want it to get back to Grey. And she didn't want to tell Grey because . . . because there was no point. What would be the benefit of torturing him with the details of why, exactly, she'd said they couldn't be together? This way, maybe it would be more of a clean break for him. She'd stopped things before they became too serious and now Grey could move on. He might be angry with her, he might come to hate her with time, but he'd move on. She could deal with everything else.

Daphne Elizabeth turned to her, holding a glittery black skirt on a padded silk hanger. "Is there any chance you might want to . . . reconcile with him? Because I think he'd be open to it—"

"Daph, we've already talked about this." Jaya tried to unhear her words. She didn't want to know Grey was open to it. She needed to be steel, hard and strong and steadfast. She couldn't afford to weaken. "Please."

"I'm sorry," Daph said, putting her skirt back in the closet and picking up a pink velvet top instead. "I just don't get it."

"It would never work." Jaya picked at a loose thread on the papasan cushion. "We're too different."

"I know, and I know what a pain in the ass Grey can be, but seriously, Jaya, I've never seen either of you happier than when you were tog—"

Jaya held up a hand, her heart squeezing in pain. But taking a page from Grey's book, she kept her face an impassive mask. "If you can't stop talking about it, I'll have to leave."

Daph looked abashed. "I'm sorry. I know. I can stop, I promise." Turning to her closet, she said, "I have literally *nothing* to wear," and immediately contradicted her statement by pulling out yet another article of clothing, this time a dress.

"I think that one looks really nice." Jaya gestured to the red-and-green gown in Daphne Elizabeth's hands, feeling a rush of relief for the change in topic. "Is it Gucci?"

"Yes, but it's totally wrong for this! I don't want to look like a Christmas decoration at a twenties-themed charity event in November! Especially not one thrown by you-know-who."

"Fair point."

Caterina had slipped thick embossed invitations to a twenties-themed yacht gala under the doors of all the seniors just an hour before. Jaya couldn't help but feel a little disquieted by it all. What game was she playing? Whatever it was, Jaya hadn't been given a rulebook. To be honest, she wasn't so sure Caterina would ever forgive her, even if Caterina should logically only be angry with Alaric and Daphne Elizabeth. Jaya had underestimated the consequences of rejecting her when she was vulnerable. Still, now that she and Grey were no longer speaking, Caterina would have no more ammunition, at least. The thought should've brought Jaya some relief, but it didn't. "She still hasn't texted you back, right?"

Daphne Elizabeth looked at her, distressed. "No, she hasn't reached out to me at all! Apparently, she just wants to pretend the text never happened."

"Hmm." This was very unusual behavior for someone like Caterina. Very, very unusual.

"I've asked Alaric about it so many times," Daph continued, "but he just keeps saying she doesn't want to talk about it. He told me I should just forget about it and move on."

Jaya knew she shouldn't say anything. It wasn't the diplomatic thing to do. But she felt a swell of irritation too powerful to ignore. "And you're okay with that?" Closing her book, she set it aside. "Come on, Daph. Can't you see what Alaric's doing here?"

Daphne Elizabeth frowned. "No, what?"

Jaya threw up her hands. Was Daph really that dim? Or was she just choosing the coward's way out, refusing to see what was right in front of her because it was easy? Because it got her what she wanted? It infuriated Jaya that she wouldn't do the honorable thing. "He's manipulating you! I haven't been here that long, but even I know that Caterina wouldn't just ignore a text like that. He's obviously lying to you or her or very likely the both of you! You're in such deep denial!"

"*Denial?*" Bright spots of red appeared on Daphne Elizabeth's pale cheeks. "He's shared so much of himself with me, Jaya. You obviously don't understand."

Jaya made a reflexive disgusted face before she could stop herself.

"What?" Daphne Elizabeth yelled. "What's the face about?"

"He's a gobshite, Daph!" Jaya couldn't help but say. She hopped up from the chair and began to pace. "And there are more important things than just going after what *you* want and doing what makes *you* happy. Sometimes you have to sacrifice your happiness for someone else, for something else bigger than you! I don't know how to get you to see that!"

Jaya stared at Daph for a long moment, blinking, not able to believe she'd really just yelled all of that at her friend.

"Maybe I don't need you to get me to see that!" Daphne Elizabeth said, pale skin mottled a rage-red.

"Fine," Jaya said, in more dignified tones, taking her book off the papasan chair. "I'm not here to be your moral compass, Daph."

"Yeah, well, I didn't ask you to be," Daphne Elizabeth shot back.

"I'd better be going."

Jaya swished out of the room, not looking back once. It was true, sometimes people needed to make their own mistakes.

But if Jaya were being honest with herself, she knew her near-constant burning, surging anger wasn't really for Daph. In fact, there was no one in particular she was mad at. Just the entire world.

# Jaya

The next weekend, Jaya was in her robe, about to begin her makeup regimen for Caterina's party. The only reason she was going was because she thought she might be able to make a sizable donation to One World—a charity Caterina obviously felt strongly about—and therefore engender feelings of forgiveness. Although Caterina hadn't done anything since the Skype incident involving Kiran, her ire felt like a hammer hanging above Jaya's head, waiting to deliver a killing blow.

Her phone buzzed on her dresser, and she saw Kiran's face pop up. He was trying to video-chat her. Feeling the heavy weight of her decision press down on her once more, Jaya answered the call and forced a polite smile. "Hello, Kiran." They'd spoken only once since the future engagement was announced. She wondered why Kiran was calling now; he seemed about as interested in talking to her as she was in talking to him.

He inclined his head. "Jaya. You'll be pleased to know the answer is a hundred and twelve."

Jaya blinked. "I . . . beg your pardon?"

Kiran looked at her like he couldn't believe she didn't understand. "You remember our conversation via email a few days ago?

I wanted the gardeners to plant the golden hibiscus shrubs to make a large entwined *RH* in the gardens for our engagement?"

"Oh yes," Jaya said, the memory flickering to life. "The . . . our estate initials. Yes, of course."

He seemed appeased that she remembered. "Well, it'll take one hundred and twelve shrubs to achieve an *RH* of the size and scope I would like. But it's well worth it, I think. I want people to experience the power of the Hegde dynasty as soon as they set foot on the grounds."

Jaya honestly didn't care. He could have two thousand shrubs and cover up the entire palace for all she cared. And yet she found herself saying, "But isn't the engagement going to be at the *Rao* palace?"

Kiran studied her coolly. "Yes, but you'll be a Hegde once we're married."

Jaya forced another smile. "Yes. Of course."

Kiran continued to study her over the phone. "I had a nice conversation with your friend Caterina."

Jaya stilled. They hadn't really talked about Caterina or the Skype call at all since it had happened. "Oh, good," she said carefully. "Caterina's very charming."

"Yes, she is. You know, it's very important who we socialize with. The friendships we keep are a mirror of our values."

Jaya found herself barely breathing. Why was he saying this? Did he know . . . something? Had Caterina somehow seen Grey and Jaya kiss that night Appa had called her? What if Kiran told Caterina about the upcoming engagement and she told Grey, just to get back at Jaya for not helping her with Daphne Elizabeth? What if Kiran pulled out of the engagement if he felt Jaya was a risk to the Hegde name?

"I agree," Jaya heard herself saying quickly. "Completely." She paused before adding, "You know, I haven't told anyone here about the engagement. I thought it would be best to do that closer to the time. I don't want people we hardly know feeling obliged to buy us presents or, worse, trying to finagle an invitation." Jaya laughed an easy laugh.

Kiran frowned slightly, and for a moment Jaya was afraid he was going to tell her he'd already told Caterina. But then he nodded. "Yes, I suppose that's fine. But that reminds me, I did want to get your input on the invitations. I really feel the font for my name should be very slightly larger than the one for yours. The Hegde name . . ."

Jaya let out a breath and sagged against her dresser as he continued to speak.

Jaya smoothed down her flapper dress—a pale green number with fringey beads hanging off the ends—and adjusted her gold carnival half-mask. The fact that it covered the top half of her face made her feel a bit more cushioned from the world at large, as if it might help disguise the pain in her eyes. She'd paired her dress with tights and ankle boots, but she was still desperate to get on the yacht, where it would be warmer. The car service had dropped her off as close to the marina as possible, which was still too long a walk in the biting air. She wasn't even sure why she was here when she could be ensconced in her room, eating ice cream and reading a book. Suddenly cozying up to Caterina didn't seem that important. Jaya just wasn't in a glitzy party mood. After what had happened with Grey and her fight with DE . . . she would feel more at home at a funeral.

Twenties-era music played energetically off Lake Rosetta. She couldn't see the yacht yet; there were too many pine trees in the way. Jaya glanced down at her ruby pendant. It didn't really go with her outfit, but she'd worn it out of some stupid sense of nostalgia for a time when Grey and she . . . Anyway. She frowned. Two more rubies had fallen, bringing the total to six remaining; fewer than half the original number. Were they falling faster now than they had before? And a thought crept into her mind— Grey's eighteenth birthday was soon. But that was silly. The one had nothing to do with the other.

She rounded a bend and was completely distracted by the vision in front of her eyes.

Lake Rosetta stretched before her, dark and vast and milky with thin patches of ice. The yacht was a 90-foot behemoth, and it had been dressed up for the occasion. Small, intimate tables on the deck were covered in glittering gold tablecloths. Twinkling strands of lights hung from every spare surface. Guests—all in costume—milled about with coupe champagne glasses and long cigarette holders, giving the impression that they really had been transported to the 1920s.

Jaya climbed aboard the yacht, the musty scent of the lake air tangling with her clothes.

Caterina's people had done a spectacular job. This dripping-with-lights-and-sparkles setup looked less like a gala and more like they'd time-hopped back to a plush speakeasy for twenties-era celebrities.

Jaya spun in a slow circle, drinking it all in, and came to a stop to find two lupine blue eyes watching her.

# Grey

Grey had had plans to sequester himself somewhere, drink a few Cokes (which were being served in the original glass bottles), and then leave early. The only reason he was here was because DE and Leo had begged and begged, unrelenting, and he didn't have the energy to fight with them any longer. They were hoping that he and Jaya would begin speaking again, he knew. He might've tried to fight his feelings for a while, but apparently they were no secret to the others.

Then he saw her. Like a twenties film star, in her green dress, her ornate half-mask, and her hair in waves. She hadn't seen him yet; she was marveling at the yacht, how it was done up. Watching the naked awe on her face, the way she loved these social shindigs in a way he could never begin to understand, Grey was sure there was an iron fist around his heart, squeezing and squeezing and squeezing.

It took a moment, but then she turned, and their eyes met. Her face lit with joy for a brief microsecond, only to be immediately replaced by . . . sadness.

Sadness?

Not irritation or weariness or, even worse, indifference, but sadness. But why would she be sad when she was the one who'd broken up with him? They kept staring at each other, neither able to look away.

Grey wanted to cinch his arms around her waist and press his mouth to hers. He knew what she'd taste like: heartbreak and hunger, regret and reconciliation.

He'd barely finished the thought when someone shoulder-checked him. He automatically grabbed the person's arm—they were a few inches shorter than him—before noticing it was Alaric.

"Watch where you're going," the dude practically sneered. The way he was looking at Grey made it obvious it hadn't been an accident.

Grey's anger surged, making him feel more alive than he had in weeks. He tightened his grip on Alaric's arm, taking note of the glass of scotch in his right hand. "Don't push me, Konig."

Suddenly Jaya was at his side, looking between them, her eyes wide. "Why don't we all—"

"Jaya and Grey!"

They turned to see Caterina bustling toward them, wearing a very slinky black-and-gold dress. Alaric tossed a last sneer at Grey as he roughly pulled away and then disappeared through the crowd. Grey heard Jaya breathe an audible sigh of relief at Caterina's approaching form, and glanced at her. She looked up at him, a tentative smile at her lips.

But before he could say anything, Caterina was upon them. Grey frowned. Her skin was too pale, her face too thin. Grey wasn't one to care about such things, but Caterina's appearance was gossip fuel at St. R's. If things were going well with her and Alaric, she was pink-cheeked and bright-eyed. When they fought (which, let's be honest, was pretty frequently), she became gaunter and gaunter until they got back together.

Grey had always wondered what Caterina saw in Alaric. The dude was kind of a loser. The way he openly stared at other girls even when he and Caterina were walking together always set Grey's teeth on edge.

"Hi, Caterina," Jaya said, and the girls air-kissed.

Caterina turned a cold smile on them both. "Thank you for coming."

"Thank you for inviting me." Jaya was obviously very good at playing Caterina's game. "This is such a wonderful thing you're doing for charity," she added warmly.

Caterina's smile turned ostentatious. "Well, I *am* set to raise more money tonight than any single person has ever done for One World. It's going to be wonderful PR for my father's company." Grey thought there was something stilted about the way she said it, as if it were vital that they got that she was doing this only for the *publicity*. Which was strange. In Grey's experience, it was the opposite: most wealthy people wanted to show what great philanthropists they were and pretended not to care about the publicity, even though they secretly craved it.

Jaya nodded seriously. "Of course. I understand." She looked around, smiling. "This yacht is so splendid!"

Caterina's smile was back, a complacent thing that barely touched her lips. "It is, isn't it? All the decor, down to the table-cloths, was my idea. The event planner wanted to go with plain black, but I told her she was ridiculous."

Jaya glanced at Grey and bit the inside of her cheek, as if she was trying not to laugh. Grey covered his answering smile with a hand, pretending he had an itch on his chin. For a moment it was like they were . . . them again. "That's . . . yes, absolutely ridiculous," Jaya said finally.

"Stay for the fireworks," Caterina said airily. "They start at nine and they're going to be absolutely magnificent."

Rahul came walking up, looking like he was wearing a much bigger guy's suit, although Grey knew for a fact that he'd had it tailor-made. Somehow it seemed to swallow him. His gaze lingered on Caterina. "Hello, Caterina."

Caterina barely spared him a glance. "Hello, Rahul. Enjoying the party so far?"

"Absolutely. Although I feel I must tell you, there's something wrong with the peach juice. It's a little bitter. And carbonated. I'm not sure how that happened."

Caterina looked at him as if he'd just told her he'd bought a knockoff Gucci handbag. "Those are bellinis. Fresh-squeezed peach juice mixed with Armand de Brignac—champagne."

Rahul's ears turned a shade of red that Grey had never seen before. "R-right, no, I—I thought it, ah, well, I should . . ." And then he just walked off.

"Anyway," Caterina said, turning back to them. "I better go! There's a reporter here from one of the nationals, and Alaric made me promise I wouldn't forget about having our picture taken. He tends to get lost without me. Ta!" She turned, shoulder blades like glass shards poking out of her back, and sashayed off.

They watched her go for a moment, then turned to each other again, as if on cue. Jaya raised a hand, as if to touch him, and then dropped it again. Grey gazed into her brown eyes behind the gold carnival half-mask she wore, soft and glowing once again with sadness. "Hi," he said.

She swallowed and pushed the mask up to the top of her head. "Hi." She gestured to the suspenders and twenties bowler hat DE had insisted he wear. "You look really nice."

"I look like a jackass."

Jaya's mouth twitched. "No one could ever say you were disingenuous." He didn't smile. "How are you?" Jaya asked, her voice just a breath. A soft breeze off the lake wrapped them up in its cold arms.

"Do you really care?" Grey asked roughly.

She looked stricken. "Of course I care."

He believed her. She cared. She still . . . cared. "Then . . . then why?" Grey asked, shaking his head, just as a group of extremely loud couples walked past them, jostling them both, pushing them closer together.

Jaya put a hand on his chest to steady herself and then jerked back, as if he were hot to the touch. She looked at him, her mouth working, no sounds actually escaping it. It seemed to Grey that she wanted to talk but that she couldn't find the words to say.

He pointed to a far corner of the yacht's deck. "Do you want to go down there? It's a bit quieter."

After a long pause, during which he fully expected her to say no, she nodded.

They walked past all the laughing, chattering people to the northern corner, which was mostly deserted. Grey watched as Jaya walked up to the railing, closing her eyes against the stiff breeze coming off the water. Her wavy hair undulated, kissing her cheeks and collarbone. She'd put something glittery on her eyelids, and they sparkled like twin stars.

As he joined her, he had a sudden aching need to put his arm around her, to feel her lay her head on his chest. She'd fit perfectly there. "So, tell me," he said, instead of saying the hundred other things he wanted to say. "You still care about me?"

Jaya turned to him, unaware of his clamoring thoughts. "Grey," she said, glancing down for a moment. "I shouldn't. I can't talk about this with you."

He swallowed. "Two weeks ago you were kissing me, Jaya. And from what I could tell, you were really into it."

She flushed and cupped her neck with a small hand, looking away.

"Well, weren't you?" he pressed when she didn't respond.

"Yes," she said quietly. "Yes, I was."

Grey loomed over her, his hand clamped around the icy metal railing so he wouldn't be tempted to grab her wrist and pull her to his chest. "So if that wasn't an act and you still care, then . . . then why can't we be together? That's all that matters, Jaya, that we feel the same way about each other."

She looked at him, a desperate fire in her eyes. "But it's *not* all that matters, Grey. Not for me. Family and dynasty have to come first. I have a duty toward my—toward the Rao name. And right now it's imperative that I fulfill that duty."

"And it's that easy for you," Grey murmured, leaning even closer. She blinked but didn't move back. Her breathing was faster, coming in short, shallow gasps. His eyes searched her face. "It's that easy for you to walk away from me."

# Jaya

If he kissed her, she wouldn't turn away. It was madness, it was thoughtless, it would be the most brazen act to do it here, on a yacht that belonged to Caterina. Caterina, who was Kiran's friend and just happened to hold a grudge against Jaya. But if Grey kissed her, Jaya would lean in and kiss him too, hungrily, desperately, like the world was ending. Looking into his searing blue eyes, Jaya wanted to do nothing more than wrap her arms around him, to press her body against his.

And then Caterina would see, and she'd tell Kiran, and Kiran would call off the engagement. That would finish off the Raos; there would be no coming back from it. There was only one ending to this story of her and Grey together, and it involved the complete destruction of her world.

Jaya stepped back from him as if she'd been shocked. What was she thinking? What was she even *doing* here?

"Jaya!"

Jaya spun from the railing, guilt and fear flaring through her, expecting to see Caterina. Instead, she saw Daphne Elizabeth clomping her way across the deck in the high-heeled button-boots, unsteady on her feet.

"H-hello, Daph," Jaya said, stealing a glance at Grey, who was glowering at the girl.

Daph looked from her to Grey. "So you guys are talking again?"

Jaya opened her mouth to say something, but nothing came. Grey was silent beside her, no help at all.

Daph waved a hand. "Okay, I get it. You don't want to tell me. Doesn't matter, because I have s-something important to say." Holding her drink aloft, Daph clumsily wedged her way between Jaya and Grey, who looked like he wanted to throw her overboard. "Move, Grey, jeez. You can bone Jaya later."

"We were in the middle of something, DE," Grey bit out.

"I've finally decided," Daph said, ignoring him. Her vowels were all slurred and running together. "You were right this whole time, Jaya." She thrust her coupe champagne glass in the air, and some pale pink liquid sloshed off the side, but she didn't notice.

"Decided what?" Jaya asked, unable to help herself.

"I've been a complete fool. He's walking around with her like they're a—a couple! They walked right by me and neither of them so much as looked at me." Daphne Elizabeth's eyes were pink around the edges. "I'm not just some . . . some doll he can toss aside when he's done playing with it. I have self-respect. Even if I haven't been acting like it." She hugged Jaya. "You're a real friend for telling me what I needed to hear, Jaya. I appreciate it."

Grey sighed and ran a frustrated hand over his face.

Jaya purposely avoided looking at him. "Ah, I'm happy for you, Daph. Really. Alaric's not even worth bothering with. But perhaps we could talk about this—"

Daph gave her a look. "Oh, I'm bothering with him all right. I'm going to go up there and talk to him and Caterina right now."

Jaya felt her pulse kick up a notch. "You can't do that," she said, grabbing Daph's arm. "Daph. This is *Caterina's* event. Firstly, you can't ruin it for her like that. And secondly—"

"She'll rip your hair right out of your scalp and use it as table-top decor," Grey added gruffly.

Jaya shot him an exasperated glance and turned back to Daph.

"I'm not looking to ruin Caterina's night. But I'm tired of just sitting around waiting for one of them to acknowledge this. If not now, then when? I just have to get it over with. We're all here, I've had some liquid courage. It's now or never. And I know me. If I wait, I'm going to let him sweet-talk me tomorrow. I need to just do it. Right now. Thanks, Jaya. I'd never have done this without your help." She began to walk off.

Jaya turned to Grey. "I have to go."

He studied her. "Do you want me to come with you?"

"No," Jaya said, trying hard to keep the regret out of her voice. "I'd better do this alone."

They glanced at each other for a long moment, the music and laughter from the other parts of the yacht fading. Then Grey nodded, once, and stepped back. Jaya swallowed a lump in her throat. They'd never speak like this again. Of that she felt sure. Before she could change her mind, she turned and hurried after Daphne Elizabeth.

Daphne Elizabeth's legs were quite a bit longer than Jaya's. Standing at the bottom of the metal stairs, Jaya saw the skirt of her burgundy dress disappearing into the top floor. Cursing softly under her breath, she ran up the stairs, dodging couples and their various twenties accessories.

The warm upper level was crowded; it was where the items for the silent auction were arranged grandly on a table: a ski trip for two to Aspen, an all-expenses-paid stay at a Tuscan villa, a collection of gilded Fabergé eggs. Jaya would catch sight of Daph's burgundy dress only to lose it again as she wove in and out of the swarm of people milling around in the middle, considering what they might bid on, or clustered around the edges by the windows, taking in the glittering view of Aspen across the water.

Then she saw Alaric's head—bobbing above the rest of the crowd as usual, his thick blond hair gelled within an inch of its life. Jaya began to push her way through the crowd, really digging in with her elbows when people wouldn't move. Amma would be aghast at her unseemly behavior, but this was important, dammit.

"Ouch!"

"Excuse *me!*"

"Hey, where's the fire, darlin'?"

Jaya ignored all the indignant shouting and kept her sights focused on Alaric's stupid, tall hair. She could not *believe* Daphne Elizabeth. Jaya was never, ever giving anyone relationship advice ever again.

She pushed her way through the small bubble of people congregated in front of Caterina and Alaric just in time to see Daph stride up to them, her head held high.

"Caterina, we need to talk," Daph said, but neither of them heard her. They were both deep in conversation with Alaric's lackey, Lachlan, and another senior girl, Spencer, Alaric's hand resting lightly on Caterina's lower back.

Jaya lunged forward and grasped at Daph's arm, but it was too late. Daphne had already said, in a louder voice, "Caterina. We need to talk."

It worked. Caterina and Alaric turned. Alaric's smile slid off his face at the same time his hand slid off Caterina's back. Caterina's expression cooled a few million degrees. "Please excuse us," she said graciously to Lachlan and Spencer, who exchanged glances and went on their merry way, probably to spread the news that there was A+ gossip fodder sprouting on the upper level.

Caterina turned back to Daphne Elizabeth, not smiling at all anymore, her steely expression made even scarier because she was still wearing her bloodred carnival half-mask, unlike Alaric or Daph. "What do you want?"

"I w-want all the lying to be over," Daph said, her voice trembling. Jaya could tell she was making a monumental effort to not slur her words. Or maybe the fear of Caterina's wrath was enough to sober her up. She turned to Alaric. "Enough's enough." To Caterina, she said, "You never responded to my—my text. It's been a long time now, Caterina, and I really think we need to talk this out."

Caterina's face was frozen behind her half-mask. "What text?"

Daph looked from her to Alaric and back again. "The . . . the text I sent you. About Alaric and me? Alaric said you didn't want—"

Alaric laughed, loud and braying. "I must've given you the wrong number, Daphne Elizabeth. Silly mistake. I'm sure we can pick this conversation up tomorrow."

Daph appeared completely confounded. "You . . . you gave me the wrong number?"

"What text?" Caterina said again, with much more menace in her voice this time.

Daph met her eyes and straightened her shoulders. "I'm sorry, Caterina," she said. "But Alaric and I began seeing each other over the summer. It . . . it kind of just happened and I'm not proud of it. I tried telling you over a text; Alaric gave me your number."

Caterina turned slowly to Alaric. Jaya could almost hear tendons creaking. In a strange, wooden voice, she said, "You were going to let Daphne Elizabeth *text* this to me? And you weren't going to say anything?"

"No," Alaric said, putting his hand on her shoulder, which she shrugged off savagely. "Of course not. I was going to tell you; it was my idea, but Daphne Elizabeth was scared."

Daph gasped. "What? Alaric!"

He regarded her blankly.

After a long, crackling pause, Daph laughed. "Oh . . . my . . . God. I'm such a fool. You really *are* a gobshite."

"A what?" Alaric said, drawing himself up to his full height.

Daph ignored him and turned to Caterina. "I'm so sorry," she said sincerely—or as sincerely as she could say that while also being plastered. "I—I consider myself a very honest person. But this . . ." She ran a hand through her short red hair, leaving it mussed. "I lost my mind. It had nothing to do with you, Caterina, and everything to do with me." Giving Alaric a disgusted look, she added, "And a bit to do with your boyfriend." Turning fully to him, she said, "I don't know what kind of spell you put on me, but it's over."

Alaric smiled arrogantly. "How can it be over when it was never begun?" He obviously thought he was being very clever.

Shaking her head, Daphne Elizabeth looked at Jaya. "Thanks," she said quietly. "For bringing me to my senses." And then she pushed through the crowd of people and clip-clopped her way downstairs.

Caterina's eyes were unreadable behind her half-mask, but her lips curved up in a little smile.

*How mature*, Jaya thought. *She's going to walk out of here, still smiling.*

Suddenly there was an enormous, earsplitting shriek. It took Jaya a moment to realize it was emanating from Caterina. She launched herself at Alaric, her fingers hooked into claws. People gasped and turned to watch as she began clawing at his face, his neck, his arms—really anything she could get her hands on—all the while screaming and calling him names. She was fury person-ified. Alaric was having no trouble holding her off, but she kept going at him anyway, her face splotchy with impotent rage.

"Well, don't just stand there!" Jaya said in her most imperious/commanding tone to a group of young men standing next to her. "Help me peel her off him!"

Her voice spurred them to action, and with their assistance, she was able to pull Caterina off Alaric. "Let him go," Jaya kept saying to Caterina, hoping she would eventually get through the rage fog. "He's not worth it. He's not worth it, Caterina."

Finally, realizing she was no match for two big guys and Jaya, Caterina slumped forward, her hair in disarray, her carnival mask askew. She ripped it off in disgust, and panting, said to Alaric, "You're the vilest specimen of the human race. I hope you know you've done this at the cost of every friend you have. I will *destroy* you."

Alaric regarded her with such cold indifference, even Jaya felt the chill. "You greatly exaggerate your sphere of influence and how loyal people are to you, Caterina." Then he, like Daph, turned and walked off, his head held high and gelled hair stiff and unyielding.

Caterina turned to address the crowd. "Please," she said, in her most dignified voice, which was impressively dignified, considering her hair was sticking up in about sixty-seven different directions and her face was still red. "Continue to bid on the items. It's for a very good cause. The fireworks will begin in a few moments."

She glanced at Jaya; there was a flicker of pain on Caterina's face that was gone as quickly as it had arrived. Then she strode off through the silent crowd, her head held high.

After a moment's hesitation, Jaya took off after Caterina and caught up with her on the stairs.

"Wait!" she said. "Caterina. Are you okay?"

The fireworks show began, but Jaya barely registered the colors or the gasps of awe from the crowd.

Caterina spun around, virtually snarling. "What do *you* think?"

she spat over the popping and booming. "I was just humiliated in a room full of my father's business acquaintances and my friends! And you know what the worst part is? You could've stopped it and you didn't, Jaya. I really thought, when we first met, that perhaps one day you'd prove yourself to be a worthy friend." Her eyes were pink at the corners. "But I was wrong. And sometimes I get really fucking tired of being disappointed."

"I'm so sorry," Jaya said. Two couples from upstairs tried to make their way down, but when they saw Caterina, they quickly turned back around and scurried up the stairs. "But maybe this is a blessing in disguise. Alaric really didn't deserve you."

"Don't act like you're my friend. Don't act like you care." Caterina narrowed her eyes. "You're just as bad as them. Maybe even worse. The well-groomed, polite, likable princess who loves her sister and her family. You fooled them all, didn't you? You're a hypocrite and a liar." Caterina ripped off her feathered headband and threw it on the ground. It was like she was divesting herself of this party, of this evening, one item at a time.

Jaya felt a small ripple of fear move through her. Was Caterina talking about whatever she'd learned from talking to Kiran? Or was she just talking about how Jaya had kept the whole Daph/ Alaric thing from her?

"Caterina . . . ," Jaya said, reaching a hand out, unsure of what, exactly, to say.

Caterina held up a hand. "I don't need your charity. It's clear where your allegiances lie." Scoffing, she added, "Enjoy the fucking fireworks." Then she turned, pushing her way through the crowd, and melted away.

Jaya looked at Caterina's feathered headband lying abandoned on the metal stairs, the feather limp and sad. She felt guilt like a knife twisting in her chest. Somehow, in the weeks prior, it had become easy to justify her lie of omission to Caterina, just like she'd justified so many others. But Jaya had never meant for Caterina to get hurt. She'd never wanted that.

She looked out over the sea of people, down to the deck where she and Grey had been talking. The space that had held him was now empty. Maybe she just had a talent for inflicting pain.

# CHAPTER 16

## Grey

"Push X! No, not Y! Push X—X!" Rahul yelled.

They were lounging in one of the entertainment rooms at St. R's a couple days later. Leo and Rahul had invited him, like they still did occasionally, and then had looked shocked when he'd accepted their invitation. Leo had quickly covered up his shock with mindless prattle, which had prompted Rahul to call him on his behavior, which had made the whole thing awkward. Grey considered just going back to his room at that point, but now he was glad he hadn't. This was . . . kind of fun.

The "game over" sound warbled, and Leo threw his controller on the oversize couch. "*Merde!*" he said, gesturing at the 110-inch 4K TV screen. "Why am I so horrible at these video games? How is this physically possible? I am a smart man, but video games—they make no sense to me." His shoulders slumped. "I have been on a losing streak lately. I am also not making the slightest bit of progress with *le magnifique* Samantha Wickers."

"You need to make progress quickly, before the factories run out of rhubarb jam," Rahul deadpanned.

Leo glared at him. "I am serious! I do not know what I am doing wrong."

Grey gave him a sympathetic half smile. "You're not doing anything wrong. I mean, jam's an unconventional strategy, but it's not *wrong*. Just keep being you. Show her you care. Sometimes you have to fight for what you want."

Leo was silent, and Grey glanced at him again to find him staring. "What?" he asked, unsettled. Had he said something socially unacceptable somehow?

"*Rien*, nothing," Leo said, shaking his head and settling against a leather throw pillow. "You are different now. You have been for some time."

Grey frowned at him. "What do you mean, 'different'?"

Leo shrugged. "You were shut down before. Then you and Jaya began to hang out and you changed. You are more . . ." He pursed his lips, apparently not able to find the right word.

"Open," Rahul said on Grey's other side.

Grey regarded the two of them. "Open," he mused. They were right. Jaya had unearthed so much of him.

Raised voices in the hallway had them pausing in their conversation. Caterina and Alaric walked in, their faces red, their voices heated. They stopped short when they saw Leo, Rahul, and Grey. Then Alaric strode to the back of the room, where the air hockey and ping-pong tables were, and Caterina followed him. A moment later, they were arguing again, their voices too low for Grey to make out what they were saying. If he had to guess, it had to do with the bombshell DE had dropped on the yacht.

"Anyway, yes," Leo said, turning back to Grey. He raised his hands, palms upward. "You are playing a game with us rather than just saying no and going to your room. You are inside rather than outside, watching." He paused. "What has changed? Are you and Jaya speaking again?"

"No," Grey said, thinking back to the night of the yacht gala. "No, we're not talking again. But . . ." It was hard to explain. Something had shifted for him that night at the gala, seeing the pain he felt mirrored in her eyes. The way she'd said she still cared about him. They'd almost kissed before DE interrupted them. And Jaya hadn't said she didn't want to be with him. She hadn't refuted that she had feelings for him; she'd said she had a duty to her family. Those were two very different things.

"You love her," Leo said simply.

Caterina yelled the word "asshole," and then there was quieter heated arguing between her and Alaric, but Grey ignored them and stared at Leo. "Love? Does love make you feel ill, like you're being tossed about on a stormy sea? Does it steal your sleep and make you feel like your insides are on fire?"

"From your symptoms, it's either love or a stomach virus," Rahul put in.

Love. That was a big word. Was he in love with Jaya? Grey didn't know. What he did know was that she'd taught him, with her steady kindness, with her unfailing warmth, that he wasn't what his father believed he was. What Grey had come to believe he was too. She'd shown him he was more than some cursed, damaged, unloved aristocrat. She'd shown him he was capable of more, that he had so much uncovered promise within him. And, weirdly enough, he'd begun to believe her.

Seeing her at the gala, seeing how much she seemed to be suffering too, Grey had felt the ice begin to thaw once again. He'd begun to realize that even if he died on his eighteenth birthday, even if the curse took him, he wanted to be the master of his fate until then. He wanted to die knowing he'd lived his life how *he* wanted to live it.

Grey turned to Leo and Rahul. "I have to fight for her," he said suddenly. Of course. It was so obvious.

"*Quoi?*" Leo said, sitting up. "What do you mean, 'fight for her'?"

Grey hopped up from the couch and began to pace. Caterina and Alaric turned to look at him for a moment before going back to their conversation. "On the yacht. It was obvious that she—she doesn't like this any more than I do. I thought I was just some side note in her life, but that's not true at all. She *wants* to be with me, she just feels like there's no solution. But I have to get her to see that there might be. We could do it together. I can't just let her slip away." If he was going to die, he was going to die happy and in love, damn it. He refused to let Jaya concede defeat for the both of them. Grey turned to Leo and Rahul, who looked fairly confused.

"Huh?" Leo said finally.

Grey laughed and ran up to them, feeling lighter than he had in weeks. "Homegoing's in two weeks. That gives me about four-teen days to work on my strategy, what exactly I'm going to say."

"Huh?" Rahul this time.

Grey grabbed him by the shoulders. "I'm going to tell her how I feel. I'm going to tell her . . . that I love her. I have to try to win her back. I *have* to."

"Ouah!" Leo yelled, jumping up and clapping Grey on the back.

"Congratulations," Rahul said, also standing and twisting his hands together awkwardly. "Um. May the force be with you."

Grey and Leo laughed. Grey could feel Caterina's and Alaric's judgmental eyes on him, but even that couldn't dim his joy.

"You're going to tell Jaya you love her?" Caterina said, folding her long arms across her torso. Next to her, Alaric smiled a patronizing smile Grey wanted to wipe off his face.

"Yes," Grey said, meeting their eyes. "Why?"

Alaric laughed. "You? And Jaya? I don't see it."

Grey felt his old, familiar insecurities begin to rear their ugly heads and tamped them down. "Sometimes people miss what's right in front of them, don't they?" he asked, pointedly looking from Alaric to Caterina and back.

Both their faces were livid as Grey, smirking, sat back down on the couch to begin a round of *Hallucination*.

# Jaya

The bell tinkled, and everyone scraped their chairs back and headed for the doors. There was a tangible note of relief, of escape. The English final had been very simple; Mr. Linski had gone easy on them, thankfully. Jaya sighed; another exam down, only three more to go today and then they'd be done with the semester. Homegoing was tomorrow and then they'd all scatter to the four winds for winter break. She'd go home and see Appa, Amma, and . . . Kiran. And, of course, the engagement preparations that were already underway. She stood and was grabbing her backpack when she felt a tap on her shoulder. Jaya turned to see Grey looking down at her.

Her heart thundered. They hadn't spoken since the yacht

gala, except for him to smile at her occasionally, taking her completely by surprise. Usually she was too astounded to respond. But he hadn't approached her at all, and he hadn't mentioned their interrupted conversation from that night. Jaya had begun to think he was letting go. It had shattered her already broken heart, but it had been for the best.

"Hi," he said, smiling.

Jaya tried to speak, only her throat closed up and not a single sound escaped. Clearing her throat, she tried again. "Hi, Grey." She lowered her eyes and moved to go around him. "Sorry, I have to leave now."

He turned to walk with her. "Are you going to Homegoing tomorrow?"

Jaya stopped and stared at him. "What?"

He stuck his hands in his pockets. A few people brushed past them toward the exit. "Homegoing. Are you going?"

"Y-yes. Daph wouldn't take no for an answer." She paused, not able to read his expression. "Why?"

"I'm going too," he said, half smiling in that way that made her heart stutter for a moment before she reminded it that it had no right to stutter that way.

"Grey," she said, shaking her head. "We're not going together."

"I didn't ask you to go with me." He grinned impishly.

Jaya stopped, surprised. "Oh. No, I suppose you didn't." She gathered herself again. "And we can't dance or talk to each other either. In fact, I should get going, as I said."

Grey continued to smile, as if he could see through her words to the real feelings lurking underneath. "Okay." He turned and sauntered out of the room.

Jaya stood looking after him for a long moment. Homegoing?

But he'd said he wasn't going. Why would he go to a social event like that? And why was he asking her if *she* was going? What had changed? Jaya's blood thrummed with a mixture of anxiety and, against her wishes, longing. She squared her shoulders against it. There was no chance of them ever becoming more. She'd made her unequivocal choice; she was going to be engaged to Kiran. It would be best if Grey left her alone.

Mr. Linski cleared his throat at the head of the class.

"Sorry," Jaya said as she forced herself to walk toward the door, her cheeks warm. She was the only person left in class. "I'll see you later, Mr. Linski."

"Have a good day," he called.

And Jaya thought, *That won't be possible for me.*

Jaya ran to her room to grab a book she needed to study for her calculus final, which was after lunch. Daph, Leo, and Rahul would all be in the dining hall already. Grey had said yesterday he was going to be studying in the library. Jaya found herself thinking of him again, of what he'd said to her in English class, of the way his eyes had looked. So blue, so bright. Seeing right through all her fortifications. *Stop it,* she told herself. *You want this to be a clean break.*

Her phone buzzed in her pocket. Setting her book on her dresser, Jaya pulled the phone from her pocket. It was Kiran, trying to video-chat her. She answered. "Hi."

"Hello, Jaya," he said formally, his face lamplit. She could see a window behind him, and a dark sky beyond. "Are you finished with your exams?"

"I have three more after lunch," she explained, "which is where I was just headed."

"And then the Homegoing dance is tomorrow." Kiran's eyes were watchful.

Jaya cocked her head. "How did you know about Homegoing?"

"You told me before," Kiran said. "Don't you remember?"

"No," Jaya replied, but it was possible she had. Things had been a little hectic the past couple of weeks. "Anyway, I was thinking about skipping it, but Daphne Elizabeth is forcing me to go. It's our last big event before the winter break, so I acquiesced." She thought about how Grey had asked if she was going, and felt a spark of something like anticipation struggling to catch. She stomped it out immediately.

"I see." Kiran smiled, but it was a grim, flat line. "I heard about one of the students there. The Emerson boy."

Jaya stiffened. This was the first time Kiran had ever mentioned Grey. And calling him a "boy"? They were the same age, for God's sake, and Grey was twice his size. "Oh yes?" she said, keeping her voice disinterestedly neutral, though her heart was beginning to pound. Had Caterina said something else to Kiran?

"I heard he had . . . ideas . . . about the two of you."

Jaya felt the blood drain from her face. "Kiran—"

"Don't worry. I know how to take care of people like that. People who can't take a hint. Is he still bothering you?"

"No," she said quickly, her grip on the phone tightening. Out in the hallway, someone called out to a friend. "Kiran, just leave him alone, okay? He's immaterial to us, to the engagement. I've already made my decision, and I choose this. I choose the alliance between our families, our estates." What if Kiran talked to Grey and found out that he and Jaya had kissed right before the engagement announcement? What if he decided Jaya was too wayward for his tastes and called off the engagement? Everything she was working toward would be gone. The Raos would be finished.

Kiran studied her, his eyes glinting. "You're right, Jaya," he said finally. "He's immaterial."

Jaya let out a breath. "Okay. Well, I should get going. I don't want to be late."

"No," Kiran said. "You don't. I'll talk to you soon."

Things were getting untenable. Jaya pressed "end" and squeezed her eyes shut for a long moment before gathering her books. As she closed the dorm room door behind her, she realized Kiran hadn't agreed to leave things alone.


Jaya made her way down the hallway to the elevator, passing Caterina's closed door. Ever since the gala, Caterina had been walking the grounds and buildings like a wraith, thinner and paler than usual. She had the flu, she told everyone. She ate meals in her room. She didn't go out with her friends. When she did emerge from her room, she and Alaric argued incessantly. Someone had even reported her behavior to the school psychologist, but Caterina had flounced into her office and then flounced right back out again, a small smile on her face as if she'd played a marvelous trick and gotten away with it.

Jaya had gone up to her one day when they passed each other on the way to classes. "Caterina. Do you want to talk?"

Caterina had looked at her blankly. "About what?"

"Come on. What happened at your party. You know."

"Talk?" Caterina had said, huffing a laugh. "Are you serious?"

Jaya had looked at her, not understanding.

"You betrayed me," Caterina had said slowly, as if explaining a difficult concept to a toddler. "You knew the whole time that

Daphne Elizabeth and Alaric were making a giant fool of me, and *you chose to do nothing*. Even though I asked you to intervene, you decided you'd rather take their side."

Jaya had felt her cheeks burn. "I'm really sorry," she'd said sincerely. "That was absolutely the wrong thing to do."

Caterina had let out a slow, steady breath, as if she was trying not to combust. And then she'd walked off before Jaya could respond, her head held high.

It was just more evidence of how deeply she'd hurt Caterina by withholding the truth. Caterina was the kind of person who surrounded herself with "friends," but was still, for all intents and purposes, alone. She trusted rarely; she thought everyone was out to get her. She'd seen something in Jaya, and in her eyes, Jaya had taken advantage of that. All of what had transpired must have reinforced to her that she was right to keep everyone at bay. And that, if nothing else, seemed like the worst tragedy of all.

Jaya sat down at her table in the dining hall with her veggie wrap and fruit smoothie. Grey was at the library, studying. Jaya always asked Daphne Elizabeth in advance what Grey's plans were; if he was at the table, she made herself scarce. When he was gone, she joined Daph and the others. It hurt her heart that this was what things had come to, but she could see no other way to help both of them along to that clean break she was after.

"Hey, Daph," she said now, eyeing the other girl with concern. "How are you?"

Daph looked tortured; her eyes had dark circles under them and her lips were dry and bloodless. "Fine. No, not fine. Crushed with guilt and remorse." She tossed a look over her shoulder at Alaric. He sat grinning around the table at his old friends, his arm slung casually around a new girl. "What was I *thinking*?"

"You were likely caught up in a fog of lust," Rahul said after chewing and swallowing his mouthful of chicken sandwich. "I saw in a documentary that falling in love can feel like snorting cocaine. It produces a similar high based on dopamine, serotonin, oxytocin, and norepinephrine. Young people are especially susceptible."

Daph gave him a withering look.

"You made a mistake," Jaya said gently, drawing Daph's attention back to her. "It happens."

Daph's nervous finger shredded a napkin into fine confetti. "I know Caterina's going to come after me. And Alaric, but who cares about him? I feel like I'm waiting for a trained assassin to take me out at any moment."

Jaya sipped her smoothie. "Maybe all of this will die a natural death over winter break. Homegoing is tomorrow. The semester's almost over."

Daph laughed a mirthless laugh, stabbing her fork listlessly into her salad. "If anything, Caterina will probably just nourish her anger over the break. Come up with something really good."

"That'll be her decision, then," Jaya said. "There's no point in worrying about something you can't control."

"That is absolutely right," Leo said, setting his pizza down and taking a seat. "You are taking the high road, DE, which is the best road of all."

Daph sighed. "I'm just glad you're going to Homegoing with me tomorrow," she said, tossing Jaya a grateful look. "I wouldn't have the courage to face them otherwise."

Jaya forced a smile, even though the thought of Homegoing made her want to curl up into a ball. "Of course."

"You're going to descend with me, right?" Daph continued. "Down the stairs? Rahul's going to be waiting for me at the bottom. You can descend even if you don't have a partner."

It was a St. Rosetta's Homegoing tradition that one of the dates would wait in the grand foyer downstairs while the other descended with great ceremony from the staircase (if you didn't have a date, you could pair up with a friend and you still got to choose whether you wanted to be a descender or a waiter). In straight relationships, it was mostly guys who waited in the foyer and girls who did the descending, but not always.

Jaya made a face. She hadn't asked anyone to escort her to Homegoing; not going with Grey would be painful enough without having the added burden of having to entertain a date. "I wasn't planning on it . . ." But seeing Daph's crestfallen expression, knowing that her friend needed to pretend that everything was special and magical even if she and Alaric weren't together anymore, she acquiesced. "Oh, all right."

Daph's eyes shone, and she looked genuinely happy again. "Thanks, Jaya. You're a good friend."

"Yes, she is." Leo glanced over at Jaya, his eyes going wide. "*Merde!* Your pendant. Almost all of the stones are gone!"

Jaya forced a smile and caressed the rose that had been steadily losing its petals. "Yeah, I know. It's, erm, old."

Three more rubies remained. Jaya knew what Grey would say if he were here—one for each day until his eighteenth birthday. She looked out across the dining hall to the big windows on the far end and wondered what he was thinking, what he was feeling right then.

• • •

"You look *beautiful*." Penelope's voice held a hushed reverence as she took in Jaya's outfit.

The next evening, with finals and exams and studying behind them, they were all getting dressed for the final bash of the semester—the Homegoing dance. Although she could barely muster enough energy to get dressed, Jaya smiled affectionately at all the girls clustered in her room. It warmed her heart to see them happy.

Eons ago, she, Penelope, Daph, Isha, and Isha's (best) friend Raina had all decided to get ready together here, in Jaya's dorm room. None of them had thought it through—the fact that five girls with all their dresses, makeup, shoes, and handbags couldn't fit comfortably into Jaya's suite had completely escaped them. Daph was currently behind the bed getting changed, and Jaya could hear Isha and Raina squealing and chattering away in the bathroom together.

Jaya turned back to the mirror and smoothed down the skirt of her peacock-blue ball gown. It was an Alexander McQueen, and she'd been besotted with it in the store a few months ago, when she'd been planning to go to Homegoing with the intention of faux-wooing Grey. The thought made her heart hurt; she muscled past it. Looking at herself in the full-length mirror now, she felt . . . foolish. Like someone who'd once been naive enough to have plans to wear this dress with confidence. Someone who'd thought she could be just another teenager at a dance. Jaya adjusted the rose pendant at her throat. Two rubies were still hanging on.

Her thoughts automatically went to Grey, and her stomach

flipped nervously. Now, more than ever, after what Kiran had said on the phone, she hoped Grey would keep his distance. She'd consider staying here, in her room, if Daph wouldn't pitch a fit.

Jaya mustered a smile for Penelope. "Thank you," Jaya said, squeezing her hand. "You look stunning too. Are there any boys you're hoping to ask to dance?"

"Well," Penelope said, her cheeks getting pinker. "Not exactly . . . not *boys*. I want to ask Trinity."

Trinity Damilus was the tall, extremely statuesque senior Penelope had sat next to on the bus ride into Aspen. Trinity's mother was the world-famous Haitian interior designer, Stéphanie Damilus. "I'm sorry, Penelope," Jaya said. "I shouldn't make assumptions like that."

"Thanks." Penelope smiled. "I'm excited. We've been flirting all semester. We're in the same music theories class."

"Then she's definitely going to say yes," Jaya said. "Not that you need it, but here's something that might help." She rummaged in her drawer and pulled out a pink diamond necklace. "I got this in Mexico a few years ago. It'll hang really nicely with your neckline. And rumor has it, it used to belong to the dukes of Moctezuma de Tultengo—an old royal family in that region."

Penelope took it, her eyes dancing. "Wow, this is *stunning*. Thank you."

Jaya waved a hand. "Don't mention it. I hardly ever wear it, and it deserves better." Was she just ensuring *other* people were happy since she had no hope of that herself? Glancing at her somewhat-haggard reflection in the mirror, Jaya decided not to look too deeply into her motivations.

Daph swished over in a strapless turquoise gown that really set off her red hair. It hugged her slim figure and fell to her feet in a silky waterfall. She and Rahul were going as friends, but as she'd put it, "that doesn't mean I should dress like some basic bitch."

Isha and Raina came out of the bathroom then, Isha dressed in a burnt-orange gown and Raina in a black one that made her look much older.

"You look gorgeous," Raina said, looking at Jaya.

Jaya gathered the strength for yet another smile. She didn't want Isha to see the depths of her fatigue, her despair. "So do the both of you." She got her little embroidered purse out of the closet. "Who's ready for the big night?" Jaya couldn't help but notice that her words fell flat, as if she were announcing the weather rather than a dance.

Jaya, Daph, Isha, Raina, and Penelope all approached the grand staircase and waited to descend one at a time. There were mostly girls at the top and boys at the bottom of the stairs, though it was hard to see or hear individual people in the glittering, boisterous mass of privileged children of billionaires, politicians, and movie stars.

The curving oak balustrade had been festooned with blue-and-silver velvet and silk ribbons and glittering flowers. Taller in her heels, Jaya could barely make out Leo waiting at the bottom, watching with glee as Samantha Wickers descended, wearing a spectacular golden gown with a sheer, flowing train. Her blue eyes looked fierce behind her eyeliner. So Sam had said yes. Jaya felt a touch of dim happiness for Leo.

Rahul was at the bottom too, standing off to the side until Daph descended, as if he were just waiting for the whole thing to be over. Jaya noticed he kept looking at Caterina (who was going with a senior boy Jaya couldn't remember the name of) at the top of the stairs and looking away, his ears pink.

Dr. Waverly, Coach Stratton, and Ms. Rivard, the psychology teacher, as well as a few other adults fixed hair clips and bow ties and zippers. Jaya kept her distance, not wanting to be fussed over.

Of their group, Penelope went down first, looking pretty and shy (Trinity was already at the bottom, waiting with a cluster of her friends. She didn't have eyes for anyone except Penelope). Then a few other girls descended, followed by two guys, and then Isha.

Jaya watched dully as Elliot waited at the bottom, looking up at Isha with what could only be described as naked adoration. All she could see was the back of Isha's head, of course, but the way her little sister held her body, shoulders back, head high, Jaya could tell she was just as smitten. What was the point? What was the point of any of it? Isha and Elliot would never work, just as she and . . . No. She didn't want to finish that thought.

Daph went next. Rahul waited for her at the bottom, completely unsmiling. But when she got to the bottom, he took her hand and placed it securely in the crook of his arm.

Caterina went after her. She swept down the stairs, beautiful and dangerous in her dark green Valentino, the one she'd modeled for all her friends and Jaya at the start of the school year so long ago. Jaya watched as Caterina's date, the senior boy with blond hair and an alarmingly square jaw, met her at the bottom and planted a deep kiss on her mouth. Caterina leaned in at first, but then muscled him away after a few seconds to see if Alaric had been watching. When she saw him deep in conversation with Portia, a senior girl, her face iced over, all emotion leaching from it at once, and she led her date off to the side.

Jaya felt her heart twinge with pain for Caterina. It wasn't her fault how things had all played out. She may be an ice queen, but underneath, she was just as soft, just as hurt, just as vulnerable as anyone else. But Jaya couldn't dwell on it, because then it was time for her own partner-less descent. *Let's get it over with.*

She put one foot on the first marble step, her eyes sweeping the hall below, which had been decorated as if for a celebrity wedding. Waterford crystal vases filled with silver branches and pale blue orchids the exact color of the silk ribbons on the stairs covered every available surface, from the credenza by the window to the small table by the door. The crystal chandelier overhead had been draped with more silk ribbons and clusters of large silk flowers.

When Jaya's gaze dropped from the chandelier, she saw him for the first time.

Grey stood in the center of a group of people, all of whom were chattering excitedly to each other, giddy with expectation and the smell of perfume. But Grey—Grey only watched her. His face was serious, but his blue eyes shone. If Elliot had had naked adoration on his face, Grey's was full of pride and respect and heartache and maybe even the beginnings of love.

Holding her breath, willing herself to not feel a single iota of any of the hundreds of emotions swirling through her like a tempest— heartbreak, misery, yearning, anguish—Jaya descended the stairs.

# Grey

Watching her glide down the stairs, Grey knew. He'd made the right decision. Fighting for Jaya, telling her he wasn't going to give up so easily, would be the best decision he'd ever made. As soon as she was done descending, she was swallowed up by a small crowd of people, all eager to talk to her.

Grey smiled when her eyes met his, before turning away. He could wait. He didn't have all the time in the world, but he had all night. Perhaps he should feel more anxious, more fearful, that his birthday was tomorrow. He'd caught a glimpse of Jaya's pendant; he'd seen there were only two rubies remaining. But he didn't feel anxious, and he didn't feel scared. Because, whatever his future held, he knew that it also held Jaya.

# Jaya

The school had arranged for transportation to take them to the ballroom so they wouldn't have to walk in the snow with their expensive shoes and clothes. Jaya looked out the window when the van holding her and a few other students (but not Grey; she'd lost track of him, and hoped to continue avoiding him the rest of the night. Seeing him, those blue eyes, was just too painful) pulled up to the entrance of the ballroom.

The ballroom was always impressive; its domed roof and ornate stone pillars brought to mind Victorian-era balls and parties. But tonight it was absolutely captivating. Projectors hidden behind trees and boulders had transformed the plain roof into a shimmering dome made entirely of stars. The pillars held thick strands of ivy and twinkle lights, and dozens of large glass lanterns filled with flickering pillar candles and fake snow lit the path up the stairs and to the heavy wooden double doors.

"Wow," Jaya whispered, one hand against the window, impressed in spite of her mood.

"Wait till you see inside," Daph said. "St. R's always goes all out for this. Come on."

She was right. Inside the doors, Jaya stood looking around. "I've seen lavish parties before, but never at a school. Never like this."

Hundreds—maybe even thousands—of strands of blue, white, and silver crystals hung from the ceilings, stopping just above their heads, catching the light and winking at Jaya as they twirled lazily. Gigantic pots holding trees that had been painted white, their trunks and branches glittering with lights, dotted the corners, while mini versions of them anchored the tables. Dozens upon dozens of oversize shining lanterns, similar to the ones outside, bordered off the enormous dance floor, which was made of polished white stone and looked like a huge piece of ice. White chandeliers of various sizes hung from the ceilings in the midst of the strands of crystals. The entire room glowed and sparkled and appeared to be made of water or vapor or dreams rather than anything solid. Other students began surging in, hand in hand, their faces shining as they went to claim tables and to dance. Isha and Elliot walked close together, their heads bent, talking. Alaric was leading a girl in a red dress out to the dance floor, his hair higher and stiffer than ever.

"Ha," Daph said, crossing her arms. "Her hair's even taller than his. Wonder if they coordinated."

Jaya had to laugh. "Yes, maybe. I wouldn't put it past Alaric to have that as a stipulation for his dates."

A tall black senior boy—Jaya thought his name might be Jake—came up to Daph to ask her to dance. After a pause, she smiled and took his hand. "I'd love to." Looking back over her shoulder at Jaya, she let herself be led out onto the floor.

Jaya felt a twinge of genuine happiness for Daph, mixed with just a hint of wistfulness. Perhaps this was the beginning of Daph's clean break. Caterina deserved one too. Speaking of which . . . Jaya looked past Alaric and the girl in the red dress. They were dancing rather close together, their bodies moving in synchrony like they'd done this a thousand times before, the girl's crimson ball-gown skirt swirling around them like blood.

And by herself, just off the dance floor, stood Caterina. The flickering flames from the lanterns cast long shadows around her and across her face; her expression was hard but otherwise inscrutable. In her high-necked ball gown, she looked like an evil queen, plotting the princess's demise. Her date was nowhere to be seen.

According to Rahul, there was a 19.68 percent chance that, if Jaya were to approach Caterina, Caterina would launch herself at Jaya as she'd done to Alaric on the yacht. Apparently, he'd tabulated all the times Caterina had "lost her temper" over the years, along with some kind of estimation algorithm that her "mean intervals between outbursts" would be sufficiently high enough to evoke a physical reaction. That number kept playing in Jaya's head as she crossed to where Caterina stood, alone outside of the lanterns bordering the edges of the dance floor.

Why, then, was Jaya doing this now? Wouldn't it be safer, more drama-free, to just leave things alone? Caterina had done nothing recently but threaten Jaya. This didn't concern her. Besides, Caterina wasn't doing anything besides staring at Alaric. And who could blame her? She and Alaric had gone out for almost three years. Surely she was entitled to some stewing.

But it was the look on her face, the utter mask of coldness, so carefully constructed, when Jaya could see in her brown eyes a very deep despair, an overpowering loneliness.

"Hi," Jaya said, trying on an easy smile in spite of the fact that she was in a very un-smiley place currently. "You look fantastic. Valentino, right?" She gestured at Caterina's green dress.

Caterina was frozen crystal. Her eyes barely flickered in her direction. "What do you want?"

Jaya turned and watched Alaric and the girl in the red dress too. Here, behind the circle of light the lanterns threw on the dance floor, it was possible to believe you were in another colder, darker dimension, looking in on happiness. "It's ridiculous how happy they look, isn't it? It won't last. Alaric isn't capable of appreciating anyone the way they deserve to be appreciated."

"No, he isn't," Caterina said.

Jaya glanced sidelong at her. "It would be easy, you know, if this had happened to me, to let it consume me. To reject all the good things about myself—how charming I am or how socially gifted or generous. To really let the hatred take me over. If it were me, I mean."

"It *isn't* you. You don't know anything about how this feels. You don't know anything about me, Jaya." Caterina looked at her, her brown eyes sparking in the dark. "You don't know what I'm capable of."

# Grey

Grey had barely walked into the ballroom and scoped out the place, looking for Jaya to ask her if they could speak soon, when his cell phone began to buzz. Frowning, he pulled it out from an interior pocket of his tux.

It was a number he didn't recognize—an international number. It wasn't from the UK, but he was seized with a sudden fear that it had something to do with his father, that something terrible had happened.

Striding quickly to the double doors that led outside, Grey pressed the "answer" button. "Hello?" He pushed the doors open and slipped out, walking down the steps lined with lanterns to a cluster of blue spruces off to the right. The chilly night air wrapped its hands around him.

"Is this Grey? Grey Emerson?" a slightly grating male voice asked in an Indian accent.

"Yes, it is." Grey frowned, looking past the spruces into the darkness beyond. In the distance, he could see the main building that held the dorms. The first-floor windows were all lit; the front office was still staffed, even tonight. St. R's took their 24/7 policy very seriously. "Who am I speaking to?"

"This is Rajkumar Kiran Hegde of Karnataka, India."

CHAPTER 17

# Jaya

"Back home, we had a young mango tree," Jaya said to Caterina after a pause. "It was absolutely gorgeous, with soft green leaves and the most beautiful textured bark. But it kept growing too close to this big banyan tree we already had. My father's gardeners tried everything they knew—they pruned it back, they tied it, they even considered moving it at one point, even though it was well over thirty feet tall and twenty feet wide then. But you know what they did in the end?"

Caterina shook her head, interested in the story in spite of herself, it seemed.

"They left it alone. They figured if the mango tree really wanted to grow so close to the banyan tree, so close that it wasn't getting any light for itself, they shouldn't interfere."

"And what happened?" Caterina folded her long, pale arms across her green silk-clad torso.

"The mango tree died. It didn't stand a chance. The banyan was unstoppable."

They looked at each other. Caterina tried to keep her face impassive, but Jaya could see the muscle under her eye twitch. "I guess I'm the mango tree in that scenario. Great work, Aesop."

"Caterina." Jaya put a hand on Caterina's slender arm, but she brushed her off. "I am so sorry I didn't tell you what was happening between Alaric and Daphne Elizabeth. I felt caught between a rock and a hard place and I completely misstepped. But I'm not going to misstep anymore. I'm here to tell you that you can't let Alaric do this to you. Don't let him strip away everything. You're *Caterina LaValle*. Last time I checked, that meant something."

Caterina glared at her, eyes burning, like she was about to launch herself at Jaya and rip her hair from her skull.

# Grey

Grey waited for more from the dude, Kiran, but there was nothing else. "Okay."

He heard laughter—snuffling, derisive, annoying. "I see. So she never told you about me."

"Who hasn't told me about you?" he asked, but somewhere deep inside him, a faint alarm was beginning to sound.

"My *fiancée*, Jaya Rao," Kiran answered. "I understand you know her?"

Grey walked a few paces deeper into the trees, his shoes sinking in the mulch. "Your fiancée? I think there's some misunderstanding here." There had to be. This was ridiculous. "Jaya never mentioned you."

"And she didn't tell me about you. I found out through other means," Kiran said easily.

Grey opened his mouth, to say what he didn't know, but

nothing came out. He put a hand out to balance himself against the cold, rough bark of a towering pine. "I don't believe you," he said, his voice sounding distant and strange even to him.

Kiran chuckled again, and the raspy, superior sound made Grey want to crumble his phone with his bare hands. "I thought you'd say that. So I've sent you something via email. Why don't you check it? I'll wait."

"How do you have my phone number? My email?"

"We have a mutual friend," Kiran said, clearly enjoying this.

# Jaya

Jaya had just braced herself for a full-body attack—trust Rahul to get it right—when Caterina's face and shoulders sagged, like she was deflating. "I'm sorry too, Jaya. I've been fairly antisocial to you."

Jaya studied Caterina's miserable, remorseful face and realized she was telling the truth. "It's okay. I understand." Taking her arm, Jaya gently led her away, past the lanterns, into a dark corner. None of the dancers noticed them; it was like they were completely invisible. They sat on an extra table that wasn't being used.

"You know what's weird?" Caterina said finally. "Part of me is upset because Alaric dumped me, but the other part is just upset because he took something—some power—away from me by doing that. I was vulnerable, and he hurt me because of it. I don't want other people to think I'm weak. I wish I didn't care, but the truth is, I do."

Jaya put her arm around Caterina. "Of course you care. It's how we're raised, isn't it? We're expected to keep up appearances no matter what. The pressure's ludicrously exhausting. It's really not fair when you think about it. We have more pressure on us by the time we're six than most adults do their entire lives. And it's only because of who our parents are. So yes. I understand." Jaya paused, considering. "You should take up kickboxing at the athletic center, take out all your frustrations with Alaric in a socially acceptable way. It feels good to blow off some steam sometimes—to let your id show, as Ms. Rivard might say."

Caterina glanced at her, a small smile at the corner of her lips. "Kickboxing *does* sound fun right about now."

"So where's your date, whatever his name is? I don't think I have any classes with him."

Caterina sighed. "Connor Davids. He took off with some of his friends. Apparently, I was being 'boring.'"

"Wanker." A brief thought flitted across Jaya's mind: *Whatever would Amma say?*

"No, he was right. I wasn't much fun tonight. Or the past couple of times we went out. The truth is, I don't think I'm ready to date yet. I might not be for a very long time." There was a pause that Jaya didn't rush to fill. She could sense Caterina had more to say. "I loved Alaric, you know," she said finally, her voice barely a breath on the air. "It wasn't perfect, but in my own way? I really fucking loved him."

"I know," Jaya said, tightening her arm around Caterina's shoulders. "I know you did."

And they sat together in the dark, wearing their pretty dresses like armor.

# Grey

"A mutual friend?" Grey frowned. "Who?"

"Alaric Konig."

"Alaric?" Grey said. "He's not my—how does he—"

"Why don't you check your email and then we can speak some more."

An owl hooted somewhere in the night. Grey took the phone from his ear and, with hands that were slightly shaking, pulled up his email app. There was a new one, unread, right at the top. He tapped it to open.

It was a PDF of a newspaper announcement. Grey read the first line, his heart sinking. *Maharaja Adip Rao and Maharani Parvati Rao announce with pleasure the engagement of their eldest daughter, Rajkumari Jaya Rao, to the heir of the Hegde house, Kiran Hegde, son of Maharaja Dilip Hegde and Maharani Aruna Hegde.*

Feeling suddenly numb, like he'd plunged into an icy lake, Grey raised the phone back to his ear. "I—I don't believe this."

"Oh, but I think you do, deep down where it matters."

Grey didn't know what to say. Not a single word came to mind.

"The engagement's been in the cards for a while. Years," Kiran said. "I'm not sure if she told you that—"

"No." His voice was a strangled whisper. "No, she didn't."

"Mm. Can't say that surprises me. You an Emerson and she a Rao? Your families have been feuding for generations. She was probably having a little laugh at you since you met," Kiran said. "Come on, Grey. Didn't you think about it? Why is she in every single one of your classes? Didn't you even consider what immense coincidence conspired to make that happen?"

"Well, I . . ." He felt colossally stupid. He'd thought it was coincidence or fate or the stars that had aligned just right to bring her to him. He straightened. "Why would she do that? And how could she have—"

"I don't know the precise whys of it all beyond that your families abhor each other," Kiran said dismissively, as if he couldn't bother with the mundane details. "But I'm sure you could find out the how easily enough if you wanted to."

Grey shook his head, as if to ward off Kiran's words. He desperately, desperately wanted to believe Kiran was a lying piece of shit. But how could he overlook the engagement announcement? It was dated right after she had broken things off with him. Was Kiran right? Had Grey just been her plaything, a way to amuse herself, while she waited for the bigger, better things in life?

DE had mentioned how Jaya had won a trophy in archery, and Grey had dismissed it because it didn't fit with the Jaya he knew. She hadn't corrected him when he'd said what an incredible stroke of luck it was that she'd ended up in virtually all his classes. And now this arrogant jerk—her future fiancé—was saying she'd set it all up. That from the moment Jaya Rao had entered his life, she'd been trying to . . . to what? What was the endgame behind her manipulations, behind all her lies?

Snow began to fall, and Grey stood, letting the flakes coat his hair, his eyelashes, letting it cover him up, bit by bit, in ice.

"It's better this way, Grey," Kiran said, almost sympathetically. "I'm sure there was always a part of you that felt like this wasn't real. Isn't it better to know the truth than to be blissfully ignorant in a complete lie?" He sounded so patronizing, a part of Grey wanted to reach through the phone and wrap his hand around his neck. But that was a distant part of him. Most of him felt nothing.

Grey took the phone from his ear and pressed "end," his fingertips cold and covered in snow. He stood for a long time, staring at nothing.

A few minutes ago he'd been wondering where Jaya was, so he could speak to her. So he could fight for her. A few minutes ago life had been relatively simple. Then he'd answered his phone. And in that instant things had gone from simple to very-not-simple. From all's-well to what-the-fuck-is-happening.

Grey glanced across the snowy darkness at the main building, lit up bright and warm. Laughter drifted out. He thought about how happy he'd felt holding Jaya's hand, how he'd felt ridiculously lucky when she turned those big brown eyes on him. He had believed everything she'd said about how the curse didn't define him, that it didn't matter to her. He had believed her when she'd said he deserved more. He'd been so sure he *knew* her. That she was steadfast and honest and her eyes would never lie to him.

Grey squeezed the phone in his hand, which, he noticed with a grim, remote interest, was shaking. Fury? Shock? Sorrow? All of those and so much more.

He turned to look back at the main building and began to pick his way there, through the cold darkness. It was time he got some answers.

He pushed in through the doors, bringing the chill winter air with him, and the receptionist, Mrs. Lucas, looked up at him in surprise. She'd been playing solitaire on her computer, a half-eaten microwaveable lasagna pushed to the side. She hurriedly shut down her game and stood. "Lord Northcliffe! Are you all right? How can I help you?"

The alarm in her voice made Grey wonder what he looked like, but only for a moment. Leaning forward on her desk, he said, "I need to know why Jaya Rao is in all my classes."

She looked at him, confused. "Princess Jaya Rao?"

"Yes." Grey was trying to keep a lid on his temper, but it felt like a volcano, urgent, seething, simmering. "Please," he said carefully, biting each word up. "Please look at her records and tell me why she's registered in my classes. Was it arranged?"

The receptionist put her reading glasses on and sat back down, opening an application on her computer. "Well," she said, still sounding discombobulated, but apparently deciding it wasn't worth it to ask questions of Grey in the mood he was in, "if there was any kind of special intention behind it, we'd have recorded it here. . . ." She clicked around for a few moments, and Grey tried to get his breathing under control. Everything felt like it hinged on what Mrs. Lucas had to say.

"Ah, here it is."

Grey held very still. "Who arranged it?"

"It appears that your father's secretary made a phone call the day before classes began to request that Jaya be put in your classes." She glanced at him. "Due to the fact that your families are old friends and Princess Jaya was new."

Grey felt like he was witnessing every single moment a thousand times because time had slowed to a standstill. "My father's secretary," he repeated slowly, in a voice as heavy and colorless as lead.

Mrs. Lucas turned back to her computer and tapped at a few keys. "Would you like me to connect you, Lord Northcliffe?"

Grey nodded numbly.

She dialed the number on her desk phone and handed the receiver to him, striding off to an interior office to give him privacy.

Grey put the phone to his ear, his hand in an iron vise around it.

It rang once.

Twice.

Three times.

"Hello?"

# Jaya

She sat next to Caterina, frowning. "Hello?" she said again. No one answered. "How odd," she said to Caterina as she began to pull the phone away from her ear.

Then he spoke.

"Jaya," Grey said, in a voice that didn't sound much like his at all. "Could you meet me outside the ballroom in five minutes?"

"Outside? Well, yes, but . . . why? What's going on?" She paused, but no answer came. "Hello?"

But he was already gone.

# Grey

He plowed through the snow, back toward the ballroom. His heart pumped furiously in his chest, his blood surging with hot, pulsing anger. She'd lied to him. From the very first day they'd met, she'd been shamelessly, flagrantly lying. Why? Because he was an easy mark, so turned inward, so obviously damaged? Because he was an Emerson and that meant he was subhuman, not worth consideration?

A brisk wind blew snow into his face, and Grey welcomed the stinging in his eyes, against his skin. While he'd been falling in love with her, she'd been someone else's. When she kissed him, she'd probably been thinking of Kiran Hegde. And on the yacht, when she'd seemed so sad, just as lonely as him, it had all been an act. It was all an act, and he'd been thoroughly fooled. Well, now it was time for her to answer a few of his questions. It was the least Jaya Rao could do.

He marched onward.

## Jaya

Jaya turned to Caterina, an anguished look taking over her face even though she was trying to stop it. Caterina's face was pale and thin and raw. She shouldn't be left alone. "Caterina . . ."

"Go," Caterina said, her chin up. "I'm fine."

Chewing on her lip, Jaya regarded her worriedly. She was anything but fine. Caterina needed a fr— Slowly, Jaya turned to study Rahul, a few yards away. Slipping off the table, she walked over to where he was standing like a footman at attention, just slightly off the dance floor. She straightened his bow tie and Rahul looked at her in surprise. "Ask her to dance," Jaya whispered to him.

"Who?" he whispered back, completely oblivious.

"Caterina," Jaya said, gesturing over to the table where she sat alone.

"Uh . . . no, I don't think so," Rahul said, and his golden-brown skin tinged bright pink.

Jaya studied him. The way he was fidgeting with his cuffs, staring at his shoes, the way his upper lip was prickling with sweat—he really, really *liked* Caterina. "You should," Jaya said, and before he could argue, she added hurriedly, "Not for yourself, but for her. She's in a bad situation right now, and she could really use a friend. Please, Rahul. You'd be doing me a giant favor."

He looked at her, his brow clouding with doubt. Adjusting his glasses, he said, "Really?"

"Really." Jaya made sure her eyes were extra wide and earnest. "I really don't want to leave her, but . . . Please?"

"What are you two whispering about?" Caterina said, in what was meant to be a snarky voice, but really just sounded croaky and kind of wilted.

Jaya raised her eyebrows at Rahul, and swallowing so his Adam's apple bobbed nervously, he stepped around her. "Um, I was wondering if . . . that is, if you're not otherwise engaged, if you'd like to dance?"

He sounded so polished and . . . sweet. Not bad, Rahul. Not bad at all. Caterina, frowning lightly, looked from him to Jaya. Jaya nodded slightly, as if to say, *Go on. What will it hurt? You'd be doing the poor guy a favor.*

Sighing, Caterina slid herself off the table. "Fine," she said, swiping her gloved fingers under her eyes and adjusting her hair clip. Her cheeks were flushed; her shoulders just a bit straighter.

Jaya knew her thought process exactly: Caterina could march back out onto the dance floor with a guy now. She could show Alaric she wasn't just crumpled in a soggy heap somewhere, having been abandoned by not just Alaric but Connor, too. She was *enjoying* the Homegoing just as much as he was, thank you very much. She was choosing to dance with boys she'd never danced with before, to try things she'd never tried before. Alaric had done her a *favor.* "I suppose one dance won't hurt."

Jaya watched them for a moment, smiling. Then, her smile fading, she walked toward the exit to find Grey. Why had he sounded the way he had? Why had he called her instead of just talking to her in person? She had no idea what he wanted to speak to her about, but a low thrumming panic in her chest told her it wasn't anything good.

When Jaya walked outside and around the building, her eyes feasted on Grey, standing still in the cut-glass night. The snow had dusted his shoulders and hair before it stopped falling, and with his blue eyes, he looked like Jack Frost, commanding the winter.

Jaya stepped through pools of starlight and around drifts of silver snow, watching Grey, who was looking at her. His gaze slipped to her pendant—probably noting the two rubies that remained—and then back up to her face. It was hard to read his expression in the muted light, but his blue eyes were unwavering, like he was studying her face for answers to questions he hadn't asked yet.

"Hi," Jaya said as she reached him, but he didn't return her greeting. Her heart thundered.

Her eyes fell to something in his hand—his phone. "What's going on?"

"Just doing some reading," Grey said in a voice like granite and ice. He held his phone out to her so she could more clearly see the screen. "Recognize this?"

On the screen, she could make out an announcement. Her engagement announcement.

Jaya looked up at him, opening her mouth, not a word escaping her lips. Her system had iced over from shock. It wasn't supposed to happen this way. She'd tried to spare him this pain as soon as she'd known what she had to do.

"How . . . ," Jaya began, not sure how to finish the question. "Who . . . ? I . . ." She tried again, her heart beginning to pound furiously as the reality of the situation began to sink in. "I can explain."

But he was already stepping away from her.

# Grey

"Such a lie." Grey kept his voice low, but it reverberated in the silent night. He walked to a nearby pine tree and studied its snow-laden needles. "Such a profound lie."

Jaya's dress rustled as she stepped forward, closer to him. Her voice was thick with tears. "I'm so sorry."

"I had to find out from Kiran Hegde that you were playing me." Jaya opened her mouth, but Grey kept going, his fury like a demon, whispering in his ear. "Our classes together! Our friendship! The concern about the pendant! The kiss! Was *any* of it real?"

She squeezed her eyes shut as if his words were causing her physical pain. "It was. I didn't—"

"You called Mrs. Lucas and pretended to be my dad's secretary. So, right from the very first day, this was all a setup. Have you been reveling in my idiocy this entire time?" Grey said, his chilly smile kissing his lips with frost.

A wind that smelled of more snow whipped around them. "No," she whispered. "No, never."

"And what about archery? Do you really have a trophy in it? Was all of the pretending to need my help just another lie?" He studied her, watched her face as it drained of color. "Right. Thought so. I have to hand it to you, though. You're good; you're very good. You really had me going, and that's not an easy thing to do. If I'd known *any* of this, I would never have—" He swallowed. "I would never have let myself fall for you."

Jaya's eyes filled with tears, almost brimming over. But she said nothing.

## Jaya

There was nothing she could say. And nothing she should say. What would telling him that she'd come to execute revenge but then ended up falling for him do? What would telling him that the engagement was a last-ditch effort at saving her family's name, her sister's honor accomplish? Perhaps if he raged against her enough, perhaps if he let the anger crescendo and swallow him, he could begin to let her go. Perhaps he could begin to make peace with their parting. It was what she'd wanted for him all along.

"What was the purpose?" he asked, his hair falling into his eyes. "Why did you do all this?"

# Grey

Twin tears splattered on Jaya's cheeks and ran down her face. "I came here with the intention of breaking your heart," she said, her voice barely a whisper. "I was told a male Emerson heir was behind the leaked pictures of Isha; I thought that meant you. When I learned that you attended St. Rosetta's, I thought it would be the perfect opportunity to get back at your family." Grey's heart squeezed in his chest as if a vengeful fist were bent on reducing it to pulp. So it was true. Everything Kiran had said was true. Jaya paused. "How did . . . how did Kiran find out about you and me? Was it Caterina?"

Grey shook his head. "Alaric. That asshole was laughing at me every time he saw us together, wasn't he?" He watched disbelief and anger cloud Jaya's eyes, but he kept going before she could respond. *He* was asking the questions right now. Bracing himself, he said, "And it's true that this engagement between you and Kiran has been in the works for years?"

Something flitted across her face. Shock? Confusion? Anger? Then it was gone, and her face was back to being a blank mask, though rivers of tears ran down her cheeks. Her voice shaking, she said, "Yes."

He felt like someone had hit him with a concrete pole, right in the chest. He almost doubled over, panting in agony. She was almost engaged. The entire time, she was almost engaged. And he was the biggest fool in the world.

He nodded at her, once. "I see." He was surprised by how calm, how in control, he sounded. "Goodbye, Jaya."

Sidestepping her, he walked briskly away, cutting a path right through the piles of snow. He didn't look back once.

# *Jaya*

Jaya stumbled off at some point. Her entire body—actually, even her soul—felt completely, thoroughly dead. Kiran had lied to Grey. He'd made it seem like he and Jaya were laughing at Grey behind his back. She felt a brief jolt of anger, at the fact that he'd called Grey, that he'd tried to hurt him, that he'd lied. She'd told him to leave Grey alone and he'd completely flouted her wishes. But how could she ignore her own hand in this? If she hadn't lied, if she hadn't set up the house of cards for Kiran to knock over, they wouldn't be in this situation at all. Jaya's anger seeped out of her. *Maybe this is for the best*, she told herself. *Grey can let you go now. He can go on with his life. This is all for the best.* Perhaps Kiran had done her a favor.

For a brief moment, she thought about Grey, watching the sunrise tomorrow by himself, afraid of the curse, filled with self-loathing, waiting for it all to end. The flare of agony she experienced was so great that she had to bury the thought immediately. She didn't have the strength for that right now, on top of everything else.

Jaya found herself back in the ballroom without remembering having made the decision to go back. People were slow-dancing or sitting at tables enjoying their custom mock-tails, blissfully unaware of the smoking wreckage of her life. Jaya walked to an empty table and then stood there, her hands at her sides, thinking nothing, feeling nothing. After some time, she began walking toward the table on the other side of the ballroom where she and Caterina had sat before. That was the only place she could bear to be right then . . . hidden in the shadows, not forced to make eye contact and smile. The table was, thankfully, empty now—Rahul and Caterina were still on the ballroom floor.

Suddenly, she realized Isha was in the dark corner with her. Her sister's face was full of concern. How long had she been there? Where did she come from? "Jaya? What are you doing back here?"

Jaya didn't answer. She just wrapped her arms around Isha and held her close.

Isha patted her back. "Are you all right?"

When she pulled back to look at Isha, Jaya tried to smile and reassure her. But, almost of its own accord, her face crumpled and tears began to stream down her cheeks. "No," she managed finally. "I'm not."

"I'll come by your room tomorrow, okay?" Isha said outside her dorm room door.

"Sounds good," Elliot replied. Jaya leaned back against Isha's headboard and closed her eyes.

A long, significant pause and then, "I should really get inside. My sister needs me."

"Yeah, sure. I'll see you, Ish."

The door closed and Isha turned out the overhead lights, switching on a small lamp on her nightstand instead. She sat on the bed at Jaya's feet, bouncing her a little. "Hi."

Jaya tried on a wan smile, but from Isha's concerned face, she wasn't sure she succeeded.

"Something happened?" Isha ventured. "With . . . Grey?"

Jaya blinked and sat up. Her beautiful dress was all crumpled and bunched around her, but she didn't have the energy to straighten it out. "How did you know that?"

Isha shrugged. "It's not hard to figure out. You look heartbroken. And the way I see it, only one boy has your heart."

Jaya looked away. "He doesn't. I'm getting engaged to Kiran."

"Did Grey find that out somehow?"

Jaya nodded. "Kiran called him. He made it seem like I was playing with Grey's heart the whole time."

"What?" Isha looked livid. "Why? That's *none* of his business—"

"Except it is," Jaya said, leaning forward. "Don't you see, Ish? Kiran will be my fiancé soon. I don't have the luxury to be 'heartbroken' over an Emerson." She tried to say it with vitriol, but her voice cracked.

Kicking off her shoes, Isha put her hand on Jaya's knee, pulling her legs up so she was sitting cross-legged. "Maybe you don't have the luxury to," she said quietly. "But you can't tell your heart what to do."

Jaya blinked away her tears. "I'm marrying Kiran," she said again, her voice high and tight. "It's what's best for the family." Without quite meaning to, she found herself echoing Grey's words from their first time in the dining hall. "It might not be easy, but it is that simple."

"Jaya, you don't even like Kiran. What's best for *you*?"

Jaya shook her head and leaned back against the headboard once more. "Immaterial."

"Jaya—"

"No. There's nothing more to say about it." Blinking, she added, "But I have to tell you something."

Isha nodded.

"I'm sorry," Jaya said, holding her sister's gaze. "I'm sorry I've been pushing you so hard to be someone you're not. I told you not to take robotics. I told you not to be with Elliot. I've been controlling and rigid and . . ." Caressing Isha's cheek, she smiled a little, as much as she could. "You did nothing wrong kissing Talin. You did nothing wrong helping those other boys in the motorcycle shop. The problem's not you. The problem's the bloody messages we're given, starting before we can even fully understand them. You're perfect the way you are, Ish. People who don't turn out how their parents or their society expects are the best people of all." Her voice broke as she finished, and she cleared her throat to continue. "So you be the best fucking robotics engineer you can be. And if people give you shit about it, give them hell. I know I will."

Isha stared at her, agog. "Jaya . . . You . . . you said 'fuck.' And 'shit.'"

Jaya stared back. "Damn right I did."

Isha laughed into the silence and leaped on Jaya. They hugged each other tight, both of them laughing, tears prickling Jaya's eyes.

Then Isha pulled back and studied Jaya's face, her own lined with worry. "So . . . um . . . What are you going to do about Grey? Are you really just going to let him think you were messing with him this entire time?"

"Grey," Jaya whispered, feeling a stab of pain deep in her heart. "I don't know. I wish I could explain to him that . . .

that I wasn't trying to be cruel. It could be my way of undoing some of the damage I've done, of making amends before we say goodbye. But he won't even speak to me. I haven't given him any reason to."

Isha studied her older sister, her jaw set. "Then *I'll* have to give him one."

# CHAPTER 18

# Grey

He was on Mount Sama, standing at the very edge, looking down over the town, the sharp rock jutting into the soles of his shoes, hurting him. The wind shrieked, an angry demoness.

Grey inched one foot forward and then the other.

The rock under him crumbled, and he fell, tumbling, his stomach not in his throat, no longer even in his body, but somewhere above him, waiting to catch up.

Grey grabbed the lip of the mountaintop with one hand, his fingers scrabbling for purchase. He couldn't hang on too long. How was he supposed to get back up? He was going to die here, alone. His body would fall into the abyss below, never to be found.

"Help!" Grey yelled, hoping someone would miraculously be walking up the path, that someone would hear him. "Help! I can't do this much longer!"

A hooded figure stepped up to him. He couldn't see the person's face.

"Oh, thank God," Grey said, relief washing over him like a warm ocean wave. "Please, take my hand. Help me up."

The person reached up to pull their hood back. Jaya's face

looked down at him, unsmiling. The wind whipped her hair around her face like a swirl of black smoke.

"Jaya?" Grey was confused. Why was she looking at him like that? Like she didn't even know him?

"It's not that I don't know you," Jaya said, apparently reading his mind. "It's that you don't know me."

"Jaya, I—"

She lifted one snow boot–clad foot up. And she brought it down, hard, on his hand.

Grey jerked awake, not even twenty minutes after he'd fallen asleep, his body covered in a thin film of sweat, and lay there, his mind curiously blank.

Bit by bit, the night came back to him, like a car crash he couldn't stop from happening. The good news was, his chest felt strangely hollow, like his heart had been scooped out. He got out of bed, brushed his teeth, showered, and got dressed. Then he slipped out of his dorm room and walked down the silent, empty hallway.

It was past midnight now—officially his birthday. Eighteen. The day his life wound down, like some broken toy. The day everything went silent and cold.

Grey stood with one palm pressed to the curved window in the West Wing tower, watching the flat black night sky, pulled taut like a shroud. Fitting, considering he felt about as dead as a person could feel while still having a pulse. He tried to tell himself it didn't matter. It didn't matter how he felt or what had happened with . . . *her* . . . because this was for the best. His father had warned him, and he'd been foolish. Grey had thought he knew better.

He almost laughed at the idea. How fucking hilarious that he'd thought, even for a moment, that he might actually get to see this day on his own terms. Jaya had made him believe that—that was the cruelest thing of all.

He closed his eyes and began to count down the hours until sunrise.

# Jaya

Jaya sat in the empty common room on a green velvet couch, drinking her coffee, her eyes bleary. It was barely four a.m., but that didn't matter. She hadn't slept at all anyway. She'd tiptoed out of Isha's room about thirty minutes ago, once she'd heard her sister's soft snores.

On the arm of the couch, the final book in Jaya's YA romance series lay open and facedown. She'd tried to read it, but her mind kept wandering. It kept flashing pictures of Grey. The way he'd looked both burning with fury and completely defeated when he confronted her. The way he'd held her close when they were dancing at the mixer so long ago. Skiing with him in Aspen. How he'd bought her the gap-year book. Their snowball fight, the way he'd kissed her until she forgot she was cold.

Where was he now? Was he waiting for the sunrise by himself somewhere? Her heart ached to be with him, not just because she wanted to see him smile at her again, but because she knew he was probably so very scared, and now, thanks to her, so very lonely. The pendant glinted at her throat. Only one ruby remained.

Jaya felt like she was wearing every feeling, every emotion on the outside of her skin. Her sweater scraped too hard against her, the coffee slid too hotly down her throat. An outsider looking at her would see a princess, poised perfectly on the edge of a settee, looking out a large picture window at the darkness beyond. But what they wouldn't know was that at any moment she might burst into tears because the night was too dark, the silence was too loud, or the world was too big.

"You're up really early."

Jaya turned to see Caterina stalking in, already dressed in a belted cream sweater and black pants, her feet clad in suede boots. Her makeup and hair were perfectly done. "What time did *you* have to wake up to look like that at four o'clock in the morning?" Jaya asked.

Caterina smiled coolly as she got herself a cup of espresso from the machine at the counter along the far wall. "I didn't go to bed at all."

"Oh." Jaya scooted over as Caterina came to sit with her on the settee. She paused. "Wait. You and Rahul . . . ?"

Caterina eyed her with disdain. "Rahul was nice to dance with, but he is not the kind of boy I date."

"Hmm." Jaya hid a faded smile behind her coffee cup.

"He is *not*," Caterina said, a little too stridently. Then, composing herself, she added, "So. Something happened with Grey."

Jaya felt her entire body contract painfully at the mention of his name. She didn't bother to ask Caterina how she knew; people like Caterina had their ways. Taking the time to smooth down her expression, Jaya said, still staring straight ahead, "Yes." Tears fell from her eyelashes, but she made no move to dry them. She was tired of pretending to be impeccable. "Alaric was updating Kiran on everything I did."

"But Alaric doesn't know—" Caterina stopped, her eyes wide.

"What?" Jaya asked, putting a hand on Caterina's arm. "Are you all right?"

"It was me," Caterina said, looking pale.

"What?" Jaya said again, stiffening.

"I . . . I was so mad at you, and I told Alaric a whole bunch of things about you and Grey, some of which I didn't even know were true, like that you were dating and that it was really shady that you were in all his classes." Looking stricken, she continued. "I didn't think anything of it. I was just venting and—God, I cannot be*lieve* that asshole! I'm so sorry, Jaya."

Jaya let out a breath. "You know what? It was mainly my fault. I can't really blame you for venting, just like I can't blame Alaric and Kiran for acting how their natures dictate. I really did want to hurt Grey at first, and if I hadn't had those intentions in the first place, none of this would've happened." She filled Caterina in on everything that had happened back home, before St. R's, and the plan she'd formulated.

Isha came upstairs in a robe in the middle of Jaya's recounting, her hair still rumpled, and sat on the couch beside her, laying her head on her big sister's shoulder.

"Family," Caterina said, smiling a little at Isha. "One would do most anything for them."

Jaya nodded. "Yes."

Caterina studied Jaya's face. "So what's the plan now?"

"I guess I'll just sit here and watch the sun rise in a couple of hours." Jaya's hands shook a little as she said the words, as she imagined Grey doing the same, fear knotting his stomach and icing his spine. Alone, thanks to her.

Isha and Caterina exchanged a glance and then Jaya felt

Caterina's eyes on her, assessing, weighing. She didn't have the energy to ask what that was about.

"Excuse me," Caterina said a few moments later, getting up abruptly and stalking away, back down the hallway.

"Yeah, um, me too," Isha said, hopping up and following her.

Jaya watched them go, frowning slightly. It was odd, but she didn't have the energy to wonder what they were doing. "Nice speaking to you," she said, and sipped her coffee morosely.

# Grey

Grey walked in the dark-cloaked forest outside the campus, ensconced in his jacket, his face hidden by the hood. There was a thick layer of bluish snow on the ground and he trudged through it, winding deeper into the trees, his boots crunching as they packed down the icy precipitation. He couldn't keep still, though he didn't know what it was he was trying to outrun. The sunrise? That was coming soon, whether he liked it or not. It was just after four thirty in the morning. His weather app told him sunrise was at 6:45 a.m. There was no outrunning this. There was no outrunning anything. Still, if he could pick anything, what would he have chosen to do on possibly the last morning of his life? An image of Jaya pressed against him as they danced together entered his head, unbidden, and he forced it away.

*Wherever you go, there you are* flashed through his mind, and he smiled grimly.

His phone beeped in his pocket and his heart thudded. He

pulled it out and felt a small prick of disappointment when he saw who it was.

DE: Hey, dude. Where are you?

Frowning, he put the phone back into his pocket. He didn't want to speak to DE right now. His phone buzzed again. And again. Annoyed, Grey slipped it back out.

DE: Dude.

DE: Grey. Hey. Dude. Where are you?

Growling in frustration, he tapped out a reply. Why?

DE: Mm, that's not exactly an answer

He waited.

DE: You need to speak with Jaya.

He stopped and leaned against a tree, his jaw hard.

DE: Grey I know you're super mad. But you had some good times with her too, right? She needs to say something before you guys go your separate ways

She had the chance to say a lot of things and never took it. Why start now?

DE: This is about closure, duh. You need it, even if you don't think you do

When he didn't respond right back, she sent another text.

DE: Why? Do you have big plans today?

Grey read it and looked up at the mountain beyond the trees. *His* mountain. What would be a worthy way to spend his last morning, his last few hours? Did he really want to die a petty bastard?

Fine, he responded. Tell her to meet me on Mt. Sama.


Grey sat back against the big boulder on the mountain and looked down at the tiny town of St. Rosetta, snow-covered shops and small buildings dotting it like thorny burrs. He could make out St. R's sprawling campus from up here too. Concealed inside it was Jaya, possibly getting ready so she could come up here and say whatever it was she wanted to say.

He thought about speaking to her. How did he feel that he'd be seeing her so soon? How did he feel that this might be their last ever conversation?

He felt close to nothing, he realized. It was like one of those magic eye pictures. If he squinted and contorted himself, he might be able to see hints of sadness, of hurt, of loneliness, of fear. But besides that? Nothing.

If Jaya had, over the course of the last few months, chipped away at the block of stone surrounding him to reveal who he was underneath, she'd also managed to scour him bare in the matter of a single night. All he felt right now was a hollow nihilism.

An icy wind whistled past him, but apart from that, there was no sound of life. He was completely alone.

# Jaya

"Come on. We're going for a walk."

Jaya realized she'd been slumped back on the couch, watching the day gradually lighten outside. She blinked her dry eyes and looked at Daphne Elizabeth, who was towering over her dressed in a big coat, pants, and a winter hat, her hands on her slim hips. Next to her was Isha's much smaller form, also completely bundled up. "What?"

"You can't just sit here like this. We're going for a walk." Daph shoved a coat at Jaya; Jaya realized it was hers. Daph and Isha must've gone into her room to get it.

"What—what time is it?"

Isha consulted her phone. "Almost five a.m."

Jaya rubbed her eyes. Her cup of cold coffee sat abandoned on the table in front of her, looking as lonely and sad as she felt. "You guys want to go for a walk *now*?" The early-morning snowball fight with Grey flashed through her mind before she could stop it, bringing with it a wave of pain.

Daph and Isha exchanged a look, unaware of her thoughts. "Yes, we do," Isha said firmly. "Come on."

Jaya felt discombobulated enough that she did as she was told, slipping on her winter coat and following her little sister and Daph meekly to the stairs. "How was your night, Daph?"

Daphne Elizabeth glanced at her as they walked downstairs. "Good. It was good. I saw Alaric dancing with Portia and, I don't know. I'm realizing maybe I just need some time to be by myself, you know? Ride that single train."

The three of them pushed through the doors and walked onto the grounds, their boots crunching the snow. The tree limbs were all weighed down, heavy, reaching down as if to touch them as they walked.

"Right. That's a good idea. A good thing to realize." She rubbed her face, confused. "And now we're going for a walk at five a.m.?" None of this was making any sense.

"Well, yeah," Daph said, pulling her hat down lower on her head. "After Isha texted me and Caterina—"

Jaya turned to Isha. "You texted them? When?"

"Last night," Isha said. She was so bundled up, Jaya could only see her eyes and her nose, the tip of which was red from the cold. "You fell asleep for a few minutes, and I knew I'd need help to get this whole Grey-plan situated."

Jaya shook her head, frowning. "Okay . . ."

"Okay, so after Isha texted us, Caterina swung by my room."

"Oh no, did she—"

"No, it wasn't as bad as you think." Daph buried her hands in the pockets of her coat and stared straight ahead as she spoke. They wound their way down a snow-covered hill and off campus toward the town of St. Rosetta. "She told me what Alaric had done. He actually was spying on you, in a sense, and sending information to that jackass Kiran. And Kiran called Grey." Daph's jaw was hard, her eyes like glittering emeralds.

"Yes, but, Daph . . . I don't like what Alaric did, but he couldn't have done it if it weren't true. If I hadn't plotted to break Grey's heart and kept things from him at every turn." She heard her voice crack.

Daph and Isha each put an arm around her, as if they'd coordinated. "You made a bad choice, I'll hand you that," Daph said. "But who am I to judge? The longer I stayed with Alaric, I . . . I lost my mind, Jaya. I wanted his attention and I thought taking him from Caterina proved—I don't know, that I was important enough to someone to make him weak." She snorted. "I'm an idiot."

Jaya stepped on a snowy bed of pine needles, feeling their spongy weight beneath her boots. "So are you and Caterina talking now?"

Daph took her arm off Jaya's shoulder and laughed. "No, are you kidding? She still wants to boil my spleen and eat it. We just temporarily reconciled to, ah, for a mission of sorts. But I did apologize to her. Again."

"What'd she say?"

"I believe her exact words were 'Fuck off and die.'"

"Savage," Isha muttered.

They were heading into the woods now. Jaya put her arm around Daph's waist and squeezed. "I'm sorry."

"Nah, it's all me. I was weak and wrong and stupid, and I'm paying the price now. As I should. I don't even know how I'm going to go about making amends for this one, but I'm going to try." She hopped over a log in her path and kept walking.

They wound deeper into the encroaching forest, along a path that was usually dirt but was now covered in snow and ice. Jaya looked up at the pines above them, her pulse picking up. She knew this path. "Where are we going, Daph? Isha?"

Isha turned to look at her. Her brown parka matched her eyes exactly, both of them a darker shade of amber in the faded light of early morning. "We're taking you to see Grey."

Jaya stopped short. "No. He doesn't want to talk to me."

Daph's face was serious. "Well, okay, maybe that's true. But he's willing to let you say your piece."

Jaya's breathing quickened. "What?"

"I texted him about thirty minutes ago." Daph shrugged. "He didn't sound too pleased about it, but he's open to it. He wants to give you the chance to say what you need to say."

Isha gestured to their right. "He's up there."

Mount Sama. Grey's mountain. She turned to look at the towering rock, dark and hooded and silent. "He's up there," she repeated in a whisper.

Isha gave her a quick hug. "Yeah. And I really think you should go talk to him. You've come all this way, Jaya. Just do it; get it off your chest."

Jaya nodded. She could make her amends now, if Grey would let her. She could try to convince him that she'd never laughed at him behind his back; that she really had fallen for him. She could spare him that small amount of pain, at least, before she reconciled herself to being Kiran's soon-to-be fiancée. "Thank you," she said to the both of them.

Daph rubbed the back of her head. "It's the least I could do. Thanks for trying to have my back before. Wish I'd listened to you sooner." Impulsively, she leaned forward and gave Jaya a hug. Jaya was so surprised, it took her a moment to return it.

Isha kissed her on the cheek.

"I love you," Jaya said to her, her voice catching. "You know that, right?"

"Better than I know anything else," Isha said solemnly.

Jaya gazed at her and then at Daphne Elizabeth, her heart brimming with love and pain, jostling for space with the trepidation and anxiety already there.

"All right, all right, now get going," Daph said, shoving Jaya gently away.

Jaya turned to go, and Isha said, "Hey, Jaya?"

"Yes?"

"Good luck. I hope he hears you."

Jaya looked back up toward the mountain and took a shuddering breath. "Thank you. I'll need it."


Jaya wound her way up to the mountaintop, puffing lightly. Her parka was warm, but the wind was still tugging at her hair and slapping her in the face, bringing tears to her eyes. Her heart pounded at the thought of coming face-to-face with Grey in just a few minutes. She was still completely gobsmacked about what Isha, Caterina, and Daph had done, and even more so that Grey had agreed to meet with her one last time. Jaya knew this was Caterina's way of making up for what Alaric had done with the information she'd given him, and in spite of herself, in spite of how bossy and invasive this was, Jaya was grateful.

She had no grand expectation that she would be able to get Grey to believe she'd never meant to hurt him, that she hadn't been playing games with him the whole time. When he'd flung all those accusations at her, she'd made no attempt to refute them. If anything, she'd *wanted* him to believe it so he could move on. Now all she hoped for was that he'd listen to her with an open mind. That he'd see she really had fallen for him. That the engagement hadn't been preplanned, and that there was a very good reason why she had to go through with it. And maybe, just maybe, he'd let her sit with him while he waited for the sun to come up. All Jaya wanted was to be there for him when the sun rose, so he didn't have to be alone. If she could do all that, she'd get engaged to Kiran with a modicum of peace.

She emerged onto the mountaintop and looked around among the boulders and rocks, her pulse thundering in her ears. At first she thought he'd decided not to come after all, and her heart sank. But then she saw him, unfolding himself slowly from where he'd been sitting against a giant boulder that was topped with snow. His red jacket, too, was covered.

"Hi," she said, walking up to him. Beyond them, the town of St. Rosetta looked like one of those little idyllic winter villages you could buy in department stores around the holidays.

He regarded her with expressionless blue eyes, so reminiscent of when they'd first met. Jaya felt a deep ache in her bones, knowing that she'd done this to him. She'd sent him back to how he used to be.

"DE said you wanted to speak to me," he said, as if he were reading a grocery list.

"Yes." Jaya brushed a few snowflakes from her hair. "Thank you for meeting me."

He didn't say anything.

"How are you, Grey?" she said, searching his eyes. "It's almost sunrise. I was thinking about you."

"I'm fine," he said shortly, but his eyes flickered to where he must know the pendant sat, safe behind her winter coat, warm against her skin. He didn't trust her anymore; he wouldn't tell her how afraid he was.

Jaya unzipped her coat just low enough to pull the pendant out, so he could see. She knew he liked to keep an eye on it, like you might a snake that had slithered in your open window. His face paled a little at the sight of the solitary ruby, sitting precariously in its socket. Still, he said nothing.

Swallowing, Jaya said, "I know we spoke last night, but . . . but I didn't say everything I wanted to say then."

Grey didn't speak or show any emotion; his arms hung loosely by his sides, his hair windblown and peppered with snow.

"There's no excuse for what I wanted to do to you when I first got to St. Rosetta's, Grey. None. It was a horrible thing, born from my rage and my pain. But I want you to know that after our fight in Aspen, I gave up on that plan completely. And this engagement with Kiran? I only agreed to it because I need to protect my sister and my family name. It's what I need to do. The night we kissed in the snow, my father called to tell me we were in trouble. I didn't tell you any of it because I wanted you to be able to move on. If you thought of me as callous, as evil, you would be able to forget me. I kept it from you, not to be deceitful, but to help you let go of me. You're . . ." She stopped, her voice catching, and blinked away her tears. She needed to say this without going to pieces. "I've never met anyone like you before. You bring so much light and warmth wherever you go. You've completely changed me, you know. You've helped bring me closer to my sister." She sniffed and kept going. "Grey, what your father's told you . . . it doesn't have to be the end. Your mother . . . You don't have to believe what he believes. You . . . you deserve to be happy." She put a finger under her eye to catch a tear. "Even if it's without me, Grey, I want you to be happy."

Grey studied her for a moment, then nodded once. His face was still distant, remote. She hadn't gotten through to him at all.

Jaya could feel the tears coming to her eyes. "Can I sit with you? So you don't have to be by yourself when the sun comes up?"

But he turned away, looking out over the edge of the mountain, a brief flash of torment lighting up his face before it went blank once more.

# Grey

If he had any heart left, it would've broken again, splintered into unrecognizable pieces. Ironically enough, Jaya had accomplished her mission after all.

As he watched her go, climb back down the way she'd come, her shoulders shaking, Grey understood that this was it. This was the memory he'd have with him as his life ended. He looked up at the sky. There was light creeping in at the edges, day slowly erasing night. His heart began to pound.

It's okay, he told himself. It was okay because he'd been prepared for this his entire life. Maybe he should thank his father
for that. There was a distant comfort in knowing that, no matter
what you did, life worked out the way it was meant to. There was
no point thrashing against the hands of fate. Grey sat back down
on the boulder to wait.

# Jaya

Tears flowing unstoppably down her face, Jaya stumbled a little bit farther down Mount Sama, her breath hitching. The only
sound she heard was the crunching of her own boots and nothing else. He'd given up on her. And maybe that was what she
deserved. But worst of all, she had the sinking feeling that he'd
given up on himself.

She walked to a small boulder and sat on it, not even bothering to sweep the snow off. Everything felt raw and painful; it felt
like the entire world was on fire.

It was over. She couldn't believe it; it was over. Grey was waiting so fearfully for the sun to rise, for whatever fate had in store
for him, and she wasn't even with him. He didn't want her with
him.

"Jaya?"

She blinked and looked up, through her tears, to see her sister's concerned face peeking out of the hood of her parka. Isha
was walking up to her, her hands buried in her pockets. "What
are you doing here? I thought you and Daph left."

"Daph did," Isha said, looking over her shoulder down at the path below them. "But I couldn't. I wanted to wait for you, just in case . . ." She let her words trail off, her face anguished. "He didn't listen?"

Jaya shook her head and bit her lip, and tears coursed down her face. "It's what I expected," she said bravely, but her voice broke, betraying her.

Isha sat next to her on the boulder and put her arm around Jaya's shoulders. "I'm sorry."

They sat together for a long minute, feeling the wind whip around them. Then Isha said, "Are you . . . ? The engagement's still on?"

Jaya wiped her face and frowned at her sister. "Of course it is. Why wouldn't it be?"

"I just thought, after talking with Grey . . ." Isha shrugged.

Jaya straightened her shoulders. "No. Nothing's changed. I still need to do this."

"Jaya." Isha waited until she met her eye, her brown eyes glimmering in the muted light of a new day. "Is that what you want for me, too?"

Jaya shook her head. "What?"

"In two years, do you want me to get engaged to, I don't know, Venkat Samagood?"

Jaya frowned, trying to remember who that was. Her brow clearing, she said, "That kid who tries to look down your shirt at every palace event? Why on earth would you—"

"If it was good for the family," Isha said, raising her eyebrows. "If something really beneficial would come from that union. Would you want me to?"

Jaya spluttered. "Of course not! You're much too good for him! You deserve to be with someone you love!"

Isha waited, her eyebrows still raised.

Jaya sighed and pushed her hair back. The pine trees around them shuddered in the brisk breeze. "It's not the same."

"Of course it is!" Isha said, frustrated. "There's not a single difference!"

"The difference is I'm your big sister!" Jaya said, throwing her hands up. "I've always known it's my duty, not just to protect the kingdom, but to protect you!" Oh, bollocks. She hadn't meant to say that last part.

Isha frowned and dug the toe of her boot into the snowy ground. "What do you mean, protect me? What does you and Kiran getting engaged have to do with me?"

"Nothing," Jaya said quickly, smoothing out her jacket. "I just meant, in general, that—"

"Jaya, please. I'm not a dummy."

Jaya looked into her little sister's face and knew she couldn't lie to her. Not anymore. Not after all they'd been through, not after how far they'd come. "I . . . Appa called me. He said there was another article in the paper about you."

Isha's face paled to match the taupe scarf around her neck. "What did it say?"

"That you . . ." Jaya cleared her throat and put her hand on Isha's. "It was stupid."

"Please tell me."

"It said that we came here, to St. Rosetta's, because you were pregnant. The entire city was in an uproar. We were losing political standing, our reputation was in shreds. The Hegdes said they'd stick by us, but Appa didn't think that would be the case for much longer."

Understanding dawned on Isha's face. Up in the trees, a

chickadee called. "And if you and Kiran got engaged, it would show the people that the Hegdes still believed in our family."

Jaya nodded. "It'd also get people focusing on something else. A royal engagement is pretty big news."

Isha took a moment, her face lost in thought as she gazed into the woods below them. Then she looked at Jaya. "No."

"No . . . ?"

"No, you still can't do this."

"Isha, it's too late—"

"You cannot sacrifice yourself for me or Appa or the kingdom or our people or anyone else, Jaya. No."

Jaya opened her mouth to respond, but Isha spoke again.

"This is *my* problem. For far too long, you've taken on all my worries as your own, and it's time to stop."

Jaya pressed her hands into the cold, unyielding surface of the boulder underneath her. "Isha, you're my little sister. I don't know how to stop."

"Try," Isha said, fire in her eyes. "How do you think I'll feel, seeing you in an unhappy marriage, knowing that it was because of me? Do you think I'll be able to live a happy life, Jaya? I'll feel so guilty, I'll probably marry some rich, powerful asshat just to make myself feel better."

"You wouldn't," Jaya said. "You shouldn't feel guilty."

Isha smiled a little. "You can't tell me how to feel, Jaya."

Jaya studied her sister's expression, her heart pounding. If Isha would feel guilty all her life, if this decision would oblige her into an unhappy marriage of her own down the road . . . "But Appa," Jaya said weakly. She ran a hand over her numb face. "I already promised him I'd do this."

"If there's one thing I know about our father," Isha said, "it's that nothing's more important to him than the happiness of his girls."

Jaya stared at her little sister in the blue light of near dawn, her thoughts whirling, tumbling in a dizzying dance through her mind. Was Isha . . . ? Was Isha right?

"So, what are you thinking?" Isha asked, her eyes searching Jaya's face after a long moment of silence. "What are you going to do?"

Jaya gazed upward, at the clouds scuttling across the slate-gray sky. "I think I need to make a phone call."

Once Isha kissed her on the cheek and walked off back down the path, Jaya reached into her pocket and pulled out her phone, feeling a sudden surge of energy, of purpose, of fury.

She video-called Kiran and waited. When he answered, a haughty smile on his face, anger spiked in her blood, a potent elixir against the despair she felt.

"Don't you cry now, Jaya," he said. "I've cleaned up your mess for you."

She stared at him. "Cleaned up my mess? Are you completely deluded?" The self-satisfied look fell off his face. She took a deep breath. "The engagement is off," she said, with as much calm authority as she could gather. She felt a brief stab of guilt at doing this to her father, at taking away the one neat solution they'd arrived upon. But Isha's words rang in her ear: *If there's one thing I know about our father, it's that nothing's more important to him than the happiness of his girls.*

Feeling bolstered, Jaya continued. "I don't want to be with you, Kiran. I don't want anything to do with you, in fact."

"You don't know what you want," he said coldly. "You forget yourself, Jaya. We're meant to be married."

"We *were* meant to be married," Jaya corrected, still speaking calmly, in spite of the adrenaline that was making her hands tremble. She pressed her free hand into the boulder, felt its steadying presence soothe her. "I made a mistake. I thought I had to sacrifice my own happiness for the longevity and reputation of my family, but I was wrong. We'll find a way to persevere without making a trade of my heart and my values."

"Is this about that *Emerson* boy?" Kiran asked.

Jaya shook her head. "Leave him out of this. You've done enough."

Kiran's nostrils flared. "If you back out of this alliance now, I will make sure that the newspapers *destroy* the Rao name. The Hegde dynasty isn't a plaything for you to toy with. Give us what you promised, or be prepared to suffer."

Jaya narrowed her eyes. "Do *not* threaten my family."

Kiran looked like he might explode with impotent fury. "Everything I have done, I have done for my title. The same cannot be said of you and your sister, Jaya." He paused, then said, "You know what? I'm *pleased* the papers ran that story on Isha. The Raos needed to be brought down a peg or two, letting their daughters get drunk and hang all over filthy garage mechanics, letting them run around in T-shirts that support anarchy and feminism. It's a disgrace!"

Jaya sat up straighter, her blood cooling as his words hooked into her brain. The way he said them, the way he was looking at her . . . defiance mixed with so much anger. How had she never seen the anger? "The picture never showed Isha's T-shirt," Jaya said slowly. "None of the papers showed her T-shirt. How do you know what she was wearing that day, Kiran?"

He met her eyes. There was a long pause, as if he were

assessing what to say next. "Yes, it was I who fed them the picture. I took it with my phone," he said finally, his tone a touch boastful. "It was the only way to protect the Hegdes' political position in Karnataka. I was thinking of my family, as any good heir should."

It was astounding; he actually still believed he was in the right. That his actions were acceptable. Jaya shook her head, her rage so great, everything in her body went silent and still. "*You* were the 'male heir' the journalist was talking about. And you kept leaking the rumors after we were gone, just in case they began to die down. You were the one who told them Isha was pregnant."

He stared back at her.

"Incredible," Jaya whispered, tugging her hair back against the wind. "So you broke my sister's heart, nearly destroyed my family's reputation and my parents' peace of mind, but that wasn't enough for you. Because of your obsession with power, you've now come after the man I love. I knew you were an ass-hole, Kiran, but I had no idea you were so bloody evil."

He opened his mouth to speak, but Jaya continued. "You will call the newspapers immediately and issue an apology to my family. You'll confess what you did—both the initial scandal and the pregnancy rumors—and say you had no right to go after a young girl, that you've made mistakes of your own, and that the Rao family name is still imbued with honor and dignity as far as you're concerned."

Kiran scoffed. "Why would I do that?"

"Because I've recorded this conversation," Jaya said simply. "I'll send it to every newspaper in India. I imagine every journalist who might be interested in—how did you put it? Oh yes—taking the Hegde family down a peg or two would clamor for this clip. Don't you think so?" She smiled a little. "Plus, once I send this to my father, I imagine he's going to have a few political moves up his sleeve that likely won't benefit the Hegdes. As I recall, the Raos are still very much the most powerful royal family in Karnataka. No thanks to you, of course. I imagine your father won't be too pleased with whatever punishment Appa metes out."

Kiran's face was absolutely furious. "You wouldn't do that. Isha was still at fault for those pictures. I didn't force her to do anything!"

"Maybe, but she was fourteen. And besides, she's not the heiress to the throne. What's *your* excuse, Kiran?"

They stared at each other, unsmiling for a long moment. Finally, Kiran said shortly, "Very well. I'll release a statement."

"I'll send you the exact wordage via email," Jaya said serenely. "Just so you're clear on what to say."

He kept staring at her. "Fine."

"Goodbye, Kiran," Jaya said, and pressed "end."

Dawn was fast encroaching. The sky was now a faded purple, and a chorus of birds began to sing. The world was waking up, bit by bit.

# Grey

He'd heard everything. Grey didn't know whether it was a weird wind pattern or if he was sitting in some kind of sound tunnel, but every word Jaya and Isha, and then Jaya and Kiran, had said had floated up to him, as if they were speaking into microphones. Jaya had ended things with Kiran. She'd told him she believed she didn't have to sacrifice herself for her family anymore. For the first time since the night before, Grey felt the stirrings of doubt. This didn't sound like an act, not at all. And then, right on the heels of that doubt came blinding, searing, painful hope.

Could it be? Could it be that these last few minutes before the sun rose could be spent with Jaya after all? That she truly felt that Grey was worth more than the traditions and values she held dear? That she really had changed, like she'd told him? Before his brain could catch up, his body had unfolded itself from the boulder. Grey was crashing down the mountain, toward Jaya's voice. He wasn't thinking of what he'd say when he got there. He just knew he had to get there.

# Jaya

The sun had begun its gradual ascent. Dawn was only minutes away. Jaya slipped her phone into her pocket, jerking her head up at the sudden sounds of branches snapping and thundering footfalls hurtling down the mountain toward her. It was Grey.

The wind whistled between them as they regarded each other silently. His face was haggard and his hair fell in his tired eyes, but his gaze didn't waver.

Jaya stood and stepped forward, closing the gap between them. She realized she had no idea what Grey was thinking. His blue eyes were as wild, as stormy, as the most tempestuous ocean, his mouth set in a hard line. "Hi," she whispered.

Grey didn't say anything. He looked like a wounded animal, unsure, afraid, suspicious. Painfully hopeful. It hurt her heart to see it, to see what she'd done. She waited, in silence, sensing that he needed it.

"Is it true?" he asked, his speech pressured, as if he couldn't stop the words from forming.

Jaya stepped forward, trying to get closer to him, but he stepped back, not letting her. She felt the pain of his lost trust but held still, respecting his need for space. "Is what true?"

He pushed a jerky hand through his hair. "Everything, all of what you said—is it true?" He took a deep, shaky breath. "You've realized you don't have to sacrifice your heart for your family?" He couldn't quite meet her eye as he said it, as if he didn't want to show how much he needed it to be true.

"Every word is true. Grey, you've made me realize things about myself, about the way I want to lead my city. You've helped me see that tradition, what people expect of me, doesn't have to be how the story ends. I have a hand in all this too. If I don't like a scene, I can rewrite it."

Jaya took a tentative step forward, testing to see if that was okay. He didn't move back. Her hand shaking, Jaya reached up to caress his jaw, waiting for him to pull back, to push her hand away. But he didn't. His eyes slipped shut.

"I love you," she whispered simply. "I'm so sorry I lied. I'm so sorry I ever wanted to hurt you. And I'm sorry that I let my fear and my rigidity force me into decisions I never should've made. But you have to believe me when I say my heart is completely, unquestionably yours, Grey. It has been for a while."

Grey's eyes opened. He sucked in a breath, and when he spoke, his voice was a low tremble. "So the engagement is off?"

Jaya took a breath. "The engagement is off."

"It might be too late," Grey said, looking somewhere past her.

He glanced down at her necklace. "Look at the rose."

She did. The single ruby that remained hung precariously out of its socket, ready to fall at any moment.

"Once that one falls, it's done. My life could be over. There might not be a chance for you and me, Jaya. It might be wisest for you to protect your heart from whatever's about to happen." He contemplated the sky, the soft pinks and golds of dawn reflected in his eyes.

"My heart is already broken when we're not together," Jaya said, fire in her voice. "Don't you see that, Grey? I want to be with you. And you want to be with me. I sent my father a text. I was going to tell him about us today. This morning, in fact. I'm ready to take the next step with you, Grey. If you'll have me still."

Grey looked out over the frozen lake. "I—I can't . . ."

"Grey."

He turned back to her.

"Do you want me? As much as I want you? Still? After everything I've done?" Her lips were trembling so much, she was barely able to get the words out.

"Of course I do," Grey said, his voice breaking as he took her face in his big hands, the pressure behind his words unstoppable, the intensity of his gaze turning her liquid. "You know I do. If this curse wasn't— You're the only one for me, Jaya. You're the only one who sees me for who I am, and when I'm with you, I actually believe in happiness—"

She closed the gap between them just as two things happened simultaneously: the sun crested over the horizon, filling the world with its golden light, and the last ruby fell, pirouetting out of its socket in a slow, graceful arc, the sunlight winking off its hard surface.

Jaya pressed her lips to Grey's gently, but then his hand was behind her head, pressing her to him with an urgency that left her breathless.

# Grey

Pulling back from her, Grey looked down at the ground. The ruby glittered in the snow between them like a minuscule, evil seed. "It fell," he said. "The last ruby, on my eighteenth birthday."

"It means nothing," Jaya said firmly. "Nothing. Look, you're still here." She gestured around them and smiled. "And it's a new day, Grey. It's a new day."

He shook his head in wonder. "I'm still here. But . . . how?"

"I don't know," Jaya said. "But, Grey . . . I don't really care. You know what really scares me? The thought of never being able to see you again."

There was no lie in her bright brown eyes. Grey smiled slowly at her, his heart thrumming and leaping. "Really?"

"Really."

He gazed out at the frozen town below them. After a long moment, he said, "That's . . . that's how I feel too." Looking at her, he added, "Besides, I have a theory."

"What's that?"

"Hold that thought. There's something I have to do first," Grey said, pulling out his phone. He dialed a number and waited while Jaya stood by him. "Father?"

"Grey? You . . . you're still—"

"Alive?" Grey smirked. "The last time I checked, yes. There's something I need to tell you."

"And what might that be?"

He looked at Jaya, and she gazed steadily back at him. "I'm not . . . I'm not damaged or a burden or any of those other things you've told me all my life. I'm not different, and I don't need to keep my distance from people." He took a breath. "And I wasn't responsible for Mother's death. How could you even have thought that about an infant? How could you have stolen all these years from me? I should've been forming friendships. I should've been laughing, engaged with the world. And instead . . . instead I locked myself away in a metaphorical tower. I thought I was a beast." Jaya squeezed his hand, and he found the strength to continue. "I want you to know that I'm done believing your bullshit. I'm done feeling like I'm not worthy of love."

"Grey, you're being utterly ridiculous. This melodrama—"

"I'm not finished. I'm renouncing my title, effective immediately. I'm emancipating myself from the family. From this moment on, I am no longer an Emerson. I'm changing my last name to Mother's."

Jaya stared at him, shocked.

"What?" his father thundered. "That is preposterous! How on earth do you imagine you'll continue paying for that expensive education of yours? Or hadn't you thought that far, you stupid boy?"

"I've been investing for a few years now. I have a bit of money socked away that you don't know about, as it turns out. I'll make my own way in this world. I don't need you, and I don't need your title. I'm my own man now. I'm writing my own story." Jaya beamed at him. "I hope someday you'll make amends for what you've done. And I hope someday you'll stop being the twisted person you became after Mother died. That's all I have to say, really. Goodbye, Father." He pressed "end" and turned to Jaya, his eyes bright. "So that's that."

She put her arms around him and he tightened his around her waist, closing his eyes to revel in the feel of her warm weight pushed up against him. The bare pendant hung lifelessly between them as the sun rose higher and higher in the sky, bathing them in its rose-gold light.

"Are you okay?" Jaya asked after a few minutes. "How do you feel?"

"How do I feel?" He pulled back and smiled down at her. "Fucking amazing. Now, do you want to hear my theory about the curse?"

Jaya nodded.

> *Mend that which is broken*
> *Repair that which is severed*
> *Or the Emerson name is forsaken*
> *And shall vanish, at last, forever.*

"I thought that meant I'd die on my eighteenth birthday, right?"

"Right," Jaya said, a small crease between her eyebrows.

"But what if it meant I'd emancipate myself instead? What if it meant the Emerson line would end because its last remaining heir would renounce his name and his title?"

The idea had only occurred to him once the sun rose and he realized he was still standing, but it made sense. These last few months, ever since he met Jaya and really understood what his father had stolen from him, he felt like he'd been moving toward this moment. Renouncing his name, emancipating himself, felt like something essential slotting into place, the last piece of the puzzle. He hadn't been able to undo the curse, but it didn't matter. He was no longer defined by his father's narrow constructs, by his cold, unyielding cruelty. Grey had shattered that stone tower; he was finally free.

"*If* the curse was even real in the first place, that's a pretty good theory," Jaya said, a half smile at her lips.

They gazed at each other, their eyes shining. A generations-long burden lifted off Grey's exhausted shoulders. He felt beams of hope, like sunlight, warming him, thawing him out again. It was done. It was over. Never again would he have to think about the curse. Never again would he have to live, afraid, in its shadow. He could go anywhere. He could be anything. He wanted to whoop and yell; he wanted to jump in the lake just to feel the shock of ice-cold water. He just wanted to *feel*.

Jaya took his hand as the wind gusted around them, making the pine trees shake. With her free hand, she pulled out her cell.

"What are you doing?"

"It's my turn now." Jaya began to dial.

# *Jaya*

"Appa, it's me," Jaya said, her heart pounding. She could feel Grey's eyes on her. "I have something to tell you. Actually, some *things*."

"Is everything okay, Jaya?"

"Yes, everything's fine. I've just had some revelations recently, and I want to share them with you." She swallowed.

"Okay . . . hold on a moment. Your mother wants to join us on the call."

"Jaya?" It was Amma's concerned voice this time. "What's going on? Is Isha okay?"

"Yes, she's fine. Everything's fine. But I have something to tell you both." She met Grey's blue eyes, steady and strong, and suddenly wasn't as anxious. "I've called off the engagement between Kiran and me. I don't want to marry him. I'm sorry." She swallowed. "I know the engagement was the perfect solution to our problems, but I've arrived at a different solution I'll tell you about in a moment. For now I want to say, I've . . . I've met someone who's become very important to me," she said, smiling. "His name is Grey. It used to be Grey Emerson."

There was a long, shocked silence.

"The Emerson boy has become *important* to you?" Appa's voice finally bellowed down the phone. "A member of the family that tried to destroy our family's reputation! And you're calling off an engagement with the Hegde heir for him? Are you mad, Jaya?"

Jaya could hear Amma's more soothing voice trying to placate her father. "Actually," she said, her voice slicing over both of theirs. "The one who leaked Isha's photographs and the one who added fuel to the fire with the pregnancy rumors was Kiran Hegde. Not the Emersons. In fact, I've already spoken to Kiran about it. He'll be issuing a public apology in the papers very soon. I think our problems are over. The Hegdes will be facing the wrath of the people now, and rightly so, I'd say."

There were spluttering noises from both her parents. Finally, Appa said, "*Kiran* leaked the pictures? He was behind the whole thing?" He was clearly apoplectic.

"Yes, but I've taken care of it, as I've said. Appa, Amma, I know the Emersons have done a lot to the Raos over the years, and the Raos have retaliated. But here's the thing—Grey isn't an Emerson anymore. He's renounced his title."

"So the boy isn't even an *aristocrat* anymore?" her father said. It was clear he was reeling from all the news she was throwing at him.

"No, he isn't," Jaya said, squeezing Grey's hand.

"But, Jaya—" her father began.

"Adip, please," Amma cut in. "Listen to what she's saying. Listen to her. Doesn't she sound happy? The one we picked for her, Kiran, has turned out to be . . ." She could hear all of Amma's etiquette training pushing against her need to really lay into Kiran. "Well. I don't think this is a bad thing. Let her be happy. Let her live her life while she's young."

Appa grumbled, but didn't disagree. Jaya plunged on. "Speaking of, I have two other things to tell you: One, Isha will be taking robotics classes while she's here at St. Rosetta's. I think it's a wonderful idea. I think she might just turn out to be the first female Rao engineer. And two: Regarding college, I'm taking a gap year after my senior year of high school. I want to travel." She took a breath and felt Grey rub his thumb over her knuckles. She gave him a grateful smile. Birds tweeted in the trees above them; mild choking sounds emanated from the phone.

"Well," Amma said finally. "I think you've rendered your father speechless, Jaya. This is . . . quite a lot of news to digest."

"I know." Jaya sighed. "I'm sorry. I'm not trying to stress you both out. However, as you know, I've been a very dutiful daughter and I've been thinking—maybe it's time I find out what *I* think about some of these things."

"Learning lessons on your own gets you hurt," her father said gruffly. "That's our job as parents, to teach you those lessons so you don't have to get hurt."

Jaya softened. "I know, Appa. And you've taught me so well. But now . . . now I want to see the world through my own eyes. It doesn't mean I don't want to come back and help you manage the estate or lead our people. I'm proud of our traditions, of my heritage, of the fact that I'm a Rao heiress. Nothing will ever change that. But I also want to find out who Jaya is besides a Rao princess." She paused. "Does that make sense?"

In the long silence that followed, Jaya met Grey's eye and shrugged. Her mouth was dry. What were her parents up to?

Finally, Appa spoke quietly. "Yes," he said. "Yes, it does. Jaya, you are brave to say all that you have said. I can't say that I agree with it all, but I do respect you for saying it. There's a lot to digest and think about, but the most important thing, I suppose, is that you must be feeling these things quite strongly to say them to us in this way."

"You'll always be our daughter, Jaya," Amma said, her voice trembling at the edges. "We have much to discuss and perhaps some things to compromise on, but the most important thing is that we just want you to be happy."

"I want that too," Jaya said, smiling. She stepped in closer to Grey and leaned her head against his chest. "I want to be happy."

# Grey

She did it. She really, really did it. She wanted to proclaim to the world how she felt about him, and the fact that they were together. It felt like a dream.

Once she ended the call, she and Grey stood together in silence for a minute, gazing at each other, contemplating the future that lay before them like a glittering, unknowable treasure chest. Then Jaya wrapped her arms around Grey's waist and looked up at him through the thick fringe of her eyelashes. "So, then. Do I have to beg for a kiss?"

"No begging necessary, Princess," Grey murmured, bringing his lips down to hers until they were just a breath apart. Every nerve ending sang in joy. "Isn't it funny? The beautiful princess did turn the beast into a man after all."

"But here's a secret," Jaya whispered against his mouth, sending waves of desire down his spine. "The beast was the handsome prince all along. He just didn't know it. Happy birthday, Grey."

When their lips met, they kissed like they had never kissed before: hunger and longing and relief and love all rolled into one ecstatic moment. When they pulled apart, Jaya studied him, her eyes sparkling. "So this is it, then."

"This is what?" Grey asked, stroking her cheek. He could hold her like this forever and never grow tired.

"Our fairy-tale ending."

Smiling, Grey said, "Happily ever after."

# Acknowledgments

Escaping into the world of *Of Curses and Kisses* was such a decadent treat that most days spent working on this book didn't even feel like work. When I wasn't actively writing about Jaya and Grey, I was thinking about them, and when I was unconscious for a third of every day, they occupied my dreams.

A big thank-you to my editor, Jen Ung, my publisher, Simon Pulse, and my agent, Thao Le, without whose belief and optimism this universe wouldn't exist.

To the writers I've met and befriended, who've kept me sane and feeling not-alone, including but not limited to: Sabina Khan, Stephanie Garber, Karen McManus, Bill Konigsberg, Roselle Lim, Kathleen Glasgow, Shea Earnshaw, Karen Strong, Sabaa Tahir, Amy Spalding, Kayla Cagan, Samira Ahmed, Mackenzi Lee, Becky Albertalli, Adam Silvera, and so many others I couldn't even hope to list them all here, I'm so happy we're all in this together.

To the bookstores, booksellers, teachers, and librarians who've championed my books from day one: Thank you so very, very much.

To my family: You're the reason I wake up feeling like I've won the lottery every single day.

To my readers: I appreciate every single one of you and your support, enthusiasm, and love. I hope you enjoy escaping into the world of St. Rosetta's as much as I have.

# About the Author

SANDHYA MENON is the *New York Times* bestselling author of several novels with lots of kissing, girl power, and swoony boys. Her books have been featured in several cool places, including the *Today Show*, *Teen Vogue*, *NPR*, *BuzzFeed*, and *Seventeen*. A full-time dog servant and part-time writer, she makes her home in the foggy mountains of Colorado. Visit her online at sandhyamenon.com